I0730780

MAN MADE

GOD 004

By Brandon Varnell

Art by Lonwa

Man Made God 004
Copyright © 2020 Brandon Varnell & Kitsune Incorporated
Illustration Copyright © 2021 Lonwa
All rights reserved.

To see Brandon Varnell's other works, or to ask for permission to use his works, visit him at www.varnell-brandon.com, facebook at www.facebook.com/AmericanKitsune, twitter at www.twitter.com/BrandonbVarnell, Patreon at https://www.patreon.com/BrandonVarnell, and instagram at www.instagram.com/brandonbvarnell.

If you'd like to know when I'm releasing a new book, you can sign up for my mailing list at https://www.varnell-brandon.com/mailing-list.

ISBN: 978-1-951904-30-2 (Paperback)
978-1-951904-29-6 (eBook)

DEDICATION

This page is made in dedication to my amazing patrons. Without them, my characters would never get lewded by so many wonderful artists:

Aaron Harris; Adam; Alarinnise; Alexander Rodriguez; Armando Pastrana; Benjamin Collins; Benjamin Morgan; Brendan Smiley; Bruce Johnson; Bryce McClay; C.L. Holgrahm; Caxey G. May; Catcrazy9; Chase Corso; Charles Dorfeuille; Christopher Gross; Cody Woodard; CosmicOrange; Dane Smith; Daniel Glasson; Dhivael; Edward Grindle; Edward Lamar Stephenson; Edward P Warmouth; Emery Moore; Ginny; Feitochan; Forrest Hansen; Forrest Hansen; Ine Airlcana; IronKing; Jacob Flores; Jacob Wojno; Jeremy Schultz; Jesus; John Patton; LarC85; Lucid Fayt; Mark Frabotta; Matthew Wallace; Max A Kramer; Michael Erwin; Michael Moneymaker; NA; Nathan S; Omegapudding; Philip Hedgepeth; Rfael Eriksen; Raymond T; Red Phoenix; Red Viking; Reent Dopychai; Repooc Ilahsram; Richard Garret; Rob McDagg; Roy Cales; Samuel Donaldson; Sean Gray; Seismic Wolf; Shotgunr12; Slim; Smudi Corp; Starwarscout Jon; Thomas; Thomas Jackson; Tim Nielsen; ToraLinkley; Travis Cox; Victor Patrick Bauer; William Crew; XY172; Yuriy Snyadanko; Zach Miller; Zach Strickland; Zenn Barger

CONTENT

TITANIA

A mysterious fairy who Adam meets in a dungeon. Guardien of the spear. She hates it when people talk about her height.

ADAM

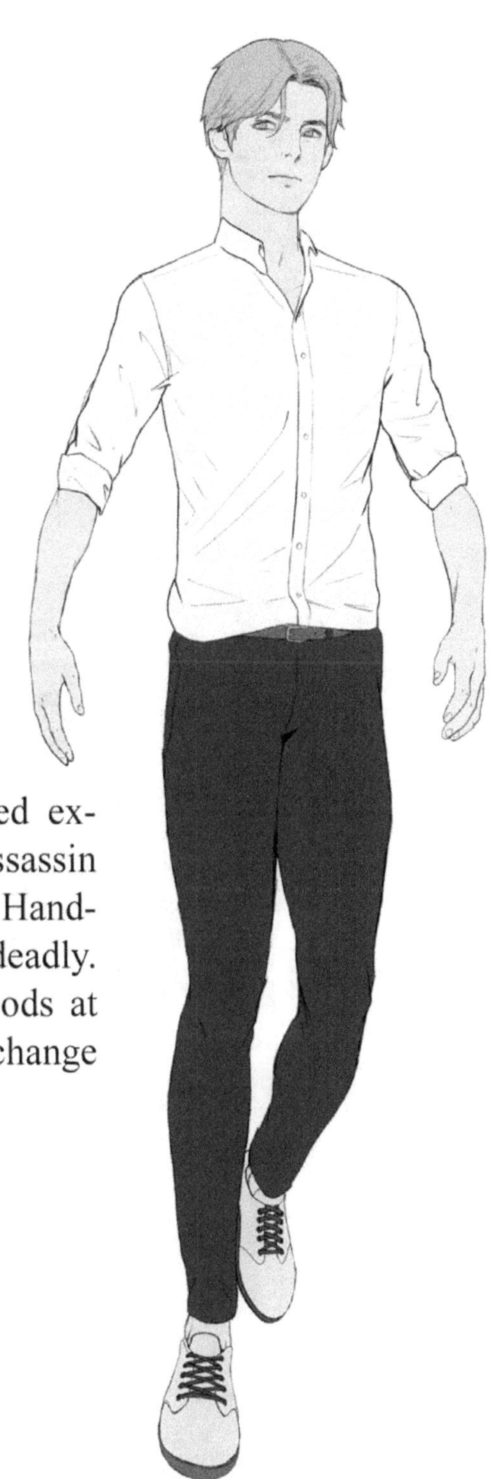

A young man trained extensively as an assassin since childhood. Handsome, confident, deadly. He enters Age of Gods at Fayte's behest in exchange for her curing Aris.

SUSAN

Fayte's best and only friend. Genius hacker. Incredibly shy. Has trouble telling people no.

FAYTE

Daughter of the Dairing Family. Fayte is intelligent and determined to fight against her fate. She is the one who pulls Adam into Age of Gods.

LILITH

Adam's most loyal suborddinate. She is a highly skilled and quiet assassin who will do anything Adam asks without question.

ARIS

Adam's lover. She used to
be rambunctious and wild,
but she became a cripple
after contracting mortems
disease. Currently in stasis.

THE GUILD ASSOCIATION

Adam walked through the busy streets of Solum. His blond hair ruffled with his movement when he shifted aside to let a group of kids run past him; it looked like they were playing tag. Several scents assaulted his nose. He looked to his left, where a number of stall vendors had set up shop and were selling a variety of foods—most of which were roasted meats. He'd read once long ago that meat was the primary element of dishes during the Middle Ages in Europe.

"Is it just me, or has it gotten busier?"

Sitting on Adam's shoulder was a slip of a woman barely a foot tall, with long hair so red it reminded him of billowing fire, vibrant green eyes, and a green dress with a slit running up the side, revealing a lot of bare leg. She wore no shoes. Her bare feet kicked back and forth.

Her name was Titania. She was a fairy who had joined his party when he was trying to leave the Village of Beginnings. From what he understood, she had been sealed away alongside the spear that was now his only weapon, though for what reason he didn't know. Titania didn't seem to know exactly why she'd been sealed away either. It was presumably to become the Guardian of the Spear and help the chosen hero who wielded it, but Adam suspected there was another reason—one not even she knew about.

They had a fairly good relationship, or so Adam liked to think, though there were times she became quite irate with him. It was usually justified so he often let it go.

"I think more players are joining the game," Adam said in response to her words.

Titania furrowed her brow. "I do not know what you mean by that? 'Joining the game'? 'Players'? Explain yourself more clearly."

"… I meant more otherworlders are coming to your world."

"Then you should have just said that."

Adam was currently logged into *Age of Gods*, the latest and most popular game in the entire world, which boasted a fully realized world nearly indistinguishable from the real world—if one excluded the swords, magic, and fantasy setting. What made this game so popular wasn't the gameplay mechanics, but how realistic the world was. Food had taste. Scents were tangible. For people who wanted to live out their wildest fantasies and go on adventures they never could in real life, this game was everything they could have possibly wanted and more.

"Yip! Yip!"

A noise on Adam's head attracted the attention of several people walking by. Sitting on his head was a small red fox with two tails. Kureha. She was a fox yokai whom he had met when traveling through the Forest of Gloom. She had been trapped within a web woven by the [Spider Queen], a fearsome 4-star monster that he could not hope to defeat at his current level. Adam had freed her, and she'd become his pet after that.

He still didn't understand the difference between a pet and a party member, but Titania assured him there were quite a few, one of which was that he controlled where Kureha's skill points went when she leveled up.

Adam, Titania, and Kureha had just returned from the Suncrest Mountain Range after several hours of hunting. He was currently in the process of trying to level up. Unfortunately, leveling up in this world was hard. Every time a person gained a level, they needed to earn twice the experience points previously required to reach the next level. That was fine in the beginning when the number of experience points was relatively small, but Adam was now at level 16 and needed 4,915,200 experience points to level up.

He was barely past the halfway mark.

On the plus side, his spear had leveled up and was now at level 11, which increased his Strength and Attack Power some.

Not that he felt they needed to be increased right now.

"You said it, Kureha. Adam says a lot of unusual things. He is a very strange man," Titania said in response to Kureha's yips, as if she could understand what the fox yokai was saying. And maybe she could. Titania was a fairy. In ancient myth, fairies were said to be capable of communing with nature, so perhaps she had some special ability that let her talk to plants and animals or something.

"I'm glad you two think I'm so strange," Adam said dryly.

"By the way, Adam, where are we going?" Titania asked.

"The general goods store. My inventory is full of useless items that I need to sell."

You could always tell a store by what kind of sign hung over the door. A blacksmith would have an anvil and hammer, a home decoration store would have a paintbrush, a potions shop would have a vial, and a general store would have a chair. The use of symbols instead of words was something that had been taken from a bygone era. The literacy rate in the Middle Ages, which he assumed this world was somehow based around, had been very low, and so rather than using names, they simply used symbols.

"Welcome to—oh, Adam! Welcome back! I'm guessing you have more items to sell?"

The soft jingling of a bell echoed around the store as Adam entered. A woman with a refreshing smile but way too much makeup greeted him. This was Jessabelle, the proprietress of this particular store.

"Hello. I do have a lot of stuff that I need to get rid of."

"Heh heh. That's good to hear. The items you bring me always sell like hot cakes! Okay. Just give me permission to view your inventory and I'll tally up the total I owe you."

A screen appeared before Adam with a soft ding.

[Jessabelle would like permission to view your inventory. Will you grant it? Yes? No?]

This screen was one of the view game-like aspects of *Age of Gods*. Titania and Kureha could see it, but only a few other NPCs like Jessabelle could see it as well. Adam didn't know how that worked. He suspected it was just one of those unrealistic aspects he needed to accept.

He granted Jessabelle permission to view his inventory, then waited for her to tally up the total. While waiting, a strange sensation passed through his crotch. He stood up straighter, spine snapping taut. The action was so sudden that Kureha and Titania were both thrown off him. While Kureha landed on the ground with a piteous whine, Titania floated next to his face and frowned at him.

"What is it? Is something wrong, Adam?"

"N-no… nothing's wrong."

"Are you sure? Your face is getting flushed. You're not catching a fever, are you? I've never heard of an otherworlder getting sick, but that doesn't mean it can't happen. You should take better care of yourself."

"Sure. I'll do that."

Adam gave Titania a weak smile as a pleasant shudder coursed through his body. He tried to control himself by taking several deep breaths as he waited for Jessabelle to finish her task. His total came up to 1,534,000 gold coins. After she paid him, Adam hurriedly left the store, went to the nearest inn, and bought a room for one night.

"I need to go," he said quickly to Titania and Kureha. "Something is happening in the real—I mean, in my world, so I'm heading back. Be good, you two."

"Just who do you think I am?!" asked Titania, seemingly angry that he had told her to be good as if he expected the opposite.

But Adam was not paying her any attention.

He had already left.

***

"Haaah… mmmm… aaaaah…"

Adam awoke to the sound of gentle moans in his ears. His rock-hard member was throbbing as something warm and wet ground against it. Opening his eyes, all he saw at first was the white ceiling overhead, but then he shifted his gaze down and found soft brown hair caressing his cheek.

"Aris…" He moaned the name as a sudden spike in pleasure raced through his body. Electricity surged through his groin.

"Mmmm. Adam, good morning."

Aris placed her hands on her chest, pushed herself up until she was straddling his stomach, and smiled down at him.

Aris Purity was a cute girl with big brown eyes, brown hair that traveled just past her shoulders, and a slender body. She was his lover, savior, and best friend all in one. Many years ago, after Adam escaped from the clutches of a man who called himself Lucifer, he had gone in search of his best friend Alexis, only to discover that she had disappeared and was considered dead by her family. In the depths of despair, he had sought death, but this girl had saved him.

She was the light that had rescued him when he was lost in darkness.

At the moment, Aris was quite naked. Her slim body was bared before him, small nipples rising perkily from her chest, soft stomach gyrating as she continued to rub herself against him. He glanced down and saw that she was leaving a wet trail on his abdominals.

"What… brought this on…?" he asked between gasps.

"Mmm… I… ahhh… hmmm… I woke up this morning… haaah… and I was so horny… Adam, I need you. I need… mmmm… I need your hot, throbbing thing inside of me. Right now."

Adam thought himself to be a man of considerable willpower and mental fortitude, but his will snapped at Aris's words, at the wanton look in her eyes, and at the smile caressing her mouth, teasing him. He'd always had a hard time denying this girl anything to begin with. To make matters worse, he had held himself back for several years because she had Mortems Disease and he didn't want to make her fatal situation worse.

Now she was cured.

He had no reason to hold back.

Aris squealed as he flipped them over. Taking his shaft in hand, Adam rubbed his length along her sodden entrance, shivering at the pleasure such a simple act evoked. She must have been grinding herself against him for quite some time. He was so sensitive just touching her felt like he was coming into contact with a livewire.

Even the most minuscule of caresses was enough to send arcs of pleasure racing through him like an electric current.

Leaning over, Adam found Aris's hands, laced his fingers through hers, and pushed them into the mattress.

"Your wish is my command," he growled in a low voice that made Aris shiver.

"Ooooh! Oh, God! Yesssss!"

Aris hissed in pleasure as he pushed himself inside of her, then began vigorously thrusting his hips. Her breathing was already labored, but it became even heavier now, headier, more wanton. She panted and moaned underneath him. Her eyes were hooded with lust, half-lidded and filled with desire. They spurred him on.

"Haaah! Hhmmmm! Mmm! Aaaah! Adam! Adam! Harder! Fuck me harder!"

Adam grunted as he increased both the pace and intensity of his thrusts, until loud smacking sounds echoed around the room. Her small chest bounced with every thrust. Her legs on either side of his body shook with the rocking motions of his hips.

Sweat formed on their skin. The glistening droplets trailed down Aris's flesh as she writhed beneath him. She hooked her legs around his waist and dug her heels into the small of his back, as if egging him on.

Aris was very enthusiastic for someone who'd only had sex once before. Last night had been their first time. He would have expected her to be sore. While he'd been far gentler with her than he had with Lilith, it had still been her first time, and he still went at it quite enthusiastically. That she seemed ready for more so early in the morning was a bit of a shock to him.

Leaning down, Adam took one of her pert nipples into his mouth. It was small and cute like the woman it belonged to. He swirled his tongue around her areola, listening to her gasps, moans, and enthusiastic cries when she told him to repeat a specific action. "Do that again!" "It feels so good!" "I think I'm losing my mind!" He paid careful attention to every word from her mouth. When he finished with one breast, he dragged his tongue across her chest, then took her other nipple into his mouth.

"Adam! Adam! I'm gonna cum! I'm gonna! I'm! I'm! Cumming!"

Aris grabbed his face between her hands and pulled him into a kiss. She filled his mouth with her tongue. He could have pushed back, but he didn't, instead letting her have her way with his mouth. He caressed her tongue with his own as his mouth became filled with her saliva and taste. At the same time, her insides clenched around him like a vice as she came. Her entire body quivered against his. The spasming sensation of her inner walls caused Adam's own orgasm. He shot his seed inside of her with several quick jerks of his hips.

I am so glad I'm sterile. I'm pretty sure she would have gotten pregnant if I wasn't.

"Haaaah… haaaah… mmmm… that was nice," Aris murmured with a sleepy smile.

"Don't go back to sleep." Adam caressed her naked hip, leaned down, and kissed her on the lips before climbing out of bed. He turned around and held out his hand. "Come on. Let's take a shower. We need to get clean so I can make breakfast."

Aris grinned as she took his hand and let him pull her off the bed. "Shower sex does sound appealing."

"We're not having sex in the shower."

"Right. Right. But if we did, I'm sure it would be fun."

"But we're not."

"Tee-hee. Whatever you say, Adam."

Despite his words to the contrary, they did end up having sex in the shower. Adam had been completely unable to withstand the sight of his lover, her body dripping with water, and he'd taken great pleasure in pounding her from behind. He would have said it was her fault for enticing him, but he knew it was as much his fault as it was her. Sure, she had pushed her cute little bottom against him, and okay, she had been grinding herself on his erect third leg and blaming it on the small size of the shower, but it wasn't like he couldn't have been firmer and stopped her if he wanted. He just... didn't want to.

Adam had known for a long time that he had a high libido. During his time in Cocytus, he had used Lilith's body to satisfy his lust more times than he could count. That had been when he was just a teenager. His body had grown since then, as had his libido, but he'd been keeping it in check for so long he'd nearly forgotten how easily he became aroused. The merest glance from Aris was now enough to make him hard enough to slice through diamonds.

Their shower ended up being a lot longer than intended. When they emerged into the living room, dressed in casual clothes, it was to find someone else waiting for them.

"Good morning, you two. You sure took your sweet time. I've already finished preparing breakfast."

Light filtered in from the balcony and illuminated the beauty before them. Her hair was long, blonde, and seemed to sparkle as she brought out a tray from the kitchen and set it on the coffee table in the living room. Her eyes were a light blue. They reminded him of sapphires. At the moment, she was wearing a red turtleneck that stretched across her expansive bust, simple pants that conformed almost lovingly to her amazing hips, and white socks. She greeted the pair with a smile.

"Good morning, Fayte!" Aris greeted the woman with a bright smile. She walked over to the woman with quick steps, surprised her with a hug, then sat down and took a deep breath. "Wow! This smells delicious! I can't wait to dig in!"

"They're just pancakes, but I hope you like them." Fayte was nothing if not adaptable, so she quickly recovered from the surprise hug and smiled at the girl. She then glanced his way. "I've also got some coffee. Two sugars. No cream."

"It seems you know what I like," Adam said, scratching the back of his neck as he walked into the room more sedately than his companion.

"Of course. We've been living together for over a month now."

Fayte Dairing was the disowned daughter of the Dairing Family—a powerful family that owned numerous business holdings and had a net worth of over one hundred billion dollars. She had been disowned by her father after refusing to marry Levon Pleonexia, the heir to another, even more powerful family. In desperation, she had accepted a bet proposed by Levon. If she could accrue half the Dairing Family's annual income, increase her reputation to match or exceed the least powerful family among the top ten most powerful families in the American Federation, and create a guild within *Age of Gods* that ranked among the top five national guilds, Levon would publicly call off the marriage and convince her father to accept her back into the family.

This bet was stacked so heavily against her it was obvious to everyone that she had next to no hope of winning, but that hadn't stopped Fayte from accepting it. She was determined the do everything in her power to win. Adam at first had thought it was an act of desperation. He understood the truth now.

Fayte was a sore loser.

She hated losing more than anything and became highly motivated when placed under duress. Whenever she lost at video games, she would challenge him again and have a new strategy in place to beat him. She was also the kind of person who preferred straightforward confrontations and hated subterfuge. Whenever they played video games and she lost their little bets, she would make lunch or dinner without complaint. It must have been this aspect of her personality that caused her to accept Levon's bet.

She wanted to beat Levon *because* he had stacked the odds so heavily against her.

That was why she brought him on. Adam was her ace in the hole. Of course, she was the reason Aris's Mortems Disease had been cured, and so he planned on doing everything within his power to help her. He was even certain now that he would have helped her even if she hadn't cured Aris.

That was how much he liked and respected this determined woman.

The three of them sat down around the L-shaped couch in the living room. Adam pilled pancakes onto three plates and served them all. There was also butter and agave, which Aris did not hesitate to load up on. He sighed.

"Aris, I know you're cured, but please make sure you're still eating healthy. Don't add too much butter. It's bad for you."

"You're my lover, Adam, not my mother. Please act like it."

"I am your lover, and that's why I worry about you. This is my right as your future husband. Please listen to me."

"Tee-hee. Okay. I guess I can listen to you this once."

"Thank you."

Aris wiped off some of the butter she had lathered onto her pancakes—there had been so much it looked like a small mountain of glistening fat—though she kept the agave. He didn't mind so much since it was a healthier alternative to regular syrups, which were high in fructose and corn syrup.

In the past, Aris had been a very willful girl who never listened to anyone. Her poor parents had often been run ragged by the rambunctious child. Adam could have held her reins back then, but he'd loved her far too much and would often spoil the girl rotten, much to her parents' dismay. It wasn't until she caught Mortems Disease that he began acting more like a mother hen. He couldn't help it. Adam just wanted Aris to live a long life so they could stay together.

"What's the plan for today?" asked Fayte. She squirmed as if uncomfortable by their conversation.

He sent her an apologetic smile before abiding by her will. "I think the first thing we should do is form our guild. We have a [Guild Creation Token], so I think we should use it right away before anyone else finds one. The earlier we can get this done, the better off we'll be."

"I agree, and I've been looking into how guilds are created in *Age of Gods*." Fayte pushed aside her now empty plate, grabbed a tablet sitting on the coffee table, and input some data. "It looks like Mystique Incorporated has been updating their website since the game launched. Last night, they added some new information about creating guilds. Here."

Adam took the tablet from Fayte and looked at the screen. Aris got on her knees and leaned over to rest her chin on his shoulder so she could read as well.

"It says here we need to register our guild with the Guild Association. We also need to buy a building that will serve as our guild headquarters," he said.

"There are several plots of land that are available to buy for people looking to create a guild," Fayte explained. "It says on their website that our guild headquarters cannot be located within the city. It doesn't say why, but if this game follows the logic of other games, it stands to reason this is to avoid getting the city caught up in a guild war."

Guild Wars were, simply put, a battle between guilds. They not only served as a means of spicing up the PvP aspect of gaming, but to settle disputes between guilds.

It wasn't just guilds who used guild wars as a means of settling disputes either. Ever since the signing of the WWIII Armistice and the creation of the virtual world, governments the world over had used Guild Wars to settle national disputes about any number of issues. Adam remembered when the American Federation had a Guild War with Taoist Union over a trade dispute. The Taoist Union had won that war, but they'd lost the one after that.

"Do you already have a plot of land selected?" asked Adam.

Fayte shook her head. "I've looked at several options, but I think we should speak to the Guild Association before choosing. I'd like to get their opinion before I make a decision."

"In that case, I think you and I should travel to the Guild Association when we log on today. Aris, you, Lilith, and Susan should head out with Titania and Kureha and do some grinding. We need to make sure to maintain a higher level than everyone else in the game," Adam instructed.

"Okay! I'll take Lilith, Sue, Titania, and Kureha out to kick some monster butt." Aris grinned as she thrust a fist into the air.

Fayte sent him a wry smile. "Aris is a very different person now that she's been cured."

But Adam shook his head. "No. This is Aris's true self. She's just gone back to being the Aris from before she got Mortems Disease."

"Wooo hoo! I am ready to kick ass and take names!" Aris continued to cheer.

Fayte raised an eyebrow at Adam, who merely shrugged and looked away.

✳✳✳

The Guild Association office was a large building made of white bricks and a red-domed roof. It looked somewhat like a cathedral and was located in what was generally considered the Craftsmen District of Solum.

This section of the city had been given that name because this area was surrounded by weavers, dyers, armorers, bookbinders, painters, masons, bakers, leatherworkers, embroiderers, cobblers, candlemakers, etc. The sound of hammers pounding at metal echoed all around them as they walked. Plumes of smoke wafted from several chimneys, filling the air with white and black. When Adam turned his head, he saw a weaver creating a basket through the window of a shop. Another building housed a couple that was working together to dye clothing. Someone was working everywhere he and Fayte looked.

Nobody else was at the Guild Association when they arrived, but that made sense. They were the only people with a [Guild Creation Token], which meant they were the only ones who could form a guild. Why would anyone else be present when there was no reason for them to be here?

They walked across a marble floor. Long tables on either side of the vast interior filled the space. Tellers stood before those tables, though all of them appeared to be in varying states of boredom, with some resting their chin on the butt of their hands and others simply leaning over, dead to the world. One of them was even sleeping. Something Adam noticed about the workers was that all of them were attractive men and women.

It must be a design of the game. People are more agreeable when the person they are talking to is attractive.

It was a sad truth of the world, but people who were considered universally attractive could get away with a lot more than people who weren't. An attractive male might not get in trouble with a woman for stalking her. A woman might get off with a warning instead of a ticket for going 245 kph down a 120 kph freeway. Being "hot," as it were, was just another weapon in a person's arsenal.

Of course, being attractive often came with its own set of problems.

Fayte was living proof of that.

They walked up to one of the tellers, a sleepy-looking woman whose head kept drooping. She didn't even seem to notice them until Fayte coughed into her hand.

"Oh… er… h-hello! Can I help you two? Are you lost?"

I guess I can't blame her for thinking we're lost. I'm sure she didn't expect someone to come here for at least another month if not longer. Guilds normally aren't created this early in the game.

"We're not lost. We're here to form a guild," Fayte said with a smile.

The woman blinked. "You are? Um, I don't know how to tell you this, but you need a [Guild Creation Token] to form a guild and… oh, my. I-I see you have one right here. Wow. So it's true. I heard there was someone who came into possession of a [Guild Creation Token], but I wasn't sure I believed… ah! Wait! Doesn't that mean you're Fayte Dairing?!"

"I am," Fayte said, nonplussed.

"I am so sorry for not recognizing you! I-I am actually a big fan of yours! Um, this might be very forward of me, but can I… please shake your hand?!"

Fayte shifted uncomfortably as the woman bowed over the table and stuck out her hand, but she was the daughter of a powerful noble family—if disowned at the moment—and so she had learned early on how to remain calm at all times. Her eyes crinkled as she held out her hand and accepted the shake. Adam could tell she was smiling behind her veil.

"Th-thank you very much!" the woman said, tears of gratitude in her eyes. The other tellers looked very jealous, especially the men.

"You are welcome," Fayte replied diplomatically.

"I'll never wash this hand again!"

Fayte's smile became fixed. "No, that's unhygienic. Please make sure to regularly wash your hand."

"If you're Miss Fayte, then wouldn't that make you Adam?" The woman turned to him. Finally.

"That's right," Adam said.

"I didn't get to see the tournament, but I heard all about what you did. Your love and loyalty toward Miss Fayte is so strong you surrendered without even putting up a fight. It sounds so romantic!" She clasped her hands together and stared between them with such an excitable look Adam imagined she had hearts in her eyes.

Adam and Fayte shifted away from each other as a strange tension settled between them. These feelings had been growing ever since Aris came out of cryosleep, but it wasn't like there was anything they could do about it. He wasn't stupid enough not to recognize that she had feelings for him. At the same time, he couldn't reciprocate those feelings because he loved Aris. That was simply all there was to it.

"Maybe we could move this along," Fayte said, trying to get back on track.

"O-oh. Right. Yes. Let's do that. So, um, you two came here to create a guild, yes? Please, follow me. There's a lot to tell you about the guild creation process, so we should go somewhere more comfortable. Oh! By the way, my name is Clarise Fontina. It's a pleasure to meet you both."

Adam hadn't been paying attention to her status information, but now that she'd introduced herself, he couldn't stop himself from looking at the status display.

Name: Clarise Fontina

Description: An excitable guild associate. She is a romantic at heart and gets easily distracted.

Lvl: 10

Health: 190/190

CREATING A GUILD

After moving out from behind the counter, Clarise led them to the end of the hall, through a small doorway in the corner with a hallway on the other side. Adam looked at one of the doors they passed. Made with burnished wood and swirling designs, it had an oblong plaque situated at about eye level with a number on it. 001. The door immediately after was 003, 005, and so on. Doors on the other side possessed even numbers.

The door they entered was 011.

A fairly spacious interior greeted them. The luxurious red carpet made this room feel very expensive. He'd once read that carpet in the Middle Ages was something only the rich could afford, which made him wonder if this was supposed to be a sign of the Guild Association's wealth. In the center of the room were two couches with the curvature of classic furniture, a table placed between them, and at the far side before a window was a desk with a neat stack of papers.

"This is one of the rooms we use here at the Guild Association when dealing with matters like the formation of a new guild, disputes between guilds, and so on. Please, make yourselves at home." Clarise opened the door wide, stepped aside, and gestured toward the couch.

"Thank you," Fayte said.

"Thanks," Adam mimicked her to be polite.

They sat down on one of the couches, and once more Adam noticed how Fayte sat as far from him as physically possible without seeming impolite. Clarise didn't sit on the couch. She walked over to the desk. First, she grabbed a small bell sitting on the desk and rang it. Then she grabbed several sheets of paper from inside of a drawer and a rather ornate quill. Only then did she sit down on the couch opposite them.

"First of all, I believe congratulations are in order." Clarise gave them both a bright smile. "You are the first people to form a guild, which comes with certain privileges that I will explain to you very soon. Before I get into that, though, let us have some tea."

"Tea?" Adam asked with a blink.

The door opened seconds after he asked and a woman dressed in the white and black frilled uniform of a maid trundled in, pushing a cart. He could only stare in surprise as the woman quietly and efficiently set out the teacups on beautifully designed plates with golden embroidery, poured some refreshing-smelling tea, added another plate, and then set a three-tiered table full of pastries in the middle. All this happened in a few seconds. Then the woman was pushing the cart back out the door, which closed shut behind her with a soft click.

"Please, help yourselves while I explained both the benefits of being the first guild and the guild creation process." Clarise gestured to the tea and cakes, then squealed to herself. "Gosh, this is so exciting! I never could have imagined that I would be the first person to help with the creation of a guild—and of all people, it's Miss Fayte's guild I'm helping create! Oh, I could honestly die happy right now."

"Please don't die on us. We still need to create our guild," Fayte said, a wry smile in her voice.

Clarise tried to regain her composure. "O-of course. Please excuse me for my loss of composure. Ahem. The tea and cakes."

Adam removed his mask and set it on the coffee table. The moment he did, there was a sharp intake of breath. He looked over to find Clarise staring at him in shock.

"Something wrong?" he asked.

"Oh, no! Not at all! I was just surprised by how hot—er, no. How handsome you are! Yes. I'm surprised by your handsomeness. I-I mean, I'm not completely surprised. I just didn't realize you would be such an attractive man! Oh, gosh! What am I saying?!"

Adam smiled wryly and reached out for his teacup as the woman buried her face in her hands. He first tried the tea with nothing. It vaguely tasted like Darjeeling, but there was a unique aroma and flavor that made it distinctly fantasy. He couldn't quite put his finger on it. The taste was just… different.

As he was drinking, Clarise gulped as Fayte reached up to remove her veil, revealing the face of a woman so beautiful he would have suspected it to have been created by polygons and pixels. It was simply too perfect for words. Clarise seemed to think so too. She was transfixed as Fayte poured some milk into her tea, stirred it, then pinched the handle between her thumb and index finger, using her middle finger to support it as she brought it to her almost too perfect lips.

As expected from a woman born into a high-class family. She must have taken all kinds of etiquette classes.

There was a way to drink tea among nobles. The tradition had been out of style for many decades, but it became renewed in the American Federation after World War III. Certain rules were followed like "don't call it high tea," or "the saucer stays on the able," and whatnot. Adam had learned a little bit about that. Some of his targets had been nobles, so it was important to know the ins and outs of noble etiquette. He hadn't used any of that knowledge in a very long time, however.

"You said you were going to explain the benefits of becoming the first guild created in your world. Can you please tell us what those benefits are now?" asked Fayte.

"Huh? O-oh! Yes! My apologies! Gosh, I don't know what came over me!" Clarise stuttered several times, more than a tad flustered, then coughed into her hand and began talking again. "The first and most obvious benefit of being the first guild is your reputation. As the first guild ever created, even people on the other continents will know of your names. I doubt there will be a single person alive who won't have heard of you very soon. With the addition of an increased reputation comes increased demand. The main purpose of a guild consists of the following: taking on quests, exploring and raiding dungeons, and defending the continent from disaster. As the first guild, you will be assigned more quests than any other. You will be given top priority on quests given to the Guild Association, of course, but people far and wide will likely come to you with quests of their own."

Adam reached out toward one of the sandwiches at the bottom tier. It was filled with thinly sliced chicken and cream cheese. The cranberry jam added a unique tartness to the food. It wasn't bad.

I wonder if I can make something similar for Alice and Fayte in the real world...

"So more quests will be given to us," Fayte murmured. "That could indeed be a great boon, though whether a small guild like ours can complete so many quests will be up in the air. What other benefits are there?"

"The second benefit is preferential treatment," Clarise answered. "This means that, aside from getting more quests from us than other guilds, when someone has a dispute with you and aims to settle it with a Guild War, you are allowed to choose the time, place, and number of members the other team can bring. Of course, you cannot abuse this particular system. A good example would be if you have one hundred members participating. You cannot make your opponents bring any less than one hundred members. However, you can force them to only bring members that have reached a certain level, which will give you a key advantage when deciding on strategies and the like."

"So let's say we have three members in our guild. We could say the other side can only bring three members between levels 10 and 15?" asked Fayte.

"Correct," said Clarise.

Adam nodded along. Knowing what level your opponents were at would help them determine what kind of skills they had, how much health they possessed, what their stats would be, and it meant they could force the other guild to leave their heaviest hitters back home. In a battle between guilds, having this kind of power could cripple the enemy forces before the fight even began.

"The third benefit has to do with the guild's location. As the first guild, not only do you have free pick of any one of our locations for a guild headquarters, but you won't have to pay any fees or taxes on your property for half a year. We normally charge between fifty to twenty percent of whatever you earn from quests and dungeon raids. That will be waived for your first six months. Of course, you will still have to pay for the costs of the materials and construction of the building, but the land will be given to you as a reward."

Now that was… interesting. While every game in this day and age had guilds, there had never been a game where guilds had to pay taxes. That was because games saw no need for this since it wasn't real. This, he guessed, was just another way in which *Age of Gods* differed.

Fayte kept a studious expression on her face as she listened, even as her hand reached for a scone. She didn't look away from Clarise as she broke a scone in half, added some clotted cream and lemon curd, then took a delicate bite.

Clarise took a sip of her tea to whet her parched throat, then continued. "The last benefit actually has to do with Guild Wars. Guild Wars are what happens when two guilds have a dispute. Let's say you and another guild discover a dungeon at the same time. You can't decide which guild has the right to explore the dungeon first. Guild Wars are meant to solve conflicts like that. The two guilds will fight over the right to explore the dungeon. Of course, it isn't just dungeon exploration rights that Guild Wars can settle. This method of settling disputes can be used for anything. You can even force a guild to disband by placing a stipulation in the contracts signed before the Guild War if both sides agree to it, or you could force a member from another guild to join yours. Stuff like that."

"So I see. And what benefit do we have in regard to Guild Wars?" asked Fayte.

Adam reached for a pastry. It was a fruit tart. The burst of flavor on his tongue didn't surprise him anymore, but the way the food revved his appetite did. He still didn't understand how he could feel hungry inside of a game.

"The benefit is that you will have a one-month grace period where you do not have to accept any challenges to take part in a Guild War," Clarise said as Adam took another bite of his tart. "While challenges can sometimes be rejected based on extenuating circumstances, there are many cases where you will be unable to reject a challenge to a Guild War. However, during this one-month grace period, you can reject every challenge that comes your way. Of course, right now your guild is the only one in existence. The one-month grace period won't start until a second guild is formed."

The woman had gone into quite a bit of depth explaining the benefits they would receive, and there were many. It seemed being the first guild in this game came with some incredible perks.

This should also help Fayte clear the second goal of her bet.

Fayte had three criteria that must be met to win her bet, and the second one was increasing her standing and reputation to match or exceed the least powerful family among the top ten most powerful families in the American Federation.

The American Federation was a country born from World War III. In the wake of WWIII, the United States, Canada, and Mexico were fractured, destabilized, and on the verge of collapse. To rebuild the foundations that had been destroyed anew, the three countries united to share land, wealth, and technology. It was thanks to this unification that the American Federation was considered the second strongest nation in the world immediately after the Taoist Union, which was powerful primarily because the former countries of China and India still boasted the largest populations in the world—even in the wake of Mortems Disease.

"Those do all sound like great benefits," Fayte said, nodding several times. Her eyes were sharp as she considered what these benefits meant for her personally. She took a sip of tea as if to give herself more time to think, then set it down and asked, "So, how do we go about creating a guild?"

"First, can you please hand me your [Guild Creation Token]?" Clarise held out her hand. Fayte removed the [Guild Creation Token] from her inventory and placed it in Clarise's outstretched hand. "This token will be returned to you once it's ready. We have to process each token so it can be used as an identifier. Speaking of, you'll want to give me a design of your guild symbol. That symbol will go on the token, your guild building, and your [Guild Identification Badge]. We can leave that aside right now since the process for that will take several days. First off, I'll need you to fill out and sign these documents."

The documents Clarise slid across the table looked like standard forms made from old parchment. It asked for things like the name of the guild leader, her second-in-command, her treasurer, her secretary, etc. It also asked for the guild name, what kind of guild it was, and where the guild would be located. Then it asked her to sign in several places.

"Have you thought of a guild name?" Adam asked. This was something they hadn't talked about, but he assumed someone like Fayte would have already come up with her own name.

"I have," Fayte said confidently as she wrote down the guild's name. Adam looked at the name, smiled, and said nothing as she filled out the rest of the forms. When she was finished, she gave the forms back to Clarise, who looked them over, nodding and "hmmhmming" several times.

"It looks like everything is in order. I'll still need you to create a design for your guild, but with this—buwah?!" Adam was certain Clarise would have done a spit take if she'd been drinking something. Her eyes grew to the size of saucers as she turned her head toward Fayte. "Th-this here says you wish to make the area surrounding Suncrest Mountain your base of operations? That place is filled with dangerous monsters! Are you sure about this?"

"Is there a problem?" asked Fayte, raising a single eyebrow.

"W-well… no. That is one of the places you can choose as a guild location, b-b-but that place is dangerous! All the monsters there are level 40 and above! It's the most dangerous zone near Solum! In fact, even on the whole Sun Continent, you're only likely to find maybe two or three areas outside of dungeons that are more dangerous, but those are closer to Sunestia!"

Sunestia was the capital city of the Sun Continent. From the maps Adam had seen, it was located on the other side of the Suncrest Mountain Range, which divided the continent in half, meaning they would have to pass through the dangerous Suncrest Mountains to reach the city. That also explained why no one else could reach the capital. The monsters they needed to fight through were simply too powerful for anyone but Adam, his companions, and the Spear God.

"Also, when someone forms a guild in a heavy monster spawning point, the monsters will be drawn to the construction work and form what's called a Stampede. These Stampedes can consist of anywhere from fifty to one hundred monsters. They'll do everything in their power to tear down your guild before it can be completed, and it will be your job to protect the construction workers while they are building your guild. Fighting against so many monsters at such a high level is suicide even for someone like you, Miss Fayte!"

It seemed this woman didn't have much confidence in them, though Adam could not blame her. She couldn't see their stats. Even if Clarise knew they were powerful, she didn't understand how powerful, and even he would admit to being a little wary of facing over fifty monsters at level 40 and above.

Fayte, however, clapped her hands. "That's perfect then!"

"What?!" Clarise shrieked.

"We can use this Stampede as a means of leveling up more quickly."

"Y-y-y-y-you mean you want to farm the monsters at Suncrest Mountain for experience points?!"

"Indeed I do. Now we're definitely building our guild headquarters there."

"B-b-b-b-b-but—!!!"

"Please make all the necessary preparations, okay?" Fayte requested of the stuttering woman with a calm, pleasant smile.

✳✳✳

Clarise spent several more minutes trying to talk Fayte out of creating a guild near the Suncrest Mountain Range, but the beautiful woman wouldn't budge, and the excitable guild associate could only capitulate to Fayte's overwhelming confidence. They left the Guild Association around half an hour later.

Adam stretched his arms above his head as they exited the building and began walking down the street. "That took a long longer than expected. I had no idea so much went into the creation of a guild."

"There is a lot that goes into creating a guild. Honestly, though, I think creating a guild in *Age of Gods* might be more involved than any other game I've played. Anyway, we should call the others and ask them to meet up with us so we can explain the situation to them," Fayte said.

"Leave that to me," Adam said as he accessed his friend's list, selected Aris's name, and hit the call button.

Her voice rang out seconds later. *"Adam! Are you done creating the guild?"*

"Sort of," Adam said vaguely. "There's still some work to do, but our part is done for now. Where are you and the others?"

"We're kicking monster butt just like you asked us to!"

"I'm guessing that means you're at the Suncrest Mountains. Come on back to Solum. We need to discuss what's going to happen from here on out."

"Yes, sir!"

Adam's lips twitched as Aris ended the call. He could almost hear the salute in her voice.

"She seems awfully excited," Fayte said.

"That girl is always excited about something." Adam smiled fondly as he thought about the past. "I remember when we were younger, she got into the habit of catching new animals to keep as pets. She would always be over the moon whenever she successfully managed to catch one. Of course, she always had a short attention span and would eventually grow bored of taking care of an animal and release it back into the wild after several weeks. I imagine living in a fantasy world like this has piqued her excitement."

"Yes, being able to explore such an expansive world like this would make anyone excited," Fayte said, an odd stiffness in her voice. Adam sighed but chose to ignore it.

It would take several hours for Aris and the others to arrive back at Solum, depending on how far into the Suncrest Mountains they were, and that was if they traveled at their fastest speed without fighting any monsters along the way. One thing Adam noticed about this game was the realistic timeframe it took to travel. He wondered if a patch would eventually be installed with an updated method of travel like teleportation pads.

Adam spent that time walking around the city with Fayte. It seemed just like any other woman, Fayte was someone who enjoyed window shopping. Even with the tension between them, her eyes still lit up like stars whenever she caught sight of something she took a fancy to, and she happily dragged him into stores that she was interested in.

However, as with all good things, this time would soon come to an end.

It happened when they had the misfortune of bumping into Levon and Connor. Adam didn't know what the two were doing in Solum. He honestly thought they would have been raiding a dungeon or taking on a quest to help them level up after their humiliating defeat at his group's hands, but maybe they had just come back from grinding their levels at a spawn point or something. He didn't know. He didn't care.

"Fayte… Adam, what a pleasant surprise. I didn't expect to run into either of you so soon after the tournament," Levon greeted with an unpleasant smile.

"The surprise is all mine, I assure you," Fayte said in a calm voice. Adam noticed she said "the surprise" and not "the pleasure," which was what one usually said during such circumstances.

"Did you just get back from the Guild Association?" asked Levon, seemingly genuinely curious. He didn't seem at all upset by what happened during the tournament, though Adam knew he must have been burning with rage on the inside. This man was so vindictive that he had tried to drive his younger sister into depression by hiring people to bully her in school when she proved to be better with the spear than him.

"We did. Our guild will be formed within the next day, I imagine," Fayte said.

Levon's smile might have looked genuine to someone who didn't know him, but it was fixed to Adam as he said, "Congratulations. I'm sure you'll make your family proud."

It was a very slight dig. Levon knew Fayte had been disowned, and by mentioning her family like this, he was basically telling her that she was a disgrace to her family name. Fayte did not react in any way other than to smile, however, showing that she was made of sterner stuff than most delicate noble women.

"Thank you. I'm certain they will be quite proud of me… eventually."

"I imagine so."

As Levon and Fayte held their patently fake congenial conversation, a devious idea popped into Adam's head.

He placed his hand on the small of Fayte's back. It was a subtle action, but it didn't go unnoticed by Levon, whose eyes narrowed in quiet rage. Fayte also straightened her spine like she'd been zapped. Adam pretended to ignore it as he leaned in as if to whisper in her ear.

"We should probably get going. I imagine Aris and the others are waiting for us," he whispered in a voice just loud enough that Levon could hear it.

"Of... Of course," Fayte said, a hitch in her voice. She took a deep breath to calm down before speaking to Levon. "You'll have to excuse me, but it seems we have some business to take care of."

"Don't let me keep you. Go do what you need to," Levon said, still smiling congenially.

Fayte gave him a stiff nod before walking off. Adam marched by her side, his hand still on her lower back. He was wearing a mask, so, unfortunately, Levon could not see his vicious smile when they passed each other, but he was certain the man could tell what he was doing. Levon's fists shook with rage.

"You can remove your hand now," Fayte said once Levon and Connor were out of sight.

"Right. Sorry." Adam removed his hand from Fayte's back.

"It's fine," Fayte mumbled. "Just never do something like that again."

"I won't. Promise."

It really wasn't fine. Even Adam recognized that he'd just pulled a jerk move. He had wanted to enrage Levon so badly that he hadn't considered how Fayte might feel about being used like that. The only reason Fayte wasn't getting upset at him was probably that she needed his help.

I'll have to find some way to apologize later.

Actions spoke louder than words, so Adam would apologize through actions first. Fayte had a sweet tooth. He could probably make crepes for dessert tonight. They were lighter fare than something like cheesecake, but they were still quite sweet and delicious, especially if he stuffed them full of cream cheese, fruits, and chocolate. If he wanted to go really light, he could replace the cream cheese with whip cream. She might like that better since it didn't have as much sugar and no fat.

They continued to the food court. Aris, Lilith, Susan, Titania, and Kureha would already be waiting for them when they arrived.

STAMPEDE

Two days went by since Fayte's and Adam's meeting with Clarise. The Guild Association handled all the matters regarding the formation of their guild, including contacting masons, blacksmiths, stonemasons, weavers, roofers, locksmiths, carpenters, and so on. While they were not required to do anything, Clarise did call Fayte to the Guild Association several times to discuss the design of their soon-to-be-built guild headquarters.

Adam, Aris, Lilith, Fayte, Kureha, Titania, and Susan spent those two days cleaning out the area that would become their new guild headquarters of monsters. All of them had gained a few levels by grinding. Aris was now at level 16. Meanwhile, Fayte, Lilith, and Susan were at level 17. He, Kureha, and Titania were at level 18. They had been keeping a lead on their levels because Adam woke up early every morning to grind before everyone else.

After the passage of two days, construction was set to begin on their guild building. The guild workers were all gathered around the construction spot and laying down the foundation. It looked like normal construction work, though the leader of this group assured them construction would be quick because they could use magic to help them build faster.

"It'll take about three hours to build your guild building. We're going to need you to protect us while we work. If a stampede comes, you'll have to stop them. I'll warn you right now that if even a single one of my workers dies, I'll pack up and leave. I'm not gonna put my men in a dangerous situation, you got me?"

The construction boss was a man named Bastion Builder. He was an overweight man with arms like tree trunks and a barrel-shaped chest. His thick beard was ruddy-colored and made Adam wonder if this man had dwarf blood in him. He looked like a dwarf had a child with a giant. Speaking of which, this man was huge, easily standing over several heads above Adam. He would have put the man at two hundred centimeters in height. He spoke in a deep voice like rumbling thunder that matched his imposing figure.

"Please rest assured, we won't let a single of your workers die," Fayte said.

"I'll be taking your word for it, lass."

As the workers continued spreading out the foundation for their building, Fayte turned to the group, eyes lit with determination. "You heard what he said. We cannot let a single monster past us."

"Lilith?" Adam turned to the woman clad in all black.

Lilith was a beautiful woman with skin as white as freshly fallen snow, dark eyes, and hair blacker than raven's feathers. She had the alluringly wide hips and a prominent bust that models everywhere would envy, but she also possessed the supple, powerful muscles of a trained warrior. As she stepped forward, her long hair, held together in a braid behind her back, jostled. Like him, Fayte, and Aris, she wore a mask that concealed the lower half of her face. Only her dark brown eyes could be seen.

"I've gathered what intel I can on stampedes and have learned that they often form when a large group of humans gathers outside of a city. These stampedes can range in size from fifty to one hundred monsters. There have also been known incidents where there was a stampede of over one thousand monsters, but those only happen once in a blue moon. Known as Pandemic Stampedes, they occur when a large group of monsters gathers to attack a human settlement."

"That sounds like an Event Quest," Susan said.

"Ah! I know about those! Event Quests are special, time-limited quests that can only be completed during a specific timeframe," Aris said.

Susan nodded. "G-generally speaking, Event Quests are large-scale events that require multiple guilds to join forces. In the case of a Pandemic Stampede, I imagine only a guild like the Pleonexia Alliance or Daggerfall Dynasty would be able to complete one on their own. In the last big game, um, Tyranny Impact, there was a similar event where a horde of several thousand undead attacked the city of Fallhaven. The Pleonexia Alliance and Daggerfall Dynasty were the only ones to complete the quest by themselves."

While all the other women in their party could have been called gorgeous, Susan Forebear was the only one Adam would have called adorable. She had light brown hair and doe-like brown eyes. Her skin was pale, but not so pale that she looked unhealthy. Her wide-eyed appearance made her seem very young and generated strangely protective instincts within Adam. He imagined most men who met her would feel the desire to shield this girl from all the horrors this world had to offer.

"So do we have a plan to deal with this?" asked Aris.

"I have seen Stampedes before," Titania added from her place on Adam's shoulder. The beautiful redhead kicked her feet back and forth as she eyed them. "There are two ways to deal with a Stampede. The first is to wipe out every monster that attacks. This is difficult but not impossible. The second method is to find the monster who created the Stampede and kill them. All Stampedes have a monster that is designated as the Leader. These Leaders are generally far stronger than the other monsters, on the same level as a dungeon boss. Given our location, you're probably looking at a 3-Star Monster. The rest will probably just be 1-Star Monsters, but they will still be at a relatively high level."

"In that case, why don't I go ahead and deal with the Leader, while the rest of you fend off the Stampede?" suggested Adam.

Aris crossed her arms and glared at him. "I think what you meant to say was: 'Aris and I will deal with the Leader,' right?"

"No. I mean just me." Adam shook his head. "Even if this is just a small Stampede consisting of fifty monsters, that's still fifty monsters we have to protect the construction workers from. We can't afford to pull too many of our forces off protection duty, especially when there are so few of us."

That was one of the downsides to being a small guild. They did not have the forces necessary to guarantee the safety of a group like those construction workers from such a large invasion of monsters. Even though all of them were individually very powerful, all the power in the world could not defend against overwhelming numbers, especially if the monsters they faced were going to be between levels 30 and 40.

"We can't afford to take away more than one person," Adam continued. "Even removing me from the equation could spell disaster here. That's why I'll cut a path straight through the Stampede, find the Leader, and kill it before the monsters can overrun you guys and attack the workers."

"I agree with Adam. He's assessed the situation quite nicely," Fayte said with a nod. "That's why, Aris, you, me, Lilith, Kureha, and Titania will stay back to protect the workers."

Aris clicked her tongue. "Fiiiine. I guess that makes sense."

Adam and Fayte shared a look, smiles hidden behind their respective coverings.

"The Stampede should only come from one direction, so at least we won't have to create a perimeter around the workers," Titania said.

Fayte nodded. "In that case, we will create a wall. Aris and Lilith fight at the front. Myself, Kureha, and Susan will be at the back to provide cover fire and deal damage to monsters further out. Meanwhile, Titania will use her songs to buff and heal us as necessary." Fayte turned to Adam. "We'll be counting on you to finish off the leader quickly."

"Please leave it to me," Adam said with a nod.

At that moment, one of the workers shouted out, "I see something in the distance!!"

Adam turned to find a cloud of rising dust several hundred meters away. He narrowed his eyes and channeled energy to enhance his vision. When he saw the massive swell of monsters like a rising tidal wave against them, even he balked. There were so many!

"It looks like this Stampede is a little bigger than a normal one," he said to the others. "I'm counting at least two hundred monsters."

It must have been because of their location. The Suncrest Mountain Range contained several monster spawning points. Adam had gone ahead and mapped them out, so he knew there were at least twenty, which was a lot more than any other location he had been to thus far. Monsters normally spawned here one at a time, but there were occasions when as many as ten monsters spawned from each point. If all twenty points spawned ten monsters each, that would make for two hundred.

Susan and Titania paled. It was hard to tell if the others were displaying the same fear, since they were all hiding their faces behind fabric, but Adam imagined even Lilith would be nervous about facing so many monsters at once.

The ground was beginning to rumble as the stampede came closer, as the dust cloud got bigger, and the monsters that had appeared as specks in the distance began gaining form. They were indistinct, blurry, but Susan could now see them as well. As a Fairy Archer Class, she had better eyesight than everyone save him.

"Adam, we'll need you to be fast. There's no way we can keep that many monsters at bay for long," Fayte said.

"Right. Guess we'd better get started then." Adam took a deep, slow breath, then smiled as he turned toward the Stampede and drew his spear.

It was time to go to work.

***

Because they didn't want to risk the workers getting caught up in their battle, the group moved further away from the construction site. The workers had finished laying down the foundation and were now in the process of actually building. It would have been interesting to watch since they were using a combination of normal and magical means to help construct the guild headquarters, but they could not risk it. Everything would be over if even one of Bastion's workers died.

Titania had cast [Scan] on as many of the monsters as she could before the battle began. All the monsters were at level 30, which meant they were weaker than what they normally fought here. Adam guessed it had something to do with how many monsters had been spawned. Maybe when more monsters spawned, their levels were decreased to accommodate for the increased number of forces.

The next moment, soft singing echoed all around them. This was not the upbeat [Song of Vigor], but the powerful [Song of Valor], which increased everyone's Physical and Magical Defense by 300%. Titania must have determined that having a powerful defense would be more useful than a powerful attack. And indeed, while being able to kill monsters faster was a strong skill, when there were so many enemies that it didn't matter how quickly they were killed, having a powerful defense would be the key to surviving longer.

Once the Stampede was less than fifty meters away, Adam bent his knees and burst forward, shooting off the ground like a rocket. He soared forward so fast that it only took a few seconds for him to reach the front of the Stampede. The hundreds of monsters filling his vision were as myriad as they were many. He caught everything from massive reptiles to gigantic cyclops charging at him. Which of these was the so-called Leader? It wasn't the one front and center, which meant it was probably further in the back.

[Blood Sacrifice]

[Energy Sweep]

-13,056; -13,056; -13,056; -13,056; -13,056; -13,056; -13,056; -13,056; -13,056; -13,056; -13,056; -13,056; -13,056; -13,056; -13,056; -13,056; -13,056; -13,056!

Adam's first attack was the AoE skill [Energy Sweep]. He swung his spear in a grand arc that sent forward a burst of energy so intense and bright it looked like a wave of light. It slammed into the front row of monsters, staggered them, and continued on to sweep through several more. While the damage it dealt was massive, all of these monsters had health ranging in the fifty thousands. The attack injured them, but none were even close to death.

[Energy Blast]

From behind Adam, Fayte raised her staff high, the tip glowing with vibrant light. She swung it down and thrust it forward a moment later, unleashing a beam of intense magical energy. The attack was so powerful that even with her heels dug in, she was pushed back by the force. However, she merely gritted her teeth and swept her beam of energy across the horde of monsters.

-23,880; -23,880!

The damage she did was even more massive than what Adam could do. Fayte had become their heaviest hitter, with a Magical Attack stat of over +15,000. When combined with her skill [Energy Blast], the amount of damage she could deal was increased by 1.5 times.

Of course, even with her incredible power, her attacks were not strong enough to kill even one of these monsters, but that was okay since there were more people in their party.

[Rain of Arrows]

-5,655; -5,655; -5,655; -5,655; -5,655; -5,655; -5,655; -5,655; -5,655; -5,655; -5,655; -5,655; -5,655; -5,655; -5,655; -5,655; -5,655; -5,655; -5,655!

Susan shot an arrow into the sky, which then multiplied into more than a dozen arrows that rained down on the Stampede. While she didn't deal as much damage as Fayte, the attack stopped several monsters in their tracks, which Adam finished off with a simple

[Slash] of his spear. Before long, he was wading deep into the enemy lines.

✻✻✻

Aris twirled her daggers excitedly as she waited for the Stampede to reach them. Watching Adam plunge headfirst into the Stampede was getting her all fired up. She honestly wanted nothing more than to rush headlong into the enemy with her lover, but she knew it was important to defend the workers while he took down the boss, so she held back. Still, though, her heart was pounding with excitement.

I've always wanted to live a life full of adventure. I couldn't do that once I got Mortems Disease, but now I can. How fun! How exciting! My heart won't stop pounding!

-10,566; -10,566!

At that moment, a loud crackle echoed around them. Aris looked up as storm clouds formed in the sky above their heads. Flashes of lightning streaked through the clouds, then gathered into one specific spot before, with another flash, dozens of lightning bolts rained down on the Stampede. The attack fried the insides of the monsters, which lit up like a light display at Christmas. This was Kureha's [Thunder Storm] attack.

Kureha didn't just end her assault with that one attack, but instead raised her first tail above her head. Fire gathered on the tip. It was so hot that Aris could feel it at her back. She was sure such an attack would have made her sweat if friendly fire were a thing, but fortunately, the creators had decided to be kind. You couldn't get hit by the attack of someone in your party. In either event, Kureha swept her tail forward and unleashed a wave of fire that overtook the incoming Stampede like a storm.

[Firestorm]

-6,916; -6,916!

Damage number signs floated over the heads of several dozen monsters. Some of the weaker monsters fell forward and tumbled across the ground, dead. The monsters behind them knocked the corpses out of the way and continued their charge, barely slowing. Fayte, Kureha, and Susan continued to launch attack after attack, whittling away at the monsters.

Until, finally, the Stampede reached Aris.

With an excited smile on her face, Aris shot forward like a bullet, so fast the world around her became a blur of indecipherable color. She didn't stop moving even as she threw herself into her first attack. Spinning on the balls of her feet, the weapons in her hands sung as she swung them around, catching several monsters.

[Spirited Twirl]

-1,066; -1,066!

Her attack didn't do nearly as much damage as the others, but she didn't let this stop her or even slow her down. She flowed from one attack to another. With a swing of both weapons, she cut into a giant reptilian creature with yellow eyes, a long tail, and four massive feet with sharp claws.

[Double Slash]

-1,400!

The monster roared and tried to attack. Aris danced out of the way as it slammed its feet on the ground where she'd been standing, then rolled across the grass several more times to avoid the stampeding feet of several other enemies. As she came to her feet, she found herself face to face with another monster, a giant cyclops. She struck it four times in quick succession with her swords.

[Dancing Swords]

-1,610; -3,220; -6,440; -12,880!

This monster must have been on its last legs because her attack caused it to fall backward with a thud so powerful it rocked the earth. The cyclops, which went by the name [One-Eyed Gigantis], did not get back up. It also squashed several other monsters flat, dealing them a good deal of damage.

Aris continued to attack, releasing shouts as she swung the swords in her hand like extensions of her arms. The monsters around her seemed to blur together as she fought them. Adrenaline pumped through her veins. She was having so much fun! The only thing that would have made this better was if Adam was by her side.

"What are you doing?! Pay attention!"

"Huh?"

Aris snapped out of her battle-induced haze as something nearly squashed her like a grape. A figure darted out in front of her and countered the attack with the [Counter] skill, dealing massive damage to the creature that jerked its paws back with a roar. She gazed at the dark-clad woman standing protectively before her. Lilith darted forward and activated [slash] several times, her dagger moving so fast even Aris couldn't see it.

-6,610; -6,610; -6,610; -6,610; -6,610; -6,610; -6,610; -6,610; -6,610; -6,610; -6,610; -6,610; -6,610; -6,610; -6,610; -6,610; -6,610!

The monster, a massive creature with the head and body of a lion, the legs of a goat, and a snake head for a tail, roared and tried to paw swipe at Lilith, but the woman proved incredibly nimble. She danced around the attack as if she could predict her enemy's moves. Then she came in with [Slash] several more times. Damage signs floated above the monster one after another until the creature died and stopped moving.

"Wow, Lilith! You're awesome!" Aris cheered.

But Lilith whirled around on her. The anger in the woman's eyes was enough to send her reeling.

"Don't get so lost in your own battle lust that you lose sight of what's happening around you! Our job isn't to attack these monsters but defend this area, to prevent them from reaching the workers! Several monsters slipped past you when you began attacking! If you only focus on one monster at a time, it only builds aggro for that single monster and the others will ignore you!"

"Oh…"

Aris quickly surveyed the area and realized what Lilith meant. A number of monsters had slipped past them and were now attacking Fayte, Susan, and Kureha, who had used AoE skills to draw their aggro. However, those three were not close-combat fighters. Their most powerful assets lay in their long-range attacks. Their magic attacks also had longer cooldown times, which meant they couldn't use them consecutively. Damage signs floated above the group as they took attacks they were unable to dodge. The only good thing about this situation was Titania, far above their heads and singing the [Song of Valor] that increased their defense. It was the only thing keeping those three alive right now.

Even then, it wasn't looking good.

"Kureha! Look out!"

A giant creature with leathery skin and horns on its head slammed into Kureha, who wasn't fast enough to move away in time. The tiny fox released a pained cry as she was thrown away. She bounced off the ground, then rolled away. Aris was able to see the fox yokai's health bar, and her face paled when she saw that it was at 400/2,400.

"I-I'm sorry," Aris said contritely. "I'll do better."

"See to it that you do," Lilith said, then sighed. "Let's help them."

"Right."

Aris turned with Lilith and burst forward to attack the Stampede that had surrounded Fayte, Susan, and Kureha. She leapt forward and swung both weapons down. She activated [Blade Dance], which allowed her to consecutively attack so long as she had MP and gave her a fifty percent chance of landing a critical hit.

-700; -700; -700; -700; -700; -2,100; -700; -700; -700; -2,100; -700; -700; -700; -700; -700; -700; -700; -700; -700; -700; -2,100; -700; -700; -700; -700; -700; -700; -700; -2,100; -700; -700; -700; -2,100; -700; -700; -700; -700; -2,100; -2,100; -700; -700; -700; -700; -700; -700; -2,100; -700; -700; -700; -700; -700; -2,100; -700; -700; -2,100; -700; -700; -700; -2,100; -700; -700; -700; -700; -700; -700; -700; -700; -700; -700; -2,100; -700; -700; -700!

Because this skill consumed five MP per attack, she quickly ran out and had to drink a [middle-grade magic potion]. Just one wasn't enough, so she downed several more in quick succession before attacking again. She flowed from one attack to another, and didn't just focus on only one enemy but every enemy within her sights. Her goal was to pull the aggro off their long-range attackers and onto her so they could have some breathing room and retreat.

Thanks to her quick work, Fayte was able to cast [Firestorm], which swept across the field and dealt an incalculable amount of damage. Several monsters were lit on fire and began running around in a panic. She then raced toward Kureha, knelt down, and used several [middle-grade health potions] on the fox yokai. This brought Kureha back up to full health. Aris would have sighed in relief, but she couldn't because Fayte's attack had pulled all the monsters' aggro back to her.

Lilith fought on the opposite end of this tiny battleground. She was creating a small hole in the monster Stampede. She leapt onto the shoulders of an ape-like monster with brown fur, slit its throat to deal an incredible -26,440 damage, then leapt off the shoulder and attacked a four-legged monster that looked like a salamander with blistering red skin. Her attack must have struck its weak point because a large -27,762 floated above the creature. That one must have been on its last leg because it died after receiving the powerful attack.

With Lilith clearing a path for them, Fayte, Susan, Kureha, and Titania darted through the opening and retreated to a safer distance. Aris was glad. She was happy her mistake hadn't cost her friends their lives. She also distinctly recalled what Adam had told her about non-player characters, how they could not be revived. Once they died, that was it. Aris promised herself she would not let that happen.

Adam, you need to hurry up, she thought as she threw herself into the fray once more.

THE HYDRA

The Boss monster that Adam faced was one he had never seen before. Aside from being nearly seven times taller than him, its leathery skin gave the four-legged monstrosity a reptilian aesthetic, though the three heads snapping their jaws at him were like nothing he'd seen from a normal reptile. While its skin was an earthy brown, each of the three heads contained a different eye color: The leftmost head had red eyes, the middle head had yellow eyes, and the furthest head had blue eyes. Because Titania was busy helping his party hold off the Stampede, she was unable to use [Scan] on this monster, but he was still able to glean some basic information about it.

It was called [Hydra].

A fierce roar unlike any other rattled Adam's bones as all three of the monster's heads angled toward him. Three different attacks spewed from its mouth. A tornado of fire barreled toward him, a bolt of lightning threatened to char him from the inside out, and numerous water bullets flew his way.

Adam shifted from an attack stance to a light-footed one almost like a rabbit as he hopped backwards on the balls of his feet. The fire burned the ground before him. Heat singed his face and caused his skin to blister. A bolt of lightning struck the spot where he had been not a split second ago, spinning around like a dancer doing a pirouette. Over a dozen water bullets attempted to penetrate his flank, but at the last second, he switched to the defensive Form Five. The spear in his hands became like the propeller of a helicopter as he spun it around to defend himself against the many water bullets.

-300; -300; -300!

Despite his impeccable defensive stance, several water bullets slammed into his chest, right shoulder, and left leg. He gritted his teeth against the pain as his health dropped from 6,775 to 5,875.

The three heads each have a separate element they can use to attack with, and they all act independently from each other. It's almost like this thing's got three separate consciousnesses rather than merely three heads. That makes its attack patterns impossible to predict.

Monsters in VRMMOs often used a form of logic programming to attack with a number of preset patterns. The monsters in *Age of Gods* were a little different in that they seemed capable of adapting, but even they began with an attack pattern that could be analyzed. However, a creature with three heads that attacked independently meant there were an infinitely higher number of ways it could attack. He would have no way of analyzing all three heads in the midst of battle.

Despite this—no, because of this—Adam felt a grin rise to his face. This was another challenge. He'd not felt this kind of insurmountable obstacle since his fight against the [Necromancer] back in the Island of Beginnings.

Since retreating would not help, Adam darted forward, pushing off the ground with his calves, thighs, and toes. He leaned forward as though using gravity to increase his forward charge.

The [Hydra] roared at him as if it could see the challenge in his eyes and was responding with one of its own. Another tornado of fire shot from its mouth. Adam timed the attack before switching to the swift Form Two. He pushed his speed to the limit, threw himself away from the firestorm, rolled across the ground, skipped to his feet, and continued forward.

[Blood Sacrifice]

[Dance of the Sakura Blossoms]

The moment he was within range, Adam activated his two most powerful skills. Half his health disappeared in an instant. Then he shifted into an attack pattern that had nothing in common with the Seven Phoenix Forms Style of the Pleonexia Family. He thrust his spear forward as he danced around one of the [Hydra's] four legs. Had someone been looking at the movements of his feet from a bird's eye view, they would have seen that it looked like he was drawing a sakura blossom in the ground.

-8,160; -24,480; -73,440; -220,320; -660,960!

Five attacks flew forward in quick succession and dealt a staggering amount of damage, but just as he expected from a Boss-level enemy, the [Hydra] was nowhere close to being finished. Adam had no idea how much health this monster had. All he knew was that the moment his attack ended, something was flying toward him at high speeds.

Adam ducked low as a shadow passed over his head. It took him a moment to realize it was a tail. By the time he discovered what had nearly knocked his head off, the [Hydra] had turned around and was throwing its hind leg at him like a horse kicking someone who surprised it from behind. With no time to dodge, Adam shifted to the powerful Form Four stance, brought the blade in close, and thrust it forward with all the strength his body possessed.

It wasn't enough.

-13,056!

-1,500!

"Gaaah!!"

Adam might have dealt some damage, but the foot slamming into him was powerful enough that he was knocked off his feet and sent hurtling backward. Working through the pain, however, he flipped his body around, skidded across the ground, and quickly downed two [middle-grade health potions] to restore the damage done to him.

On any other occasion, Adam would have preferred to dodge such an attack. That was his forte. However, it seemed this monster had a wide attack range and was using that to its advantage. Its feet were simply so big that his approach of dodging with the bare minimum amount of movements was ill-suited to fighting it.

This monster was a bad matchup for him.

I can't afford to let myself take too many hits. I have no idea how much health this monster has. For all I know, I could run out of health potions before I finish whittling down its health.

With narrowed eyes, Adam darted forward again. The [Hydra] fired a bolt of lightning from its middle mouth. He tried to dodge, but Adam became surprised when the lightning bolt suddenly curved around and nearly slammed into him from behind. Only his quick reflexes saved him from certain death.

Its lightning attack can track me?!

The previous attack it unleashed couldn't do that, which meant it probably had more than one technique for each head. Adam would have to be even more careful from now on.

Continuing his run, he dodged fire and water attacks as well, then reached the [Hydra]. It tried to squash him flat. At the very last moment, Adam fell backwards into a slide that allowed him to barely avoid being turned into a pancake. The foot slammed into the ground behind him. He winced at the sound and the feeling reverberating through his body, even as he skipped back to his feet and thrust his spear forward in an [Energy Thrust] that pierced his enemy's leg.

-13,872!

A loud roar of anguish echoed around Adam as he removed his spear from monster flesh and leapt back. The [Hydra] rampaged as it tried to squish him with its four feet. It looked almost like it was hopping around. Adam switched once more to the speedy Form Two and darted away from each and every attack.

He never noticed the tail until it was too late.

-3,420!

"Aaaaah!"

Adam screamed as something struck his spine so hard it felt like it was being snapped. He struck the ground face first and rolled across it like a tumbleweed. The world spun around him. After rolling to a stop, he scrambled to his feet and darted away just in time to avoid being burned to death. An explosion of fire went up where he'd been standing. The attack was so close he received -2,000 damage for simply being near it.

"Haah… haaaah… dammit…"

Because he was low on health, Adam had no choice but to take more [middle-grade health potions]. To make matters worse, [Blood Sacrifice] had worn off and it would take thirty seconds before it was ready for use again. And as if that wasn't bad enough, the [Hydra] had turned all three heads in his direction.

Fire, lightning, and water arced toward him, and Adam put everything he had into dodging. He rolled across the ground to avoid the fire tornado and used his spear as a grounding rod to defeat the lightning, then backpedaled while darting from left to right, avoiding the water bullets that slammed into the ground where he'd been standing a split-second prior.

Those water bullets were no joke. Someone else might have assumed they weren't as deadly because it was just water, but each bullet that struck the ground left a small crater. The ground was harder than his bones. If any of those struck him, they would no doubt do an incredible amount of damage. He couldn't afford to get hit even once.

He was eventually able to activate [Blood Sacrifice] again, and he dashed forward to close the distance before once more activating both it and [Dance of the Sakura Blossoms] to deal a massive amount of damage. Yet even though his attack took away almost one million health points, the [Hydra] remained standing, showing that it was in no way a glass cannon. How much health did this thing have? Adam would have liked to know. He cursed the fact that Titania already had her hands full helping his party.

The battle continued, [Blood Sacrifice] wore off, and Adam received several more attacks that forced him to use several more [middle-grade health potions]. He estimated that he'd done around 2.5 million points worth of damage, which meant this thing was likely on par with the headmaster of the magic academy. The overwhelming odds made him smile. That last fight had been him and his entire party facing off against a mage of unparalleled ability, but this time it was just him against an overwhelmingly powerful monster.

How could he not be having fun?

Blood pumped through his veins. His perception of the world seemed to slow down. Excitement and fear coursed through him in equal measure. There was a very good chance he could die here and now, but that was what made this moment so worthwhile. So fun. So exciting. Content though he was with a life of peace, he would not deny that part of him desired fighting against and overcoming strong enemies like this.

He activated [Blood Sacrifice] and [Dance of the Cherry Blossoms] once more, attacking and dealing nearly one million points of damage. This battle had become one of attrition. Who would succumb first? Would the [Hydra] run out of health, or would Adam run out of potions? Time lost all of its meaning as he attacked the monster with everything he had.

Yet the moment Adam got within attacking distance, the monster did something he didn't expect. It launched fire at the ground around its feet.

-1,600!

Adam flinched as he was blown backward by the flames and lit on fire. The number -10 began appearing periodically over his head as flames danced across his body. He grimaced and rolled across the ground to put out the fire, downed a [middle-grade health potion], and used what time [Blood Sacrifice] had remaining to attack. He still couldn't use [Dance of the Sakura Blossoms], so he struck with using [Slash] and [Thrust] while in the Form Three stance for power and stability.

-13,380; -12,240; -12,240; -13,380!

Because he didn't want to get hit by that attack again, he didn't stick around near the front. He traveled toward the back, leapt onto its tail, and raced up the monster's spine. It began bucking like a bronco when it noticed him. Adam jabbed his spear into its hard leather back and clung to the shaft like his life depended on it. The shaking eventually stopped as the creature tired itself out. Then

Adam raced toward all three heads and launched his only long-range attack.

[Energy Sweep]

-30,056; -30,056; -30,056!

His attack hit all three heads. He looked at the three number signs floating above each head, then grinned. He had finally found this thing's weakness, and lucky him, his ultimate attack had just finished its cooldown time.

[Dance of the Sakura Blossoms]

Adam aimed at the fire headfirst. His attacks did nearly three times the damage they had done when he was on the ground. It was so obvious looking back in hindsight, but it seemed these heads were the [Hydra's] biggest weakness. The moment he finished his attack, the fire elemental head split open at the neck and peeled off. A loud crashing sound echoed around Adam moments later as the head struck the ground with a thunderous boom.

[Firestorm]

A wave of flames swept across the land, incinerating the ground, turning grass to ash, and burning the bodies of multiple monsters. Standing in the epicenter of this incredible attack was Fayte. She took several heavy breaths as her shoulders heaved. Sweat ran down her face as several damage signs appeared above her foes' heads.

-23,880; -23,880; -23,880; -23,880; -23,880; -23,880; -23,880; -23,880; -23,880; -23,880; -23,880; -23,880; -23,880; -23,880; -23,880; -23,880!

Even though she was doing so much damage, the monsters continued to charge at them; there were so many that she couldn't see the end of them. To make matters worse, because she was their highest damage dealer, she also pulled the most aggro, making the monsters more aggressive toward her than anyone else in her party.

A massive dog with two heads, black fur, and crimson eyes broke through the crowd of monsters and lunged at her. Fayte launched an [Energy Bolt] that slammed into its face. This was not enough to stop the monster. Its name was [Orthros]. It was not a boss monster like the creature Adam was fighting, but it was a 2-star enemy, which meant it had much higher stats than the other mob monsters she had been fighting.

[Counter]

Before [Orthros] could take a bit out of her, Lilith appeared before the creature and used her unique skill. [Counter] was a skill specific to Lilith that allowed her to redirect enemy attacks and strike with a powerful counterattack that did 500% more damage than what her enemy did. As she used her dagger to smoothly turn aside [Orthros's] face, the woman plunged her dagger into its eye all the way to the hilt.

-25,000!

A large number sign floated above [Orthros's] head. It was not enough to kill the monster, which thrashed and tried to take a bit out of Lilith, but the Assassin-class player easily evaded the attack, leapt onto the monster's head, and began plunging her dagger into its body over and over while activating [Slash]. More damage signs appeared above [Orthros]. Lilith's attacks angered the beast. One of its heads reared up and tried to take a bite out of her, but she deftly moved to the side and activated another one of her skills.

[Pinpoint Strike]

-27,762!

Fayte didn't know how this technique worked, but she knew it allowed Lilith to attack the enemy's weak point, thus dealing many times more damage than normal. Sadly, [Pinpoint Strike] was also a skill that had a longer cooldown time, so she was forced to continue leaping from head-to-head and striking with a regular [Slash] until the monster's health went down to zero.

Of course, Fayte was not going to stand around and let her companion do all the attacking. She pointed her staff at [Orthros] and fired off a [Thunder Bolt] that struck its flank. A gigantic -52,536 appeared above the monster, which reared back in pain. Fayte didn't let up, firing a [Fireball] followed by [Wind Hammer]. The fire attack struck [Orthros] in the face. Following the fire attack's wake was the wind attack, which took the shape of a giant hammer that crashed into the monster with enough power to knock it onto its back. Its Magical Defense must have been lower than Fayte's for her attack to work.

-26,440!

Lilith followed up on Fayte's attack and slid her dagger across [Orthros's] throat. The monster shuddered for several seconds before its eyes dimmed and its body stopped moving. As it slumped onto the ground, Lilith leapt off and quickly dashed toward the next nearby enemy trying to sneak past them—a giant ram of some kind—and pulled its aggro to her with [Slash].

Fayte used that moment to look at the other battles taking place all around her. Kureha and Titania were sticking close together. It looked like Kureha was trying to protect the fairy, though Titania didn't appear to be drawing any aggro. Meanwhile, darting around the entire battlefield was Aris. The young woman was using her incredible speed advantage to race across the flat plain and launch attack after attack on enemies too slow to react. Doing this pulled a lot of aggro, but that also meant these monsters wouldn't continue charging toward the construction site.

The construction of their guild house was progressing smoothly. It was predominantly white but accented with blue roofing and awnings. Everything had been built on an elevated platform with stairs leading to the door. They had even already added a flag with her guild's symbol on it. The flag fluttered in the breeze. But while the main building had been built, they still needed to construct the surrounding garden and fence everything in. From what Fayte understood, the garden was built to create a repelling barrier that kept monsters at bay, though she didn't know how that worked.

Fayte wasn't able to stay idle for longer than a few seconds, however, and she quickly threw herself back into the fray. She targeted the monsters chasing after Aris. There must have been two dozen of them. Lightning flashed from her tip as she fired off a [Chain Lightning] attack. A bolt of lightning leapt from her staff, struck a monster, then leapt to another monster, then another and another, creating a thick chain of lightning that connected over a dozen monsters together.

-44,576; -44,576!

[Chain Lightning] was a powerful attack that had a small chance of stunning an enemy. While it was only 10%, that was enough to stun one of the monsters chasing Aris, and the young woman wasn't one to miss such a perfect chance. She activated her [Blade Dance] skill and struck the monster with a relentless barrage of nonstop attacks.

-700; -700; -700; -700; -3,500; -700; -3,500; -3,500; -700; -700; -3,500; -3,500; -3,500; -700; -700; -700; -700; -3,500; -700; -3,500; -700; -3,500; -3,500; -700; -700; -3,500; -700; -700; -700; -700; -700; -3,500; -3,500; -3,500; -3,500; -700; -700; -3,500; -700; -700; -700; -700; -3,500; -3,500; -700; -3,500; -3,500; -700; -3,500; -700; -700; -700; -3,500; -700!

The girl was quite the piece of work. Her relentless assault tore away its health swiftly despite the fact that she couldn't do nearly as much damage as Fayte or Lilith could. Aris's character class appeared to be one built with speedy attacks in mind. She made up for her lack of power by being able to strike nearly a dozen times for every one of Fayte's attacks.

The monster Aris was attacking looked like a Triceratops. Three thick horns sat on its head, it possessed a parrot-like beak for a mouth, and its skin was a leathery gray. Height-wise, it wasn't too much taller than a person. What it lacked in height, however, it made up for in girth. The thing was easily several times longer and thicker than any human she had ever met. Despite its imposing size, Aris was easily tearing into the monster with great zeal.

-18,850!

Just then, a large damage sign appeared above the creature as an object became embedded into the monster's eyes. It was an arrow. Fayte turned toward where the arrow had come from and saw Susan standing several dozen meters away. She was kneeling on the ground, bow in hand as she smoothly removed an arrow from her quiver, notched it, and fired another attack.

This attack did not do any damage. It struck another monster that had come charging in toward Aris, then sprouted vines that grew so thick they could wrap around the monster's arms, legs, and buried themselves into the ground. That was Susan's skill [Nature Arrow]. It was a skill unique to the Fairy Archer Class, an attack that infused the power of nature into an arrow and created vines that were powerful enough to trap an enemy for 120 seconds. The monster now trapped in a tangle of vines looked like an earth golem. It was a monster three times the size of a person, with an earthy brown color, a single glowing green eye, and plants sprouting from its body.

The moment Fayte saw it become trapped, she launched her own attacks. [Fireball] and [Thunder Bolt] struck the monster head-on. Each attack tore away a massive amount of health, not enough to kill it sadly, but enough to draw all its aggro to her. The vines burned away from her attack and the golem lumbered toward her. Fayte was not afraid as she launched an [Energy Blast] from the tip of her staff. It struck the monster in the face and sent it stumbling backward.

[Quick Sand]

Fayte tapped her staff against the ground. A faint line of magical power ran through the ground, toward the monster that had just managed to get free of the vines. The area around the monster's feet turned into sand. Unable to bear its weight, the sand gave way, and the monster slowly sank into the depths until it was buried up to its neck.

[Fireball]

[Thunder Bolt]

That was the moment Kureha struck the creature with two of her attacks. A bolt of lightning slammed into the monster's flank and did a nice -12,012 points of damage, then a fireball exploded in its face and did a further -6,916 damage. Its health must have already been close to zero because that was enough to kill it. The monster's corpse quickly sank beneath the quicksand.

Fayte ran out of MP as the battle continued and was forced to consume several [middle-grade magic potions]. Beyond her lack of MP, her exhaustion was beginning to get to her. She didn't know how long they had been fighting, but this was easily the longest battle she'd ever been in. If something wasn't done soon, she and the others might succumb to exhaustion.

Just as she was beginning to really worry, the monsters all stopped attacking and looked toward something in the distance. Fayte didn't understand what was happening at first, but then she saw where they were looking, at Adam and the headless corpse of a massive creature. Had he done it? Did he defeat the Boss of this Stampede? As if to answer her silent query, all the monsters they had been battling raced back toward the Suncrest Mountain Range with their tails tucked between their legs.

Ding!

[Congratulations! Your party has successfully fended off a Stampede! Number of monsters defeated: 46 out of 250. Experience points earned: 22,650,780. Items dropped: 233. Items will be distributed to players based on their contribution in battle. Player who contributed the most: Fayte. Fayte gets ⅓ of the items received from Stampede. Items have been placed into inventory. Inventory full. Cannot carry all the items. The Guild House contains an [item box]. Items unable to fit inside the inventory have been placed into the item box. You may check them whenever you are inside the Guild House.]

Ding!

[Congratulations! You have leveled up! You are now at level 18! +1,600 HP! +7,960 MP! +5 SP!]

Ding!

[Congratulations! Lilith has leveled up! She is now at level 18! +600 HP! +200 MP! +5 SP!]

Ding!

[Congratulations! Little_Su has leveled up! She is now at level 18! +500 HP! +200 MP! +5 SP!]

Ding!

[Congratulations! Aris has leveled up! She is now at level 17! +400 HP! +200 MP! +5 SP!]

Ding!

[Congratulations! Aris has leveled up! She is now at level 18! +400 HP! +200 MP! +5 SP!]

Ding!

[Congratulations! Titania has leveled up! She is now at level 19! +200 HP! +10,500 MP! +10 SP!]

Ding!

[Congratulations! Kureha has leveled up! She is now at level 19! +700 HP! +9,100 MP! +10 SP!]

Ding!

[Congratulations. Your Guild House has been built. You are now the leader of the first established Guild in Age of Gods. *An international announcement will be made regarding your new status as the leader of the game's first-ever Guild.]*

Ding!

[This is an international announcement. The player Changing_Fayte has established Age of Gods' first guild: Destiny's Overture. Her guild has thus been awarded one hundred million gold coins to use as she sees fit. As the first guild established, she also has the right to refuse all challenges for one month after the creation of a second guild, will receive more quests than any other guild, and has been allowed to create a Guild House free of charge.

We hope the knowledge of the rewards granted will motivate other players to find fame, fortune, and glory as they explore the ancient and mysterious Forgotten Realm.

DESTINY'S OVERTURE

As the one in charge of all their virtual holdings, Levon Pleonexia dealt with everything regarding games. As the latest VRMMO, *Age of Gods* was completely within his jurisdiction, and he was allowed carte blanche to do whatever he wanted within it. His father had told him privately that this was a test to see whether or not he was worthy of becoming the head of the Pleonexia Family. Levon had to prove his worth by showing off his talent at managing their current largest business venture.

Virtual Reality had changed the face of businesses everywhere. With the World War III Treaties of Non-Aggression in place, disputes of all kinds could only ever be settled in the virtual world. Of course, it wasn't necessarily true that all disputes were settled there. Levon himself had dealt with a number of problematic issues in the real world. On paper, however, issues between individuals, companies, and even countries could only be solved virtually.

A good example of this was the dispute between Italica and France five years ago, which had been a mining dispute over the rights to a new mine that had been discovered on the border between these two vassal states. To determine who would get the mining rights, the two vassal states had played a game—a first-person shooter called *Fall in the Line of Duty*. The dispute ended in Italica's victory, giving them complete access to the mine. There had been many other such disagreements. All of them were decided in the same way.

Right now, the only disagreement Levon was interested in settling was the one between him and Fayte.

"Let's get this meeting started. I would like to hear your reports now," Levon said as he stared at the five people sitting at the long table with him. While the room they were in was large, it seemed even larger than it actually was because of the numerous glass windows that spanned two of the walls, opening the space up. The long table was pure black but sparkled as if freshly polished. Several unoccupied chairs were arrayed around the table where the six of them sat, and hanging from the ceiling was a 3D holographic projector—something created from the latest technology.

The room was otherwise barren.

"Our cash flow has increased by .5% ever since you implemented the new policy that branch guilds must begin searching for and exploring new instance dungeons," Gaia said. She sat on his right, looking sharp in her all-black business suit. "So far, they have not found many dungeons. One was discovered close to Watershore. It's not very high level, however. The monsters' levels range from ten to fifteen and even the boss is only a 1-Star monster called [Starmite]. There was another found ten kilometers west of a tiny hamlet with more powerful monsters. Levels range in the twenties. I've sent many of our branch guilds there to grind their levels and clear the dungeon."

Gaia was not only a member of the Element Four but also his secretary/bodyguard in the real world—not that he believed he needed one. Her skin was dark like obsidian, as were her eyes and perfectly straight hair. She rarely changed facial expressions. This made her seem cold and unfeeling, but he knew that not to be the case. She was a woman who had dedicated her life to him and always acted in ways she believed would benefit him. That was why she hated Fayte. Levon knew Gaia believed Fayte was unworthy of him and would often tell him so. She just didn't understand. A woman as beautiful as Fayte could belong to no one but Levon. No one else was even close to being worthy of her.

"That is a tempting offer, but I'm gonna have to pass."

"Because what Fayte has given me is something you never could."

Levon sucked in a breath as a grating voice penetrated the darkest corners of his mind, causing his vision to seep red. He still remembered Adam's words even now. They clawed at his carefully crafted mental defenses, wearing him down and making him angry. Just the other day, one of his captains had said something that set him off. It hadn't been anything bad. Just a simple remark about the tournament that had taken place, but it had been enough to send Levon into a rage. The man had not been fired, but his pay had been docked and he would certainly be regretting ever opening his fat mouth in Levon's presence for the rest of his life.

Despite his anger, Levon was able to keep a lid on it and listen to Gaia's report.

"Given that you're in charge of an area with weaker enemies to begin with, I'm not surprised there aren't many powerful dungeons. Don't let this discourage you. *Age of Gods* is not your average game. I'm certain there are as of yet unexplored areas close to Watershore that could prove incredibly useful. It's also a great area to train new recruits," Levon said.

"Yes, sir," Gaia said with a nod.

"And what of the rest of you?" Levon looked at his other four commanders.

"I've recently begun exploring the area east of Solum," said Thor God of Thunder. Despite being named after the famous God of Thunder from Norse Mythology, this man looked like a slob. His face was masked by a five o'clock shadow and surrounded by dirty blond hair that looked unkept. It was too bad. He would have been attractive if he took better care of himself, but he probably didn't care about his looks. Rumors abound about how this man had slept with more than half the woman in the Pleonexia Alliance.

"Have you found anything?" asked Levon, folding his hands in front of him.

"I've found a forest that I believe is an instance dungeon." Thor God of Thunder scratched at his beard. "It's a forest covered in a thick fog that decreases visibility and causes confusion. We haven't been able to get too deep into it. I suspect in order to explore this forest, we'll need to have a craftsman create items that can fend off statuses like Confusion, or find an item that does the same thing."

There were many craftsmen in Solum, but none of them had the talent to create items that did much more than raise someone's defense. The most powerful item a person could buy right now was a pendant that slowly regenerated HP. Even then, it could only regenerate +1 HP every ten seconds. An item like that was all but useless inside of a dungeon like the one Thor was describing.

"Ignore the forest for now and keep expanding east," Levon instructed.

"Yessir," Thor said with an idle wave of his hand. His lazy tone caused Gaia to glare at him, but the man didn't seem to care.

"Ymir? What do you have for me?" asked Levon, turning to the man whose face appeared to have been chiseled from ice. Despite how cold his face was—no, *because* his face looked so cold—the man possessed a chilling beauty. He had the kind of feminine looks that made it easy to mistake him for a woman, but that just enhanced the aesthetic of a hauntingly beautiful man.

The man, Ymir, said nothing at first. This man was always abnormally quiet and slow to respond. While Gaia hated this about him, Levon appreciated it. He believed the man was carefully pondering what to say because he wanted to present only the most relevant information to him.

"You will be pleased to know that not only did I discover an instance dungeon near the westernmost edge of the Suncrest Mountain Range, but the Boss monster I battled there dropped a [Guild Creation Token]."

The words caused a jolt to run through the entire group. Connor Sword straightened in his seat, Flame Emperor frowned at Ymir, Gaia furrowed her brow as if angry that the person who found the current most important item in the game hadn't been her, and Thor God of Thunder whistled in awe.

"Damn, bruh. You work fast," Thor said.

Levon placed his hands on the table and clasped them together to keep his emotions carefully locked away. He didn't want his subordinates to see him shaking with excitement. As their leader, he needed to remain calm at all times.

"It's been two weeks since Fayte formed the Guild, Destiny's Overture. Not a single person has found a [Guild Creation Token] since then," Levon murmured.

In every game since the conception of the virtual world, the [Guild Creation Token] that was hardest to find was the first closely followed by the second and third. Once the first three were discovered, [Guild Creation Tokens] became common. Those first three were important since they always came with certain perks. Of course, the one who got the most perks was the first guild created, which was why the top guilds were always rushing to find a [Guild Creation Token] before anyone else.

"Good job, Ymir. Let me know if there's any reward you want. You deserve it."

Ymir nodded but didn't say anything. Levon was certain the man would eventually think of something he wanted and talk to him in private. With that settled, they could move on to other matters.

"Flame Emperor? Anything to report?" he asked.

"Nothing of note." Flame Emperor shook his head. "We have discovered a total of six instance dungeons. All of them contain monsters ranging from level 15 to level 20. They will be good for training new recruits, but they won't yield any items that will be very useful to use."

Flame Emperor was Fayte Dairing's older brother, though they looked nothing alike. His hair was brown, eyes a steel gray, and he possessed a straight nose. His jawline was all hard angles and edges. Most people would have been surprised to learn this man had any relation to Fayte, though anyone who knew the truth of the matter wouldn't be surprised by how different their appearance was. Dressed in a sharp business suit with a long trench coat made of crimson threads, the man looked identical to his game avatar.

"Understood. Keep up the good work." Levon nodded at Flame Emperor before turning to everyone. "With the [Guild Creation Token] in our hands, we can go ahead and form the Pleonexia Alliance in-game. However, before we do that, I believe we need to talk about the new updates that were announced earlier this morning..."

✳✳✳

"GRRRAAAAAA!"

The 3-Star monster [Giant Feral Cyclops] towered over everything else within the mountain pass. It was a creature that stood on two legs and had a vaguely humanoid shape, but its arms were much too long, hanging past its knees. Likewise, its face did not look very human. It had a mouth and a nose, but it only possessed one eye and there was a large horn on the left side of its head. Wearing just a loincloth to protect its modesty, the monster before him was a burly creature of rippling muscles that flexed as it swung the club in its left hand down.

Adam grinned as he leapt off the ground and landed feet first on the wall. He didn't stay there for long. He used his sharp vision to locate footholds that he could use to push off, allowing him to ascend the wall as if he was running on it. The little fox yokai on his head yipped as she dug her nails into his scalp, but Adam ignored it.

The club struck the ground and caused the earth to quake. Stones were overturned, the ground burst open, and a large crack traveled through the pass. Everything shook. Even the walls along either side of the pass rumbled as though being shaken apart. Several cracks appeared in the wall Adam was running up, forcing the stones to loosen and sending several hurtling down to him, but he used his inhuman reflexes to leap from foothold to foothold, avoiding the stones.

"This monster is quite powerful," Titania said as she flew by his head.

"Very powerful," Adam agreed. "I think this monster might also have the highest level of any non-boss monster I've ever fought."

The [Giant Feral Cyclops] was at level 40. Its stats were consequently all much higher than the average monster. Adam had been fighting this thing for almost an hour, but he had only managed to reduce half its health.

Adam eventually reached a point where he was standing at a higher elevation than the [Giant Feral Cyclops's] head. He dug his toes into his foothold and pushed off, leaping into the air and descending toward his enemy in a parabolic arc.

"Now, Kureha!"

"Yip!"

-110,484!

Kureha pointed her second tail at the monster and fired a bolt of lightning from the tip. The [Thunder Bolt] struck the [Giant Feral Cyclops] right in the eye, causing it to scream and stagger backward as it covered its eye with a hand and rubbed it furiously. Thanks to Titania singing the [Song of Vigor] in the background, Kureha's attack did a staggering amount of damage, though it was just a drop in the bucket for this monster.

Adam soon landed on the [Giant Feral Cyclops's] shoulder and ran toward its head, having already learned earlier in their fight that this was its weakness.

[Blood Sacrifice]

[Dance of the Sakura Blossoms]

-36,840; -110,520; -331,560; -994,680; -2,984,040!

Because Adam attacked its weak point, the amount of damage he did was doubled. Since he was using one skill that doubled his Physical Attack and another that stacked damage by three with every consecutive attack, the amount of damage he did would have killed any normal monster. The [Giant Feral Cyclops's] health was only reduced to about a fourth of what it had been.

The monster recovered before Adam could launch another attack. It reached over and attempted to squash him, so Adam hopped away from its head, then leapt off its shoulder entirely. He flinched upon landing on the ground. Dropping from a height like that did -150 damage and caused his spine to feel like it was being compressed, but he quickly downed a [middle-grade health potion] to heal from the fall and using [Blood Sacrifice], which sacrificed half his HP to increase his Physical Attack stat.

Adam gained some distance from the [Giant Feral Cyclops] as it tried to stomp him flat. The power of its stomps was such that Adam could not afford to be near them, lest he be knocked off balance by the resulting earthquake. He was mindful of the giant crack now running through the middle of the pass. It was easily fifty meters long and maybe eight wide. He could see the bottom, so it wasn't very deep, but he didn't want to fall in and risk trapping himself.

"Adam! It's about to use [Feral Beam]!" Titania warned him.

Indeed, the [Giant Feral Cyclops's] eye was glowing an angry, hellish crimson. He had already seen this attack once and knew better than to let it hit. It compressed a ton of magical energy into its eye, then released it as a beam that could incinerate anything in its path. The attack did three times the damage of its Magical Attack stat, which was +5,600, meaning it would do -16,800 to someone unprotected by armor. Adam's own Magical Defense was +3,000 and he had +7,100 health. He would die if an attack like that hit him even once.

Adam waited until the beam was fired to leap aside, running along the wall of the pass to avoid the beam. The [Giant Feral Cyclops] started its attack closer to its feet, but it swiftly raised its head. The compressed beam of energy tore through the ground like a hot knife through butter. Explosions rocked the air and forced Adam to dig his toes and fingers into the pass wall as he was struck by the shockwave. His fingers almost slipped more than once. He only just managed to hang on. Titania was also forced to grab his clothes, lest she get blown away.

Once the attack settled down, Adam once more began jumping from one foothold to another, and then repeated the attack pattern he and Kureha had created.

Well, that was the plan. The [Giant Feral Cyclops] didn't seem to have gotten the memo when it turned to him and thrust out a palm.

"Shit! Titania! Switch to defense!"

Titania switched from the [Song of Vigor] to the [Song of Valor], which increased her party's Physical and Magical Defense by 300%, meaning his Physical Defense was now +18,780.

-1,220!

Even though his Physical Defense was ridiculously high for someone with such a low level, the attack still did damage. As the air was driven from his lungs, Adam was launched through the air, slammed into the mountain wall, and caused the granite to indent around him. He felt like he'd swallowed his tongue. Even though he only experienced a small percentage of the pain he would in the real world, that didn't mean an attack of this caliber didn't hurt. This monster had a Physical Attack stat of over +10,000, and [Palm Thrust] did twice that.

"Are you okay, Adam?!" asked a worried Titania.

"I'm… cough cough… fine."

Adam downed another [middle-grade health potion], then gave one to Kureha. She hadn't been that monster's target, but she still received damage.

"Its attack pattern must have changed," Adam said.

"What should we do?" asked Titania.

"Yip!"

"We should attack it with everything we've got. Boost my stats with [Song of Vigor]."

"Okay."

Titania began singing [Song of Vigor] once more as Adam dropped to the ground and raced toward the [Feral Giant Cyclops]. This creature of course tried to squash him as one might a bug, but Adam danced around its foot, then leapt onto the appendage and activated the two skills whose cooldown times he'd been waiting to end.

[Blood Sacrifice]

[Dance of the Sakura Blossoms]

-12,280; -36,840; -110,520; -331,560; -994,680!

The attack didn't do nearly as much damage because he hadn't struck the monster's weakness, but this didn't stop him. Immediately after using his most powerful skill, Adam released a combination of [Thrust] and [Slash] to deal even more damage. The [Giant Feral Cyclops] shook him off and tried to stomp on him, but he darted out from underneath it, leapt onto its foot again, and continued to attack.

-29,472; -27,630; -29,472; -27,630; -29,472; -27,630; -29,472; -27,630; -29,472; -27,630!

His continuous attacks whittled away the [Giant Feral Cyclops's] HP until it released one final scream before stumbling backward. It tried to grab the ledge of the pass to keep itself upright, but then it fell onto its back. The sound of its head cracking against the ground echoed throughout the pass like thunder.

Adam breathed heavily as he landed on the ground beside it. His shoulders heaved as he gasped for breath.

"Haaaah… haaaah… well… that was fun."

"Only you could call fighting such a powerful creature fun," Titania muttered.

Ding!

[Congratulations! You have defeated the 3-Star [Giant Feral Cyclops]! [Giant Feral Cyclops] has dropped the items [Earth Defense Ring], [Cyclopean Mace], [Giant Monster Femur], [Cyclops Eye], [Cyclops Horn], and 120,000 gold coins! +1,500,000 experience points! +200,000 ability points! +500,000 reputation points!]

Ding!

Congratulations! You have leveled up! You are now at level 19! +1,500 HP! +400 MP! +5 SP!]

Adam smiled when he saw that he'd finally earned enough experience points to level up. He had been grinding every morning for the past two weeks to reach this level. It was nice to see that all of his work had finally paid off.

"Congratulations on leveling up. You're now one level away from reaching level 20," Titania said.

"Thanks," Adam said.

After putting his skill points into his Strength stat, Adam traveled out of the pass and made his way back toward their guild house. They avoided areas that were heavy with monsters. His goal had been met, so he didn't feel the need to fight anything else. He also needed to return to the real world and cook breakfast.

"You know, reaching level 20 is considered something of a landmark for you otherworlders," Titania continued. "Once you reach level 20, you will be able to choose a secondary class. Have you given any thought into what class you'll select?"

Adam shook his head. "I haven't yet. I want to see what kind of classes are available before selecting one."

"That's probably a good idea. Knowing you, you'll likely stumble upon an advanced secondary class that's not offered in the initial class listings," Titania said in a dry tone.

Adam just smiled.

They soon reached Destiny's Overture's guild house. Built on an elevated platform and surrounded by a fenced-off garden, the building did not look very defensible. This had been done on purpose. The guild house had several defenses that could be activated, though they were all basic right now. Bastion Builder had told them they could have upgrades built into the guild floor plan to increase their defenses once they had enough money, but all the good upgrades cost upwards of 15,000,000 gold. Fayte had so far only upgraded the doors and walls with [Magicore]—a type of magical ore that could absorb magical attacks to a certain degree. It wasn't good against physical attacks, but it was common practice to break through enemy strongholds with a barrage of magic.

Adam heard the sound of running water when he entered the garden. A small stream gently flowed between a variety of colorful flora. He walked over a wooden bridge and enjoyed the feeling of his hair rustling in the wind as the scent of flowers filled the air. The garden was something Fayte had designed during the planning stage. It had a wide variety of plants, including various types of flowers, but it also had an herb garden. Adam had grinned when he realized Fayte wanted to try cooking in the game world. He wondered if she'd choose Chef as her secondary class.

The building itself was large but quaint at the same time, lacking in the majestic grandeur of guild halls of larger guilds like the Pleonexia Alliance, Daggerfall Dynasty, and even the Rising Phoenix Alliance. The tiles on the gabled roof were blue as were the windows and awnings. White stones had been used in the construction of its walls. It didn't have many decorations. Fluttering in the wind was a flag at the very top and situated right above the door was a crest with the symbol of Destiny's Overture.

The symbol for Destiny's Overture was of a woman riding a horse. Epona. Adam had not known anything about this woman when Fayte introduced their symbol, but he'd done some research after Fayte told him who it represented. Epona was a Celtic goddess. Her name contained an allusion to the horse. "Epos" meant horse in Celtic, while "ona" meant on. As an Earth goddess, she was hailed for her grounding nature, and was particularly needed during times of crisis or flux in life. Adam wondered if perhaps Fayte was hoping to draw strength from such a symbol.

She didn't seem the symbolic type to him, but perhaps she wanted this woman as her symbol to motivate herself. That sounded like her.

Adam entered the guild building. It was locked, but everyone who was part of the guild could unlock it without the need for a key. He entered a narrow hallway. There was a staircase on the other end of the hall and several doors on the left and right between the entrance and the stairs.

He turned to Titania and took Kureha off his shoulders. "All right, you two. I'm heading back to my world."

"Safe travels." Titania waved him off.

"Yip, yip!" Kureha waved at him with her tails.

Adam logged off *Age of Gods* and woke up in his room. He stared at the ceiling, then looked down at the naked girl sleeping on his chest. Aris was peacefully dosing away, releasing soft, cute snores. The sensation of her warm body against his aroused him. Adam had enough willpower not to act on his base emotions, however, and so, after kissing her forehead, he quietly slipped out from underneath the young woman, got dressed, and headed for the door. He took one last look at Aris as she shifted around before burying her face into the pillow.

Fayte was not awake yet, or she would have been in the kitchen, which was empty and lacked the scent of fresh cooking. He glanced at the clock. It read 5:35 am. He was a little early. Adam often stayed in the virtual world until six or seven o'clock. Making his way into the kitchen, he rummaged through the fridge and grabbed everything he needed to make banana pancakes.

"Bananas, eggs, protein powder, some vanilla extract... I think that's everything," Adam mumbled.

Banana pancakes were easy to make. It was literally just bananas mixed with eggs, though he liked to add some extra ingredients to make it healthier and tastier. He turned on the stove, set a pan on top, and used a non-stick cooking spray to liberally coat the pan. He mixed the ingredients until the batter was nice and thick, then poured some into the pan and watched it cook.

"Adam?" a voice asked from beyond the kitchen.

Adam turned his head. "Aris. Sorry. Did I wake you?"

Aris wore a sleepy grin as she walked over to him. "You did. Tee-hee. You know I can't sleep without my favorite pillow."

"My bad," Adam said dryly. So he'd been relegated to pillow now, had he? He was fine with that. "How can I make it up to you?"

Aris adopted a thinking pose. "Hmmm. How about... giving me some morning protein."

Adam would have asked her what she meant, but Aris had the dirtiest mind he'd ever known, and so he already understood what she wanted. He would have told her no. But as if to head his rejection off, Aris suddenly lunged forward and hampered his mouth before he could deny her. A tongue forced its way past his lips and teeth. Adam could do nothing except surrender to the enthusiastic woman's lewd kisses, especially when she reached between his legs and rubbed him through his pants until the rushing blood caused his manhood to stiffen.

"Mmmm. That's what I want. So big," Aris murmured.

"Aris…"

"Shhh. Just let me have some breakfast."

Adam wondered if he should stop her, but if he was being honest, he enjoyed sex as much as she did, and he'd never been able to deny this woman when she wanted something. So he said nothing as she knelt before him. He remained silent when she pulled down his sweatpants and boxers in one go. He did try to keep an eye on the pancakes as they cooked, but it was hard when Aris began rubbing his dick against her cheek.

"Such a strong, masculine scent. I really love this smell. Tee-hee. Did you react to that? Look at how it's twitching. How cute."

"Aris… you are incorrigible."

"I am. Thanks for noticing."

Adam struggled to maintain his mind as Aris liberally coated his cock in saliva. She dragged her tongue from the base to the head, sending jolts of agonizing pleasure straight to his brain. It felt electric. Part of him wanted nothing more than to place his hands on Aris's head and guide her actions, but he was still cooking. Damn it. Had she done this on purpose? It wouldn't have surprised him. Aris had always possessed a mischievous streak for as long as he had known her and loved playing pranks.

As the pleasure he felt mounted, a voice rang out from the living room.

"I smell something good. Adam, is that you cooking?"

Adam's eyes widened. It was Fayte!

MISCHIEF

What do I do?

Adam had never been in a situation like this before. Aris was still kneeling in front of him, licking him like his shaft like a lollipop. She swirled her tongue around his length, liberally coating it in her oral fluids. The electric feeling of her moist tongue on his hot shaft was enough to distract him and weaken his legs. And just outside of the kitchen was Fayte. He could see her just fine through the small gap in the wall. On the other hand, Fayte could see him but not Aris or what the girl was doing, but all it would take for her to spot what was happening would be to walk around the corner.

What should I do?

In all his years of life, Adam could count the number of times he had panicked on one hand. The first time had been when the Pleonexia Family had ambushed him and Lexi, forcing them away from each other. The second time had been during his escape from Cocytus. The third time had been when he discovered that Lexi had gone missing several years ago and was presumed dead. And the last time was when Aris contracted Mortems Disease.

And now, Adam was on the verge of panic once more.

"Adam?" Fayte called again, looking at him through the small gap. It was maybe only three feet wide and two tall, just enough to see from his face to his waist.

"Y-yes? What is it?" he asked.

"Are you okay? Your voice sounds… strained."

"I'm fiiiine!" Adam's voice rose in pitch as his entire length was engulfed by something hot, soft, and wet. He looked down to find Aris had taken him into her mouth. She was staring up at him with a mischievous twinkle in her eyes. He glared at her, but still responded to Fayte. "Don't worry. I'm just… cooking."

"… Do you need any help?"

"No, no! I've got this! You just… just… oooh… um… sit in the living room and check the latest updates on *Age of Gods*, please."

"Well, okay. I'll do that. But don't be afraid to ask for help if you need anything."

"I wooooOON'T!"

"Adam?"

"It's fine! Everything's fine! I just touched the hot stove!"

As Adam created excuses for his sudden groan, he glared down at the young woman whose nose was firmly pressed against his crotch. He didn't know how she knew how to deepthroat someone, but he'd felt her throat softening as she took all of him inside of her mouth, felt the way her throat conformed around his length. Adam knew he wasn't the biggest guy around, but twenty centimeters was still twenty centimeters.

What do you think you're doing?! Adam's eyes seemed to say as he stared at her.

What am I doing? What's it look like I'm doing? I'm getting my daily protein. Tee-hee. Aris looked right back at him.

Adam and Aris had known each other for years and were closer than most people. He had dearly loved her ever since she was young, and he had spent three whole years of his life staying by her side after she got sick. Their shared time together meant they could communicate with nothing more than eye contact.

Stop it! Fayte is in the other room!

Good. Maybe she'll come into this room, see what's going on, and decide to join us.

In what twisted alternate reality would that ever happen?!

Maybe it could happen in this one.

Realizing Aris had no intention of surrendering, Adam decided his time would be better spent trying to focus on his cooking. He looked at the pancake currently on the pan. It was ready to be flipped. He grabbed the spatula with a shaky hand, slid it underneath the pancake, and flipped it—not carefully enough it seemed. He grimaced, though whether that was because the pancake almost fell out of the pan or because Aris had just licked the underside of his shaft, not even he knew.

"Haaah… mmmm… hrrrrnnn…"

Adam tried to keep his pleasure-filled groans to a minimum as he cooked and Aris sucked him off. This was absolutely mortifying, and yet, at the same time, he could not help but feel incredibly aroused by the situation. Fayte was just a room away. Not even a room. The living room and kitchen were connected. He could see Fayte through the small window, sitting on the couch as she went through some information on her tablet, though she would look back at him every so often.

The concern in her eyes was completely unwarranted.

But he couldn't tell her that.

The first pancake was done, so Adam took it off the pan and added more batter, all the while trying to ignore the way his cock throbbed in Aris's mouth. He was close. So close. When had Aris become such a pro at sucking dick? Was she really just that talented, or was he maybe that inexperienced? He didn't know. His mind was going blank.

The second pancake finished about the same time Adam did. His knees buckled and threatened to pitch him forward as he shot several spurts of cum straight down Aris's throat. He pressed his hands against the counter and leaned over, allowing him to see Aris better from his new position. Her throat bobbed as she guzzled down his sperm with ease. He was both impressed and a little mortified. She had mentioned masturbating to him many times not so long ago, but this nymphomaniac side of her was still something he wasn't used to seeing.

This girl is… way too erotic for her own good.

Once she finished milking him, Aris let go of his dick with a surprisingly loud pop. He had to look at Fayte because he was afraid she had heard that, but she was still facing away from him, reading from her tablet. He looked back at Aris just in time to see her kissing his dick. Then she dried him off, pulled his sweats back up, stood to her feet, and patted him on the cheek with a satisfied smile.

Her expression reminded him of a Cheshire cat from a story he'd once read.

"Looks like the coffee is done," Aris said in a voice loud enough for Fayte to hear. "Would you like some coffee, Fayte?"

"Aris? Are you in there too? And yes, please. I could use some coffee right about now."

"Tee-hee. I've been helping Adam cook. One cup of coffee coming up."

Adam, mind numb from the explosion of ecstasy and eroticism he'd just experienced, turned back to the pancakes. He flipped the one currently on the pan. The other side was a nice golden brown. It was almost hard to believe this pancake was made from just eggs, bananas, protein powder, and vanilla extract. Meanwhile, Aris grabbed three mugs from a cabinet overhead, poured three cups of coffee, and brought them out to the living room.

"Here you are, Fayte."

Fayte looked up from her tablet and smiled at Aris. "Thank you."

Aris grinned back as she sat down. "What are you doing?"

"Well, I was looking up the forums, but now I'm on Mystique Incorporated's website. It looks like there's been a game update."

"You mean like a DLC patch?"

"Kinda like that, yeah."

Adam finished making the pancakes as the women spoke, placed them all on a tray, and walked into the living room. He set the tray on the coffee table, then went back into the kitchen to grab forks, knives, and plates, which he placed before the two.

"Thanks, Adam!"

"Thank you."

"You're both welcome." Adam sighed as he slumped onto the couch beside Aris.

Fayte gave him a concerned frown. "Are you sure you're feeling okay? You look tired."

He tossed her a graceless smile. "I'm fine. Just a bit exhausted from dealing with a mischievous minx this morning."

While Fayte tilted her head in obvious confusion, Aris grinned and winked at him. He sighed again. Much as he didn't want to admit it, this was definitely the Aris he had known from before, but with a new nympho side to her—or rather, a nympho side that she was only now showing to him. It made him wonder how long she'd kept this side of her repressed.

Nobody spoke for a moment as they ate breakfast. The only sounds were those of tableware clinking against plates and chewing. Fayte's eyes did widen briefly as she tried the food, but she still didn't speak, just increased the speed she ate. Adam had made twelve pancakes, and all twelve were quickly consumed by them.

The pancakes had a light vanilla and banana flavor that paired well together. The protein powder he used was tasteless and didn't add anything to either the flavor profile or texture. This allowed the umami from the banana and vanilla to shine. Adam used to make these for Aris when they were younger, but he had to stop after her mouth became incapable of chewing solid foods. It was nice to make this once again.

"Wow! That was delicious! I've never had pancakes like that before!"

"They're made with bananas. Bananas can be used as a substitute for flour in some cases because they're high in starch, though it does add a slight banana flavor to anything you make. I used vanilla because they pair well together," Adam explained.

Fayte nodded. "I've heard of that, though I have never tried it myself. Maybe I should consider making something similar?"

"Can I help if you do?" asked Aris.

"Of course," Fayte said with a smile.

The light conversation gave Adam the moment he needed to recover from his orgasm. He sipped some coffee as the women talked. Aris had added exactly two cubes of sugar and just a bit of whole milk. She knew how he liked his coffee. After setting the mug back down, he turned to Fayte.

"You mentioned something about *Age of Gods* getting an update?" he prodded.

"Oh, yes. Here. Read this article. It explains everything you need to know about the update in detail."

Fayte handed over her tablet to Adam, who set the device on his lap, grabbed his coffee once more, and took periodic sips as he read.

"New updates to Age of Gods *are being added. Updates are as follows:*

-   Secondary Classes will become available to characters up-on reaching level 20. A list of Secondary Classes will be given to all characters upon reaching this level. Updates have already been in-stalled.

-   Time Compression System. The Time Compression System is a new program that will be implemented to enhance gameplay by compressing time within the game by 14X that of real-time.

The Time Compression System will be implemented on January 1st at 0000 hours eastern standard time. Players are requested to log out before the update takes place. Players still in-game will be forcibly logged out.

Adam's brow furrowed as he finished reading. He set the tablet on the coffee table and glanced at Fayte.

"The Secondary Class update was something I expected since Titania mentioned it this morning, but I'm a little confused by the Time Compression System. Is it what I think it is?"

Fayte nodded. "Probably."

"Time Compression…" Adam murmured with a frown. "I've heard of such concepts before. It's impossible to truly compress time, but you can compress a person's perception of time by accelerating their consciousness many times over. If you accelerate a person's consciousness by ten times, they can perceive the world ten times faster than normal, which makes everything seem like it's moving in slow motion."

"It's like overclocking a CPU!" Aris exclaimed.

"In a way, yes. The human brain is kinda like the CPU of a computer. However…"

"It's dangerous, right?" Aris said.

"I'm not sure. Theories have been put forth regarding this idea, and many of them claim they are too dangerous to implement because they put a strain on the mind of whoever is having their thoughts accelerated." Adam glanced from Aris to Fayte. "What are your thoughts?"

Fayte was sipping her coffee when he questioned her, but she set the mug down, crossed her arms, and leaned back on the couch, thinking. She only spoke after nearly thirty seconds. "I'm not sure. This update was posted sometime last night and has already received a lot of criticism from scientists warning others about the dangers of time compression. However, I'm not really sure it's dangerous. I read an article written by the creator of *Age of Gods*. It states the device used in this game is fundamentally different from other devices used in the past. The device we use to play *Age of Gods* connects wirelessly at the quantum level to your brain cells to send images, sounds, and sensations, while simultaneously canceling out your own senses of reality. Because it's a quantum connection and not a physiological one like standard gaming devices, it doesn't place a burden on your brain cells." She smiled in self-deprecation. "Well, that's what I read, but I didn't really understand it much."

Adam felt a chill crawl down his spine. Something about this all felt sinister to him, though he couldn't put his finger on why he felt this way. He pushed those dark feelings to the back of his mind and focused on the present.

"The Secondary Class updates aren't big, but this Time Compression System is huge. If it really does accelerate time within

Age of Gods like I think it does, then one day in the outside world will equal fourteen days in the game. That's going to seriously mess up some people's sense of time."

"I don't think people will care about that," Aris said thoughtfully. "I mean, so many people are already practically living in the game world, right? Being able to spend even more time in the game without having to constantly log out to get food, water, or go to the bathroom would make any fanatical gamer ecstatic, I would think."

"I know a lot of gamers who will definitely be pleased by this," Fayte agreed.

"The update won't happen until January first, so we've got about a month before the update happens," Adam said. It was currently November 29th. Thinking about it now, he had spent pretty much all of November with Fayte.

"I wonder why the update is happening so late?" Aris pondered out loud.

"It might have something to do with the next bit of news I have to tell you," Fayte said, expression turning a bit grave.

"What is it? Did something happen?" asked Adam.

"Early this morning, the Pleonexia Alliance and Auspicious Inc. officially formed guilds within *Age of Gods*," Fayte said, making Adam realize why she looked so bitter. It seemed their one-month grace period had officially begun.

***

Adam, Aris, and Fayte logged into *Age of Gods* after finishing breakfast. They didn't bother traveling to their bedrooms and just logged on while sitting on the couch in the living room. Nobody was there aside from them, and they had already grown to trust each other. As they appeared inside of the guild house for Destiny's Overture, they discovered that both Susan and Lilith were already present.

"You are just soooo cute!" Lilith said as she rubbed Kureha's belly. The little fox was rolled onto its back, and she was leaning over it. While Adam couldn't see her face, hidden as it was behind her mask, he could imagine the smile she wore.

"That girl used to be so dignified. I wonder what happened?" Titania asked.

"Lilith just likes cute things… I guess," said Susan.

Susan was sitting on the couch, while Titania sat on the armrest. Both watched as Lilith pampered the happily yipping Kureha. The one who saw them first was Susan, whose eyes strayed toward them a few seconds after they appeared.

"Ah! Fayte, Adam, Aris. Welcome back."

"Eeep!" Lilith leapt to her feet after she heard Susan call Adam's name. She didn't turn around to face them, but her shoulders quivered a little.

"Morning, Sue, Lilith, Titania," Fayte said with a smile.

"Mrrr. Mrrr."

"Of course, good morning to you too, Kureha."

"Morning, everyone!" Aris greeted the group much more casually.

"Morning," said Adam.

With everyone now present, the group gathered around the meeting room, though it looked a lot more like a living room. The floor was made of polished wood, a rug had been placed in the very center, where two couches and a table sat. The table was a low-standing one, almost like a coffee table, but not quite. A fireplace sat to their left, a fire merrily crackling inside. Hanging over their heads was a chandelier that provided a bright illumination.

Adam thought this place looked much more like a home than a guild headquarters, but perhaps that was what Fayte wanted from her guild—a place to call home.

"There's a lot we need to talk about now, so let's get to it. Our one-month grace period has finally started. The Pleonexia Alliance formed early this morning. I'm sure Levon will be doing everything he possibly can to establish a strong presence, and he's most certainly going to begin looking to strengthen his members. We need to figure out what we're going to do about this," Fayte said. She wasn't wearing her veil at the moment, so her beautiful face was on full display. Aris had also taken off her veil, though Adam and Lilith kept their faces hidden.

She was sitting on the couch with Susan and Titania. Adam sat in between Aris and Lilith. Curled up on his lap was Kureha, mrring softly as he stroked her fur. He could feel Lilith burning a hole into his hands with her eyes.

"Why must we do anything?" asked Titania. Because she didn't live in the real world, she didn't know about the bet Fayte had with Levon. Fayte had to explain the situation to her, and by the time she was done, the little fairy was frowning at the entire group. "So I see. This does sound like a problem. Why did you not tell me earlier?"

"It never really came up." Fayte shrugged her delicate shoulders.

"I suppose not, though I am not pleased to know that I am the only one who didn't know about this." Titania looked seconds away from pouting, but she released a slow breath and uncrossed her arms. "In either event, if this Pleonexia Alliance is so much bigger than us, then there are only two things we can do."

"Recruit more people or increase our levels so much it doesn't matter how large Levon's forces are," Adam said for her. Titania nodded.

"I don't want to increase our numbers," Fayte said with a frown. She reached up and caressed her lips in thought, drawing a line across her lower lip with an index finger. "Having a larger force certainly has its benefits, but it also comes with many problems, not the least of which is you can't know every member in your guild. There's too great a chance Levon or someone else might try to slip a spy into our ranks."

"True."

While technology had come a long way, it wasn't like there was any invention that could force someone into silence. Blackmail notwithstanding, you couldn't make someone do something they didn't want to, which meant there was always a chance someone who joined them would betray them, either for money or something else.

This sort of tactic was also something the Pleonexia Family was well-known for. They had put several companies out of business by discovering and exploiting their secrets with spies and the like. No one had been able to find any evidence of duplicity, but everyone knew it was the only way the Pleonexia Family could have put so many companies six feet under.

"Adam, what do you think we should do?" asked Fayte.

"Hmmm." Adam closed his eyes and thought for a moment. What could they do? "So far, we have been taking quests from the Guild Association, which has increased our reputation, filled our coffers, and given us some pretty good experience... but I don't know if quests like this will be enough to raise our levels as quickly as we need to."

There were several types of quests found in VRMMORPGs like *Age of Gods*. Kill quests, escort quests, defense quests, gathering quests, delivery quests, and destroy quests.

Kill quests were fairly straightforward. A player's job was to find a specific monster and kill it. Sometimes they were requested to kill a certain number of monsters, or maybe the monster they were requested to kill was a unique monster not typically found within a specific region. Quests like this used to be the bread and butter of MMORPGs before the age of virtual reality took hold. While they were still important for leveling up, they had taken a backseat to the PvP aspect of multiplayer games.

The other quests were also all pretty standard. Escort quests involved protecting someone (typically an NPC) as they traveled to their destination. Defense quests were all about defending a location from enemy forces—a good example of this was a quest they had taken not long ago to defend a small city from an invasion of [drakes] that had flown down from a nearby mountain. Gathering quests had players finding specific items like herbs for alchemy ingredients, ore for forging swords, or meat for food. Delivery quests were likewise about delivering items to someone. These often came with a time limit, so players had to be careful. The last quest type were destruction quests, which were similar to kill quests, except players were asked to destroy a specific location, typically a fortress. These were the rarest quest. Destiny's Overture had only been given one destruction quest, which had them storming a fortress that had been invaded by a monster army.

At the moment, their levels looked like this:

Name: Adam

Class: Seven Forms Spearman

Lvl: 19

SP: 0

AP: 1,700

Experience: 290/19,660,800

Reputation: 1,572,000

Strength: +1,225

Constitution: +300

Dexterity: +100

Intelligence: +100

Speed: +100

Physical Attack: +6,275

Health: 7,100/7,100

Hit-rate: 1,000%

MP: 570/570

Movement: +1,606

Comprehension: +2

Physical Defense: +6,260

Magic Defense: +3,000

Dodge-Rate: ???

Magic Attack: +500

Resistances:

Fire: 50%

Water: 50%

Earth: 50%

Wind: 50%

Darkness: 50%

Slashing: 50%

Skill List:

Skill Name: Slash

Description: A skill where the player swings his or her

sword and attacks the enemy!

Current lvl: 5 MAXED

Ability: Causes 150% damage to enemy if it hits

MP Cost: 1

Cooldown time: 0 seconds

Skill Name: Thrust

Description: A basic skill where the player thrusts his or her sword at the enemy!

Current lvl: 5 MAXED

Ability: Causes 160% damage with a 5% chance at getting a critical hit

MP Cost: 5

Cooldown time: 1 second

Skill Name: Blood Sacrifice

Description: By sacrificing 50% of your blood (HP), you have gained the ability to increase the damage you do

Current lvl: 5 MAXED

Ability: Causes x3 attack power increase for 60 seconds

Disregards skill cooldown times, allowing the user to attack with every skill without limit until Blood Sacrifice wears off

MP Cost: 20

Special limit: Drops HP by half

Cooldown time: 30 seconds

Skill Name: Dance of Sakura Blossoms

Description: A skill only Adam can use

Attacks with numerous spear thrusts that eventually forms the shape of a sakura blossom

Current lvl: 10 MAXED

Ability: Release a constant stream of attacks, has a x3 damage increase for every hit, damage stacks, and resets when Adam misses an attack.

Hit-Rate: 100%

MP Cost: 100

Cooldown time: 30 seconds

Skill Name: Energy Sweep

Description: The wielder of Seven Forms Spearman infuses his energy into a sweeping swing and releases a powerful attack that extends past his natural range.

Current level: 10 MAXED

Ability: Attacks every enemy within five yards of the user.

Does 300% damage

MP Cost: 50

Cooldown Time: 10 Seconds

Skill Name: Energy Thrust

Description: The wielder of the Seven Forms Spearman infuses his energy into a thrust that ignores all defenses and armor.

Current level: 8

AP needed to reach level 9: 512,000

Ability: Ignores enemy's defenses and armor to deal critical damage

420% damage dealt

MP Cost: 50

Cooldown Time: 10 Seconds

Equipment:

Item Name: Goddess of Creation Spear

Lvl: 15

Experience points needed to level up: 5,912,512/81,920,000

Item Type: Spear

Grade: 5-Star

Use Requirements: Can only be equipped by Adam. Cannot be thrown away, cannot be given away, and cannot be unequipped.

Description: The Goddess of Creation Spear was created eons ago by the Goddess of Creation and recently discovered by Adam. It has recognized Adam as its master and cannot be used by anyone else.

Abilities: Physical Attack+150; Strength+150

Special ability: Sentient Growth

Item Name: Dragon Bone Cuirass

Item Type: Armor

Grade: 2-Star

Use Requirements: Can be equipped by Warriors level 10 and above.

Description: This chestplate was made from the bones of a powerful dragon. Not only does it look stylish, but it offers solid defensive abilities and some special stats.

Abilities: Defense+200; Constitution+100; 25% resistance to slashing, fire, earth, wind, and darkness damage

Item Name: Dragon Bone Gauntlets

Item Type: Armor

Grade: 2-Star

Use Requirements: Can be equipped by Warriors level 10 and above.

Description: These gauntlets are made from the bones of a powerful dragon. Not only are they stylish, but they offer solid defensive abilities and resistance to elemental damage.

Abilities: Defense+50; Constitution+10; 10% resistance to slashing, fire, earth, wind, and darkness damage

Item Name: Goddess of Creation Greaves

Item Type: Armor

Use requirements: Can only be equipped by the wielder of the Goddess of Creation's Spear.

Description: These greaves are made from an unknown material. They were created by the Goddess of Creation and can only be worn by the chosen wielder of her spear.

Abilities: Constitution+150%; Physical Defense+200%; Magical Defense:+200%; Speed+200%

Special abilities: 60 seconds of Flight; Double Jump

Item Name: Reflection Bangle

Item Type: Accessory

Grade: 3-Star

Use Requirements: Character must be level 15 or higher.

Description: This bangle has been enchanted with reflection magic. Anyone wearing this bangle has a 10% chance of reflecting a physical or magical attack back at their opponent.

Abilities: 10% chance of casting reflection.

Name: Kureha

Class: Fox Yokai

Lvl: 19

SP: 0

AP: 657,100

Experience: 14,165,416/52,428,800

Strength: +10

Constitution: +350

Dexterity: +100

Intelligence: +930

Speed: +200

Physical Attack: +10

Health: 2,400/2,400

Hit-rate: 100%

MP: 25,680/25,680

Movement: +400

Physical Defense: +350

Magic Defense: +1,400

Dodge-Rate: 100%

Magic Attack: +3,720

Skills:

Skill Name: Fireball

Description: Kureha has incredible control over fire thanks to her first tail. She can create fire through the power in her tails and launch a fireball at opponents.

Current lvl: 5 MAXED

Ability: Deals 250% damage

Has a 55% chance of causing burn damage

MP Cost: 100

Cooldown Time: 10-seconds

Skill Name: Firestorm

Description: Kureha has incredible control over fire thanks to her first tail. She can create fire through the power in her tails to unleash a powerful storm of fire.

Current lvl: 5 MAXED

Ability: Deals 190% damage to all enemies within a 5-yard radius

Has a 55% of causing burn

MP cost: 100

Cooldown Time: 10-seconds

Skill Name: Thunder Bolt

Description: Kureha's second tail has the power to control lightning. She can launch a powerful lightning bolt at her enemies.

Current lvl: 5 MAXED

Ability: Deals 330% damage of Magical Attack to one

enemy

MP Cost: 100

Cooldown Time: 10-seconds

Skill Name: Thunder Storm

Description: Kureha's second tail has the power to control

lighting. By gathering magical power into her tails, she can

create a massive thunderstorm that rains down on enemies from

above.

Current level: 5 MAXED

Ability: Deals 290% damage of Magical Attack to multiple

enemies within a 10-yard radius

MP Cost: 100

Cooldown time: 10 seconds

Name: Titania

Class: Guardian of the Spear

Lvl: 19

SP: 0

AP: 883,620

Experience:14,164,112/52,428,800

Strength: +10

Constitution: +200

Dexterity: +100

Intelligence: +1,050

Speed: +100

Physical Attack: +10

Health: 2,400/2,400

Hit-rate: 200%

MP: 51,200/51,200

Movement: +500

Comprehension: +10

Physical Defense: +400

Magical Defense: +600

Dodge-Rate: 200%

Magic Attack: +2,080

Luck: +1

Skills:

Skill Name: Song of Refreshing Rain

Description: A song that Titania can sing. When sung, this song will constantly replenish +10 HP of all party members for as long as it is being sung.

Current lvl: 5 MAXED

Ability: Indefinitely heals +30 HP every one second for as long as Titania is singing.

MP Cost: 50 MP per second

Cooldown time: 0 seconds

Skill Name: Song of Vigor

Description: A song that Titania sings to increase the strength of her companions. When sung, this song will increase the Physical Attack and Magical Attack of every companion.

Current lvl: 5 MAXED

Ability: Raise the Strength of all allies by 300%.

MP Cost: 50 per second

Cooldown Time: 0 seconds

Skill Name: Song of Valor

Description: A song that Titania sings to increase the defensive abilities of her allies. Physical Defense and Magical Defense doubles for as long as this song is being sung.

Current lvl: 5 MAXED

Ability: Increases Physical Defense and Magical Defense stat of all Titania's party members by 300%

MP Cost: 50 per second

Cooldown Time: 0 seconds

Skill Name: Scan

Description: Titania can scan any enemy regardless of level and send that information to all members of her party.

Current lvl: MAXED

Ability: Reveals an enemy's stats

Can only be used on one enemy at a time

MP Cost: 100

Cooldown Time: 0 seconds

Name: Changing_Fayte

Class: Elemental Master

Lvl: 18

SP: 0

AP: 460,600

Experience: 12,402,380/39,321,600

Reputation: 1,250,000

Strength: +5

Constitution: +400

Dexterity: +100

Intelligence: +995

Speed: +100

Physical Attack: +5

Health: 5,160/5,160

Hit-Rate: 200%

MP: 18,845/18,845

Movement: +200

Physical Defense: +3,000

Magical Defense: +7,000

Dodge-Rate: 200%

Magical Attack: +15,920

Resistances:

145% Fire

145% Earth

145% Water

145% Wind

145% Lightning

145% Light

145% Darkness

Item Name: Alexandra's Staff

Item Type: Magic Staff

Grade: 4-Star

Use Requirements: Can only be used by Elemental Masters

Description: This staff was carved by Alexandra herself. When she was young, she discovered the fabled Tree of Life and was gifted one of its branches by the tree itself. This staff was carved from that branch and contains incredibly potent magical power.

Abilities: Intelligence+200%; MP+250%; Magic Attack+200%

Item Name: Enchanted Elemental Robes

Item Type: Clothes

Grade: 4-Star

Use Requirements: Can only be used by Elemental Masters

Description: These robes were created from threads of magical silk and enchanted with incredible defensive powers.

Abilities: Constitution+100%; Physical Defense+200%; Magical Defense+200%; 75% damage resistance for all elements

Item Name: Enchanted Elemental Shirt

Item Type: Clothes

Grade: 4-Star

Use requirements: Can only be used by Elemental Masters.

Description: This shirt was created from threads of magical silk and enchanted to protect people against elemental attacks.

Abilities: Magical Defense+300; Physical Defense+300; 15% damage resistance for all elements

Item Name: Enchanted Elemental Pants

Item Type: Clothes

Grade: 4-Star

Use requirements: Can only be used by Elemental Masters

Description: A pair of pants created from threads of magical silk. They provide a boost to one's magic defense and elemental resistance.

Abilities: Magical Defense+150; Physical Defense+150; 10% damage resistance for all elements

Item Name: Enchanted Elemental Veil

Item Type: Clothes

Grade: 4-Star

Use requirements: Can only be used by Elemental Masters

Description: This veil was made from threads of magical silk. It doesn't just hide your face. It also provides you with a unique skill and defense against magic.

Abilities: Magic Defense+50; Defense+50

Unique Ability: Mind Reading

Item Name: Enchanted Elemental Boots

Item Type: Clothes

Grade: 4-Star

Use requirements: Can only be used by Elemental Masters.

Description: These boots were made from the leather of a dragon and enchanted to offer a boost to the wearer's physical and magical defense, as well as resistance to elemental damage.

Abilities: Constitution+100; Physical Defense+100; Magical Defense+100; 50% damage resistance to all elements

Name: Aris_Lancer

Class: Blade Dancer

Lvl: 18

SP: 0

AP: 256,000

Experience: 10,170,870/39,321,600

Reputation: 496,000

Strength: +185

Constitution: +100

Dexterity: +100

MP: +20

Speed: +6,400

Physical Attack: +1,140

Health: 2,640/2,640

Hit-Rate: 100%

MP: 480/480

Movement: +51,200

Luck: +10

Physical Defense: +320

Magical Defense: +320

Dodge-Rate: 100%

Magic Attack: +20

Skills:

Skill Name: Slashing

Description: A basic skill where the player swings his or her

sword and attacks the enemy!

Current lvl: 5 MAXED

Ability: Causes 150% physical damage to enemy if it hits

MP Cost: 1

Cooldown time: 0 seconds

Skill Name: Thrust

Description: A basic skill where the player thrusts his or

her sword at the enemy!

Current lvl: 5 MAXED

Ability: Causes 160% physical damage with a 10% chance

at getting a critical hit

MP Cost: 5

Cooldown time: 1 second

Skill Name: Blade Dance

Description: A skill unique to the player Aris_Lancer.

Allows for continuous attacks without pause.

Current lvl: 10 MAXED

Ability: Can constantly attack and hit every time without pausing to use another attack

Chances of landing a critical strike are 100%

Skill can be disrupted if attacked

If skill is disrupted, the attack ends and cooldown time is initiated

MP Cost: 5 MP per attack

Cooldown time: 30 seconds

Skill Name: Double Slash

Description: User attacks with both weapons at the same time.

Current lvl: 1

AP needed to reach next lvl: 4,000

Ability: Deals x2 damage

MP Cost: 100

Cooldown time: 15 seconds

Skill Name: Tornado Dance

Description: A sword technique where the player spins around and attacks everyone surrounding them.

Current lvl: 1

AP needed to reach next lvl: 3,000

Ability: 100% damage all enemies surrounding player

MP Cost: 50

Cooldown time: 20 seconds

Skill Name: Dancing Swords

Description: A sword technique that lets the user attack with four thrusts one after the other in quick succession.

Current lvl: 1

AP needed to reach next lvl: 4,000

Ability: Deals 200% damage with every successful attack

Damage is stacked

MP Consumption 50

Cooldown time: 15 seconds

Equipment:

Item Name: Blade Dancer Falchions x2

Item Type: Sword

Grade: 4-Star

Use Requirements: Can only be equipped by Blade Dancers

Description: These swords were once wielded by an aspiring hero. They were forged by the dwarves and given to a man who aided them in their time of need.

Abilities: Physical Attack+200 x2; Speed+200 x2

Item Name: Blade Dancer Sandals

Item Type: Clothing

Grade: 4-Star

Use Requirements: Can only be equipped by Blade Dancers

Description: The sandals of a Blade Dancer do not provide much protection, but they do provide a boost to speed.

Abilities: Physical Defense+50; Magical Defense+50; Speed+200%

Item Name: Blade Dancer Top

Item Type: Clothing

Grade: 4-Star

Use Requirements: Can only be equipped by Blade Dancers

Description: The Blade Dancer shirt does not have a high defense, but it boosts speed by a lot.

Abilities: Physical Defense+50; Magical Defense+50 Speed+200%

Item Name: Blade Dancer Gloves

Item Type: Clothing

Grade: 4-Star

Use Requirements: Can only be equipped by Blade Dancers

Description: Blade Dancer gloves offer a speed boost and some basic protection.

Abilities: Physical Defense+50; Magical Defense+50; Speed+200%

Item Name: Blade Dancer Skirt

Item Type: Clothing

Grade: 4-Star

Use Requirements: Can only be equipped by Blade Dancers

Description: A skirt worn by Blade Dancers. Gives a significant boost to speed.

Abilities: Physical Defense+50; Magical Defense+50; Speed+200%

Item Name: Veil

Item Type: Accessory

Grade: 1-Star

Use Requirements: Can be equipped by anyone

Description: A simple cloth veil.

Abilities: It can hide your face from view

Item Name: Dancer's Anklet

Item Type: Accessory

Grade: 2-Star

Use Requirements: Can only be equipped by the Blade Dancer Class

Description: An anklet for Blade Dancer's that increases their Physical Attack

Abilities: Physical Attack+100

Name: Lilith

Class: Demon Knight Assassin

Lvl: 18

SP: 0

AP: +5,020

Experience: 11,990,616/39,321,600

Reputation: +605,000

Strength: +800

Constitution: +200

Dexterity: +200

Intelligence: +105

Speed: +100

Physical Attack: +6,650

Health: 1,975/1,975

Hit-Rate: ???

MP: 495/495

Movement: +800

Physical Defense: +825

Magical Defense: +825

Dodge-Rate: 26,920%

Magic Attack: +200

Skills:

Skill Name: Hide

Description: A skill that allows Assassins to hide their presence.

Current lvl: 5 MAXED

Ability: Makes Assassin invisible to everyone 10 levels above their own

Skill breaks if Assassin moves

Ability lasts indefinitely

MP Cost: 5

Cooldown time: 5 seconds

Skill Name: Throat Slit

Description: Coming up behind an enemy, the Assassin slits their opponent's throats.

Current lvl: 5 MAXED

Ability: Causes 400% damage

Has a 25% chance of causing instant death

X4 critical damage dealt if enemy is unaware of your presence

MP Cost: 10

Cooldown time: 10 seconds

Skill Name: Slash

Description: A basic skill where the player swings his or her sword and attacks the enemy!

Current lvl: 5 MAXED

Ability: Causes 150% damage to enemy if it hits

MP Cost: 1

Cooldown time: 0 seconds

Skill Name: Counter

Description: A skill that Lilith learned because she was already naturally predisposed to using it. Allows user to counter enemy attacks.

Current lvl: 5 MAXED

Ability: Redirects attack from enemy and strikes with counterattack

Does 320% damage

Requirements: Users must have precise timing when countering. If your timing is off, the one who suffers from the critical damage will be the user.

MP Cost: 5

Cooldown time: 15-seconds

Skill Name: Shadow Masking

Description: Uses the shadows to remain unseen even while moving.

Current lvl: 5 MAXED

Ability: Offers complete invisibility against opponents 50 levels higher until MP runs out

MP Cost: 10 MP per second

Cooldown time: 60-seconds

Skill Name: Pinpoint Strike

Description: Everybody has a weak point. This skill shows you your enemy's weakest points.

Current lvl: 5 MAXED

Ability: Shows the weak points of your enemy. Deals 500% damage when weak point is struck.

MP Cost: 30

Cooldown time: 10-seconds

Skill Name: Dual-wielding

Description: This passive skill allows users to wield two weapons at the same time. Demon Knight Assassins can only wield weapons of the dagger class.

Current lvl: 1

AP needed to reach next lvl: 5,000

Ability: Wielder deals 110% damage if the weapons being wielded are the same

MP Cost: N/A

Cooldown Time: N/A

Skill Name: Blade Extension

Description: Channeling mana into your dagger causes the blade to extend in a surprise attack.

Current lvl: 1 MAXED

Ability: Blade can grow up to three yards long

MP Cost: 60

Cooldown time: 10

Name: Little_Su

Class: Fairy Archer

Lvl: 18

SP: 0

AP: 150

Experience: 12,434,640/39,321,600

Strength: +750

Man Made God 004

Constitution: +100

Dexterity: +100

Intelligence: +100

Speed: +100

Physical Attack: +3,900

Health: 2,020/2,020

Hit-Rate: 200%

MP: 510/510

Movement: +700

Luck: +3

Physical Defense: +1,370

Magical Defense: +500

Dodge-Rate: 150%

Magic Attack: +500

Skills:

Skill Name: Deadeye

Description: Archers can increase their hit-rate and critical
hit-rate by increasing their perceptions through the Deadeye
skill.

Current lvl: 5 MAXED

Increases Hit-rate to 110%

Deals x2 critical damage

MP Cost: 5

Cooldown time: 5-seconds

Skill Name: Rain of Arrows

Description: Archers who learn this skill can fire a hailstorm of arrows that deals damage to multiple enemies.

Current lvl: 5 MAXED

Ability: Causes 150% damage to all enemies within 15 yards of targeted enemy

MP Cost: 5

Cooldown time: 10-second

Skill Name: Fairy Shot

Description: A skill that can only be used by someone of the Fairy Archer Class. Increases accuracy and damage dealt by arrows.

Current lvl: 5 MAXED

Ability: Increases accuracy by 100%. If enemy is hit, x4 critical damage is dealt

MP Cost: 10

Cooldown time: 10-seconds

Skill Name: Light Arrow

Description: A skill used by the Fairy Archer Class. Infuses arrow with the power of light.

Current lvl: 5 MAXED

Ability: Deals 500% damage to undead and enemies of the darkness element

MP Cost: 20

Cooldown time: 10-seconds

Skill Name: Nature Arrow

Description: A skill used by someone with the Fairy Archer Class. Infuses the power of nature into the arrow.

Current lvl: 1

AP needed to reach next lvl: 2,000

Ability: When an enemy is struck by a Nature Arrow, they become entrapped in vines for 60 seconds

MP Cost: 30

Cooldown time: 10 seconds

Equipment:

Item Name: Advanced Compound Bow

Item Type: Bow

Grade: 2-star

Use requirements: Can only be equipped by Archers

Description: A bow given to beginner Archers

Abilities: Physical Attack+200

Item Name: Ranger's Jerkin

Item Type: Armor

Grade: 2-star

Use requirements: Can be equipped by Archers level 15 and higher

Description: This is the jerkin used by rangers, a group of archers who specialize in wandering through the wilderness

Abilities: Physical Defense+300; Movement+300

Item Name: Ranger Boots

Item Type: Armor

Grade: 2-Star

Use requirements: Can only be equipped by Archers level 10 and above

Description: These boots are worn by Rangers, people who wander the wilderness and protect others from monsters

Abilities: Physical Defense+20; Speed+25

"I think… we should try going after a powerful monster like the [Spider Queen] or the [Undead King]," Adam said at last, causing Titania, who had been sipping tea, to do a spit take.

S-RANK QUEST

Titania gawked at Adam like she couldn't believe what she had just heard. She even went so far as to put her pinky in her ear as though digging out earwax before asking, "I-I am sorry. I seem to have heard something phenomenally stupid. Could you please repeat that? I must have heard wrong."

Adam sighed. "No, you heard right. I think we should go after the [Spider Queen] and [Undead King]."

"Are you crazy?!" Titania exploded. "No, don't answer that. I already know you're crazy. I knew that from the moment we first met. Are you insane?! Do you really think we can defeat monsters as powerful as the Thirteen Lords of Chaos? We wouldn't stand a chance as we are now."

"I think we might stand a chance. Our stats are pretty good now," Adam said.

"Stats aren't everything and you know it. Also, our stats might be better than they were, but they pale in comparison to the enemies you want us to fight," Titania said.

Aris, Fayte, Lilith, and Susan watched the back and forth between Adam and Titania like it was a ping pong tournament. Their heads swiveled back and forth, from one to the other. None of them had interrupted the argument yet, but soon Fayte cleared her throat to catch their attention.

"I'm afraid I don't know much about these Thirteen Lords of Chaos beyond what little you've told me. Can you fill me in? Just how powerful are they?"

"Every member of the Thirteen Lords of Chaos is a 4-Star monster with a level of no less than ninety. You can expect them to have at least over one billion health points and a number of powerful attacks that would kill us in one hit as we are right now. For example, all of the [Spider Queen's] attacks do no less than fourteen thousand points of damage," Titania explained.

After listening to Titania's explanation, Fayte turned to Adam with a dry expression that caused him to look away. He couldn't bear to see her looking at him like he was a reckless fool.

"Adam," Fayte said in a patient voice. "You realize there's no way we can defeat a monster of that caliber right now. Why are you suggesting we fight them?"

"We need to get stronger—stronger than anyone else in the game." Scratching his elbow, Adam turned to Fayte with a serious expression. "Right now we are barely keeping our lead thanks to the hidden classes we acquired. However, hidden classes and skills can only do so much. We're still outnumbered by the larger guilds. Unless we can become so powerful individually that we can take on entire armies, we're not going to survive when Levon Pleonexia comes after us."

"Well, you're not wrong," Fayte admitted with a frown.

Aris raised her hand. "I'm with Adam. I think we should fight these Lords of Chaos. It sounds fun."

"Of course you're on Adam's side," Fayte grumbled. Susan giggled a little, which caused everyone to look at her. The poor girl squeaked when she noticed all the attention on her and burrowed backward into the couch, but Fayte just smiled at the girl. "What do you think, Su?"

"M-me? Oh. Um. You know I... I think you both have good points," Susan said hesitantly. Fayte prodded her to continue, which caused the youngest of them to come out of her shell a bit more. "Adam is right. We do need to get much stronger. A lot of the top players have already caught up to our level, and it won't be long before those under them do as well. However, I don't think we should rush it either. Fighting someone like the [Spider Queen] might yield a lot of experience points, but it also comes with harsh consequences if we die."

Adam rubbed the back of his neck. He hadn't thought of that, but Susan was right. If they died, players would lose all of their experience points and drop a level. They'd be in an even worse position than before if that happened. There was also Kureha and

Titania to consider. If they died, that was it. Unlike other games where NPC party members could be revived when the player died, they didn't do that in this game.

"I guess I didn't think of the consequences," Adam said with a small sigh. "Still, we can't afford to just take normal quests. They don't give us enough experience to level up quickly. If only we could find another dungeon like the Magic Academy."

The Magic Academy had monsters that were all at a very high level, but the one Adam was most interested in was the boss. Alexandra Mystique had been a level 50 4-Star enemy. She was powerful enough that she gave them a lot of experience points for defeating her, but she wasn't so powerful that they couldn't win. Adam firmly believed they could defeat her even more easily now that they all had a hidden class and had leveled up.

"Maybe we should head over to the Guild Association and see if they have any special quests for us?" suggested Fayte.

Quests in this world were given to them by the Guild Association, who was in charge of managing all the quests people from across the continent had for guilds. Whenever they wanted new quests, they headed over to the Guild Association office in Solum and perused through a variety of quests until they found one they wanted.

"I think it's a good idea," Susan said.

"It's a much better idea than going after monsters we have no hope of defeating," Titania added with a sour look at Adam.

"I'm fine with it," Lilith said quietly. At some point, she had snatched Kureha from Adam's lap and was stroking the fox yokai's delicate fur. She looked so content that Adam couldn't bring himself to take Kureha back.

"I still think Adam's idea is better, but if that's what everyone else has decided on, then I'll agree to it," Aris said with a pout as she crossed her arms.

Everyone turned to look at Adam next. He felt like their stares were putting him on the spot, but he knew what they wanted from him. Some part of him still believed fighting powerful enemies like the [Spider Queen] would yield the best results. The rest of him understood that he just really wanted to fight her. Adam disliked the fact that he had been forced to flee last time, so now he wanted to go back and defeat her.

He had always been a sore loser.

"Let's see what quests are available at the Guild Association," he said at last with a sigh.

This was why he normally played solo.

✱✱✱

There were a total of twenty-four rooms inside of their guild house. Seventeen of them were bedrooms located on the second floor. On the first floor were the kitchen, living room, a unisex bath, a vault for their items and gold, and a training hall. Among the rooms available, the training hall was the largest. It was 100 meters across and 80 meters wide. It looked a lot like the kind of training halls people expected to see at places where people practiced fencing, with soft mats on the floor to lessen the harshness of impacts when falling and an array of basic weapons hanging from racks. Adam was a little surprised they had something like this in *Age of Gods*.

Of course, he and the others were heading up to the third floor.

Unlike the first two floors, which were dedicated to living space and sleeping, the third floor only had two rooms.

The smaller of the two was an office. Fayte used it to store various files regarding their activities, taxes, maps, and other items that were necessary to run a guild. One of the more interesting facets of this game was that guilds in *Age of Gods* were run a lot like companies in the real world. Running a guild was just like running a business.

Of course, Adam and the others were not headed for the office but the last room.

Larger than the office but smaller than the training hall on floor one, the room they walked into looked like a simple unadorned space that served no purpose. The only thing this room had was a small platform at its very center. If someone were to look at it, they would have said it looked like a magic circle, and indeed, it was covered in all kinds of magical-looking symbols that Adam couldn't make heads or tails of.

"All right. Let's get on the [Warp Pad] and head to the Guild Association," Fayte said.

[Warp Pads] were, according to lore, lost magic that transported people from one pad to another corresponding pad. The term "lost magic" made it sound like it was something that no longer existed. In this case, however, what it meant was there was no one alive who could create more of these [Warp Pads]. There were apparently only a few hundred of them in existence and they cost a pretty penny of 4.5 billion gold coins. The only reason they had one was that it was part of their reward for forming the first guild.

They all stepped onto the [Warp Pad], which activated with a thrum. Adam felt the hairs on his neck and arm stand on end. He blinked once, and in that time, the area around them had changed. No longer were they standing inside of an unadorned room. Now they were inside of a smaller room made of stone.

"Let's go," Fayte said.

They exited through the only door, traveled up a flight of stairs, and emerged into the guild hall of the Guild Association. Outside of the employees who worked there, Adam, Aris, Fayte, Kureha, Lilith, Susan, and Titania were the only ones present. According to Fayte, only the Pleonexia Family had formed a guild on this continent aside from them.

Clarise was standing in her usual spot behind the counter along with the other workers. Her eyes brightened when she spotted them, a smile split her face, and she raised her hand to wave them over. The group traveled to her. She clasped her hands and bowed her head when they reached her.

"Welcome to the Guild Association, all of you. I'm guessing you're here for a new quest?" she asked.

"Yes, though we want something different from the ones we have taken thus far," Fayte said.

"Oh?" Clarise cocked her head to the side.

"We want a quest that will yield a high number of experience points. I don't mind if we don't make as much money. Do you have anything like that?" she asked.

"Hmm." Clarise crossed her arms and hummed in thought. "We do have a few quests like that… but these quests are far above your current level. I can't really recommend taking them."

"May we see them?" asked Fayte.

"Well… I suppose you can take a look at them," Clarise said after a moment's hesitation.

Quests in *Age of Gods* were listed by the optimal level needed to complete them. They were often grouped into levels of five, with the lowest quests being 10 to 15 levels, and the highest currently being 45 to 50 levels. Adam didn't know if 50 was the level cap, or if it meant there wouldn't be any higher-ranked quests until someone reached level 50.

They followed Clarise to the same office where Fayte signed the contract that made their guild official. Everyone sat down on the couches. Adam found himself sitting between Aris and Susan. He didn't know how that happened since Susan tended to stick next to Fayte like glue, but when he looked her way, she offered a tentative smile even as she blushed. He smiled back.

"Here are the current highest-level quests we can offer," Clarise said as she came back from the desk and placed a stack of papers on the coffee table. She leaned back with a frown and placed her left leg over her right. "I normally would never even let you see these quests until you reached an appropriate level, but you've all proven that you can take on quests far above your current levels."

This has to be our Reputation at work.

Reputation was, in a nutshell, the opinion people had about a person as a result of social evaluation on a set criterion based on their performance. Completing quests and killing monsters with a 1-Star or above ranking were the easiest ways to accumulate Reputation. If a person's reputation was high enough, they could be granted quests above their current level, gain more favors from merchants, and receive higher rewards for the same quest than someone who had a lower reputation.

Their average Reputation as a guild was currently 1.2 million. That was more than high enough for Clarise to decide they could accept quests above their level.

Fayte grabbed a paper from the top stack. It was a type of papyrus paper or maybe something made from goat skin. Lacking in the perfectly sharp edges and smooth surface of paper in the real world, this was yellowed with age and had a crinkled feel.

"A powerful monster army is threatening our village. Please send your strongest warriors past haste to help us. Reward: ten million experience points, one hundred thousand ability points, and two million gold coins. Level required to participate: Forty-five to fifty," Fayte read out loud. She glanced down at the bottom of the page. "It says this must be completed in four days. What happens if no one accepts the quest?"

"If no one accepts the quest within four days, then Solum's mayor will deploy his army to quell the monsters. That's what we have been doing since before the otherworlders arrived. However, doing this puts a massive strain on our forces. Only a few of our numbers are at the level required to accept quests like this, so we always end up losing a lot of people." Clarise paused, then leaned over and cupped a hand to her mouth as if about to share a secret. "The last time a monster army appeared, our army and the entire village was wiped out."

"Do monster armies appear often?" asked Aris.

"Quite often, though most of them aren't very powerful," Clarise confessed. "This particular army just happens to be incredibly strong. All of them are level 40 and above. There's also an entire army of them, so you can assume there are around ten to twenty thousand."

"… Let's set this one aside for now." Fayte placed the quest on the table before picking up another one. "Quests like that usually require either multiple medium-sized guilds to form a raid party or a larger guild to accept the quest. We only have seven members, so I'm not sure we're equipped to deal with this."

"What about this one?" asked Aris before clearing her throat and reading off the quest she had grabbed. "Help. A ship full of undead pirates is attacking Hargeon Harbor. Please find this ship and destroy it. Reward: twelve million experience points, five hundred thousand ability points, and two million gold coins. Level required to participate: 45 to 50."

"We might be able to do that one. It also offers more experience points as a reward," Adam said.

"Which means it is probably even more difficult than the monster army quest," Fayte added.

"The monsters are probably at a higher level than the ones we'll face if we go up against the monster army, but there will be less of them." Adam rubbed his jaw in thought. "The ships used in this world are galleons. They're typically around five hundred tons. That means they'll have a total of about one hundred and eighty men. If we assume every pirate is at level 50, then we should be able to defeat them if we play it smart."

"Hmmm. Where is Hargeon Harbor?" asked Fayte.

"It's about ten days east of here," Clarise supplied helpfully.

"So it would take ten days to reach." Fayte grimaced. "Let's add it to the maybe pile."

Adam understood where Fayte was coming from. Ten days in the game world was the same as ten days in the real world, meaning they wouldn't be gaining experience for ten whole days. In that time, who knew how much experience the other players would gain. Of course, given how hard it was for players in this game to level up, Adam imagined Levon and the others were in the same boat, but the worry that they might be overtaken was always present.

They went through several more quests, but all of them were either too difficult or too far away. Trying to hide his frustration, Adam reached out to the last quest on the table, glanced at it, and nearly did a double-take.

"A dungeon with unknown but powerful monsters has recently been discovered. The soldiers Mayor Paxton sent in to investigate never returned. Your job is to investigate the dungeon and, if possible, clear it. Reward: Thirty million experience points, five million ability points, and eight million gold coins. Level required to participate: 45 to 50.”

“That sounds like the most dangerous job present,” Titania said with a dry voice.

“But it’s also the closest one here. It says the dungeon is only located three days away. Also, thirty million experience points are enough to let you, Aris, Susan, and Lilith level up with a single quest. I think we should take it,” Adam defended his choice.

“I don’t know…” Fayte bit her lip. There was a heavy risk involved with a quest like this. At the same time, this was easily the best quest they could ever hope to receive. It was true that a quest like this would let everyone but Adam, Titania, and Kureha level up.

“I think we should do it,” Aris said.

“Why am I not surprised you agree with Adam?” Titania asked, rolling her eyes.

“Because you know Adam is right?” Aris offered.

“Because you’re both idiots,” Titania shot back.

“I also believe we should accept this quest,” Lilith said in a quiet voice.

“You are just as bad as Aris!” Titania snapped.

“Let’s hold a vote. All those in favor of accepting this quest, raise your hand,” Fayte said.

Neither Fayte nor Titania raised their hands, but Adam, Lilith, and Aris did raise their hands. A fourth hand suddenly rose into the air, causing everyone to look at Susan, whose shoulders were scrunched as she timidly looked at everyone present.

"Su?" Fayte spoke in a questioning tone like she couldn't believe what she was seeing.

"W-we'll never get anywhere if we don't do something," Susan defended herself. "We need to get stronger, right? I'm aware there will be risks involved, but if we take the safe route, we'll never be any stronger than everyone else. Wasn't it because we took so many risks that you and Lilith gained your hidden classes?"

"I… yes, you're right," Fayte said at last, sighing. "I forgot that completing our goals was going to come with high risks. If I can't afford to take risks now, I'll never be able to take them later when I really need to. Okay, we will take this quest."

"Are you all sure about this?" asked Clarise. "I know I'm the one who's letting you take on this quest, but please understand there's a very high risk involved. You otherworlders might not die, but you'll still drop an entire level if you're defeated."

"We're sure," Fayte said for all of them.

"Guess that's it then," Titania lamented with a groan. "Why oh why did I join this group?"

With their quest decided, the group traveled back to the guild house. Their goal now was to go through their inventory and select what items they should bring on this quest. Dealing with logistics was important even for small guilds like them.

The vault was a large space filled to the brim with shelves and chests, all of which looked stuffed to bursting with items. Chests contained items like potions. Each chest was made with some kind of magic that allowed them to hold more of a single item than any inventory space ever could. The chestmaker who built them said that each chest could hold up to ten thousand of any one item.

"We should definitely take [high-grade health potions] and [high mana potions] with us, but what else do we need?" asked Fayte as she pulled [high-grade health potions] from the chest and set them on the ground. They were elaborate vials filled with sparkling red liquid. Gold traversed the glass and held the cap in place. The [high mana potions] that Susan was removing from the chest next to Fayte's looked the same, but they contained blue liquid instead of red.

[High-grade health potions] recovered a total of +1,500 health and [high mana potions] restored +1,000 magic points. They were currently the most powerful recovery items Adam had seen. He hoped they would find something like an [elixir] or similar item, however, since even the [advanced health potion] was not powerful enough to restore him to full health after he used [Blood Sacrifice].

"We'll want to carry tents, of course," Adam said. "If we can clear out a spawning point of monsters, we can use the tent to remain safe when we log out."

"We should also bring buffing items," Aris added. "I know we have Titania and her songs, and they work great, but we might need some extra oomph if we end up facing a super strong enemy."

Adam had already pulled out fifty [tents]. A person's inventory could only hold ten. Since he didn't know how long it would take them to clear this dungeon, he felt it was best if all of them carried the maximum number they could

"We should also have [cure-alls] on us. We've got enough that all of us can carry one hundred each." After removing all the [high-grade health potions] they would need, Fayte moved over to the chest containing the [cure-alls] and began removing those as well. She had spared no expense in making sure they were fully stocked on every recovery item currently available.

Once they were stocked up on every item they needed, the group sans Titania and Kureha logged off. It was twelve o'clock by the time they finished stocking up. They all needed to eat lunch.

As Adam opened his eyes and surveyed the living room, he realized why *Age of Gods'* creator had decided to implement a time compression system. Given how realistic this game was, it would be very difficult to complete quests in a timely fashion. By compressing time so one day on the outside equaled ten or even twenty days on the inside, players could take on quests that would involve traveling fast distances and complete them all within just one or two real-time days.

"Mmmmmaaaaaaaaaah…"

Stretching beside him as she sat up, Aris released a loud yawn and raised her arms above her head. She smacked her pink lips several times. When she noticed Adam watching her, she smiled and leaned over to kiss him. Sitting on Aris's opposite side, Fayte frowned and looked away.

"Adam… I'm hungry," Aris said, her stomach gurgling at the same time.

"I'll make something," Fayte offered.

"I can make something," Adam said, standing up.

Fayte raised a hand and smiled. "You're always cooking for us now. Let me do the cooking this time. I have to show off my skills every once in a while, or you two might forget how skilled of a chef I am."

Adam had been cooking breakfast, lunch, and dinner ever since Aris had woken up. That was because he wanted to be the one who cooked for Aris. It was something he had been doing for several years now, and it was basically his pride that he could cook for the girl he loved. But he did recognize that Fayte also enjoyed cooking.

He gracefully backed down. "Okay. I guess I'll sit here and wait patiently."

Fayte looked pleased and said, "I'll have lunch made soon. Why don't you two just play some Street King V while you wait?"

"Ooooh! That's a good idea," Aris said, sending a grin Adam's way. "I still haven't gotten my revenge on you for my previous loss."

"If you think you can beat me, you're more than welcome to try," Adam said with a smile.

"Oh, it's on now! Let's do this!" Aris pumped a fist into the air before walking to the television and setting up the old-school console.

The rest of Adam's time in the real world was spent beating Aris at Street King and eating the delicious sandwiches Fayte made.

DANGEROUS WATERS

It took two days to reach the dungeon mentioned in the quest. Adam, Aris, Fayte, Lilith, and Susan traveled east just like the map told them to. None of them had ever been out this way. Watershore. Hope Village. The Deadlands. Even the magic academy. All of it was located to the west of Solum.

Much of their journey took them across a vast plain that seemed to stretch on forever, though that was something of an oxymoron since they ended up entering a forest after a day of travel. The group rode on horseback to speed up their travels. Even then, it still took a long time before they reached the forest spoken of in the quest.

Everyone logged out after Adam set up a [tent] for Kureha and Titania. His fairy companion had complained about how they were leaving again and Kureha whined, but it wasn't like they could stick around. Their bodies didn't stop working just because they were playing video games. They had to use the restroom, eat, hydrate, and move around or their bodies would grow lazy.

Adam and Aris made dinner that night—orange-glazed pork chops with salad, red wine, and a small parfait for dessert. Fayte had complimented them on their cooking.

"You two really are quite the pair. Even your cooking complements each other."

While Aris had beamed brightly at the words like she'd been paid the highest compliment, Adam had seen the loneliness in Fayte's eyes. He wondered what he could do to make her less lonely. There was nothing he could think of, however. His mind kept drawing a blank every time. He'd only briefly entertained the thought of trying to set her up with one of his assassins, but the very thought made his blood run cold. Besides, Fayte was currently trying to get out of a marriage. She didn't need someone meddling in her relationships right now.

After getting some sleep, the group logged back into *Age of Gods* and entered the forest. The forest's name was the Weeping Willow Forest. According to rumors Fayte had gathered when preparing for the journey (courtesy of Clarise), the Weeping Willow Forest was known as such because of the harmless [Weeping Willow] monster that made this place its home. There was only one of them located deep within the forest's very center. If someone found the [Weeping Willow], they would be awarded its sap, which gave someone one thousand skill points when ingested—or so the rumor went.

While one thousand skill points wasn't a lot of Adam, plenty of other players would kill to get one hundred skill points. It was more than enough to upgrade the average skill several times.

Of course, no one had seen this monster in many years. Adam wasn't even sure it existed.

Many of the monsters located within the forest were around level 30 to 37. As expected of a forest, the monsters there mostly consisted of plant types like the [succubus flower] and animal types such as the [man eating bear], but there were also the [treants]. They were technically a plant. In fact, [treants] were nothing more than gigantic trees. However, according to Titania's [Scan], they were listed as a wood-type monster.

Among the many varieties of monsters, the [treant] was the least numerous, but also the most dangerous. They were massive trees over twenty stories tall. A single swing from their branches did around -1,000 points of damage and was guaranteed to knock a player off their feet. Every [treant] had the same glowing red eyes, a gaping maw in their bark like that of a snarling mouth, and numerous roots and branches they used to attack with. The non-star ones could only use physical attacks. However, there was the occasional 1-Star [treant] who could use magic.

None of that mattered to Adam and his party.

Having dealt with monsters far more powerful than this, the group made short work of all the monsters within the forest and continued on without much delay. It was a far cry from when they had journeyed to the magic academy and struggled against the [storm wolf] monster, which tended to hunt in packs. Adam was sure that if they chose to return that way, they would make short work of the [storm wolf] pack that had ambushed them last time.

"Hyyaaaaa!"

Adam stabbed the spear in his hand forward to activate the [thrust] skill and impale the [man eating bear] on it. A large number sign floated above the monster's head. These monsters had a total of about 20,000 health, and his attack had just shaved away the last bit of it. The monster groaned and fell back with a dull thud. Adam paid no attention to the corpse and turned to the next monster.

A large group of monsters was crawling out of the woodworks to confront them, but he, Aris, and Lilith were working as a team to keep them from coming near their long-range attackers. Aris used her speed to attack monsters whenever they tried to break through their formation, Lilith used her significant attack power to deal incredible amounts of damage, and Adam played whichever role was needed at any given time.

In the center of their defense formation were Fayte, Kureha, and Susan. While Susan fired arrow after arrow into the horde of monsters, Fayte and Kureha were casting their magic spells. Since most of the monsters were plant types, they used [Fireball] and [Firestorm] to decimate the groups wholesale. Plant types were weak against fire. As the sweltering heat from their attacks caused sweat to break on Adam's skin, Titania hid between them all and sang [Song of Valor] to increase their attack power.

"That's the last of them. Phew. I feel like I got a real good workout in," Aris said after she finished cutting up the last [succubus flower]. They looked like plants with a green lady sprouting from inside its petals. Most of their techniques were based on seduction skills and were used to confuse targets into attacking their comrades. Too bad for them Adam's party was far too strong for their skills to work.

Skills that created status effects like [Confusion] were reliant on your stats being higher than your enemy's stats. [Confusion], for example, was a skill that took the caster's Intelligence stat and pitted it against whoever the spell was being cast on. If the caster's Intelligence was higher than their opponent's, the spell would work, but if it wasn't, the spell would fail. And of course, a spell wasn't always guaranteed to work even if the caster's Intelligence was higher. There was just a higher chance of success.

"I believe we should keep moving," Fayte said.

Adam nodded. "No sense in standing around here."

"Fine. Fine. It's not like I disagree, though I wish you two would at least let me bask in my sense of accomplishment," said Aris as she threw her hands into the air.

The two shared a brief smile, invisible through their mask and veil respectively, but then continued on. Their party formation was simple. Adam stood at the front and took on any monsters that attacked head-on. Aris was beside him to act as his support. Lilith guarded the back. In the center were the long-range attackers. Since this was a forest and they didn't know from which direction an attack would come from, they had decided this was the most useful formation.

They wandered through the forest for what felt like several more hours before Susan suddenly pointed at something ahead of them. "I-I think I see something!"

The group looked ahead. They didn't see anything right away, but as they pushed aside some branches, they finally saw what Susan had likely seen. A massive lake. So large was the lake that Adam couldn't even see to the other side, which meant it must have easily been several hundred meters across. That was bigger than most lakes in the real world. And situated in the very center of that lake was an island with something like an archway standing in the very center.

"Is that it?" asked Aris.

"Looks like it," Adam nodded. "That's definitely the dungeon we came here to conquer."

***

The lake was huge, and it didn't look like there was a bridge they could use to get across it. Adam searched the area for some sign of how they were supposed to cross over the water, but he found absolutely nothing, which caused him to frown.

"M-maybe we're supposed to swim across?" suggested Susan.

"I wouldn't recommend that," said Titania.

"Why not?" asked Fayte.

"Adam, throw a rock into the water," Titania instructed.

While he didn't know why she wanted him to do that, he obliged. His throw was quite impressive. The stone skipped across the water's surface several times—until a massive creature burst up in a spray of water. Susan shrieked as Aris, Fayte, and Lilith stiffened in shock. Kureha yipped and growled at the creature, easily fifteen times the size of a normal human. Its black and white blubbery skin looked glossy and slick. There were barnacles attached to its skin here and there. Gleaming red eyes the size of a human head stared viciously at them before the creature dove back into the water and disappeared.

"What the heck was that?" asked Aris.

"A [freshwater orca]," answered Titania as she cast [Scan] on the creature before it disappeared.

Name: Freshwater Orca

Description: A great whale that somehow found its way here from the ocean. Over time, it adapted to freshwater. It is a very powerful predator that will eat anything within its territory.

Class: 1-Star

Lvl: 40

HP: 600,500/600,500

MP: 100,000/100,000

Strength: +5,000

Constitution: +4,000

Dexterity: +100

Intelligence: +50

Speed: +600

Skills:

Skill Name: Swim

Description: The ability to swim through the water at
incredible speed

+200 boost to speed when in water

MP Cost: None

Cooldown time: 0-seconds

Skill Name: Fin Attack

Description: Smacks unsuspecting swimmers with its fin

Attack does 100% damage

MP Cost: 100

Cooldown time: 1 second

Skill Name: Geyser

Description: Sprays water from its spout at speeds so fast it
can cut through steel

Damage = Physical Attack * 3

Has a 10% chance of instantly killing enemy

MP Cost: 2,000

Cooldown time: 120 seconds

Skill Name: Lightning Resistance

Description: The freshwater orca's skin acts as insulation,
making it resistant to lightning attacks

Lightning attacks only do 50% normal damage

MP Cost: 0

Cooldown time: 0 seconds

This was the first time Adam had ever seen a water enemy before. He hadn't been expecting something so incredibly powerful either. Even though it was only a 1-Star monster, its stats were far above the average. He wondered if it had something to do with the creature's species, so obviously based on the killer whales of his world, which had been driven to near extinction in the past.

"This is definitely a problem," Fayte muttered.

"Underwater enemies are always difficult to deal with. It's impossible to use most of our attacks underwater, and we can only hold our breath for a limited amount of time. Even if we had the lung capacity of an Olympic swimmer, we would eventually have to surface, and they could attack us when we come up for air," Adam said.

"So we can't even get over there?" asked Susan.

"I'm sure there's a way to get over there," Adam assured Susan. "We just have to find out."

"Let's explore the lake's edge," Fayte suggested. "Maybe we'll find some means we can use to cross the lake."

It wasn't like anyone else had a better idea, and so the group moved off, walking around the lake's edge in search of something they could use. They ran into the occasional monster, but none of them were hard to deal with. The problem was they couldn't find what they were looking for. Adam had been hoping that maybe they would find a bridge if they traveled to the other side, or at least some kind of hidden mechanism they could use to cross the lake, but all they found was a whole lot of nothing.

"Maybe this quest is impossible to complete," lamented Fayte.

"I doubt it's impossible, but it will certainly be difficult with our current levels and abilities," Titania said. She crossed her arms as she sat on Adam's shoulder. "In cases like this, you would want someone who either specializes in water magic or underwater fighting to deal with the [freshwater orca] while the rest of us swim across the lake unimpeded."

"There are classes that specialize in underwater fighting?" asked Adam.

Titania gave an almost absent nod. "When I was much younger, I joined the party of a young man whose class was Diver. He had the ability to dive deep into the water and use a variety of weapons with the same skill underwater as someone else on land. The Diver skill also granted him an incredible lung capacity. He could remain underwater for two hours before needing to surface. Of course, a class like that comes with limitations. All of his skills were useless on land and his stats dropped by twenty-five percent."

"So it was a class with a very specific skillset that could only be used for underwater battles," Fayte concluded.

"Yes," Titania said.

It took one whole day to travel from one side of the lake to the other. The group had to clear out the enemies around them and set up a tent for Titania and Kureha several times so the rest of them could eat, sleep, and bathe. Yet no matter how much they searched, they didn't find anything that would let them cross the lake. It seemed like this quest was one meant specifically for someone with a class that let them fight underwater.

"I think I have an idea," Aris said during their second day there.

"You do?" Fayte looked at the girl in surprise.

Aris grinned as a mischievous twinkle entered her eyes. Adam, having known her the longest, understood what that look meant. She only had this look when she was about to do something she thought was fun... but was actually very stupid. When was the last time she gave him this look? Not counting the morning she gave him a blowjob in the kitchen while Fayte sat on the couch in the living room, it must have been two months before her parents contracted Mortems Disease. She had decided she wanted to fly and attempted to do so by creating paper wings and leaping off the roof of their house.

Adam still remembered the scolding her parents had given them, her for doing something so dumb, and him for going along with her whims.

"Whatever you're planning, I don't think it will work," he said.

"You don't know that," Aris countered. "It could work."

"It won't."

"We'll never know unless I try."

As Adam and Aris argued, Fayte, Susan, Lilith, Kureha, and Titania looked back and forth between the two. There was no heat behind their argument. However, it was clear they both disagreed and neither side was willing to give up. Adam didn't want Aris doing something that could potentially hurt her, while Aris wanted to try something she'd never done before… even if it blew up in her face.

Finally, Aris placed her hands on her hips and sighed. "Look, Adam, I understand that you want to protect me, but this is just a game."

"Just a game?" Titania muttered in a dark tone.

That tone worried Adam, but he ignored it for now. He needed to convince Aris that her idea, whatever it was, wouldn't work.

"That may be so, but I still don't want you to do anything reckless."

"It's no more reckless than you fighting against enemies thirty levels above you." Adam grew silent since he had no rebuttal, but he didn't like the fact that she was using his own actions against him. Aris sighed, then smiled. "Look, I really do get that you're worried. However, we need to do something. If this works, then good, but if it doesn't, all that will happen is I'll lose a level and resurrect at the cathedral in Solum. Please, let me do my part to help out."

Adam really wished he could just deny this girl, that he could be stern and tell her no, but Adam had never been able to outright deny her anything. It was the reason he had let her try to fly way back then even though he knew it wouldn't work. She was his one weakness. His Kryptonite. As she stared at him with those big, doe-like eyes, wide with innocence and imploring him to let her help, he felt his will crumble.

"That's not fair. You know I can't deny you anything when you look at me like that."

"Tee-hee. I know. Why do you think I mastered this look?"

"What was that?"

"Nothing."

Since it looked like the two of them were finished, Fayte stepped forward to get between them. "Since it looks like you've worked out your issues, Aris, why don't you tell us what your plan is?"

"Of course." Aris nodded, placed her hands on her hips, and proudly puffed out her small chest. "My plan is to use my Speed stat to run across the water's surface and draw the [freshwater orca's] attention. While it's chasing after me, the rest of you will swim across the water. I'll join you once everyone has made it onto the island."

Everyone stared at Aris as she looked at the group with pride. She clearly thought her idea was amazing. However, judging from the look on almost everyone's face—except for Titania's, who looked thoughtful—no one else agreed with her. Fayte decided to voice what they were all thinking.

"That sounds like a horrible idea."

"What?! Why?! What's so bad about it?"

"Susan, can you explain this?" asked Fayte.

"Y-you want me to explain this?!" Susan asked with a startled squeak.

"You know more about this subject than I do," Fayte told her with a gentle smile.

"W-well, okay. I'll do my best." Susan turned to the others, placed a hand on her chest, and took a deep breath before beginning. "So... there was a group once that ran several experiments to see if it was possible to run across water. It was theorized that humans *could* run across the water if they ran fast enough. The idea put forth proposed that each time their feet slapped the water's surface, it would provide an inertial force from the water, and if they retracted their feet fast enough before the water collapsed, they could continue moving. However, moving fast enough to run across water is a feat beyond human ability. The research shows you'd need to run at least thirty meters per second."

Adam was a little surprised Susan knew so much about such an obscure subject, but he realized this was likely something she had researched for fun while stuck inside her house. Susan was a very sheltered child from what he understood. He could picture her sitting at her computer, scrolling through articles on the internet.

Susan's father was Eugine Forebear. He was not a business tycoon like the head of most families but a powerful politician who rose to prominence when he was just twenty. It was thanks to his remarkable policies that the American Federation had managed to recover so many of their assets after World War III and Mortems Disease ravaged the world. He operated numerous charities for families who had lost relatives to war and disease, making him very popular among the people. Thanks to his popularity, he not only received a lot of donations, but many powerful families like the Pleonexia Family tried to get in his good graces by offering favors.

Adam did not know much about the man himself. Everything he had learned was something he'd discovered with a simple web search. There were a lot of articles on him.

Why would a man like that let his daughter marry Connor Sword? Surely he knows what kind of person Connor is? No, I guess he wouldn't. He and Levon have hidden their darkness so deep few people can see it. Even I only saw it because I was in the way. So long as Eugine doesn't attempt to get in his way, Connor will keep up his public facade for as long as he needs to.

Thinking about Susan reminded Adam that he had yet to ask for her help. He wanted to use her talents as a hacker to hide any and all information about him and Aris so Levon could never find it. That would be something he could do after this mission, however. It wasn't an immediate problem since most players used fake names.

"Excuse me," Titania's voice cut through his thoughts and the argument taking place. She fluttered off his shoulder and floated between the group, hands on her hips as she glared at them all. "Since all of you are so dead set on arguing, I feel like I should mention that Aris's idea actually has merit."

"It does?" asked Fayte in surprise.

"Of course it does." Titania looked at her as if wondering why she couldn't see it. "I knew someone who could run across the water. He had a Movement stat of +10,000. Aris's Speed is more than enough to run across the water like he did."

The fairy's words reminded Adam of something important. *Age of Gods* was a game, and it didn't necessarily follow real-world logic. Aris's ridiculous Speed and Movement stats were proof of this, which meant it could very well be possible for the girl to run across the water's surface.

Nobody could contest Titania, who was the most knowledgeable person they knew. Thus, Aris was allowed to try out her idea.

The person in question wore a cheerful grin as she did some stretches to limber up. Adam's heart pounded in his chest as she adopted a kneeling position as though getting ready to run the hundred-meter dash. She placed her hands on the ground, put her dominant foot forward, and then disappeared. Adam blinked. All that was left to show signs that someone had been there were the footprints on the ground.

A sound caught his attention seconds later. It was the sound of splashing. He looked at the lake and saw several splashes appear all across the lake, but he still couldn't catch sight of Aris. That was when he realized something he'd forgotten in his worry.

His lover's Movement stat was +56,000.

The Speed stat was a measure of how fast someone could move, while Movement indicated how quickly someone could cover a specific distance. The two stats were linked together because a person's speed affected their movement. With a Speed of over +6,000 and a movement of +56,000, Aris could travel close to one hundred meters per second, more than fast enough to run across water according to the theory Susan had mentioned.

While Adam could only see the splashes Aris left in her wake, the [freshwater orca] must have had some means of keeping track of anything that moved above water. It burst from the surface and tried to swallow Aris whole. The person in question appeared above the monster, having jumped high into the air. As the monster opened its mouth wide, Aris unsheathed her swords and began spinning so fast that she created something like a tornado. She hacked into the monster, which released a cry of pain. Aris then landed on its snout and pushed off, smacking into the water and taking off once more.

"It looks like she really can run on water," Fayte muttered.

"Wow," Susan said in agreement.

Adam was also in awe, but he knew now wasn't the time to be stunned. "We should hurry and swim to the island. We don't know how long Aris can keep that thing at bay."

"Right," Fayte agreed.

"You'll want to remove your armor," Titania said. "It will weigh you down. Your robes, in particular, will grow quite heavy and might cause you to drown."

Fayte grimaced, but she didn't disagree and unequipped her clothing, leaving her in nothing but white underwear. Adam looked away out of respect. However, he still caught a glimpse of her gorgeous white skin and generous proportions before turning the other way. Susan and Lilith also removed their clothes, though Susan was far more reluctant. Her figure seemed childish compared to Fayte's. The way she covered her small chest made him wonder if she was perhaps insecure about her figure. He tried not to look at her either as he unequipped his own armor, which disappeared into his inventory.

Now in nothing but their undergarments, Adam, Aris, Fayte, and Lilith rushed into the lake and began swimming. He glanced at Kureha, who sat on his head. She seemed content to just let him carry her. Titania had it even easier since she could fly.

The group continued unimpeded. Aris had drawn the [freshwater orca] far away from them. He could just barely see their battle on the other side of the lake as several geysers of water erupted, but he did his best to simply focus on his breast strokes and keeping up his speed. It was only after a little while that he noticed one of them was lagging behind.

It was Susan.

He didn't know if she didn't know how to swim, or if she just wasn't a very strong swimmer, but she was struggling to keep up with them and was even slowing down. Adam quickly turned around and swam to Susan before presenting his back to her.

"Get on. I'll help you swim to shore."

"I-I couldn't burden you like that."

"We don't really have time to waffle here. Please, just get on."

"O-okay."

The way she so easily agreed to do what he asked was just proof that Susan was a pushover. She swam up and wrapped her arms around his neck. He felt only a brief spike of arousal as her chest pushed against his back. They might have been small, but his lovers weren't much bigger. He clamped down on those feelings and began kicking once more. Since he had someone hanging off him, he couldn't breaststroke and switched to simply paddling. Fortunately, with his Strength stat, he swam faster than most people even while paddling.

Adam quickly caught up to Fayte, then kept pace with her. It looked like they would reach the island soon.

"Look out!"

Yet just as it seemed like everything would go their way, Titania screamed seconds before several massive tentacles burst through the surface of the lake.

THE NAUGHTY NAUTILUS

"What is this—kyaaaah!"

"Noooooooo!"

"D-dammit! Master!"

The numerous tentacles that burst from the water's surface clearly belonged to some kind of Cephalopoda, though Adam couldn't tell which kind. It wasn't an octopus. A squid? Cuttlefish? Nautiloid? The tentacles were thick and leathery, but they didn't have any suction pods attached to them, and the spaded tip made him think it was some kind of devil.

"Titania! Cast [Scan]!" Adam shouted as one of the tentacles latched onto his leg and hauled him above the water's surface. It was about as thick as his torso, and it looked like it got thicker the further into the water it went. He couldn't see what this thing belonged to, meaning it was so deep underneath the surface that no light reached it.

"R-right! Just give me a second!"

Titania was busy dodging tentacles that were trying to grab her as she ascended higher into the air. She was fortunate she was so small. The tentacles couldn't get a good grip on her. They thrashed and lashed out, but she wove through them, ascending higher and higher, until she was far out of their reach.

The other girls weren't so lucky.

Adam wondered if maybe there was a glitch in the game. The tentacles that had wrapped around the girls had done so in a manner so erotic it reminded him of those eroge from the early 2000s. Fayte's breasts stood out like round melons as a thinner part of the tentacles wrapped around them, causing them to look like they were about to pop out of her bra. Lilith was in a similar position, but the tentacles had wrapped around her thighs and was forcing her legs apart. She was practically spread eagle by this point. Even poor Susan had the things running all over her body. Matters were only exacerbated by the fact that all of them were in their underwear.

Adam's eyes popped wide open when one of the tentacles brushed against his crotch. Gnashing his teeth together, he activated [Thrust] and impaled his spear into the tentacle.

-10,040!

The tentacle didn't make a sound as it jerked back like it had been shocked. Adam twisted his body and around and used [Slash] on the tentacle holding him.

-9,412!

Adam found himself free falling as the tentacle let go of him, but he didn't just let himself fall back into the water. First, he activated [Double Jump] to ascended higher, then used [Flight] to reach the nearest girl. It was Susan. Spinning around like a dreidel, he used [Energy Sweep] since it was the easiest to activate right now.

-18,825!

A crescent wave of energy sliced into the tentacle, which dropped Susan. Adam still had flight activated, so he was able to catch the screaming girl in his arms, though his flight deactivated seconds later and they both fell into the water. He broke the surface quickly, a coughing Susan clinging to his neck.

"You okay, Su?" asked Adam.

Susan didn't say anything because she was still coughing, but she did nod once as if to try and reassure him.

At that moment, Titania finally activated [Scan] on the creature that was attacking them.

Name: Naughty Nautilus

Description: A Cephalopoda that was raised by a perverse mage who wanted to drown the world in pleasure. After the mage died, the nautilus made its way to this lake, where it slumbered for hundreds of years. It has a habit of groping people.

Class: 2-Star

Lvl: 30

Main Body:

HP: 120,000/120,000

MP: 30,000/30,000

Strength: +600

Constitution: +400

Dexterity: +1,000

Intelligence: +500

Speed: +1,200

Tentacles:

HP: 30,000/30,000

Skills:

Skill Name: Swim

Description: The ability to swim through the water at

incredible speed

+200 boost to speed when in water

MP Cost: None

Cooldown time: 0 seconds

Skill Name: Tentacle Grab

Description: The nautilus grabs players with its tentacles

and refuses to let go

Players are stuck until someone either breaks them free,

they break themselves free, or the nautilus runs out of MP

MP Cost: 10 MP per second

Skill Name: Grope

Description: The nautilus touches players inappropriately

while secreting an aphrodisiac

Aphrodisiac effect ends only when the Naughty Nautilus is killed or runs out of MP
Drains +500 MP per second
MP Cost: None

Skill Name: Physical Immunity
Description: The nautilus's shell is durable to the point that physical attacks don't work on it
Negates all physical damage
MP Cost: None

Adam felt his eye twitching as he read the description for this creature. Whoever made this [Naughty Nautilus] must have been an incredibly depraved programmer. However, since it didn't seem to have much health and none of its attacks did physical damage, he could easily kill the creature.

[Blood Sacrifice]

After activating his greatest trump card, Adam released Susan and dove under the water without any hesitation. He used his Strength stat to his advantage, kicking his legs so hard that he was propelled down toward the depths at a speed normal humans could never hope to achieve. The water grew darker and colder as all light vanished. Adam channeled energy into his eyes, granting him a unique form of night vision. It was a skill he had in real life. Adam still found it a bit weird that he could use abilities from his real life in the game, but he wasn't going to look a gift horse in the mouth.

He soon found the monster attacking them.

It was indeed a nautiloid of some kind—a rather huge one at that. He couldn't accurately judge its full size, but its body was ensconced in a massive shell easily ten or fifteen square meters in size. The shell was one of those spiral variations. Its face was sticking out of the end, dozens if not hundreds of tentacles emerging from it. Most of them were going above water, but the [Naughty Nautilus] must have spotted him because several came his way.

-79,065!

Adam didn't hesitate to thrust his spear in front of him and use [Energy Thrust] to sheer his way through the tentacle. Now that he was this close, he could hear the monster's scream of pain. It was a shrill sound that he wouldn't have expected from a creature like this, but then again, he wasn't sure what kind of sound an underwater monster was supposed to make. Either way, he didn't stop swimming toward it.

[Blood Sacrifice] wore off before Adam could reach his foe, but he'd already shaved away plenty of its health. He reached the creature and used [Slash] against its outer shell.

-0; -0; -0; -0; -0; -0; -0; -0; -0; -0!

Adam grimaced when he saw his attacks do nothing, only now recalling one of this creature's skills. [Physical Immunity]. What a troublesome ability.

His lungs were burning by now. He knew that if he didn't defeat this creature soon, he might not get another chance. He swam toward the front. Adam felt sick to his stomach the moment he laid eyes on the [Naughty Nautilus's] gaping maw, briefly visible behind the swarm of tentacles writhing around it. A massive eye tracked him as he swam and several tentacles tried to wrap around him, but he cut them apart by activating [Slash] several times in rapid succession. With spots appearing before his eyes, Adam used all of his strength to attack the monster's head, activating every skill in his arsenal save [Blood Sacrifice], which was still in cooldown, and [Dance of the Sakura Blossoms], which he couldn't activate because he wasn't standing on solid ground.

-26,355; -18,825; -10;040; -9,412; -9,412; -9,412; -9,412; -9,412; -9,412; -9,412!

His attacks landed in quick succession and rapidly depleted the monster's health until it reached zero. The [Naughty Nautilus] shrieked and thrashed, giving what amounted to death throes as its cries made the water vibrate. Its body seemed to shrivel as it retracted all its tentacles and curled into its shell. Then the tentacles and the body itself seemed to grow stale before it crumbled into mud. Soon only the shell remained.

Ding!

[Congratulations! You have defeated the 2-Star monster [Naughty Nautilus]! [Naughty Nautilus] has dropped the items [Giant Shell], [Secret Pleasure Manual], [Fisherman's Spear], [Shell Shield], and 250,000 gold coins. +250,000 experience points! +120,000 ability points!]

Adam sighed in relief and closed his eyes as he realized he'd won. He didn't even realize he was falling unconscious or that his health was rapidly dropping from being underwater for so long.

✱✱✱

Fayte felt like a waterlogged cat as she dragged herself onto the shore. They had reached the island, though it had taken a lot of effort. She'd have thought they wouldn't have so much trouble with Aris distracting the [freshwater orca], though she understood now that her thoughts were far too optimistic. Of course there would be other monsters in this lake.

She looked at the lake from where she stood, far from the water's edge. Susan was sitting on the sand, arms behind her as she took deep breaths. Fayte had helped Susan swim to shore after Adam killed the [naughty nautilus]. Kureha, Titania, and Lilith were also present. The only ones missing were Aris and Adam.

Ding!

[Aris_Lancer has died. Her level has been reset to 17. She has been resurrected at the Solum Cathedral.]

The announcement screen that appeared before Fayte sent shock rippling through her. She knew there had been a possibility, given the dangerous action Aris was taking, but she guessed some part of her had never wanted to entertain the idea that any of them could die. The only consolation she had was that *Age of Gods* was a game.

"I-I can't believe Aris died," Susan mumbled.

"Me neither," Fayte said.

"She's always seemed so strong and indomitable. Kinda like Adam."

"I bet she gets it from him. Speaking of Adam, why hasn't he come back up yet?" Fayte realized only now that they were discussing him that Adam still hadn't emerged from the water's surface.

Titania grimaced. "He may be drowning… even you otherworlders can only hold your breath for so long. If he exceeded his time limit, then he might have lost consciousness and is in the process of dying."

"What?!" Fayte shouted in shock.

A loud splash caused her to turn back toward the lake. Ripples were spreading across the water from where someone had jumped in. She noticed Lilith was gone, so the woman must have rushed in to help Adam. The fanatic loyalty she displayed even now startled Fayte, but she understood the woman better after eavesdropping on Adam's conversation with Aris about his past. She didn't know everything. However, they surely had a deep and complex history together.

Fayte felt like she was on pins and needles as she waited for Lilith to emerge. She paced back and forth, heedless of the three sets of eyes on her, trying hard to calm the frantic heart beating within her chest.

Yet it didn't stop pounding.

It wouldn't calm down no matter what she did.

Lilith finally broke the water's surface. She wasn't alone. Adam was with her, but it was clear from the way she dragged him by the arm that he was unconscious. Fayte rushed over just as the woman came ashore and carried Adam to dry land. She knelt before the man as Lilith set him down and checked his stats.

Name: Adam

Class: Seven Forms Spearman

Lvl: 19

HP: 10/7,100

MP: 430/570

Status Ailments: Unconscious; Drowned

"I've never seen his health so low. What do we do?" asked Fayte.

"Calm down," Titania said. "First, use [high-grade health potions] to restore his health. Unfortunately, drowned is a unique status ailment that can't be fixed with a [cure-all]. There are only two ways to fix it. One is to wait until the effects wear off. The other is to force the water out of him by performing mouth-to-mouth resuscitation."

Fayte hadn't known there were unique ailments like that, but it did make sense. Drowning wasn't like being poisoned, put to sleep with magic, or suffering from confusion. It happened when the body attempted to breathe underwater and sucked water into the lungs. She glanced at Adam, whose face was far paler than she had ever seen. It didn't look like he was breathing either.

"Do any of you know CPR?" asked Fayte. It was not something she had studied since she never saw the need to. Lilith silently shook her head, but Susan raised her hand.

"I-I do."

Though surprised that her timid friend knew CPR, she knew now wasn't the time to say anything. She moved back and gestured to Adam.

"Then we'll be counting on you, Su."

Susan gulped at the pressure being placed on her, but she inched forward nonetheless until she was kneeling beside Adam. She took a deep breath before getting to work. Susan first tilted Adam's head back to lift his chin, then checked to see if he was breathing. He wasn't. She placed her hands, one atop the other, in the middle of his chest, then used her body weight to compress his chest several times. Nothing happened. However, Susan wasn't deterred as she pinched his nose shut, placed her mouth over his, and delivered two breaths before compressing his chest once more.

Through her worry, Fayte could not help but briefly admire Susan as she worked. There was no hint of the normally shy Susan as she tried her best to breathe life into Adam again. Her face was set in a mask of concentration, eyes narrowed with determination. She wondered if the girl even knew what she looked like at the moment.

Probably not, Fayte mused to herself.

Nearly one agonizing minute went by with nothing to show for it. Fayte wondered if this would even work, but just as doubt began creeping into her thoughts, Adam coughed, water burbling from his mouth. Susan moved back as he rolled onto his side and began spewing water like a faucet.

"Master, are you okay?!" Lilith was by his side in an instant. Fayte almost felt like the woman had teleported. She rubbed Adam's back, and Fayte felt a small tinge of annoyance embed itself within her heart. She knew these two had some history as assassins together. However, Adam belonged to Aris now. Lilith really had no right acting so close to him.

"I-I'm fine," Adam said through his coughs. "Thanks… for the save… I owe you one."

"I… I did not do anything," Lilith admitted with great reluctance. "Susan is the one who saved you."

"That so?"

"Eep!"

Susan's back went ramrod straight as Adam turned his gaze onto her. She was sitting with her calves underneath her butt, hands on her calves. Her face went bright red. Adam wasn't wearing his mask right now, which meant all of them could see the warm smile on his face. It was such a lustrous, honest expression that Fayte couldn't help but be enraptured by it. She felt like she could have stared at that smile until the end of time.

Come on, Fayte. Get a grip. Now is not the time to think about that. You've got to focus on the task at hand. Besides, Adam is dating Aris.

"Thank you, Su," Adam said, voice laced with sincerity.

"Y-you're welcome," Susan said softly.

While Fayte did wish Adam would smile at her and thank her, she couldn't find it in herself to take this moment away from Susan. The girl had always been timid and seriously lacking in self-confidence. She had lived a very sheltered life, and she was too good a girl to gain a rebellious streak, so she'd never done anything that would go against her father's wishes. It had caused her to become very meek. She needed moments like this to help bolster her confidence.

Kureha, having realized Adam was going to be okay, came up and began licking his fingers. Adam placed his hand on the fox yokai's head and began stroking her fur. The strange mrrring sounds that Kureha produced were adorable. Fayte could understand why Lilith was so taken with the little fox.

"By the way…" Adam began again, looking at all the faces surrounding him. "… where is Aris?"

***

"My bad. I sorta goofed up and fell in the water while I was running. That stupid fish came right in and swallowed me whole. Tee-hee."

"Don't 'tee-hee' me! You said you'd be okay!"

"I know. I know. And I'm sorry. If I hadn't tripped, I'm sure I would have been fine, but, well, these things happen, you know? It's not like any of us can predict every possible outcome. Besides, I can't really die in here. You know that."

"Even if you can't die for real, I felt like my heart stopped when Fayte told me you resurrected at the cathedral."

"I-I am sorry about that. I really didn't mean to worry you."

"Haaaah. No. I'm sorry. I got carried away. Since you've been resurrected in Solum, I don't think you'll make it in time to join us. I recommend heading to the guild house and waiting for us there. If possible, try to do some grinding around the Suncrest Mountains to regain your level. However, don't be too reckless. We really can't afford to have your level drop like this again."

"Got it. Good luck clearing the dungeon, Adam."

"Yeah. Thanks."

Adam sighed as he ended the friend chat, then turned to look at everyone else. Everyone had equipped their outfits once more. Fayte was dressed in her elemental mage outfit, Susan was wearing her archer clothes, and Lilith had donned the getup of a dark clansman assassin. Adam had also donned his armor once more. He never realized how naked he had felt not wearing this armor until he put it back on.

"Well, you all heard what's happening. Aris won't be joining us now."

"What happened was a shame, but I think we should also be grateful to Aris," Fayte said. "We never would have been able to reach this point without her help. Adam, you need to make sure you thank her when you log out."

"You're right. I'll be sure to thank her later today," he said. Adam did feel bad for getting worked up like he had. Aris was just so precious to him that he felt like he needed to constantly protect her. It was hard for him to not treat her like a glass figurine, especially since she had Mortems Disease until just recently. Looking after her was a several-year ingrained habit. Shaking his head, he got back on track. "What time is it?"

"It's about fourteen hundred, Mas—erm, Adam," answered Lilith.

Lilith had already called him "master" several times since he'd woken up, but fortunately, no one seemed to have noticed. Adam could only hope the panic from seeing him almost drown had prevented them from really focusing on the woman's words.

"So we only have a few hours left to play before we need to log out," Adam murmured.

"I doubt we'll get far, but I do think we should at least check out the dungeon to see what we're dealing with," Fayte said.

"You're right."

Adam and everyone else agreed, so they all turned toward the structure in the center of the island. It was a series of archways and crumbling walls built in a circle. As they walked underneath one of several arches, they all spotted the stone stairs in the very center of the structure. It was a spiral staircase leading down.

"Guess it only makes sense that this dungeon would be underground," Adam said. "Let's get into formation before heading down. Lilith, take the rear. Susan, Fayte, Kureha, and Titania will be in the center, and I'll be the vanguard. Titania, be ready to begin singing at a moment's notice."

"You don't need to tell me twice," Titania said.

The group made their way down the stairs, traveling deeper, deeper, and deeper still. Torches sprang to life as they walked, illuminating their steps. Adam didn't know how far these stairs went, but it felt like hours of simply listening to the sounds of their own footsteps before they finally reached the bottom. What they found after passing through a small entryway was something that went beyond all of their expectations.

"What… is all this?" asked Susan.

"Is this really a dungeon?" Fayte wondered out loud.

Adam and Lilith remained silent, but they shared the other two's sentiments.

The dungeon did not look like a dungeon at all. They were standing on a bluff that overlooked a world of fire and brimstone. Boiling lava flowed at the bottom, and it looked like there were only several paths they could take, narrow walkways with no guardrail to keep them from falling off. Several towering structures stood in the distance. They were structures of stone with towering spires and large contraptions extending from their base. Adam couldn't make heads or tails of it. Several large creatures with green skin and hulking bodies appeared to be toiling away.

"This is far more than just a dungeon," Titania said gravely. "You see those massive monsters in the distance. Those are [trolls]. They were one of the War Demon's favorite monsters to use during sieges because of their brute strength. I remember hearing stories about how he would throw hundreds of [trolls] at the gates of various strongholds belonging to the races of light, forcing them to act as a battering ram. When they broke through, the [trolls] would rampage through the stronghold. They were the perfect siege weapons because they can both absorb a lot of damage and deal a lot of damage."

"So, they're basically a combination of tank and DPS," Fayte said.

Those were old gamer terms. Tanks were essentially meat shields, designed to draw aggro, absorb damage, and protect their teammates. DPS was short for "damage per second" and was the amount of damage a weapon, other equipment, or player could do against an enemy. The term could be used to either describe a class or a weapon's capability. A tank DPS was basically someone who could take incredible damage and deal it all back several fold.

"Can you [Scan] them from here?" asked Adam.

"Yes. Hold on a moment," Titania said as she cast [Scan].

Name: Troll

Description: Trolls are monsters used by the War Demon as part of his forces. They were the backbone of his army and were used to great effect during sieges. Many people feared trolls because of their high health and high attack power. The only upside is that trolls are slow and stupid.

Class: 1-Star

Lvl: 50

HP: 3,500,000/3,500,000

MP: 3,000/3,000

Strength: 6,000

Constitution: 10,000

Dexterity: 50

Intelligence: 5

Speed: 10

Skills:

Skill Name: Bash

Description: Troll bashes players with club or fists

Damage = Physical Attack * two

MP: 50

Cooldown Time: 0

Skill Name: Sweep
Description: The troll uses whatever weapon it has on hand
to sweep opponents away
Damage = Physical Attack
Deals damage to anyone within range of attack
100% chance of knocking enemies off their feet
MP Cost: 10
Cooldown Time: 0 seconds

This creature only had two attacks, but that hardly mattered in this case. Both attacks dealt a lot of damage, which meant none of them could afford to get hit even once. Adam counted at least fifteen [trolls] in the area. There was also more than just [trolls]. He couldn't see them very well, but there were a lot of small monsters walking around the [trolls'] feet.

"What are those monsters?" asked Adam.

Titania squinted her eyes. "I cannot see them very well, but if I had to guess, I would say they are [low-class demons]. Those are another part of the War Demon's forces. He had hundreds of thousands of them under his command. They were his foot soldiers. Fortunately, they are very weak. A normal human at the same level can defeat at least a dozen of them on their own. The problem is they're very numerous. Whenever you face a [low-level demon], you're not just facing a mere dozen but hundreds if not thousands at a time. I should also mention the term 'low-level' is meant to signify their position in the hierarchy and not their actual level."

Adam listened to Titania with a small frown as he studied the layout of this dungeon. There were two dozen walkways that led to the fortress in the very center. The fortress itself looked like something a demon would have created, with colossal spires that were jagged and gave an ominous aura. He wondered if the War Demon was located inside. He hoped not because it meant they would not be able to complete this quest.

Since they had done what they came to do right now, the group traveled back up the stairs, set up a tent for Kureha and Titania, and logged out for the day.

DEMONIC OPERATION

Adam, Fayte, Susan, and Lilith logged back into *Age of Gods* the next day. They traveled back into the dungeon with Kureha and Titania, stood on the bluff overlooking what now seemed to him like an assembled army, and observed them.

"I count at least two dozen [trolls]," Adam said at last. He was kneeling near the edge of the cliff, one hand propped on his knee, eyes narrowed. "I can't tell how many [low-level demons] there are, but there must be at least several thousand."

"Would you like me to see if I can get closer to [Scan] them?" asked Titania.

Adam shook his head. "Not yet. We don't want to risk being discovered before we can create a plan, and honestly, it doesn't matter how many of them there are. Even if there were ten thousand, it wouldn't change anything."

In a quest where the objective was to clear the dungeon, the only option they had going forward was to defeat every monster in this area, find the boss, and defeat them. Failure to do so means failing the mission. They couldn't afford to lose when Fayte had so much riding on her shoulders, and there were few things Adam hated more than losing.

"Observing any longer isn't going to help us. Let's come up with a plan," Adam said at last.

The group gathered around. Lilith stood on Adam's right, Susan on his left, and Fayte directly across from him. Kureha and Titania were not on his head and shoulder respectively right now. Kureha stood near his feet, while Titania was floating in the air, her translucent wings fluttering.

A strong smell of brimstone filled the air around them, making it difficult to breathe. Adam had no problem. Susan and Fayte, however, had never dealt with a stench quite this bad and looked put out. Kureha had it the worst. She was a fox yokai, so her nose was dozens of times more sensitive than anyone else's. She was on the floor with her hands covering her snout.

"Do you have any ideas?" asked Fayte. As a woman determined to control the fate of her life, Fayte had studied everything from business management to diplomacy to how PvP battles between guilds typically worked. She had not studied warfare, however, since it wasn't something she believed she would need in this day and age where war had been banned. Tactics against a horde of monsters like this were beyond her field of expertise.

"I've got a few." Adam nodded before looking at the woman on his right. "Lilith?"

"Yes."

Lilith took what looked like a stick out of her inventory. It was called [Treant Branch] and was a crafting item that could be used in the creation of wands and staffs for magic classes. She knelt on the ground, took branch to dirt, and began drawing. Like a knife, she cut through the dirt to create a map approximately shaped like the dungeon they found themselves in. She finished the drawing by attaching the pathways that led to the exact center where all the monsters were located.

"In a battle where a small group is outnumbered so heavily, there are only a few ways for the smaller group to win. Can you guess what those ways are?" asked Adam. Fayte shook her head, but Susan was quivering in place. He looked at the girl who seemed like she had something she wanted to say but was too shy to say it. Smiling, he said, "Do you know, Su?"

"Eh? Ah, um…" Susan became startled when he called on her, but she quickly produced the answer he was looking for. "You can either defeat them with an overwhelming use of force like a nuclear warhead, something that can kill them all even if you only have a few people, or you can force them to fight you in smaller groups. It doesn't matter if there are a hundred thousand monsters arrayed against you. If you can fight them all one-on-one, then you stand a better chance of winning than if you fought them a hundred thousand against one.”

“That’s exactly it. Good job, Su,” Adam complimented.

“That’s our Susan for you,” Fayte said.

Susan tilted her head to look at the ground. It was a little hard to see her face, so he didn’t know what kind of expression she was making, but the tips of her ears were bright red.

“We can’t use the first option,” Adam said, getting them all back on track. “Even though we are powerful, none of us are so powerful that we can simply plow through all these enemies regardless of their numbers and expect to come out on top. That means we need to use the second method.”

“I’m guessing you’ve got a plan?” asked Fayte.

Nodding, Adam said, “It’s not much of one, but I do have something in mind. You see, I learned during my time on the Island of Beginnings that it was possible to damage the environment...”

After Adam explained his plan, the group went off to put the plan into action. They traveled down from the bluff and walked along the pathway leading to the walkways that stood over boiling lava. Adam wanted to wipe the sweat from his face. It was scorching! He glanced over the edge of the cliff, saw the bubbling magma below, felt the heat rising from it, and felt sweat drenching his back.

It’s so freaking hot! This reminds me of the mission I’d been sent on to kill a weapons dealer who’d stashed all of his munitions in a volcano. Idiot. Who the hell stores live ammunition in a volcano anyway? This mission might be even worse. At least that base had air conditioning.

They soon reached the first of many walkways. Now that they were closer, Adam judged the walkway to be about three meters wide and maybe fifty long. It looked to be made from hardened magma, though just how the magma had hardened to form a bridge was beyond him. Was it naturally formed, or had someone created it with magic?

He turned to look at the others. "I'm off."

"Be careful," Fayte said.

"Don't worry. I will."

Using his superior speed, Adam blasted off the ground and raced across the walkway. He was alone. Not even Kureha and Titania were with him. They were waiting by the other three. This was Adam's mission alone. As the strongest one among them, he was the only one who could accomplish this task and hope to survive.

After crossing the bridge, he made his way toward the edge of the monster encampment. There were a lot of rocky outcroppings, so he hid behind one of them and peered out from around it. Only a few [low-level demons] were close by. He counted six of them standing guard, though two of them looked like they were squabbling over something.

The [low-level demons] had a very humanoid shape, with two legs, two arms, and a head possessing a human-like face, but that was where the similarities ended. They're skin was like ash. Their eyes were a gleaming crimson. There was no white in their eyes, just a dark black surrounding the blood-colored iris. Some of them had horns, a few had a tail, and there were even some that had wings. All of them wore basic leather armor and carried dual-pronged spears.

Adam couldn't tell what level they were at since Titania was unable to use [Scan] on such small monsters from so far away, but he assumed their level to be only slightly weaker than the [trolls].

He took a deep breath, held it, the burst into action.

[Blood Sacrifice]

Adam rushed from around the rocky outcropping and charged at his first victim. The [low-level demon] spotted him coming, of course, and it immediately shifted into a fighting stance, but Adam was on it before it could mount a proper defense. He was gratified to see the monster's eyes widen seconds before he attacked.

[Dance of the Sakura Blossom]

-18,825; -56,475; -169,425; -508,275; -1,524,825!

Because Adam didn't know how much health a [low-level demon] had, he went all out from the very beginning, activating his strongest skill to deal so much damage there was no hope of this monster surviving. Just like he expected, the [low-level demon] dropped like a sack of bricks after his attack.

Ding!

[Congratulations! You have killed a [low-level demon]! Items dropped: [Demonic Spear]. +300,000 experience points!]

Adam didn't pay much attention to the announcement and turned to face the next enemy. The other six [low-level demons] had noticed him by now. They turned in his directions, spears drawn, but they didn't move quite yet. There was surprise etched clear on their faces.

"What is a human doing here?!"

"How did a human find this place?!"

"Whatever! It doesn't matter! Let's kill him so he can't tell anyone else about us!"

Adam was a little shocked to find monsters were capable of speech, but he didn't have time to let his surprise get the best of him. The five remaining enemies closed the distance between them and thrust out their spears at the same time. Adam switched to the defensive Form Five and repelled their attacks like a tortoise hiding in its shell. Once their attacks were properly defended against, he threw himself forward and attacked in earnest.

-56,475; -56,475; -56,475; -56,475; -56,475!

Adam spun around and swung his spear in a wide slash to activate [Energy Sweep]. A blue crescent wave of power erupted from his spear, cut through the five [low-level demons] and continued, slamming into a rock wall after dealing a great deal of damage. This, unfortunately, was not enough to defeat these monsters. They remained standing, though they did react in an oddly human manner.

"Gyaaaah! That hurts!"

"What kind of attack was that?!"

"A spearman who can use AoE skills?! What kind of unfair advantage is that?!"

This was only his second time fighting against humanoid creatures. The first was his battle against Alexandra. However, she had been a 4-Star Boss and a former human at that. He expected her to be a bit more animated, but these guys were acting with the same amount of personality.

Whatever. It doesn't matter.

Adam shunted this matter to the side and attacked them in earnest. He only had a bit of time remaining before [Blood Sacrifice] entered its cooldown period, so he attacked the group of [low-level demons] with a series of [slash] and [thrust] attacks. He didn't let them attack either. Using both the tip and butt of his spear, Adam forced all five monsters to remain on the defensive as he whittled away at their health.

-28,237; -28,237; -28,237; -28,237; -28,237; -28,237; -28,237; -28,237; -28,237; -28,237; -28,237; -28,237; -28,237; -28,237!

Even while in the midst of combat, Adam kept careful track of how much damage he did to each monster. The first one dropped after he dealt around two hundred thousand points of damage. With that as the basis, Adam attacked the others in earnest.

The [low-level demons] tried their best to fight back. It was no use. They were clearly not well-trained even if their levels were high. The way they wielded their spears was clumsy and uncoordinated, as if their only understanding of how to use a spear was to thrust it at the enemy, but of course, that was only the most basic of the basics. Adam constantly switched between the defensive Form Five and the aggressive Form Seven.

Form Seven of the Pleonexia Family's Seven Spear Forms was decidedly the most aggressive of them all. When using this form, Adam put all of his weight and power behind his attacks. He didn't just rely on the strength of his arms. His legs, his core, the muscles in his back and butt, all of them were used to deliver punishing attacks that sent his enemies stumbling. As he launched his attacks, a strange roar echoed from his spear. It sounded like an enraged dragon.

-28,237; -28,237; -28,237; -28,237; -28,237; -28,237; -28,237; -28,237; -28,237; -28,237; -28,237; -28,237; -28,237; -28,237!

Ding!

[Congratulations! You have defeated five [low-level demons]! Items dropped: x5 [Demonic Spear]. +1,500,000 experience points!]

After all of his opponents lay dead before him, Adam took a deep breath, went to wipe the sweat from his forehead, then grimaced when his hand came into contact with his mask. No wonder he felt so stifled. Wearing a mask in this heat was a terrible idea. He briefly considered taking it off. Susan had already seen his face now when she performed CPR on him, so it wasn't like it mattered, but then he considered something else.

If these demons knew what he looked like, could that cause problems for him in the future? Had this been a normal game, he would have said no, but this wasn't a normal game. Nothing about this game was average. For all he knew, showing his face to these monsters would paint a target on his back and, more importantly, his comrades' backs.

I'll keep the mask on for now, he decided.

Continuing on, Adam strolled casually into the main encampment where nearly a hundred [low-level demons] were wandering around. Some were eating by a blazing campfire, others were moving supplies, and a few were barking out orders to others. It was quite the bustling little enemy stronghold. However, everything came to a stop when they spotted him.

Time seemed to stand still for a moment as he stared back at the shocked monsters. Even the nearby [trolls] had stopped what they were doing to look at him like they weren't sure what to make of him.

"Good evening," Adam said in a cheery voice. "How would you all like to die today?"

That snapped the monsters out of their stupor.

"It's a human!"

"What the hell is a human doing here?!"

"Does it matter?!"

"Yeah, yeah! Who cares?!"

"Let's kill him!"

An alarm bell sounded out somewhere in the distance. Adam looked up to see a [low-level demon] ringing an alarm from one of several watchtowers. The other monsters were all brandishing their weapons as they raced toward him now. Seeing this, Adam turned tail and fled. He raced back the way he had come, toward the walkway.

"Don't let him escape!"

"After him!"

"Kill the human!!!"

Adam easily outpaced the monsters chasing him, but he made sure to remain in their sights so they wouldn't lose him. He was soon racing across the walkway. On the opposite end were his companions. Titania was already singing the [Song of Vigor] to increase their power. Fayte and Kureha likewise looked like they were had prepared their spells.

He was almost halfway across the walkway when his pursuers caught up and began running across the walkway as well. There was a limit to how many could fit on these walkways since they were only about three meters across. Six [low-level demons] ran shoulder to shoulder. By the time Adam had reached his companions, there were maybe a hundred of them on the walkway.

"Now, you two! Do it now!"

Kureha and Fayte didn't need to be told twice. One raised her staff into the air and the other her tail.

[Thunder Bolt]

Kureha's attack hit first. A crackling ball of lightning exploded above her tail and struck the walkway with enough force to leave cracks in the ground. Several [low-level demons] were struck and thrown off the side. The cracks spread, but the walkway didn't fall, and the [low-level demons] were still running across it. Several [trolls] had also begun lumbering over the walkway.

[Wind Hammer]

Unlike Kureha, who used a lightning spell, Fayte raised her staff high above her head, the wind congealing around it, taking shape. It transformed into a massive hammer that was easily fifteen meters tall and maybe two meters across. With a gruff grunt, she swung her staff down. The hammer went with it.

When the hammer met the walkway, an intense explosion of wind buffeted Adam's hair. More importantly, the attack caused the walkway to shatter. It started where she struck, then spread across the ground, quickly overtaking the army of [low-level demons] and [trolls]. The monsters who'd been on the walkway screeched in shock and surprise when they plummeted into the lava.

Ding!

[Congratulations! You have defeated 100 [low-level demons] and 10 [trolls]. Items dropped: x100 [Demonic Spears], x20 [troll pelts], x10 [troll eyes], and 5,000,235 gold coins. +50,000,000 experience points!]

Ding!

[Congratulations! Kureha has leveled up! She is now at level 20! +700 HP! +9,300 MP! +10 SP!]

Ding!

[Congratulations! Titania has leveled up! She is now at level 20! +400 HP! +10,600 MP! +10 SP!]

Ding!

[Congratulations! Lilith has leveled up! She is now at level 19! +600 HP! +210 MP! +5 SP!]

Ding!

[Congratulations! Changing_Fayte has leveled up! She is now at level 19! +1,600 HP! +7,960 MP! +5 SP!]

Ding!

[Congratulations! Little_Su has leveled up! She is now at level 19! +500 HP! +200 MP! +5 SP!]

A string of announcements marked everyone except Adam leveling up, but while this was indeed something worth celebrating, they couldn't afford to let themselves be distracted right now. They were at the crucial stage of their operation. If they wanted to make it out of this ordeal alive, then they needed to act fast.

"I'm sure our enemies will try to attack us from the other bridges now." Adam hefted his spear over his shoulder and turned to the group. "Fayte, Kureha, and Titania, I want you three to head to the next bridge over, wait for our enemies, and blow out the bridge. Try to take out as many of them as you can. Meanwhile, Lilith, Susan, and I will head to the next two bridges and defend those locations until you three can arrive and destroy them. You already destroyed the furthest bridges, right?"

"We did. We'll try to finish our task as quickly as we can." Fayte placed a hand against her chest as if to emphasize her words. "Meanwhile, you try not to take too many reckless actions, okay?"

"I'll do my best," Adam said.

The group rushed off. They reached the next bridge relatively quickly. There, Fayte, Kureha, and Titania remained, while Lilith, Susan, and Adam made their way to the next one. There were no enemies coming this way yet, but Adam was certain that would change.

"I'll leave you two here. Su, provide Lilith with long-range support please."

Susan nodded, but then worried her lower lip. "I'll do my best, but will you be okay on your own?"

"Don't worry about me. I'll be fine."

Adam thought maybe he'd been resisting the impulse for too long, and that's why he did it, but he didn't even realize he had reached out to Susan until his hand landed on her soft hair. His fingers glided through her brown locks. What kind of shampoo did she use? It must have been some high-quality stuff to give it such a silky feel. Susan's cheeks heated up until they looked like a furnace.

"Um… Adam…?"

"Ah. I'm sorry." Adam retracted his hand. "I acted without thinking. That was my bad."

"No, um, it's fine. I didn't mind," Susan said after a moment.

Adam gave her a troubled smile, even though he knew she couldn't see it, then turned around and raced off toward the next bridge. He couldn't afford to deal with this now.

It didn't take more than maybe a minute to reach the bridge. Like the previous one, this one didn't have any enemies at it yet. It was a little wider than the other bridges. He guessed it was maybe five meters across instead of three.

Walking toward the center, Adam thought briefly about his actions toward Susan. He didn't understand why she evoked such a strong desire to protect her. He at first thought maybe it was because she made him think of Aris when she was younger, but the two were absolutely nothing alike. Aris had always been a wild child. Meanwhile, Susan was meek and obedient. They couldn't have been more different if they tried.

A large horde of monsters suddenly appeared by the opposite side of the bridge. Adam shook his thoughts about Susan off and readied himself for battle. The monsters were already beginning to run across the walkway, and so he downed a [high-grade health potion] set himself in a defensive stance, and activated his unique skill.

[Blood Sacrifice]

The screeching enemies soon crashed into Adam, who remained unmovable like a mountain as he spun around the spear in his hand, blocking several attacks before unleashing his own.

[Energy Sweep]

-56,475; -56,475!

[Energy Thrust]

-79,065!

[Slash]

-28,237; -28,237!

Adam blocked a spear with his own, twisted his wrist until the enemy spear impaled the ground, and jabbed the [low-level demon] through the chest. This monster was one with two horns and a tail. It was already weakened from Adam's previous assault, and so it died when his [thrust] pierced its chest.

Several more [low-level demons] tried to flank him while another several attempted to sneak past him. Adam activated [double jump] to avoid being caught between two attacks, landed in front of the monsters trying to reach the other side, and kicked them off the walkway. They fell into the boiling magma with desperate screams.

Of course, while he attacked like it was going out of style, Adam was on the receiving end of many attacks himself.

-1,300!

-2,000!

-300!

His health dropped rapidly as he received a number of attacks that tore into his mind. Not even his prodigious ability to dodge could save him when there was so little room to maneuver. A slash to the arm. A cut to the leg. One of his enemies even stabbed him with a spear. Adam would retreat quickly and down several [high-grade health potions] in rapid succession before jumping forward to halt the enemies' advance.

Ding!

[Congratulations! You have defeated 150 [low-level demons] and 12 [trolls] Items dropped: x300 [Demonic Spears], x24 [troll pelt], x12 [troll blood]. Inventory is full. Cannot fit items. Items have been sent to storage. +75,000,000 experience points!]

Ding!

[Congratulations! Adam has leveled up! You are now at level 20! +1,500 HP! +400 MP! +5 SP!]

Ding!

[Congratulations! You are the first person to reach level 20! You can now unlock a second class. Secondary classes are non-combat classes such as Blacksmith, Chef, Mapmaker, Squire, and Diplomat. They offer a wide variety of non-combat skills. The secondary class menu is currently unavailable. You cannot select a secondary class as of right now. The secondary class menu will

update on December 1st. As both an apology and a conciliatory reward, you have been awarded +200 SP. Please use them wisely.]

Ding!

[You can learn new skills! Be sure to check your status to see what new skills you can use!]

Ding!

[By reaching level 20, you have increased the level cap on your old skills. You can now increase the level for all of your skills except unique skills by 5.]

Adam couldn't pay much attention to the announcements, or to the subsequent announcements as Fayte, Lilith, Kureha, and Susan all leveled up once again. He was still beset on all sides by enemies. Sweat stung his eyes as he continued to viciously hold the line, but even though he tried his best, the number of monsters arrayed against him was endless. They came in waves. Adam was forced back over and over, retreating little by little.

-900!

-1,000!

-1,300!

-500!

Adam downed a [high-grade health potion], then another one to recover some of his lost health. He didn't have time to take one more. Two [low-level demons] attacked him in a frontal assault. He fended off their attacks, spinning the spear in his hand around as he shifted into the defensive Form Five. Then he launched [Energy Sweep], which didn't do nearly as much damage as he wished since [Blood Sacrifice] had worn off some time ago. He was waiting for the cooldown time to end, but thirty seconds felt like forever in a life and death battle.

-2,100!

Adam felt pain sear his stomach as a spear punched straight through it. His Dodge-Rate meant nothing here since he didn't even have room to maneuver. He removed the spear with a grunt, then activated [Energy Thrust] and stabbed his own spear through the head of the [low-level demon] that attacked him. His attack ignored the creature's defense and did several times the damage of his Physical Attack stat, ending the monster's life.

If only it was the only monster he had to worry about.

Ding!

[Congratulations! You have defeated 90 [low-level demons] and 10 [trolls]! Items dropped: x180 [Demonic Spears], x15 [troll pelts]. Inventory is full. Cannot fit items. Items have been sent to storage. +52,000,000 experience points!]

Ding!

Congratulations! Titania has leveled up! She is now at level 21! +400 HP! +10,600 MP! +10 SP!]

A shadow suddenly overtook him. Two legs like gigantic tree trunks appeared in his vision. Adam looked up to find a massive [troll] looming above him. It took up the entire walkway, though several [low-level demons] scurried around its feet to get at Adam. The monstrous creature looked down at him with a smile that promised nothing but pain.

TROLLING FOR TROUBLE

This was the first time Adam had faced a [troll] head-on. It looked even bigger up close. He guessed it was maybe ten meters tall. Though its gut protruded from its stomach, the rest of it was covered in thick, corded muscles. A thick club the size of a tree trunk was clenched tightly in its left hand. As it gripped the weapon, the muscles on its leathery green arms flexed, showcasing the explosive strength it possessed. It raised one leg, then brought it down, squashing flat one of the [low-level demons] trying to walk past it.

The walkway shook.

Adam felt his lips split into a twisted smile as the blood pumping through his veins accelerated. He could already tell this was going to be a challenge on his own.

Racing forward despite knowing it was stupid, Adam activated his two greatest skills.

[Blood Sacrifice]

[Dance of the Sakura Blossoms]

-18,945; -56,835; -170,505—

Before Adam was able to complete his attack, the [troll] swung its club to smack him away. He was forced to stop mid-attack and lowered his body until his back was pressed to the hard, hot ground. The club passed by so close he could almost feel it grazing his nose. As it passed, he leaped to his feet and kept attacking. Unfortunately, [Dance of the Sakura Blossoms] had entered its cooldown period, so he was forced to rely on his other skills.

[Energy Thrust]

-79,569!

[Thrust]

-30,312!

He thrust his spear forward twice in quick succession. The first attack released a burst of blue energy that penetrated deep into the monster's thick hide, while the second attack was just a regular thrust. While both attacks did a good deal of damage, it was just a drop in the bucket for this creature with over two million health points. It also didn't seem to do much more than enrage it.

Its roar rattling Adam's bones, the [troll] raised the club above its head and swung it down. Adam evaded. The attack slammed into the walkway, causing it to rumble and shake. Cracks spread from the point of impact. Some of them were large enough that Adam worried this creature might destroy the walkway on its own.

While he was attacking the troll, a handful of [low-level demons] tried to slip past them, but Adam would not let that happen. He leapt back, away from the [troll], and attacked the [low-level demons] with an [Energy Sweep]. Several of them flew off the walkway and fell, screaming, into the bubbling magma below, but the rest were drawn to him and attacked. Now he had to deal with the [troll], which was coming at him with a series of powerful swings, and the [low-level demons].

This is getting fun! I'd forgotten how fun a life and death battle could be! It's amazing that a game of all things could bring this thrill back!

It was an act of desperation, but Adam jumped into the air. He activated [Double Jump] to ascend higher. The [troll] couldn't stop its swings and continued attacking even though he was no longer there. Its attacks struck the [low-level demons], knocking them off the walkway. They screeched as they fell to their deaths. Meanwhile, Adam landed on the [troll's] shoulder.

Not one to miss an opportunity, Adam thrust his spear directly into the monster's eye.

[Thrust]

-10,104!

"GRRRRAAAAAAAAAHHHHHHH!"

[Blood Sacrifice] had run out of time and was now cooling down, so his attack didn't do much damage, but it still enraged the [troll]. It flailed around on the walkway as though attempting to force Adam off. He gritted his teeth and kept a firm grip on his spear to avoid falling, though that hardly did anything when his spear slipped from the eye. Kicking off the monster's shoulder, he landed on the ground several meters away. The [troll] continued to flail as it covered its eye.

Adam rushed forward and began peppering it with attacks. This might be his only chance to really deal any serious damage. He used [Slash] and [Thrust] constantly while using the Form Seven style of the Pleonexia Family's spearman style. His attacks still did very little damage to the monster. That wasn't a big deal, however. His goal was not dropping its health until it died. He kept backing away, until he was right next to the edge of the walkway, then slipped around its legs and kicked the creature as hard as he could.

-1!

His kick didn't do any damage, but it did tilt the [troll] forward. With a ferocious scream that sounded like terror, the [troll] pitched off the walkway, falling into the magma below with a loud splash. It continued to thrash even as the magma melted its skin, revealing the bones and muscle sinew that quickly burnt to a crisp as its fatty tissue ignited. It eventually sank below the surface. The last Adam saw was its hand as it tried to claw its way out.

"Haaaah… haaaah… hoooo…"

Adam was breathing heavily, and he wanted to rest a moment, but there were more [trolls] and [low-level demons] coming across the walkway. He raced back to the center of the walkway, adopted the Form Five stance, and prepared himself to deal with these monsters, even though his muscles were shaking with exhaustion.

Despite how tired he was, the smile that split his face was a mile long. He could feel it tugging at his lips.

It's a very good thing I'm wearing a mask...

"Adam! Hurry back over here! We're ready!"

Turning at the sound of the shout, Adam looked over to see Fayte, Lilith, Kureha, Susan, and Titania standing at the end of the walkway. He was a bit disappointed that his solo battle would end here, but he burst into a sprint toward his comrades. His leg muscles burned with the strain as he quickly cleared the distance. The moment he did, Kureha and Fayte unleashed their magical attacks that destroyed the walkway, and with it, all the monsters that had been attempting to cross it.

Ding!

[Congratulations! You have defeated 236 [low-level demons] and 34 [trolls]! Items dropped: x474 [Demonic Spears], x120 [troll pelt], x60 [troll eyes]. Inventory is full. Cannot fit items. Items have been sent to storage. +125,360,000 experience points!]

Ding!

[Congratulations! Adam has leveled up! You are now at level 21! +1,500 HP! +400 MP! +5 SP!

Ding!

[Congratulations! Lilith has leveled up! She is now at level 21! +600 HP! +210 MP! +5 SP!]

Ding!

[Congratulations! Changing_Fayte has leveled up! She is now at level 21! +1,600 HP! +7,960 MP! +5 SP!]

Ding!

[Congratulations! Little_Su has leveled up! She is now at level 21! +500 HP! +200 MP! +5 SP!]

"Looks like we all leveled up quite a bit," Adam said.

Fayre nodded. "It seems farming enemies like this is the best way to level up."

"It helps that the enemies in this dungeon give us a lot of experience points. I don't think we'd do nearly as well with other monsters."

"It's probably because this is a high-ranking quest," Susan said.

"Quests and rankings do not have anything to do with it," Titania refuted them, arms crossed as she fluttered her wings. "It's the type of monsters we are fighting and their level respective to our own. We are currently at a very low level. Meanwhile, these monsters are not only beasts who were personally used by the War Demon during the Demon Lord's war against the goddesses, but they are all over twenty levels higher than our own. These two factors mean they yield far more experience than other monsters."

"It looks like our expert has spoken," Adam said in a wry voice. He shook his head. "In either event, we should hurry up and move onto the next stage of our plan."

"Guess it's time to clean up," Fayte agreed.

The first stage of their plan involved using the environment and their ability to destroy it to demolish as much of the enemy force as possible. The second stage was mopping up the rest of the forces the old-fashioned way.

They moved quickly, reaching the next walkway, which was already littered with [low-level demons]. Adam couldn't see any more [trolls] coming. He assumed they had all been destroyed during stage one of their plan.

[Energy Sweep]

-18,945; -18,945; -18,945; -18,945; -18,945; -18,945; -18,945; -18,945; -18,945; -18,945; -18,945; -18,945!

Adam swung the spear and released a wave of energy that hit all the nearby [low-level demons], causing many to stumble and a few to even fall over the walkway. Most of his foes recovered quickly and attacked. He moved into the defensive Form Five and deflected their attacks with his spear.

The fact that he could do this and not receive damage was proof of the game's combat system working in his favor. It was just like Titania had said. Stats in the game were not the end all be all and only helped determine specific factors like health, damage dealt, and how often a person could hit or be hit. What really mattered in this world was superior skills.

[Counter]

-12,000!

While Adam was busy defending against several [low-level demons], another one tried to attack in his blind spot, but Lilith appeared before them and used her unique skill to counter its attack. As the creature staggered back from the damage she'd done, Lilith charged forward and swung the dagger in her hand so quickly it was nothing but a blur. Her enemy could do nothing but back away under the woman's relentless assault.

-3,600; -3,600; -3,600; -3,600; -3,600; -3,600; -3,600; -3,600; -3,600; -3,600; -3,600; -3,600; -3,600; -3,600!

While her attacks were not enough to kill the [low-level demon] any time soon, she had forced it back until it was standing close to the walkway's ledge. Spinning on the balls of her feet, Lilith launched a kick. Her heel struck the monster's chest. The [low-level demon] was lifted off its feet and pitched over the edge, disappearing into the magma with a splash.

With Adam and Lilith at the front, drawing all the enemies' aggro, Fayte, Susan, and Kureha were free to launch long-range attacks from the back. They used area of effect skills that dealt damage to multiple targets instead of just one. Their attacks were also aimed at the enemies standing near the edge of the walkway instead of the walkway itself.

[Chain Lightning]

-133,372; -133,372; -133,372; -133,372; -133,372; -133,372; -133,372; -133,372; -133,372; -133,372!

A bolt of lightning flew from Fayte's staff. It struck one enemy, frying them, then leapt to another enemy, another, and another, until ten [low-level demons] were connected through a lightning chain. The single attack was so powerful that all ten were felled within a single hit.

[Thunder Storm]

-32,712; -32,712!

While her attack didn't do as much damage, Kureha's [Thunder Storm] dealt damage to more enemies. Lightning poured from her second tail. The lightning flew into the sky, where a large storm cloud gathered. There was a flash of light. A peel of thunder.

The sound echoed all around them before multiple lightning bolts rained down from above.

[Rain of Arrows]

-16,965; -16,965!

Susan raised her bow into the sky, pulled back the arrow she had notched, and released it. The arrow disappeared into the distance. It seemed as though she had wasted a shot. That assumption only lasted for a moment before a brief flash signified a coming storm in the form of nearly a hundred arrows. Raining down from above like hail, the arrows penetrated the flesh of her foes, causing them to scream in pain and rage.

And behind them all was Titania, whose voice rang clear and sweet as she sang the [Song of Vigor], boosting their attack power. She had her eyes closed and hands clasped together as if praying for their victory.

Adam and Lilith continued to move forward across the walkway, utilizing teamwork to keep any enemies from slipping past them as they watched each other's back. Adam acted as the vanguard, plowing through enemy after enemy with his straightforward assault. Lilith danced around him. Her dagger flashed as she attacked any enemy within reach. It wasn't long before they reached the other side, though by the time they did, all the enemies were dead.

Ding!

[Congratulations! You have defeated 69 [low-level demons]! Items dropped: x138 [Demonic Spears]. Inventory is full. Cannot fit items. Items have been sent to storage. +24,159,522 experience points.]

That appeared to be the last of their enemies, so Adam took that moment to finally look at his stats. He had two hundred and ten status points to use. He decided to place fifty-five of them into his Strength stat, thus increasing his Strength to +1,300, then put one hundred into his Speed and the rest into his Intelligence. While he wasn't a magic class, MP was used by all classes for their attacks. He understood the importance of having more MP, even if he didn't need a high Magical Attack.

Adam briefly pondered looking over his skill list since he had received an announcement that he had new skills and the level cap for his old skills was gone, but he'd decided not to. They were not in a situation that would allow him to really ponder his new skills. He decided to instead focus his energy on the task at hand.

"All the enemies are defeated. Does that mean we're finished?" asked Fayte.

Adam shook his head. "I don't think so. If we had cleared the dungeon, an announcement would have been made. The fact that it's not means there is still at least one enemy somewhere."

"Do you think it's the boss?" asked Susan.

"It is most certainly whoever is in charge here." Titania, having apparently had enough flying around, landed on Adam's shoulder and sat down. "[Trolls] and [low-level demons] like that are not smart enough to gather in such numbers, and a [troll] would never listen to a [low-level demon] since they are so much weaker. There must be at least a [high-level demon] somewhere."

"If there's a boss around here, they're probably in the middle of this island," Adam said.

"Then what are we waiting for? Let's go," said Fayte.

There was something eerie about walking through a camp with no one present. It was almost like a ghost town. The tents, campfires, and supplies remained where they had been left before the battle began. Adam looked into one of the cooking pots out of curiosity and wrinkled his nose when he saw what looked like flies and lizard tails floating in the bubbling liquid. The rancid smell wafting from it didn't help make the food—if it could be called that—seem any more appetizing.

One thing Adam noticed as they walked through the camp were the pickaxes embedded into the walls and what looked like old-fashioned mining equipment. There were wheelbarrows filled with rocks and dirt, tunnels being carved into the rock walls, and numerous levers and pulleys. Adam realized only now that he had gotten a glimpse of them that the towers were actually massive blast furnaces.

"What do you think was going on here?" asked Fayte as she, too, studied the blast furnaces with interest.

"It looks like this was a mining operation," answered Titania. "See those blast furnaces? They are used for the refining of ores. Most of the ones you find in human cities can only refine basic ores like [iron], [lead], [copper], and [steel], but these ones here are meant for refining [magicore], [oricalchum], and [adamantite].

Those are the three strongest ores in existence. In the past, they were used by the dwarves to produce some of the best armor and weapons in the world. However, the technology to refine those ores should have been lost. I wonder how these monsters learned the refinement process…?"

Titania went silent, her brow furrowing in deep thought. Nobody interrupted her, however, as they had arrived at their destination.

What appeared to be an abandoned structure stood in the center of the island, a series of ruined walls and archways that were crumbled in places created a semi-circle. No longer hardened rock, the floor was instead made of black stone.

In the very center of this crumbling structure stood a man.

Though Adam called him a man, he was not human. He stood nearly fifty centimeters above Adam himself, possessed skin the color of ash, and had two horns growing on his forehead. Large wings protruded from his back. They looked like angel wings, but they were pitch black and covered in blood, lending them a demonic aesthetic. With the head of an owl, his massive, glowing red eyes looked horrifying as he stared the group down, tracking them as they stepped forward.

"I had wondered what the noise was all about. So a couple of humans have intruded on our operation. And you have defeated all the forces under my command. I must commend you. However, your adventure ends here."

The demon, for that was all he could be, was dressed in pitch-black armor that had strange symbols and lines like veins covering its surface. The lines glowed a bloody crimson. Embedded into the ground before him was a large claymore with jagged edges running along the blade. Taking the weapon by its hilt, the demon lifted the claymore like it weighed less than a feather and swung it around. Each swing produced a blast of wind that slammed into Adam and the others.

"Titania," Adam said.

"Already on it," Titania informed him as she cast [Scan].

Name: Andras

Description: A commander who served under the War Demon during the war against the four goddesses. He is an excellent leader and very skilled with both a sword and magic.

Class: 3-Star

Lvl: 65

Health: 15,560,000/15,560,000

MP: 1,255,000/1,255,000

Strength: 10,000

Constitution: 10,000

Dexterity: 1,200

Intelligence: 2,000

Speed: 1,600

Skills:

Skill Name: Slash

Description: A slashing attack that does 600% damage 100% chance of causing the bleed status effect

MP Cost: 600

Cooldown time: 0 seconds

Skill Name: Thrust

Description: A thrust technique that causes critical 1,200%

damage

Ignores all defenses

MP Cost: 1,000

Cooldown time: 5 seconds

Skill Name: Kamikaze

Description: A suicide attack used by Andras as a last

resort

Causes internal combustion within the blood to detonate

the body

Creates an explosion that deals 100,000 damage to anyone

caught within the last radius

Blast radius is twenty meters

MP Cost: 1,000,000

Skill Name: Midnight Draw

Description: A quick draw technique enhanced with the

power of darkness

Does 10,000 damage to a single person no matter the

opponent's level

Has a 100% chance of bisecting opponent

MP Cost: 6,000

Cooldown Time: 30 seconds

Skill Name: Stalwart Defense
Description: A sword technique that creates an
impenetrable barrier for 10 seconds
No damage can be dealt when this technique is active
Can even block offensive spells
MP Cost: 5,500
Cooldown time: 30 seconds

Adam could hardly believe how powerful this guy was. Even though he was only a 3-Star enemy, his stats were far higher than even [Alexandra Mystique's], and that woman had been a 4-Star opponent. Was this the difference between a human and a demon? He had been informed by Titania that humans were supposedly the weakest race in this game, so perhaps that was simply a reflection of their stats. A 4-Star human simply couldn't compare to a 3-Star demon.

"Let's go, Lilith!" Adam shouted.

"Yes, Master!"

Titania began to sing [Song of Vigor] as Adam and Lilith raced across the ground and closed the distance between them and this owl demon. The demon did not even bother to move. It simply watched them with its haunting crimson eyes.

[Blood Sacrifice]

[Dance of the Sakura Blossoms]

-59,850; -179,550; -538,650—

[Andras's] eyes widened as Adam attacked with his most powerful skills right off the bat. He finally seemed to realize what kind of danger he was in, for he leapt into the air before Adam could finish his technique. The second to last attack for [Dance of the Sakura Blossoms] missed and entered a cooldown time. Adam glared up at the owl-like demon, who twisted his head in a very owlish manner.

"I see you are much more formidable than I suspected. I meant to take that attack head-on without flinching so you can see the difference between us and despair, but it seems I cannot—"

[Andras] was unable to finish his sentence as Lilith appeared above him. While Adam had attacked head-on, Lilith had deviated to the side and used her incredible nimbleness to race up the crumbling wall. As the owl demon kept its eyes on Adam, she leapt in a parabolic arc that took her directly to him.

[Pinpoint Strike]

-10,080!

Her attack targeted the creature's weak points, dealing a good deal of damage. [Andras] screamed, though whether in anger, pain, or both was not something Adam knew. Lilith landed back on the ground as he whirled on her. When that happened, Fayte and Kureha unleashed their own attacks. Two lightning bolts streaked through the air.

Had this been a weaker opponent, those attacks would have surely hit and done extraordinary damage, but this was not some random enemy. [Andras] spun around and swung his sword so fast none of them could see it move. The lightning was sliced in half. Adam had never seen someone do this before, so even he could not stop his eyes from widening as he watched it happen.

What the hell?! All he did was use a simple [Slash]. Are you telling me the most basic attack in a player's arsenal can be used to cut lightning?!

Adam wondered if maybe these monsters had a similar ability to level up their techniques. He had noticed that [Slash] did different amounts of damage depending on the monster in question. This guy, for instance, did 600% damage, which was six times more damage than his Strength stat. Perhaps when a player reached this level with their skills, they would be able to cut through lightning too.

Adam was not given time to contemplate this further as [Andras] dive-bombed toward him, forcing him to leap aside as the man tried to cut him in twain. The claymore in his hand produced a loud boom as if it was rending the air. Gritting his teeth as the wind hit him, Adam leaped forward and activated [Thrust], but Andras was so fast he moved out of range before Adam could hit him.

"It seems you are not the most dangerous opponent," [Andras] said to Adam while turning around. **"When faced with a balanced party, it is important to first go after the mages and healers."**

Adam's eyes went wide as [Andras] turned toward Fayte, Kureha, Susan, and Titania. He raced forward to protect them, but Adam already knew he wouldn't make it in time. [Andras] was simply too fast. He reached the group in what felt like a split second and swooped down to cut Titania, who he must have deemed the most problematic.

[Counter]

-134,600!

"GAAAAHHH!!!"

Yet just before he could attack, as though she had been waiting for the opportunity, Lilith appeared from within her [Shadow Masking] skill and used a perfectly executed [Counter]. The timing it must have required to pull that off astonished even Adam. All he caught was a brief flash of sparks.

[Andras] shrieked as he backed off, flying back into the sky where no one could attack him. The moment he did that, Susan released the arrow she'd been holding, which flew forward, pierced his chest, and sprouted vines that entangled him.

"A Fairy Archer skill?! It seems I really have underestimated you humans!"

[Andras] fell to the ground, and none of them were willing to miss an opportunity to bombard their enemy with attacks. Kureha unleashed a powerful fireball that exploded when it struck [Andras] and electricity crackled along Fayte's staff seconds before she unleashed [Thunder Bolt], which punched clean through the explosion to strike at [Andras].

Adam knew better than to assume that would defeat [Andras], and so he rushed through the fire and attacked with [Dance of the Sakura Blossoms]. Even though [Blood Sacrifice] had entered its cooldown period, this was still his greatest attack. Yet when he struck [Andras], his first attack clanged off the demon. Adam stumbled back, confused. It was only as the smoke and flames cleared that he realized there was something like a black shield of flashing swords surrounding [Andras].

It was his defense skill [Stalwart Defense].

"You filthy humans have angered me greatly. Prepare yourselves! From this moment on, I will attack with everything I have! I will make you suffer for this humiliation!"

A DEMON'S ANGER

Adam understood how bad their situation was immediately after [Andras] gave them that proclamation, but their helplessness really showed itself when he began attacking.

The first big issue was that [Andras] was an aerial fighter. He flew through the skies, descended swiftly toward the ground, and attacked quickly before retreating. It was in some ways similar to the blitzkrieg tactics of the Germans during World War II. However, this was an attack from the air. The only one among them who could fly was Adam, but there was a time limit on his ability, and he wasn't well-versed in aerial combat.

Second among the issues was the power [Andras] possessed. Just one attack was enough to kill them in a single hit, which meant they couldn't afford to get hit even once. That proved exceedingly difficult as [Andras] swooped down from above like a bird of prey. He could attack from a full three hundred and sixty degrees and had a near-limitless variety of angles.

The third issue was simply the amount of HP this monster had. Aside from the fact that it was insanely difficult just to deal any damage to this guy, he could absorb what damage they did do like a sponge.

Adam was finally beginning to understand why this quest was for people from level 45 to 50.

Even someone at that level might not be enough to defeat [Andras].

"He's coming in from your left," shouted Fayte.

"Lilith!" Adam shouted in return.

"Leave it to me, Master!"

If anyone had something to say about Lilith's form of address, they kept it to themselves as [Andras] swooped down. Lilith had already interposed herself between him and Titania. Her stance was tense, the muscles of her arms and legs visibly coiled like springs ready to burst.

[Andras] already knew all about her [Counter] ability. He swerved at the last second to avoid her—but that put him right in Susan's line of sight.

"I got you!"

With a shout of triumph, Susan released an arrow that penetrated the demon's flank. She had used the [Fairy Shot] skill. While it didn't look like anything had happened, the number sign that floated above [Andras] was a whopping -56,550. [Fairy Shot] was a skill with a 100% accuracy range and did x5 times critical damage. When stacked on top of Titania's [Song of Vigor], the amount of power behind it was most impressive.

"Hurk!"

[Andras] was also thrown off course thanks to the impact. He went into an uncontrolled spin, and Adam chose that moment to leap out and engage him in a melee battle. His [Blood Sacrifice] had gone back into cooldown mode, so he stuck with simple techniques, but despite spinning out of control, his opponent managed to activate [Stalwart Defense] at the last second and block his attacks. Fortunately, the skill only lasted for a limited amount of time.

"Fayte! Kureha! Attack him now!" Adam shouted as he leapt back.

[Andras] had been properly grounded thanks to Adam keeping him occupied, and he could no longer use his unique defense skill since it had entered its cooldown time. Fayte and Kureha released their respective skills. Fayte's [Wind Hammer] slammed into [Andras] and knocked him to the ground. She then activated [Quicksand]. As his body sunk into the sand, Kureha launched a [Fireball] that slammed into the sand and hardened it.

-47,760!

-28,200!

While the damage they dealt was nice, the importance of their tactic was that they had managed to keep him from moving. Adam used that opportunity. He burst forward, finally activating [Blood

Sacrifice] as its cooldown time ended, and then used [Dance of the Sakura Blossom].

-59,850; -179,550; -538,650; 1,615,950; -4,849,850!

It was the first time Adam had been able to land an attack since their initial bout, but it deprived [Andras] of more than half his HP. Sadly, he was able to free himself from [Quicksand] shortly after Adam finished his attack and took to the skies once more. That was not to say he was out of reach. Lilith once more raced along the walls and leapt up to attack. Her blade flashed in the light as she swung it, but unlike last time, her attack was parried this time. [Andras] swung his sword so hard that Lilith was knocked back and slammed into the ground.

-500!

"Ack!"

Lilith gasped for breath as her back hit the ground. His had not been an attack, so the damage she sustained was from the fall and not [Andras], but the attack had paralyzed her, and the demon quickly swooped down to capitalize on what happened. Adam was fortunate enough to reach her in time. After interposing himself between them, he adopted the defensive Form Five stance and spun his spear so quickly it looked like a solid shield in front of him.

[Andras] flapped his wings to generate lift and flew over Adam's head, landed on the ground behind them, and tried to impale the still downed Lilith with his claymore. He might have succeeded if Susan didn't fire an arrow at his face. With perfect situational awareness, [Andras] moved the blade to block the arrow before it could hit him. This gave Adam enough time to rush forward and attack the demon with his spear.

The fierce melee battle that followed left Adam gasping for breath. [Andras] was a stellar swordsman. It was like the demon had the cognitive ability to read Adam's every move. Adam used [Thrust], but it was brushed aside with a simple swing of [Andras's] claymore. He spun around and tried to turn his thrust into multiple [Slash] attacks, but those were blocked when [Andras] placed a hand against the flat of his blade and used a form of two-handed blocking. As if to add insult to injury, the moment Adam's attack ended, [Andras] struck back with ten times the ferocity.

Adam ducked underneath a swing that nearly bisected him. As he bent his spine so far back it was nearly parallel with the ground, he placed a hand on the cold stone and tried to kick [Andras] in the chest. It didn't work. The demon leapt back and swung his claymore to take off Adam's foot, and though he pulled it back in time, the attack was so close Adam could feel the wind brush against his pant legs.

While Adam distracted [Andras], Fayte once more used [Quicksand] to try and trap him, but the owl demon clearly knew better now and flew into the air before he could get stuck. At that moment, Susan peppered him with a hailstorm of arrows that the winged demon avoided by the skin of his teeth. She did not relent despite how little her attacks did. Even as he evaded them, she moved away from Fayte, Kureha, and Titania to get a better angle for her shots.

Adam knew they needed to end this soon. They had managed to survive up to this point, but the longer this battle went on, the more likely one of them was to die. The problem was that [Andras] was simply far too smart. Unlike a normal boss monster in a typical MMORPG, this one seemed perfectly capable of deviating from any set attack pattern. He fought like a normal person would. That meant they couldn't rely on discovering an attack pattern to predict his actions. This also explained why he never fell for the same trick twice.

They tried trapping him with [Quicksand] several times, but he was on guard ever since the first successful attempt. [Andras] probably understood that it would all be over the moment he was trapped. Adam would use [Blood Sacrifice] and [Dance of the Sakura Blossom] to finish him off, so he'd been wary for traps like that.

Even traps using other skills had failed. They had attempted to knock him off his feet with [Wind Hammer]. Kureha and Susan halted his advance with arrows and magic, then Adam and Lilith engaged him at the same time, but all that was a distraction for Fayte to use her magic to knock him down. It didn't work. The moment she created the hammer, [Andras] disengaged from Adam and Lilith and took to the skies.

In short, they were at an impasse.

However, it could not remain as such for much longer.

Adam had once discovered the limits of the human mind during his battle with the [necromancer] back when he had just started playing *Age of Gods*. He had forced his mind to the utmost limit of what it could endure and nearly broke from the stress. Fayte and Susan were just normal people. They did not have his or Lilith's incredible mental faculties, so they would not last very long. He feared they would break mentally if something wasn't done soon.

He glanced at the pair to find them already straining to keep track of [Andras] as he flew through the sky. They were reaching their limit.

"Lilith! We're going all out here!"

"Yes, Master!"

Lilith hopped onto Adam's shoulders as he activated [Double Jump] to gain height, then [Flight] to bring him close to [Andras]. Lilith leapt into the air as Adam attacked the demon with a series of spins. Each attack was blocked, but Adam was swinging his spear down, slamming it against the claymore and using the resulting momentum to keep himself from falling even after [Flight] wore off. His relentless barrage of attacks seemed like they would force [Andras] to the ground.

"Fool! The sky is my domain! Do not think you can defeat me here!"

[Andras] roared as he swung his claymore to attack Adam, but he activated [Double Jump] one more time, but this time he slipped behind his opponent. Adam then did the unthinkable. He dropped the spear, wrapped his arms around [Andras's] waist, and pinned the man's arms to his side.

"W-what are you doing?!"

That was the moment Lilith descended. She had jumped high into the air, high enough to give Adam enough time to pull off this trick.

-84,798!

Lilith stabbed her dagger into [Andras's] weak point, the center of his chest, as she landed on top of him. She planted her feet on his stomach, held on with one hand, and used [Slash] to continuously assault him.

-20,190; -20,190; -20,190; -20,190!

"Get off me!!"

They were able to deal a significant amount of damage before [Andras] could throw them off, but it wasn't as much as Adam would have wanted. He landed on the ground and picked up his spear. At that moment, Kureha and Fayte hit [Andras] with a double dose of lightning. He hadn't been able to dodge because of his and Lilith's coordinated assault.

-37,224!

-157,608

"Nggg!"

[Andras] went wide-eyed as he fell to the ground and didn't get up. Arcs of blue lightning coiled around his body. Adam quickly realized he was stunned and decided not to look a gift horse in the mouth.

[Blood Sacrifice]

[Dance of the Sakura Blossom]

-59,850; -179,550; -538,650; 1,615,950; -4,849,850!

Adam unleashed his most powerful attack, and while his health didn't reach zero, [Andras] was definitely on his last leg.

This battle would not go on much longer.

However, it was when someone was on their last leg that they were at their most dangerous.

"Damn you! If I can't kill you all, I'll at least make sure to take as many of you as I can with me!"

Adam didn't know what this demon was doing until his ashen skin turned a blistering red. His eyes widened.

"Everyone, move! He's using [Kamikaze]!"

No one needed to be told twice; everyone quickly raced away from [Andras], ducked behind one of the crumbling walls, and were just in time to avoid the explosion. Adam had somehow gotten close to Susan. He was hiding just a few meters from her, behind a crumbling wall. Susan had managed to get behind the pillar for an archway. However, while the wall held, the pillar was destroyed from the force of the detonation. Adam watched in shock as Susan screamed in surprise, even as she was lifted off her feet and pitched over the edge of the island.

"SSUUUU!!"

Fayte thought her heart was going to stop when she saw Susan fall over the edge. She was hiding behind another wall on the opposite side of Susan and Adam. When [Andras] decided to blow himself up, she had hunkered down behind the wall to protect herself. She only looked up after the explosion died down, and she was just in time to see her best friend fall.

Even though she cried out, she knew there was nothing she could do. She also understood that this was a game. Susan wouldn't die permanently and would revive in the cathedral, but it still hurt to see something like this happen to her friend, and she knew that falling in magma would leave lasting mental trauma on the girl.

She reached out her hand, even though she knew it was useless.

And in that moment, Adam did something she never thought he'd do.

He leapt over the edge after Susan.

Ding!

[Congratulations! You have defeated the 3-Star [Andras]! Items dropped: [Orichalcum Greatsword], [Orichalcum Grieves], [Orichalcum Gauntlets], [Oricalchum Chestplate], [Oricalchum Coil], and 6,000,000 gold coins. Inventory is full. Items have been sent to guild storage. +16,000,000 experience points. +6,000,000 ability points. +2,500,000 Reputation.]

Adam grimaced when the stupid announcement popup window appeared in front of his face. It had the worst timing ever! Looking past it, he saw found Susan still falling, eyes closed. It looked like she had lost consciousness. Perhaps her fear had been so great that she had passed out.

"SUUUU!"

Adam shouted at the top of his lungs, projecting his voice straight from his diaphragm. Susan jerked at the sound and opened her eyes. He reached out to her the moment she did.

"GRAB MY HAND!!"

Susan gave him a confused look like she didn't understand at first, but then she looked around and became aware of their situation. She began screaming and flailing in a panic.

"SUSAN! GRAB MY HAND! HURRY!"

Perhaps something in his tone or maybe the volume of his voice set her off, but she desperately reached out to grab his hand. Their first attempt missed, which caused Susan to nearly panic again, but Adam stretched his arm as far as it could go and grabbed her hand, then yanked her into his chest.

Okay. So, I've got her, but all that means is we'll die together. Now what, Adam? Come on! Think! Think!

This had not been his smartest idea. He honestly didn't know what he was thinking when he jumped after Susan. It was like his body had reacted before his mind could tell him it was a bad idea, but regardless, they were now in this situation, and he needed to think of a way out of it. A quick glance revealed they were still relatively close to the island. They were also about halfway between the top and the bubbling magma below.

Reacting with desperation, Adam spun his body around and used [Thrust] to impale his spear into the island's sediment. Had this been real life, either his spear would have bounced off or snapped under his and Susan's combined weight. What happened instead was the spear impaled the island and halted their downward momentum.

Adam groaned in pain as his arm was pulled from its socket. A damage number floated above his head, but it was small enough for him to ignore it.

"Su, are you okay?"

The first thing Adam needed to do was check on Susan and see how she was doing. The girl was clinging to him like a spider monkey, her arms around his neck and her legs around his waist. She had buried her face into his neck and his skin was becoming stained with tears. She was obviously not okay.

"Su?"

"I… I'm… fine…" Susan croaked.

Adam accepted her words at face value since he couldn't do anything else right now. He craned his neck to look at their surroundings, wondering if there was anything they could use to either climb up or…

"Oh?" Adam spotted something about a meter below them. "Su, it looks like there's a ledge just a bit below us. I'm going to climb down to it, so I want you to hold on as tightly as you can. Keep your eyes closed if you need to. I'll tell you when you can open them."

"O-okay…"

The ledge itself didn't seem very big, but he realized that most of it was hidden by an overhang. He would have to do some tricky maneuvering if he wanted to climb down that while Susan clung to his chest.

The first thing Adam did was move across the spear until he was close enough to touch the rock wall. He looked for a clear handhold. There was one just to the spear's left, a small crevice that

he dug his fingers into. Once he was sure of his purchase, he pried the spear from the wall, placed it on his back, and latched onto a rock jutting from the wall close to the crevice his other hand was in.

Free soloing was a form of technical rock climbing where climbers climbed without ropes, harnesses, or other protective equipment. Adam had been trained in this style of rock climbing. He'd once killed a target who owned a mansion on a cliff. To reach it, Adam had been forced to climb up the cliffside where security was weakest to avoid detection. Free soloing required smooth hand and feet coordination, balance, flexibility, and agility to climb up or down a surface. It also required an analytical mind. It wasn't enough to just search for handholds to climb down. You had to observe the rock wall and discover a route you could take to reach your destination.

Adam's muscles in his arms, legs, and core burned as he slowly climbed down the rock wall, the scent of brimstone clogging his nose and the magma's heat making sweat burst on his skin. He had already calculated the best path he could take without being able to see what lie beyond the overhang. As he climbed, one of the rocks protruding from the surface cracked and he nearly lost his footing. Susan whimpered against his chest. Gritting his teeth as sweat stained his brow, Adam kept going until he reached the overhang.

Now for the hard part...

"Keep a tight hold of me," he said to Susan. She said nothing in return, but she nodded against his chest and tightened her hold. He wouldn't say the feeling of her body pressed against his wasn't distracting, but Adam had a strong enough will that he could ignore it.

Adam took a slow breath, then let his feet hang. With nothing more than the strength of his arms, he began lowering himself along the overhang. He grabbed onto a rock that seemed stable enough, then reached for another rock just a little lower. It felt like hours had ticked by, but it was probably only a few minutes before he was dangling above the overhang.

Now that he was this close, he could see that the overhang was much bigger than he first suspected. It was like something had carved away at this section of the island. The overhang curved inward at a near-horizontal incline, which meant it would be hard if not impossible to actually climb with another person attached to him. He looked down. The ledge was just half a meter below.

I should be able to make it.

"Don't be surprised if you suddenly feel a moment of weightlessness," he said to Susan right before he swung them both forward and let go. Susan squeaked in shock and fear as she pressed deeper into his chest, but Adam didn't let that bother him. His feet hit the ground. He flinched as he bent his knees to absorb as much of the impact as possible.

It's a very good thing this is just an avatar. Even I would be in pain if this was real life.

"Su… we're safe now," Adam said. Susan just kept her arms and legs wrapped tightly around him. He sighed.

Waiting for her to calm down, Adam took a look at their new surroundings. The ledge was a lot bigger than he'd expected, and perhaps because they were hidden somewhat, it wasn't as hot here. Further in was what appeared to be a tunnel. It was such an incredible stroke of good fortune that Adam wondered if Susan's +1 for Luck wasn't responsible for it.

At some point, without Adam really realizing it, he had begun stroking Susan's hair. This seemed to calm her down, so he kept it up. Her silent tears eventually stopped.

"Are you feeling better now?" he asked.

"Y-yes. I'm… sorry… for, um, you know," Susan said. She removed her face from his chest and slowly lowered herself onto solid ground. Her knees wobbled a bit, but she forced them to carry her weight. Her eyes were red from crying, but her ears were red from embarrassment.

"Don't let it worry you. Anyway, it appears there's a tunnel over there. Since we can't go back up the way we came, let's see if we can find a way to the surface through there," Adam said.

"O-okay."

"ADAM! SUSAN!"

Just as Adam and Susan were getting ready to head into the tunnel, a voice cried out to them. They turned around as Titania flitted into view. She turned her head toward them seconds before disappearing from their sight, then quickly darted back in their direction. The relief on her face was palpable.

"You two are okay! I hope you both understand how worried everyone was when they saw you go over that ledge. Fayte and Lilith are nearly inconsolable. Also, Adam, do you not think that leaping off a cliff like that is rather reckless? I understand you otherworlders don't die like we do, but you should still consider the mental trauma we get from seeing you act like that."

Titania had crossed her arms as she came to a stop in front of Adam's face and lectured him. While her words were scolding, he felt like they were just expressions of the worry Titania felt, so they lacked any real heat.

"I'm sorry for worrying everyone, but I didn't have much of a choice. Su would have died if I did nothing. I'd rather not have that on my conscience." Adam shrugged. "I'll call Fayte and Lilith through the player chat to let them know we're okay. In the meantime, I think we should head into that tunnel. It might lead back to the surface."

While Titania looked like she wanted to say more, she stopped herself and merely sighed. Adam called Fayte to let her and Lilith know that he and Susan were okay. Then the three of them entered the tunnel.

It was dark at first, but as their eyes adjusted to the light, they discovered that small crystals were sticking out of the walls, illuminating the path before them. He glanced at one of the crystals. It was actually a cluster of three or more. He wondered what they were.

Titania gasped. "That's [Magicore]!"

"[Magicore]? The ore used in the production of powerful weapons and armor with magical properties?" asked Adam.

"Yes." Titania nodded. "And there are quite a few clusters. There must be a [Magicore] vein here."

"Hmmm."

Adam didn't say anything but continued on. The path they took seemed rather twisted. Sometimes they traveled down, sometimes they traveled up, and sometimes it felt like they were going in circles. As they walked, Adam glanced at Susan, who followed meekly behind him.

"Are you doing okay, Su?"

"Huh? Oh, yeah. I'm fine." Susan seemed startled when he talked to her, but she responded with a patently fake smile.

"It's okay to not be fine, you know?" Adam sighed. "If you need to cry, then cry. I won't think any less of you."

Susan looked like she might tear up, but then she shook her head. "No. I don't really feel like crying, but I... I do want to apologize... for being so useless..."

"Useless?"

"Back during our battle with [Andras], and even before during our battle with [Alexandra Mystique], I barely contributed anything to those fights. Even though you got me this amazing class, I haven't done anything worth mentioning." Susan looked down in depression.

Adam could have said a lot of things. He could have reassured her, could have told her she wasn't a burden, but he knew that wouldn't help. Susan already had it in her head that she was a waste of space. He didn't know where her belief came from. There were a lot of people who, despite seeming to have everything, suffered from depression and a lack of confidence.

"Hey, Su, when we get to the real world, can I ask for your help?" asked Adam.

"There you go with that 'real world' talk again. You do realize this world is also real, don't you?" said Titania.

"You want… my help?" asked Susan, blinking.

"Fayte said you're a skilled hacker. I would like your help protecting myself and Aris from Levon in the event that he discovers what we look like and attempts to find us in the real," said Adam.

"Are you two ignoring me?!" Titania demanded to know.

"For now," Adam admitted.

"H-how rude!"

"I… I can help you," Susan said. Her eyes brightened a moment later. "I'd be more than happy to help you."

Adam resisted the urge to rub her head. "Thanks, I'll be counting on you."

"Haaaaaah. I hate how you ignore me whenever you think it's convenient," Titania muttered bitterly.

"Sorry."

"I know you're not sorry at all. Stop being patronizing."

The tunnel they had been walking through soon opened into what seemed like a spiral that traveled both up and down. Adam felt like he was looking inside a conch shell. It was much brighter inside this area, and the reason became apparent as they looked around. Hundreds if not thousands of [Magicore] clusters were sticking out of the walls. Several wheelbarrows were filled to the brim with clusters that had already been mined. Tools lay discarded on the ground.

"So beautiful," Susan murmured.

Adam couldn't disagree, as the sight before them of thousands of glittering clusters of glowing ore was indeed extraordinary. The many clusters emitted bright lights that refracted off each other to create a rainbow of colors. You'd never see something like this in the real world.

"This… this is a mining operation!" Titania exclaimed. "A rather large-scale one at that."

"It's almost as if [Andras] was preparing for another war," Adam mused.

"[Andras] would not do anything without the War Demon's permission, which means the War Demon is gathering supplies, troops, and mining ore to create weapons." Titania bit her thumb. "I don't like this. It seems like the War Demon is on the move after many thousands of years of inactivity."

The question Adam had was whether the War Demon was planning to wage war against humanity on his own, or was his activity the result of the Demon Lord reawakening? In old-school MMOs, the Demon Lord being resurrected was a very standard plot, but since the face of virtual reality had changed after World War III, plotlines like that had disappeared in favor of open-world PvP. The PvE aspect these days had taken a backseat for the most part and was mostly added for flavor and to create monthly events.

"Whatever the case is, we've completed our mission and now know what the demons were doing here. Let's see about mining as much of this [Magicore] as we can. When we get back to Solum, we'll inform the Guild Association of our findings and have them mine the rest," Adam said.

"So you want to take these as our spoils of war? You are an awfully greedy man," Titania said.

"I'm just looking out for me and mine," Adam replied with a sardonic grin hidden behind his mask.

NEW SKILLS

"Y-y-you fought against a commander of the War Demon's army?!"

Adam and Fayte just finished debriefing Clarise on their completed mission. They were sitting on the couch alongside Lilith, Susan, Titania, Kureha, and Aris—who had met them in Solum after their mission concluded. Opposite them was Clarise, who had shot to her feet and slammed her hands onto the coffee table after they mentioned their fight with [Andras]. The woman looked like she'd been broadsided.

Well, isn't she surprised.

"That is what I just said," Adam said dryly.

"S-sorry." Clarise turned red all the way to her ears and sat back down, seeming both astonished and flustered. "I'm just... shocked. There's been no sign of demons in many years, and now, all of a sudden, we've learned that there was an entire battalion of [low-level demons] and [trolls] just a few days travel from us. To top it off, they were being led by one of the War Demon's top commanders. I don't remember much about [Andras], but there are records that state he's an indomitable swordsman who killed many soldiers on the battlefield."

"We know it must come as a shock to you," Fayte assured the woman. "It came as a surprise to us as well."

"Do you know what they were doing there?" asked Clarise.

"They were mining this." Adam removed something from his storage, a large crystalline chunk of ore that contained an almost rainbow sheen. He set the chunk on the table. It released a dull thunk, though that was nothing compared to Clarise, who produced a sound not unlike an animal as it was being strangled.

"Th-th-th-th-th-THIS IS [magicore]! And very high quality [magicore] at that! You say the demons were mining this?!"

"The dungeon we were asked to clear has a large deposit of [magicore]. Titania thinks there might be a [magicore vein] there. I'd personally suggest getting some people together and traveling there to set up a mining operation. The demons are all gone, so it shouldn't be a problem," said Adam.

"That's a good idea. I should definitely contact the leader of the Guild Association and let him know about the [magicore]. If there really is a vein there… anyway, he'll be the one to deal with this. It's way too much for me. I'm just a normal guild employee."

Clarise seemed pretty overwhelmed, though Adam didn't blame her. It wasn't every day a group informed you that a force of demons was mining an all-important ore just a few days travel from your city. In either event, now that they had returned, it was time to get their reward.

"So, I would say this completes our quest, wouldn't you?" asked Adam.

Clarise nodded. "It most definitely does. You've all done a great job. I honestly can't thank you enough. Here's your reward."

Ding!

[Congratulations! You have completed the quest: [Clear Out High-Level Dungeon]. Your rewards are as follows: +30,000,000 experience points, +5,000,000 ability points, and 8,000,000 gold coins.]

Ding!

[Congratulations! Aris_Lancer has leveled up! She is now at level 18! +400 HP! +40 MP! +5 SP!]

Ding!

[Congratulations! Kureha has leveled up! She is now at level 22! +700 HP! +9,400 MP! +10 SP!]

Ding!

[Congratulations! Titania has leveled up! She is now at level 22! +400 HP! +10,700 MP! +10 SP!]

Several announcements arrived in rapid succession, announcing that several of them had leveled up. Aris went back to level 18 after losing her previous level, which he guessed meant they were back at square one. They would need to bring her level up soon. She was the only person who hadn't broken through to level 20 now.

After their meeting with Clarise, the group traveled back to their guild house. Adam found himself sitting on the couch in the living room with Lilith and Titania. Kureha and Aris were also present, but they were playing around on the floor. Aris was rubbing Kureha's belly as the fox yokai released pleased whines. Lilith glared jealousy at the carefree girl.

Kureha had 20 status points that he hadn't allocated yet. He wondered where he should put them. Her Intelligence stat was already very high, so he didn't think she needed more in there right now. Strength was useless to her since she was a magic-user. Between Constitution, Dexterity, Intelligence, and Speed, which one was the most important right now?

"Hey, is it just me, or does Kureha look a little different...?" asked Aris suddenly.

Adam looked at Kureha to see if anything was different. Nothing stood out to him at first, but then he glanced at her tails and realized what had changed.

"Oh! Kureha has gained her third tail," Titania said at last.

Indeed, sticking out of Kureha's hindquarters was not two but three bushy red foxtails. They waved back and forth as Aris continued to rub her belly. Adam found himself briefly mesmerized by them before he snapped out of it.

"I think you mentioned something like that before," Adam said. "Something about how fox yokai gain more tails the higher their level is?"

"That's right. A fox yokai's level can be determined by the number of tails they have. All fox yokai start off with two tails. This differentiates them from regular foxes. After they reach level 20, they gain their third tail. If you look at her skill list, she should have more skills available now."

Adam hurriedly pulled up Kureha's skill set and immediately found several changes. The first was that all of her old skills were no longer maxed out. They could be leveled up more now, but even more astonishing than that was the new skills she possessed. There were quite a few.

Kureha's Skills:

Skill Name: Fireball

Description: Kureha has incredible control over fire thanks to her first tail. She can create fire through the power in her tail and launch a fireball at opponents.

Current lvl: 5

Ability points needed to reach next lvl: 50,000

Ability: Deals 250% damage of Magical Attack

Has a 55% chance of causing burn damage

MP Cost: 100

Cooldown Time: 10-seconds

Skill Name: Firestorm

Description: Kureha has incredible control over fire thanks to her first tail. She can create fire through the power in her tails to unleash a powerful storm of fire.

Current lvl: 5

Ability points needed to reach next level: 50,000

Ability: Deals 190% damage to all enemies within a 5-yard radius

Has a 55% of causing burn

MP cost: 100

Cooldown Time: 10-seconds

Skill Name: Fire Whip

Description: Kureha sprouts a whip of fire from her first tail and uses it to lash at her enemy. This skill remains active for as long as Kureha pumps magic points into it.

Current lvl: 1

Ability points needed to reach next lvl: 15,000

MP Cost: 100 MP per every 1-second skill is active

Cooldown time: 15-seconds

Skill Name: Thunder Bolt

Description: Kureha's second tail has the power to control lightning. She can launch a powerful thunderbolt at her enemies.

Current lvl: 5

Ability points needed to reach next level: 60,000

Ability: Deals 330% damage to one enemy

MP Cost: 100 MP

Cooldown Time: 10-seconds

Skill Name: Thunder Storm

Description: Kureha's second tail has the power to control lighting. By gathering magical power into her tail, she can create a massive thunderstorm that rains down on enemies from above.

Current lvl: 5

Ability points needed to reach next lvl: 60,000

Ability: Deals 290% damage to multiple enemies within a 10-yard radius

MP Cost: 100

Cooldown time: 10-seconds

Skill Name: Blinding Flash

Description: This is not an attack. Kureha releases a flash of lightning so bright it blinds all the enemies around her. Does not affect allies.

Current lvl: 1

Ability points needed to reach next lvl: 15,000

Ability: Has a 50% chance of blinding enemies at the same level or lower

Has a 25% chance of blinding enemies 10 levels higher

Has a 10% chance of blinding enemies 20 levels higher

Has a 0% chance of blinding enemies 30 levels higher

MP Cost: 1,000

Cooldown Time: 5-seconds

Skill Name: Water Spear

Description: Kureha's third tail has the power to manipulate water. By manipulating water molecules in the air, she creates a spear that can pierce through all but the most powerful of substances.

Currently lvl: 1

Ability points needed to reach next lvl: 10,000

Ability: Deals 100% water damage

Ignores 50% of enemies' defenses

MP Cost: 1,000

Cooldown time: 5-seconds

Skill Name: Overflowing Cascade

Description: With the power of her third tail, Kureha draws a massive amount of water from the atmosphere and creates a waterfall that sweeps away her enemies.

Current lvl: 1

Ability points needed to reach next lvl: 10,000

Ability: Does 200% water damage

Has a 50% chance of sweeping away an enemy

Chance of sweeping enemy away decreases to 25% if the enemy's Constitution is higher than Kureha's

MP Cost: 2,000

Cooldown time: 10-seconds

Skill Name: Hidden Mist

Description: Kureha creates a thick mist that blinds enemies.

Current lvl: 1

Ability points needed to reach next lvl: 15,000

Ability: Creates a mist with a 10-meter radius around Kureha

All enemies within the mist are affected by the blind status effect

Mist lasts for 30 seconds

MP Cost: 2,000

Cooldown time: 30-seconds

"Those are some very powerful abilities," Lilith said. She didn't speak very often, so the fact that she was talking now was a testament to her astonishment—not that Adam blamed her. These abilities were very useful.

"They are. What's more, she currently has a lot of ability points, so I can upgrade all of her current skills as well," Adam said.

"We should also upgrade our own skills," Lilith added.

"Right."

"Oh! Are you talking about upgrading your skills?" Aris scooped Kureha off the ground and sat on the couch next to them. She leaned over and looked at Kureha's skillset, whistling before she looked down at the little fox yokai with a grin. "Aren't you super powerful!"

"Ha ha ha! That's right! I am super powerful! Be sure to praise me lots and lots, Big Sister!"

No one said anything when a young, female voice emerged from Kureha's mouth. Aris stopped rubbing the fox yokai's belly, Lilith was still wearing her mask, but Adam could tell her mouth was agape, and he was fairly certain his own mouth was similarly dropped.

"Oh, my gosh! Did you just talk?! You can talk?!" Aris shouted in shock. Her voice was so loud that Susan and Fayte, who were currently checking to see what items they had acquired, came bursting through the doorway seconds later, having heard the sound.

"I heard shouting. What's going on?" asked Fayte.

"T-talk! Kureha can talk!" Aris shouted.

Fayte blinked. "Um, what?"

"Ah! Big Sister Fayte!" Kureha leapt out of Aris's lap and trotted over to Fayte, who had frozen alongside Susan the moment she spoke. The little yokai wore a foxy grin as she looked up at the stunned woman. "Listen. Listen. I can talk now. Isn't it great? Are you surprised, Big Sister Fayte? You are, right? You're totally surprised."

"Ah… um…" Fayte looked at Adam, Aris, and Lilith, none of whom knew quite what to say in this situation, then glanced down at the little fox grinning up at her. She pinched her hand as if to see if she was dreaming. When it became clear that she wasn't, she took a calming breath, knelt down, and smiled as she rubbed Kureha's head. "Yes, I am very surprised."

"Hee hee."

Titania sat on the armrest with her arms crossed. "I told you, didn't I? Fox yokai are different from normal monsters. They are divine beasts created by the Moon Goddess. They're perfectly capable of speaking once they reach a high enough level."

"Did you say something like that?" asked Adam.

"I did."

"Well, I honestly don't remember."

While all of them were surprised that Kureha could suddenly speak, they got over it eventually and spent several hours talking. Fayte and Susan had gone over the items they acquired from their last quest. They had a lot of [Demonic Spears] and parts salvaged from the [Trolls] like [troll blood] and [troll eyes].

"I'm going to sell most of what we acquired. It's not like we have any use for them," Fayte said.

"[Troll blood] and [troll eyes] are important ingredients for alchemists—the people who make potions," Titania said. She tilted her head. "If I remember correctly, [troll blood] is a catalyst used in potions meant to buff a character's offensive stats like Strength and Constitution. The most well-known potion made with [troll blood] is called [Strength of the Undying] and it boosts a person's Strength and Constitution by two hundred percent for a duration of sixty seconds."

"You certainly know a lot about alchemy and potions," Fayte said.

Titania puffed out her chest. "Not to brag or anything, but I did a lot of traveling before becoming the Guardian of the Spear. One of my companions during a journey I took to the Ruins of Na'al was an alchemist who was looking for a rare ingredient called [Heart Flower]. She was a very precocious child. Loved to talk. I learned a lot about alchemy from her, even if I didn't necessarily want to."

"If possible, I would like the armor that [Andras] was wearing," Adam added.

"That's fine," Fayte said, nodding. "I looked the armor over. It's meant for a swordsman, but I think you can wear it as well. That said, it requires a level of at least 30 to 40, so you'll have to wait until you reach an appropriate level."

"Ah. Well, I guess I can wait."

"I believe there are several alchemists in Solum who will pay a premium for [troll blood] since it's so rare these days," Titania continued.

"I'll talk to Clarise and ask her about introducing us to some alchemists we can sell the ingredients to. Something else we need to do is sell off those spears."

While Fayte and Titania continued to talk, Adam upgraded all of Kureha's skills. He first put her status points into her Constitution, then brought all of her original skills—[Fireball], [Firestorm], [Thunder Bolt], and [Thunder Storm]—up to level 10. That cost 5,440,000 ability points, which meant he had 17,217,100 ability points left. He put several more ability points to upgrade [Water Spear] and [Overflowing Cascade] to level 10, leaving him with just 6,977,100 ability points left, which he put into [Blinding Mist], having judged it to be the most useful among her current abilities. He didn't have enough to max the skill, so he settled for bringing it to level 9. He was left with 3,137,100 ability points left.

After upgrading Kureha's status and skillset, Adam opened his own status screen, then selected his skillset. Just like Kureha, his skills all had their level caps removed—except, he noticed with some wry amusement, [Blood Sacrifice] and [Dance of the Sakura Blossoms]. He remembered the announcement stating he couldn't upgrade his unique skills. Adam wondered if this was some kind of limit the *Age of Gods'* system had put on him to make sure his abilities weren't too overpowered.

He first maxed out [Slash] and [Thrust] again. They were the least powerful of all his skills, but they were also the ones with the shortest cooldown time and therefore his main methods of attack. It cost 1,600,000 ability points to upgrade them both. After that, he upgraded [Energy Sweep] and [Energy Thrust], which could be upgraded to level 15. It cost 12,000,000 to upgrade them both, so that left him with just 418,700. As he was getting ready to close the status menu, he caught sight of something that made him pause.

[List of new skills available to learn.]

Adam hesitated a moment, then pressed on the icon, which flashed, disappeared, and was replaced with a list of seven skills that he could learn. His eyes widened when he saw the skills available.

Skills Available to Learn:

Form One: A deceptive and poisonous offensive stance that allows the player to create a web of attacks, trapping enemies and leaving them unable to move without being hit.

Ability points required to learn: 100,000

Form Two: An offensive stance that relies on speed. The user thrusts his or her spear so fast that he forms spear shadows. This stance also increases the user's speed many times over and allows them to dodge seemingly undodgeable attacks.

Ability points required to learn: 200,000

Form Three: A stance that relies on attacking from multiple angles and using the momentum of one's own swings to increase their attack speed until after images form in the air.

Ability points required to learn: 300,000

Form Four: This power stance offers increased attack power in exchange for decreased mobility. While in this stance, the user's Speed and Movement are decreased, but their Strength and Attack Power are increased.
Ability points required to learn 400,000

Form Five: This stance was made with defense in mind. The user spins their spear so fast that it forms a shield around them, deflecting incoming attacks. It can block everything from weapons to magic.
Ability points required to learn: 500,000

Form Six: A stance that epitomizes the vigors of life just like a Phoenix. This stance uses the friction from intense swinging to produce a brilliant flame that increases the user's Attack Power.
Ability points required to learn: 600,000

Form Seven: The most powerful offensive stance among the seven stances available to player Adam. This stance only offers a single attack, a thrust so powerful that it penetrates all defenses and unleashes Attack Power akin to an enraged dragon.
Ability points required to learn: 700,000

Adam finished reading the skillset, mind almost numb. All of these skills were ones that he had learned in real life. They were the stances used by the Seven Forms Style of Spearmanship taught by the Pleonexia Family. He had already hypothesized that *Age of Gods* somehow pulled information from his mind to produce unique skills like this, but seeing this skill list all but confirmed it for him. Rather than be happy, he was worried.

After all, if this game could pull out information from his mind to create these skills, what else could it pull out?

He suddenly felt very exposed.

And more importantly, was there some overlord watching what was happening in this game, cataloging every detail about the people playing?

"Adam, are you okay?" Aris suddenly asked, having noticed how silent he had become.

"Oh, yes. I'm fine." Adam shook his head, then smiled at everyone, who he only now realized were looking at him with worry. "It's nothing to worry about. Really. I was looking at the new skills that were being offered to me after reaching level 20. Fayte, Lilith, Susan. You three should also have a list of new skills that you can learn. I recommend looking at them when you have time."

Fayte quickly called up her skillset, blinking several times as she pressed something on her screen. "You're right. I have five new skills available. [Fire Dragon], [Lightning Dragon], [Wind Spear], [Giant Waterfall], and [Earth Entrapment]. They cost a lot of ability points to learn. I'll probably learn a few of them, but I'd also like to increase the levels for some of my current skills."

"A-Adam?" A timid voice caught his attention.

"Yes?" He looked at Susan. She was sitting on one of the chairs instead of the couch. For whatever reason, she was not wearing her boots. Her bare feet were placed on the edge of the chair as she sat with her knees drawn into her chest.

"Um, I also have some new skills available. I'd like to get some... but I was hoping that... um... maybe you could... help me?" she asked.

"Susan..." Fayte's eyes widened. She wasn't wearing her veil right now, so her surprise was clear for all to see, though he didn't know if she was surprised by the fact that Susan had asked for help or that she specifically asked for *his* help.

Adam smiled as he stood up. "I don't mind. Let me see what skills you can learn."

"Th-thank you." Susan's cheeks turned pink as he walked over to her.

Aris pouted. "I want you to help me with my skills too."

"You don't have any new skills to learn," Adam fired back. "Come back once you've reached level 20."

"Arrrrrg! I can't believe I died to that stupid whale! What the heck?! I didn't even last long enough to enter the dungeon! So not fair!" Aris bemoaned her unfortunate fate, gripping her head in lamentation.

Adam ignored the young woman for now as he leaned over Susan. Perhaps it was because he had become a bit more aware of her after their near-death experience in the dungeon, but the refreshing scent of her hair drifted over to him. It was easy enough to ignore. Still, the fact that he noticed it meant she had become more important to him than he was comfortable admitting.

"You do have quite a few skills," Adam said after looking at her skill list. "I've only got seven, but you have twenty."

"The Fairy Archer Class's most powerful asset is its versatility," Titania offered an explanation. "Fairy Archers have many skills. Not all of them are related to archery either."

"I've noticed," Adam said. He leaned in closer. Susan squeaked at the proximity, but he was focused entirely on her skill list now. "Let's see... I think the four most useful skills to you right now is [Rapid Fire], [Long Shot], [Farsight], and [Bow Blocking]."

There were plenty of other useful skills as well like [Ballista], which was an attack that ignored an enemy's defense to deal several times more damage than a normal attack, or [Poison Arrow], which infused an arrow with venom and inflicted the poisoned status effect. He had determined these four skills were the most useful, however, because each one offered something that could be used in different circumstances. [Rapid Fire] to shoot enemies at close-range, [Long Shot] to snipe enemies from a distance, [Farsight] so she could act as their scout, and [Bow Blocking] so she could defend herself in the event that she was forced into a close-range fight.

When Adam offered his opinion, Susan breathed a sigh of relief. He gave her a confused look, but she smiled at him.

"Those are the same skills I thought would be the most useful."

"I guess great minds think alike."

"O-oh, no. I'm not... that great..."

Susan reacted to his words like a turtle attempting to hide in her shell, or in this case, her shirt. Really, this girl was just too cute. He was almost tempted to tease her some, but he didn't want to make her feel uncomfortable. Besides, Aris was looking at them with that oddly contemplative expression he'd seen a few times before. He didn't know what she was thinking, but he didn't want to give her imagination any fuel.

"Fayte, what time is it?" he asked.

"It's… just a bit after four," Fayte answered.

"We should probably log out then."

"Yeah. We need to get started on dinner."

The group unanimously chose to log out. Adam, Aris, and Fayte woke up together on the couch in her living room. Adam offered to make them dinner, but he was vetoed by both Aris and Fayte. The two had apparently decided to cook something together. He watched them as they worked in the kitchen. Aris was giggling at something and Fayte wore an indulgent smile as they kneaded some dough.

I wonder what they're making...

He thought about asking, but his phone began ringing before he could. He looked at the caller ID. It was Lilith.

"Lilith? Has something happened?"

Adam was worried that something might have happened. Lilith was currently looking after his old apartment, and she wasn't supposed to call except in emergencies like the apartment being discovered. His worries proved to be unfounded, however, when Lilith spoke.

"No. I wanted your help."

"You want… my help?"

Lilith had never asked for his help before, always offering to serve him or help him. Hearing her say she wanted his help was enough to leave him stunned.

"Well, this is a first. What did you want my help with?"

"I also have several new skills. Ten, to be precise. However, Age of Gods is the first game I have ever played, so I do not know what skills to pick. Astaroth has given me his advice... but I would rather have yours."

The scent of baking bread coming from the kitchen almost distracted him, but he focused on his conversation with Lilith. It was the first time she had asked for his help. He also owed her a lot for sticking by his side all this time even though he had abandoned her once before. Adam had no reason to refuse, nor did he want to.

"Tell me what your skills are and what they do. I'll see if I can help you out."

"Yes, Master."

Adam spent the rest of his time until dinner helping Lilith select new skills.

A SHORT BREAK

After completing their quest for the Guild Association, everyone in Destiny's Overture decided to take a break the next day, which meant Adam did not log into *Age of Gods* early in the morning to grind for experience points—not that grinding had been doing much for him these days. Raising his level in *Age of Gods* had become increasingly difficult. It was honestly a blessing in disguise when Clarise allowed them to take that quest to clear out the dungeon. They'd been able to farm far more experience points like that than they ever had before.

Lying in bed, Adam stared at the ceiling and wondered what he should do now that he wasn't playing. Because of how much energy his body produced, he only needed two hours of sleep to run at peak efficiency. It wasn't possible for him to get more sleep either. His body just didn't work like that. Once he was awake, he couldn't simply fall back to sleep.

"Mmmm hmmmm… Adam… zzzz…"

Adam smiled as he glanced at the naked girl using his shoulder as a pillow. Aris's eyes were closed, and her breathing was deep. The rise and fall of her shoulders let him know she was fast asleep. Her nipples against his skin and the warmth of her body brought him unprecedented pleasure. He placed his hand on her bare hip and rubbed her skin, enjoying the silky softness. As he did, his body reacted, quickly growing hard.

That reminds me, isn't this girl always waking me up with a blowjob? It's only fair that I return the favor.

Rolling over, Adam observed the girl as she flopped onto her back. While her chest was very modest, much smaller than Fayte's certainly, they still had enough weight to jiggle. He was tempted to kiss her chest and take her small nipples into his mouth… but that wasn't what he wanted to do just yet.

After placing a single kiss on her cheek, he moved down, letting his lips trail across her throat, her chest, and down to her stomach. Her belly was tight. Anyone but Adam would have been surprised by how flat her stomach was. Mortems Disease often ate into the body, destroying a person's muscles. Aris should have been nothing but flab. However, her belly was as tight and toned as it had always been.

Adam kissed her belly button several times, then looked up. Aris was still asleep, but now her cheeks were red, and her breathing had grown heavy. Her brow was furrowed as if suffering from unknown frustration.

With a grin, Adam continued moving down, then hooked his arms underneath her legs and spread them apart. She was already a little wet. Trace amounts of her juices caused her lips to glisten. He leaned down and took in her scent, then placed his mouth directly over her and gave Aris a long, languid kiss.

"Mmm… haaaah… aaaahn…"

Aris moaned in her sleep, but that just spurred Adam on more. He buried his tongue inside of her, listening to the sounds she made, letting his tongue brush against the areas that pleased her the most. He rubbed his tongue against the spongy interior close to her entrance, the fabled G-spot, which made Aris writhe in her sleep. It did not take more than a minute before her lips were puffy with arousal. After nibbling on her outer labia for a moment, Adam removed Aris's clit from within her folds. It was such a small thing. He placed his middle finger over it and began moving his hand in concentric circles.

"Haaaah… mmmm… nnnnmmm… haaaaaah… aaaaahn…"

Adam glanced at Aris's face to see that she was still caught within the throes of sleep. He went back down and continued to play with her clit and folds. He used his thumbs to spread her lips apart, leaned forward, and pressed his mouth against her clit, flicking his tongue back and forth.

"Mmmmm!"

Aris bucked her hips against his mouth. Adam would have chortled if his face wasn't full of Aris just then. He continued to lick

her. At the same time, he reached forward and pressed his finger against her sodden entrance, slowly pushing it inside of her. He only went up to the second knuckle. He curled his finger and caressed the inside of her spongy walls.

"Haaaaah! Haaaaah! Hhhnnnn!! Oooooh!"

Aris's eyes snapped open as her entire body shuddered from head to toe. Her legs suddenly locked around Adam's head, driving him further into her. She had quite the powerful set of legs too. It felt like she was trying to squish his head. They remained like that for several seconds before, as Aris's shudders subsided, her legs' grip on his head slackened.

Adam's face was wet when he removed it from between her thighs. He wiped his mouth with his fingers, then sucked them clean, aware of Aris's blinking eyes on him.

"Good morning, Aris. Sleep well?"

"I was until a certain someone woke me up."

"Are you complaining?"

"Of course not." Aris grabbed Adam's arms and pulled him until he was hovering over her. With a smile, she placed her arms around his neck. "It was a good wake-up call."

"You do this to me so much. Thought I'd return the favor."

"Mmmm. I do appreciate that. Now, gimme a kiss."

Adam did not resist Aris's command as he leaned down and kissed her, pushing his tongue inside of her small mouth. Their kiss was languid and slow. Aris rubbed her tongue against his, stirring up all kinds of emotions and saliva between them.

"Mmm… haaah… Adam…"

"Do you want it?"

"I do…"

"In that case…" Adam retracted himself and sat up until he was straddling just her legs. "… Turn around and show me that cute, little ass of yours."

Aris's eyes gleamed as she rolled over. It took some work because her legs were underneath him, but once she was lying on her stomach, Aris curled her legs inward and lifted her backside until her butt was sticking in the air. Her inner thighs were drenched in a combination of his saliva, the juices from her orgasm, and sweat. Her puffy lips quivered as if in anticipation… though he imagined it was probably just the contrast between the cold air and her hot body.

"This is… the first time you've been so demanding," Aris muttered, her breathing heavy.

"You like it when I'm demanding like this?"

"I love it."

"Hmmm."

Adam placed his hands on Aris's cheeks and began massaging them, Aris moaning as she wiggled her butt. He spread her cheeks apart and looked at her puckered hole. It was a lovely pink color. He was tempted to see what it'd be like to have anal sex with her, but he was after something different this time. In either event, when and if they had butt sex, he wanted to find some way to penetrate both her holes at once.

Guess I should think about investing in some toys…

"You ready?" he asked.

"I've been ready since you woke me up. Hurry up and give it to me."

"Wow. Impatient much?"

"It's because you made me so—oooh!"

Aris arched her back as Adam pushed his way inside of her, moving his hips forward slowly until his crotch was pressed against her buttcheeks. The way she conformed around him, the feel of her insides stretching to accommodate his girth, and the warm, spongy wetness rubbing against him was enough that he almost felt like he would release his load right then. He held this position for a moment, then quickly retracted his hips and slammed them forward. A loud slapping sound echoed around the room.

"Ooooh! Aaaahn! Haaaahn! Hhhnnnn! Adam! S-so deep! You're… gonna… haaah… haaah… it feels like… mmmm!… like you're gonna split me in half!"

"I'm. Gonna. Split you. In half? Sounds bad. Maybe I should stop?"

"Do that and I'll kick you—aaaahn!"

"Just kidding."

Adam increased the speed and power of his thrusts until Aris's butt was forced down. Now lying flat on the bed, Aris could do nothing but bury her face into the pillow as she moaned. Adam pressed a hand against her back. He rubbed her skin. She was covered in sweat. A certain scent permeated the air. The muscles of her back seemed to convulse as he applied light pressure to certain parts that forced her muscles to relax.

"N-no fair… that's… mmmm… cheating…"

"All's fair in love and sex."

"That's not how that saying goooOOOOOH!"

Aris's entire body seemed to lock up. Her insides, already quite warm and tight, felt like they were trying to milk him, but he wasn't ready to cum just yet. As Aris rode out her second orgasm, Adam leaned down, slid his hand underneath her, and began rubbing her clit with fast, furious strokes.

"NNNNNGGGGG!"

He enjoyed the way Aris's third orgasm hit immediately after the second. It felt like her insides were becoming a vice that rubbed against every centimeter of his length. After she finished cumming, he placed the hand she had cum on near her face.

"Suck it off," he ordered.

Aris's ears turned red as she stuck his finger in her mouth and swirled her tongue around it. Her tongue was small, soft, and wet. The finger fellatio caused Adam's arousal to spike, and after pistoning into her several more times as if driving her body into the bed, he finally came inside of her. The feeling of release was greater than any he'd ever had before. Was it because of how much more commanding he was being? There was admittedly something pleasant about being in command of this young woman.

Maybe I'm a sadist?

"Haaah… haaaah…"

"Heeeh…. Hoooooh…"

Adam rolled over until he was lying on his back, his breathing deep and even. Sweat covered his chest and ran down his face. He glanced at his still-hard length, drenched in his and Aris's nectar, but then his vision was blocked by Aris as she crawled on top of him. She lay against his chest like a cat stretching out. She pushed her butt back until he was sandwiched between her cheeks, then gyrated her hips to rub his still-hard shaft.

"Hee-hee. Adam, you were pretty naughty this morning."

"I learned all about being naughty from you."

"I know. I'm quite proud of myself. However, I'm not satisfied yet. I hope you're not done."

Aris reached down and grabbed his length, stroking it with her soft fingers. Then she leaned down and began licking the sweat off his chest. Adam shuddered only slightly at the sensation of her tongue. He thought seeing her drag her small, soft pink tongue across his skin was even more erotic than feeling it. Throwing his head back, he released a strained groan, though it turned into a yelp when Aris bit his nipple.

"Minx!"

"Hee-hee. Thank you for the compliment."

After having her way with his nipples, Aris sat up, lifted her hips, and lined himself up with his shaft. Adam watched as she lowered herself onto him. He felt he was a bit girthier than most, not that he had anyone to compare to, and her lips stretched to accommodate him. The sight of his dick disappearing inside of her aroused him even more. Liquid dripped from her to stain his length, which slowly disappeared until their hips joined together.

"Mmmm. I feel so full. Hey, Adam. You've cum inside me quite a bit. Think I'll get pregnant?"

"No." The answer was immediate as he placed his hands on her hips. "You don't need to worry about getting pregnant with me."

Adam was sterile thanks to all the experiments that had been done to him as a child, so he couldn't get anyone pregnant, but even if that wasn't the case, Mortems Disease had already ravaged Aris's womb. Her body might be healed, but he didn't think she would ever be able to bear children. There was also a chance any kids she had would also be susceptible to Mortems Disease. It was better if they didn't have kids.

"That's… too bad…" Aris moaned as she ground her hips against him, sending lightning shooting to his brain. "I… I wouldn't mind… having your children…"

"I guess… it wouldn't be so bad…" Adam said, though he knew the truth. They would never be able to have kids.

He didn't say anything else, grabbing her hips and letting Aris ride him to several more orgasms.

***

Fresh out of the shower, Adam and Aris entered the living room to find Fayte sitting on the couch with a tablet in her hand. Three mugs sat on the table, though only one of them was full right now.

"Good morning, you two," Fayte smiled at them both.

Fayte was dressed in black yoga pants and a red sports bra. Her hair was tied into a ponytail, something he didn't see often, but he thought this sporty appearance looked nice. The ponytail meant he could see her slender neck and the gentle slope of her shoulders. Her skin glistened a little. He imagined she just got back from the small gym located on the ground floor. She wasn't wearing shoes, which were on the rack by the door, and her toes curled against the carpet as she read whatever was on her tablet.

"Morning, Fayte!"

Aris bounced across the room, the ends of her Harajuku cardigan flapping around her. The cardigan was primarily white, but decorating the bottom was a depiction of mountains, clouds, and rivers painted in monochrome. The sleeves similarly featured unique designs. To the unknowing eye, they would have looked like swirls, but Adam understood they symbolized waves. Underneath her cardigan was a black shirt that showed off her belly button and shorts of the same color that didn't even cover most of her thighs.

Adam's outfit consisted of simple slacks and a white collared shirt. He had rolled up the sleeves. Aris had stated she enjoyed seeing his forearms, so he always kept his shirts like this. Aris sat down on the couch as he walked over.

"Should I get started on breakfast?" he asked.

"I was actually thinking I should make breakfast this time." Fayte set the tablet down and smiled. "You should take a look at the forum I found so we can discuss it while we eat. I hope you don't mind."

"I don't mind."

"Can I help make breakfast?" inquired Aris.

Fayte shook her head. "Not this time."

Standing up with the grace of an aristocrat, Fayte made her way into the kitchen, where she began rummaging through the fridge for ingredients. Adam took the seat she had left. It was still warm. He reached over and grabbed the tablet, bringing it up so he could read.

"This forum contains a list of all the guilds that have been created and what level the top ten players have reached." He paused, then spoke in a louder voice. "I see now why you wanted me to read this."

"We can discuss it once I'm done making breakfast. Please keep reading," Fayte said.

Adam did just that. Aris leaned against him as she also read the forum, which discussed the guilds and top players in the game. It looked like Daggerfall Dynasty had created a guild the other day, but they were fifth on the listing of guilds—at least internationally. Auspicious Inc. had established a guild just a few days after Destiny's Overture, and following them was the Pleonexia Alliance and Wrathful Asura—a powerful Taoist Union guild owned and operated by a corporation called Qiquan. Nationally, they were the third guild to be created.

"Look at this! It seems we're not the first people to reach level 20!" Aris exclaimed.

"What are you talking about? You're still at level 18," Adam said.

"Hee-hee. I know that, but you, Fayte, Susan, and Lilith are all over level 20."

Aris didn't seem to mind that she was only at level 18, but it bothered Adam because he knew they would need more strength if they wanted to defend themselves against the Pleonexia Alliance when they decided to attack. He put that thought aside for now, however, and instead read the listing of all the most powerful players from top to bottom.

"Lin Akamine reached level 21 yesterday and the Spear God is at level 20 now. No surprises there. Levon, Connor, and his Four Elements are all at level 19. I doubt we'll have to worry about them attacking us until they reach level 20. Let's see… Daggerfall and his brothers are also at level 19 and… huh… the Twelve Celestial Beasts are also all at level 20."

"Who are the Twelve Celestial Beasts?" asked Aris.

"They're the top members of Wrathful Asura," Fayte answered as she walked out of the kitchen with a tray in her hands. She had made them scrambled eggs. The scent of cheese drifted from the tray, which she set before them. "Wrathful Asura is the most powerful Taoist Union guild today. They're top members are called the Twelve Celestial Beasts. They're based on the twelve animals of the Chinese zodiac."

"Ooooh. I see."

Fayte went back into the kitchen, then came out balancing three plates with utensils in one arm and a pitcher of coffee in the other. She set the coffee down, placed the plates and utensils in front of them, then sat down herself. Meanwhile, Adam poured him and Aris a cup of coffee. He also refilled Fayte's since hers was only half full.

"You said you wanted to discuss this with us?" Adam pressed as they began eating.

Fayte swallowed a bit of her food, nodded, and said, "Yes. So far, we have managed to maintain a strong lead. Our guild might be small, but we are more powerful than everyone else level-wise. However, I don't think it's enough. Normally, Levon acts meticulously and only after gathering all the information he needs, but after what happened during the tournament, I believe he will simply bring the full power of his guild to bear the moment our one-month grace period expires."

"You're probably right." Adam knew Levon well enough to understand what kind of person he was even better than Fayte. "I was thinking about that too. Our last mission was a great way to farm experience, but we should think about becoming more efficient."

"It seems you're thinking about the same thing I am," Fayte said with a nod.

"What's going on now? What are you two talking about?" asked Aris.

"We're talking about dividing our forces into two parties and taking on more high-level quests," Adam said. "When you form a party with others, the experience you gain is shared between all of you. Let's say you've got five people in a party. That experience will be split five ways. This means that if you earn fifty thousand experience points, you each only get ten thousand. But let's say you only have two people in your party..."

"You'd both receive twenty-five thousand, right?" guessed Aris.

"Correct." Nodding, Adam scooped some eggs onto his fork and stuck it in his mouth. The taste of cheese filled his tongue, but it wasn't overpowering, and the hints of salt and pepper created a sharp contrast that brought out the umami of the cheese and eggs. "When grinding in high-level dungeons, it's standard for groups to form larger parties. The enemies are often higher level than you are, so you need to band together to defeat them, but this also means you're not getting as many experience points as you can. However, we are strong enough that I think we can afford to split our forces and accept high-level quests like the previous one. If we had done that quest with only two or three people, we could have reached level 22 if not level 23."

"Got it. Yeah. That makes sense."

"I'm planning to take Aris on a quest," Adam added to Fayte. "She's the only one who hasn't reached level 20 yet, so I'd like to help her gain as many experience points as possible. I was thinking you, Lilith, Susan, Titania, and Kureha could take on a different quest."

Fayte cupped her chin in thought. "I'd normally not recommend just the two of you going off on your own… but you are the strongest one among us. I guess if anyone can take on a dungeon with just two people, it would be you. All right. I'll have the others join me on a quest while you and Aris do your own quest."

"Thank you."

"Of course, today we are relaxing," Fayte added. "We worked hard and gained a lot of levels, so I think we deserve to take a break."

"I agree."

Rest was an important part of training. If all a person did was train, they would eventually break. Even Lucifer had understood that and given them rest days, though that only consisted of sitting inside of an empty cell and getting three meals. Many of his comrades had still broken from the strain.

Lucifer hadn't much cared about his guinea pigs.

"Are you doing anything, Fayte?" asked Aris.

"Hmmm." Fayte tilted her head. "I was thinking of seeing if I could meet up with Susan and going to the mall… but she's currently busy with some personal issues."

"Then how about we go to the mall?" suggested Aris.

"You mean the three of us?" asked Fayte.

Aris giggled. "Of course! You and I can do some shopping, and of course, we need someone to carry our bags."

"Ah. So I'm becoming the pack mule, am I?" asked Adam with a wry smile.

"That's right. Do you have a problem with that?" asked Aris.

"Nope. None."

"Good. Then let's get ready to leave after breakfast."

With their plans decided, Adam, Aris, and Fayte finished eating. Fayte took a quick rinse, got dressed in her baggy clothes and veil, and they left the apartment together. They took Adam's car to a not-as-well-known locale called the New York Strip. Most people who wanted to hit the town went to New York City Town Square Mall. This out-of-the-way shopping district was further from New York City's center, closer to the outskirts. Its out-of-the-way location meant it wasn't as populous as the mall.

Adam followed the women as they looked through the windows of stores to see if there was anything interesting. A lot of the clothing stores only sold last year's fashion. Most nobles would never be caught dead in places like this, but Aris and Fayte shared none of those compunctions as they wandered into several shops to try on different outfits.

Many of the workers at the stores they visited seemed completely taken in with Aris's beauty and vivacious personality. Quite a few of the workers would try to force specific outfits on her. Adam had to put a stop to a few pushy men who looked like they were gonna try hitting on her. Of course, they only focused on Aris while Fayte was still wearing her veil. All attention was drawn to her the moment she removed it, though she rarely did even during their shopping excursion.

The three eventually found a food court to sit at. Adam gratefully placed all the bags he had been carrying on the floor and sat down. As he did, a monitor built into the table lit up, showing them a list of restaurants and their menus. They each ordered something from a different restaurant.

Adam paid for all of it, of course.

Their drinks eventually came. Aris's eyes shone like diamonds as she eyed the soda. Adam was finally allowing her to drink carbonated beverages.

"Say, I have a question," Aris said suddenly before taking a sip of her drink. She paused at the fizzy beverage, then slurped loudly as if trying to suck the cup dry.

"What is it?" asked Fayte as she drank her green tea. She had to move her veil to one side as she drank.

"You remember how older MMOs always had a unique story you're supposed to follow?"

"Yes. What about them?"

"I was just wondering why none of the new VRMMOs do that?"

"It's because of why VRMMOs were created." Fayte set her cup down, leaned back, and crossed her arms. "VRMMOs, or virtual reality massively multiplayer online games, were created for the sole purpose of settling disputes. Since its purpose is different than the MMOs of yesteryear, a lot of the older features that creators deemed unnecessary were removed. The storyline feature is one of those features that were done away with. Of course, there are still stories and plots within each game, but the game itself is now more about the PvP aspect than the PvE one."

"Ooooh. That makes sense. Still, it's kind of sad that VRMMOs decided to remove an overarching story from their games," Aris said.

"I can't disagree. I did rather enjoy the storyline of games like War of Worldcraft and Dogma of the Dragon."

"Right! Those were great games! But they were great because the story was so engaging and fun to follow. It just feels like these new VRMMOs lost something when the creators decided they didn't need a main storyline anymore!"

Adam listened to the women talk, happy to just see how much they were enjoying themselves. The two got along very well. He even wondered if this was how sisters acted, though he was certain his own thoughts were favorably skewed toward wanting these two to get along like family. Aris, after all, had no one but him until recently.

In either event, this was a rare break for them.

Their food soon arrived. Aris and Fayte continued to talk about video games while they ate, until it was time to leave.

THE PROPOSITION OF A DEVIOUS MIND

Adam, Aris, and Fayte returned home several hours later with a number of shopping bags in hand. They had gotten several new outfits. Most of the shopping had been for Aris, who only possessed a few sets of clothing. Aris never had the need to own more than a few sets before. What use did a woman with Mortems Disease have for clothes? Those had been her thoughts at the time. Now that she was cured, the previously gloomy beliefs she held had evaporated like a puddle of water on a clear summer's day in Arizona.

So much has changed.

It was late evening. Adam sat on the couch, watching the setting sun through the sliding glass door that led to the balcony. Aris was fast asleep. She was curled up on the couch, her head resting on his lap, an indolent smile lighting up her face more than the sun ever could. All Adam could do was gently smile as he stroked the young woman's hair.

"Looks like someone is tuckered out. Here. Thought you might like something to drink," Fayte said as she came around to the couch, two mugs in hand. He couldn't see what they contained from his position. All he saw was the steam rising from the surface as she held one of the mugs out to him. But the smell suggested it was somewhat sweet.

"Thank you." He took the mug from her. It wasn't a regular mug but one of those self-heating mugs. There was a heating pad on the bottom that was charged via solar energy. He looked inside to see what she had made him. He blinked when all he saw was heavy whipped cream. "Dessert coffee?"

"It's another personal recipe of mine." Fayte sat down on the other side of Aris, placed her feet onto the couch, and held her mug in both hands. "I mixed in two tablespoons of whiskey, half a tablespoon of sugar, and a little bit of cinnamon. The cream is sprinkled with a dusting of ginger."

"Sounds truly decadent."

Adam brought the mug to his lips. The bold flavor of coffee hit his tongue and mixed with the burning sensation of the whiskey, which was somewhat softened by the whipped cream. He was instantly taken with it.

It had been a long time since he'd had anything to drink, though not because he wasn't able to. The drinking age in the American Federation was eighteen. It had changed after the war because a lot of younger people were becoming alcoholics. The horrors of World War III and watching as people you loved died from disease had caused many a young man or woman to drown their sorrows in alcohol, which had of course caused issues at the time, but even placing a ban on the stuff had only exacerbated the matter. People had revolted and the black market thrived during that time. In the end, the government had changed the legal drinking age.

"Pffft!"

Adam paused after taking a sip of his drink to frown at the woman beside him. Fayte was no longer looking his way. Her shoulders were shaking and the tips of her ears had turned red.

"Something funny?" he asked.

"N-no…"

"You're a terrible liar. What's got you laughing at me?"

"It's… your face…"

"Excuse me?"

"On… your face…"

"On my…?" Adam reached up and realized what she was talking about when he felt the whipped cream around his mouth. "Ah." He wiped it off with a finger, then licked his finger. "Is me having a beard really that amusing?"

"S-sorry. I don't think it'd normally be that funny, but… I don't know. You're such a… a serious figure that seeing you with a silly-looking whipped cream beard feels out of character."

"And you find that funny?"

"… Yes."

"Well… so long as you're amused, I guess it's fine." Adam blew out a breath.

"My apologies." Fayte simply smiled at him.

"I'm sure you're one hundred percent not sorry."

Her smile grew wider. "I'm a little surprised you came out with me today? I thought you were trying to be cautious."

"I am. Why do you think I had us go to the New York Strip instead of something like the New York City Town Square Mall?"

"I'm not su—oh. The New York Strip doesn't have social cameras."

Social Cameras were another invention born after the war. World War III had changed so many lives, and not for the better. There had been a time after the signing of the armistice where crime ran rampant. The Social Cameras were the government's attempt to curtail crime, and while many people had complained at first, crime rates had indeed dropped as a result.

"Correct. It is possible that Levon has people observing the social cameras that litter almost every square meter of New York City. That means we can't go to places that have them like the convenience store and areas with high traffic. But there are some places we can go. In any case, I have something I'd like to discuss with you now, if you don't mind."

After composing herself, Fayte turned back to face him. She took a sip of her mug and came away with a beard much like him. He didn't say anything though. His revenge would come after his conversation, and it was sure to be swift and brutal. Who was it that said revenge was a dish best served cold?

"What did you want to talk about?"

"The first goal of your bet," Adam said. Fayte straightened as though suddenly more alert. "I thought that'd get your attention. We're making good money in the game. I'm sure when the money exchange system is announced, you'll have yourself a tidy fortune… but it still won't be enough. I'm sure you know this? Even if we keep earning money like this, we won't make enough to reach your second goal."

At present, they had roughly 195,000,000 gold coins, which would maybe come out to around 97.5 million dollars of real-world currency. In-game currency was always less valuable than real-world currency. That was another reason people who wanted to make a living gaming had to completely leave behind the real world. You simply couldn't earn enough to live if you half-assed it. A lot of it also depended on what the particular currency you were converting the in-game currency to was worth. Right now, the American Federation's Credit was competing with the Taoist Union's Yingbi for the second most powerful form of currency after the European Union's Lamna. This meant the in-game gold coins would probably be worth less than half of the Credit.

"I… am aware of that," Fayte mumbled.

"I've been thinking of ways to help you earn more money outside of the game. From what I understand, Levon never stipulated that you had to only earn money through in-game currency, which means we can find other avenues of accruing income."

Fayte's eyes sharpened a little. "I never thought of doing that before. It's a good idea. I'm guessing you already have a plan? You're not the type to bring this up otherwise."

"I have two plans. One is a short-term means of earning a lot of money. The other is a long-term method." Aris shifted on his lap. He paused, thinking she might have woken up, but then she mumbled under her breath, smacked her lips, and settled back down. "The first thing I'm going to do is sell my blood to the doctor who became Aris's primary care physician after she got Mortems Disease, or rather, I'm going to sell it to her boss using her as an intermediary."

"I… Oh. I see." Fayte licked her lips, eyes quivering just slightly. "You… would really go that far for me?"

"I told you this before, didn't I? That I'm going to make sure you win that bet. Nothing on this Earth is going to stop me from making that happen," Adam said, determined.

Fayte turned away. Her shoulders were shaking, but it was not from mirth this time. Adam pretended not to notice as the woman wiped a few errant tears from her eyes, composing herself before looking back at him. This woman was strong. And he knew she didn't want to show weakness, so the least he could do was feign ignorance.

"Thank you. This means a lot to me," said Fayte, her voice ephemeral and soft, a gentle windchime-like sound that tickled the ear. Adam felt the urge to reach out, cup her cheek, and stroke her soft skin with his thumb. His left hand twitched. It took some effort on his part not to commit such an intimate act.

"You're welcome." Adam smiled at the woman, but then the smile left as he moved on to the next topic. "The long-term plan has to do with that device you used to cure Aris. I think we should let Dr. Sofocor—that's Aris's primary care physician—take it. We'll let her study the pod alongside several other medical experts to see if they can replicate it."

"And we'll sell the rights to do this for a high price?" asked Fayte.

"No. You'll let them do it for free," Adam said.

Fayte's eyes grew wide and round, but it wasn't because she was shocked. She was. Of course she was. No one did anything for free in this day and age. The shock came because she had understood what Adam was after with the second idea from the moment he proposed it.

"The second goal," Fayte murmured.

"Right. Your second goal." Adam nodded. "To earn a reputation that puts you, as an individual, on a level playing field with the weakest among the top ten most powerful families in the American Federation. This isn't a goal that can be done easily. You *might* be able to accomplish this in the game. In fact, I'd already say you are well on your way toward earning an impressive reputation. *However,* what if you discovered the cure for Mortems Disease? And what if you decided to donate that cure rather than sell it for an outrageous fee?"

"And what if it became public knowledge," Fayte finished Adam's thoughts, shaking her head as a helpless smile warmed her fair face. "I see what you're planning. Yes, that would pretty much propel me to the top. Forget ranking above the tenth most powerful family in the American Federation. Not even the Pleonexia Family would be able to look down their noses at me."

"Exactly. At that point, you would be such a well-known figure that Levon won't be able to even touch you. And if it becomes common knowledge that he forced you into an unfair bet, knowing you had no choice but to take it because of what happened between you and your father..." Adam trailed off to let Fayte reach her own conclusions.

"You are a frightening man," Fayte said at last. "I never would have thought of doing all this on my own."

"That's because you're only thinking about how you can achieve your goals by playing *Age of Gods*. I'm not sure how Levon worded that bet to you, but to me, it doesn't sound like he ever said you could only achieve these goals through the game."

Fayte worried her lower lip in thought. "You're not wrong. He never said I had to reach all three goals by playing *Age of Gods*. I guess... I just assumed they had to be done through *Age of Gods* because of the third goal."

"The third goal was likely a red herring meant to make you think you could only win the bet by playing *Age of Gods*. In either event, I was thinking about scheduling an appointment to meet with Dr. Sofocor. I need to make more of the, ahem, medicine to sell her before I do, which might take some time since I have to go back to my apartment and create what will amount to a bulk order. When I do, I'll take you with me and we can negotiate how we're going to let her study your miracle device."

The sun had gone down by the time they finished talking. Their empty coffee mugs sat on the table beside them. Despite the hour becoming so late, Adam wasn't tired, a consequence of being who and what he was—a genetically modified human being with incredible esper powers. He'd probably stay up late tonight, running his hands through Aris's hair until he fell asleep. That was what he'd done ever since Adam began living with Aris—even before she'd contracted Mortems Disease.

Even though so much has changed, I guess some things will forever remain the same.

"Adam. Thank you. I mean that." Fayte's eyes shone with unshed tears as she gave him the most heartfelt smile he'd ever seen. It lit up the entire room and stole his breath away. "I never had any intention of giving up, but I always knew the chances of me winning this bet was basically zero. Now, however, I truly believe I can win and attain my freedom. Thank you."

Adam didn't say anything at first. Fayte frowned in confusion. But then he leaned over, reached out, and gently traced his finger along the edge of her mouth. Fayte's cheeks and ears turned red as Adam brought the cream now on his finger to his mouth and licked it clean. Her eyes never left his finger. And her face grew an even brighter shade as she watched him.

"You're welcome," he said with a simple grin.

Fayte could only blush.

***

Adam woke up Aris, who grumpily complained as he led her to the bathroom, helped brush her teeth, and got her changed into her pajamas. The girl was only half-awake as she performed these acts. Her haphazard manner led to him doing most of the work, but he had grown used to looking after Aris and enjoyed it when she relied on him.

She fell asleep not long after they climbed into bed. Going out for so long had exhausted her. It was proof that even though she was doing much better, she still hadn't fully recovered.

As he stroked her hair, the phone sitting on his nightstand began vibrating. He grabbed it and looked at the caller ID. The person calling was a new phone number.

"Hello? This is Adam speaking," he said after accepting the call.

"Ah!" A soft gasp came over the other line. *"A-Adam? Is that really you?"*

"Yes, Su. It's me."

"I-I knew that. I guess I'm just... surprised. You sound the same as you do in the game. Eheheh."

Adam was tempted to point out that their in-game avatars were identical to their real-life bodies—so very tempted—but Susan was a timid young woman, and he didn't want her to feel like he was being condescending. There was also that strange but unmistakable desire to protect her. If he didn't know any better, he would have said it was an esper power.

"Thank you for calling. I know I asked you to call me really late at night."

"I-it's no trouble."

Before they had logged off the other day, Adam had requested Susan call him and even gave her his phone number. The number and phone were just throwaways in any case. Even if someone hacked her phone and discovered his number, he could toss it and get a new one.

"So, about what we discussed the other day…"

"I, um, I already took the liberty of looking at yours and Aris's profiles in the American Federation identification registry. Your, um, about your registry…"

"Haaah. I figured you'd notice it was a forgery," Adam said. He paused for a brief moment to consider what he should tell her. "I'm an orphan, so I was never registered as a citizen… to the best of my knowledge. That registration I have is a very convincing fake I had a friend make for me."

"O-oh. I see. Sorry if I dug up some bad memories."

"You're fine. Anyway, is it possible for you to alter the documents to provide false information?"

"It can certainly be done… but I'm not so sure that's a good idea."

"Why not?"

There was a poignant pause from the other end. Adam almost absently twirled Aris's hair around his index finger as he waited for Susan to speak. He was a natural-born killer, and he was good at infiltrating various bases and territories, but he had very little knowledge when it came to altering someone's identification. That was not his forte.

All he could do was kill people.

"The government has several backup drives stored in a separate location that contain copies of all the information in their online database. The drives are located on a server that isn't connected to the web, so they can't be accessed from the outside. If I were to alter your personal information online, the information in their servers would still have the original info."

"Which means they would know someone hacked them," Adam said.

"Yes."

Adam released a heavy sigh as he realized how difficult it would be to cover his tracks. Various governments around the world had become far stricter about security and information. Ostensibly, this was done to prevent crimes before they could occur. Nobody wanted a repeat of the spark that initiated World War III, or for some terrorist cell to spring up from the ether.

That was why most places had social cameras, why having your identification registered with the government was mandatory, and why they had such a secure backup drive filled with all that data. Of course, there were always people who slipped through the cracks like Adam, but the government had become very adept at keeping tabs on their citizens.

Of course, that was only the surface reason. The real reason was one Adam didn't want to contemplate.

"Is there anything that can be done to help protect Aris?" asked Adam.

"I-I've already taken the liberty of setting up a backdoor program that will alert me if anyone accesses your information," Susan said. *"If someone does look into you through this method, I'll know about it, and I can track them through their IP address. I should be able to find them even if they're using a VPN or simply bouncing their signal between multiple addresses."*

"That's pretty impressive."

Adam didn't quite understand everything Susan just told him, but Bael was an expert hacker and would often speak technical computer jargon at him. He was sure the man would be impressed if he heard Susan speak.

"It... it's not that impressive," Susan said, sounding embarrassed.

"No. It is impressive. I mean that. Thank you, Su."

"... You're welcome."

Since it was almost midnight, Adam didn't keep Susan any longer than that. He said goodnight and hung up the phone. As he lay there, Adam thought about what Susan had done for him. He really owed her now.

I wonder if there's anything I can do for her...

As Adam drifted off, he promised himself that he would come to her aid whenever she needed him.

***

Adam did not log into *Age of Gods* immediately after waking up. He had sex with Aris instead.

He was afraid sex was becoming something he was addicted to, or perhaps it would be more accurate to say he was addicted to Aris? There was something about the act, about how Aris moved her nubile body to an unseen rhythm as she rode him to an orgasm, about her cries as he thrust into her from behind, that just drove him wild. The scent of their sweat mingled as they made love. The sound of their cries echoed around the room as they embraced. Slick bodies. A beautiful dance of conjoined flesh and multiple hickeys.

"You're becoming quite the animal," Aris said after they finished their shower. She wore simple pink pajama pants and one of his shirts. Since it was so baggy, the shirt hung off her shoulders, but he thought it was a good look for her. But maybe he only thought that way because he felt like her wearing his clothes made her his?

It was something to think about.

"If I've become an animal, then you are the one who made me like this," Adam said.

"Hee-hee. Don't worry. I'll take responsibility for corrupting you."

Adam said nothing as they entered the living room. Fayte was already awake and standing in the kitchen, which he could see through the small window. He wondered why. It was so early, not even 6:00 am yet. He would have thought she'd prefer to sleep in.

It wasn't until they made eye contact that he understood the truth.

She had woken up because of him.

Because of them.

Fayte took one look into his eyes, then her cheeks grew red, and she looked away. It was both a sign of embarrassment, but also perhaps one of shame. Of longing? He couldn't tell. Adam knew there was something between them, something neither of them were acknowledging, and the longer it went on like this, the more obvious it was becoming.

He wondered how long it would be before they had no choice *but* to confront this elephant hiding in their closet.

He wondered what would happen when they did.

He was worried.

"Morning, Fayte!" Aris said as she bounced into the living room.

"Morning, Aris. Adam, good morning," Fayte greeted.

"Good morning," Adam said. "Already making breakfast?"

"Just simple oatmeal with some raisins and sliced apples," Fayte said.

Adam watched as Fayte came into the living room with three bowls of oatmeal. It did look delicious. The oats had been cooked to a strangely golden-brown color, which he realized was brown sugar that had been caramelized. His thoughts, however, were on the woman herself. Should he apologize? No. That would have been addressing the elephant they had been ignoring. For the sake of keeping everything peaceful, Adam knew he couldn't say anything.

Unfortunately, Aris didn't seem to have gotten that memo.

"Is the reason you're waking up so early because Adam and I were too loud?" she asked.

If Adam or Fayte had been drinking anything, they would have definitely spat it out, or choked on it.

"Aris!" Adam shouted.

"Hee-hee. Should I have not brought this up? I'm sorry."

Adam's right eye twitched as Aris rapped her knuckles against her head as though proclaiming it empty, but he knew the truth. This girl was forcing the elephant to be acknowledged. He didn't know why… yet. Perhaps he would have to speak with her about this. That, however, would be for when they were alone.

"It's… fine," Fayte said, struggling to maintain a diplomatic expression. He'd never seen such a look of forced politeness. "You two have been getting, uh, a little rambunctious."

"We'll keep it down from now on," Adam said, then quickly switched topics. "Anyway, about today. You remember the plan?"

Fayte nodded as Aris began eating her oatmeal. "Yes. We're going to the Guild Association to pick up two quests—one for you and Aris, and the other for me, Lilith, Kureha, Titania, and Susan. We should be able to farm more experience points with fewer players in our party. Guess that means we'll be disbanding our current party."

Their current party was the one they had created after their first in-game meeting. Adam was the party leader, so he would be disbanding the party.

"That's right. We probably won't see each other in-game for a few days since missions take so long, so make sure you and the others stay safe."

"Mmm. We will."

Adam, Aris, and Fayte finished eating, then logged into *Age of Gods*. Lilith was surprisingly not present when they first arrived. Adam wondered if perhaps Astaroth had her doing some task for him. What surprised him even more was the lack of Titania and Kureha, who were literally always present when they first arrived.

"No one's here," Fayte mumbled in confusion.

"Hello? Titania? Kureha?" Aris called out. "Is anybody here?"

Nobody arrived at first, but then they heard loud thumping from upstairs. The trio looked at each other. Should they go upstairs and see where that sound was coming from? It clearly did not belong to a fox or a barely one-foot-tall fairy. Adam cocked his head to one side as he listened intently to the sound.

"Footsteps? Human footsteps," he mumbled, eyes narrowing. "Judging how light they are, I'd say they're from a child... or a really short person."

The footsteps were coming down the stairs now. He could hear them drifting over from the hallway.

Before they could decide on a course of action, Titania flew in through the open doorway. Adam thought he saw something else in the door. It was large and fuzzy. Tails? Ears? Whatever they were, they disappeared behind the door a moment later as Titania greeted them.

"It is about time you showed up. I was beginning to wonder if you people would ever come back," she said, arms crossed.

Adam shrugged. "Even we need a break from adventuring sometime."

"Hello, Titania," Aris greeted. "Where's Kureha?"

"About that... I have a surprise for you."

"A surprise?" Fayte asked.

With a surprisingly devious smile, Titania turned back to the door. "You can come out now, Kureha."

Adam, Aris, and Fayte looked toward the door, expecting to see a small fox with three tails walk out. What they found instead was a little girl no older than maybe nine or ten. She had skin whiter than freshly fallen snow, soft hair that was dark like midnight, and large eyes that made him think she was of Asian descent. Her small nose was a bit red. She wore something that resembled a furisode—a kimono distinguishable by its long sleeves. She wore no shoes, so her tiny feet padded along the floor.

"Welcome home, Big Brother!" the girl exclaimed.

Silence pervaded the guild house, though it only lasted for a single second.

"HUH?!" Adam, Aris, and Fayte all shouted at the same time.

KUREHA'S HUMAN FORM

"I told you before, didn't I? I said that Kureha was a fox yokai, and that she'd eventually gain a human form," Titania said as if it should have been obvious this would happen.

Only a few minutes had passed since Adam, Aris, and Fayte logged into *Age of Gods*, and during that time, Titania had taken to explaining who the little girl was. Of course, Adam had already come to the conclusion that the tiny child was Kureha. That didn't stop him from feeling shocked. He was still surprised enough that he hadn't been able to form proper sentences during Titania's explanation.

"All fox yokai gain a human form after reaching a certain level. That level is 20, which is when they gain their third tail. The third tail is kind of like a rite of passage for fox yokai," Titania explained as she floated before the group, wings fluttering.

Adam, Aris, Fayte, and Kureha were now sitting on the couch. Well, Kureha had plopped herself onto Adam's lap. He glanced at the child sitting on him and wondered what kind of problems this little one would bring. An ache was already forming behind his skull. The dull throb made him want to rub his forehead, though he refrained.

"You did tell me that, but I didn't think it would happen for a while yet." He gave Titania a mild look of reproach. "You never specified what level they gained a human form."

"No, I suppose I did not, did I?" Titania smiled at him, and it was so devious that Adam realized she'd done this on purpose.

"I hope you don't mind if I ask a question," Fayte suddenly interjected, staring at Titania.

"Go ahead." Titania gestured toward her.

"If Kureha gained her human form at level 20, then why didn't she transform after reaching level 20? She's level 22 now."

"A good question, but one with a simple answer." Titania crossed her arms. "She couldn't... or rather, she didn't have the time. Fox yokai gain the ability to have a human form after reaching level 20, but it still requires them to create it. You do not think Kureha could create a human form in the middle of a dangerous mission, do you? Of course not. Kureha didn't begin creating the form you see now until after all of you returned to your world."

Adam glanced down at Kureha again. She was leaning her back against his chest, smiling like she didn't have a care in the world. Her three fluffy tails had curled around his left leg and were soft to the touch. He'd never felt a fox's fur before, but he somehow thought hers was far softer. With her kimono-like gown, dark hair, and pale skin, Adam thought she looked like a miniature shrine maiden from Japan.

"So you made your current body, Kureha?" asked Aris.

"That's right, Big Sister! Kureha made this body all on her own!" Kureha thrust out her chest and smiled. "Aren't I amazing?!"

"Did you forget that I helped you?" Titania asked, voice dry.

"You're very amazing," Aris said, reaching out to rub the girl's hair. Kureha giggled and leaned into the young woman's touch.

Titania sighed as she was summarily ignored. Adam could only smile. Everyone seemed to have selective hearing when it came to her. They only chose to hear the words they wanted to, and they ignored everything they didn't care for. Adam wondered if maybe he should ease up on the teasing a bit.

Still, I'm very surprised. I honestly thought the whole "gains a human form after reaching a certain level" thing was just in-game lore that didn't mean anything. I should have known better. This game has been upending all my expectations so far.

Adam wanted to ask Titania more questions, but someone appeared in the living room as if by magic. Lilith looked at them all with a cool expression. Like Adam, she never took off her veil. Now that he was thinking about it, he and Lilith were the only ones who still wore something to cover their face no matter where they were.

"Welcome back," Adam said.

"I am ba... ck?"

Adam noticed the pause in the woman's words and realized that she was now staring at Kureha. Lilith was obviously trying to deduce who this little girl sitting on her master's lap was. Her brows were furrowed as she glared at the child with a look so intense any normal kid would have run away in tears.

"Lilith, this is Kureha," Adam re-introduced them.

Kureha's eyes lit up. "Ah! Hello, Big Sis Lilth!"

Adam's lips trembled as he tried to contain his mirth. It seemed Kureha was unable to properly say "Lilith." He thought it was cute.

"S-so cute…"

And, apparently, so did Lilith.

Adam took some time to explain Kureha's new form to Lilith, who accepted the explanation easily enough. She didn't even seem to be phased, now that he thought about it. The assassin seemed more interested in petting the now human-shaped Kureha's head than his explanation.

Susan arrived several minutes later, and Adam had to explain everything all over again. At least she reacted as he'd expected. Susan was shocked to learn that Kureha had gained a human form and asked all kinds of questions, leaning toward Adam with a look of such excitement that she reminded him of a dog whose master had finally returned after a long day at work. She only realized how invasive she was being several minutes later. After which, she stuttered and began apologizing over and over again.

"I forgot to mention this, but now that she has gained a human form, she also has a beast form. If you look at her status screen, you'll see them under her skill list. She can wear equipment now too," Titania said.

Since Adam was curious, he opened Kureha's status screen.

Name: Kureha

Class: Fox Yokai

Lvl: 22

SP: 0

AP: 3,137,100

Experience: 14,165,416/52,428,800

Strength: +10

Constitution: +370

Dexterity: +100

Intelligence: +940

Speed: +200

Physical Attack: +10

Health: 3,800/3,800

Hit-rate: 100%

MP: 44,380/44,380

Movement: +400

Physical Defense: +420

Magical Defense: +1,580

Dodge-Rate: 100%

Magic Attack: +3,760

Kureha's Skills:

Skill Name: Fireball

Description: Kureha has incredible control over fire thanks to her first tail. She can create fire through the power in her tail and launch a fireball at opponents.

Current lvl: 10 MAXED

Ability: Deals 500% damage

Has a 100% chance of causing burn damage

MP Cost: 5,000

Cooldown Time: 10-seconds

Skill Name: Firestorm

Description: Kureha has incredible control over fire thanks to her first tail. She can create fire through the power in her tail to unleash a powerful storm of fire.

Current lvl: 10 MAXED

Ability: Deals 380% damage to all enemies within a 15-yard radius

Has a 100% of causing burn

MP cost: 4,000

Cooldown Time: 10-seconds

Skill Name: Fire Whip

Description: Kureha sprouts a whip of fire from her first tail and uses it to lash at the enemy. This skill remains active for as long as Kureha pumps magic points into it.

Current lvl: 1

Ability points needed to reach next lvl: 15,000

MP Cost: 100 MP per every second skill is active

Cooldown time: 15-seconds

Skill Name: Thunder Bolt

Description: Kureha's second tail has the power to control lightning. She can launch a powerful lightning bolt at her enemies.

Current lvl: 10 MAXED

Ability: Deals 660% damage to one enemy

MP Cost: 6,000 MP

Cooldown Time: 10-seconds

Skill Name: Thunder Storm

Description: Kureha's second tail has the power to control lighting. By gathering magical power into her tail, she can create a massive thunderstorm that rains down on enemies from above.

Current lvl: 10 MAXED

Ability: Deals 580% damage to multiple enemies within a 10-yard radius

MP Cost: 7,000

Cooldown time: 10seconds

Skill Name: Blinding Flash

Description: This is not an attack. Kureha releases a flash of lightning so bright it blinds all the enemies around her. Does not affect allies.

Current lvl: 1

Ability points needed to reach next lvl: 15,000

Ability: Has a 50% chance of blinding enemies at the same level or lower

Has a 25% chance of blinding enemies 10 levels higher

Has a 10% chance of blinding enemies 20 levels higher

Has a 0% chance of blinding enemies 30 levels higher

Skill Name: Water Spear

Description: Kureha's third tail has the power to manipulate water. By manipulating water molecules in the air, she creates a spear that can pierce through all but the most powerful of substances.

Currently lvl: 10 MAXED

Ability: Deals 200% water damage

Ignores 60% of enemies' defenses

MP Cost: 3,000

Cooldown time: 5-seconds

Skill Name: Overflowing Cascade

Description: With the power of her third tail, Kureha draws a massive amount of water from the atmosphere and creates a waterfall that sweeps away her enemies.

Current lvl: 10 MAXED

Ability: Does 300% water damage

Has a 60% chance of sweeping away an enemy

Chance of sweeping enemy away decreases to 30% if the enemy's Constitution is higher than Kureha's

MP Cost: 5,000

Cooldown time: 10-seconds

Skill Name: Blinding Mist

Description: Kureha creates a thick mist that blinds enemies.

Current lvl: 9

Ability Points needed to reach next lvl: 3,500,000

Ability: Creates a mist with a 19-meter radius around Kureha

All enemies within the mist are affected by the blind status effect

Mist lasts for 60-seconds

MP Cost: 3,900

Cooldown time: 15-seconds

Skill Name: Beast Mode

Description: Kureha can transform into a large fox. Her size can vary depending on what she wants.

Ability: Kureha can transform into a fox

While in Beast Mode, all of her physical stats (i.e., Strength, Constitution, Dexterity, Physical Attack, Physical Defense, Hit-Rate, Dodge-Rate, Speed, and Movement) are doubled

Beast Mode lasts until Kureha decides to change into her human form

MP Cost: 10,000

Cooldown Time: 12-hours

Equipment:

Item Name: Child's Kimono

Item Type: Clothes

Grade: 1-Star

Use Requirements: Can only be worn by children.

Description: This kimono was fashioned from [Man Eating Spider] silk and has decent defensive capabilities.

Abilities: Physical Defense+50; Magical Defense+100

Adam took a moment to admire her new stats, which had grown so much after their dungeon clearing quest, then glanced at her skill list. All her skills were fairly impressive, but it was the skill at the bottom that really caught his attention. Beast Mode. It sounded like the kind of trump card ability people used when they were in a pinch. Unfortunately, he didn't think this skill would be all that useful since her Strength stat was honestly pathetic.

Maybe I should have focused on increasing her physical abilities too.

He pursed his lips. There was no use crying over spilled milk. Her Beast Mode was an incredible ability, but it wasn't some be all end all skill, and he still believed her magical abilities were far more useful.

He also noticed that she did indeed have an equipment list now, something she didn't have before. She was only wearing the [child's kimono], however, and he didn't know how much equipment she could use. Adam decided they would check out a store soon and get her some more defensible outfits and maybe even a weapon.

"I believe we should head out now," Adam stated. "We're going to split into groups of two, with me and Aris in one group and the rest of you in another. My goal is to help Aris reach level 20. I want the rest of you to continue doing your best to level up in the meantime."

"I hate to put a rain on your parade, but Kureha and I cannot be removed from your party." Titania crossed her arms. "I am the Guardian of the Spear, which means I can only be in the party of whoever wields the spear in your hand. And Kureha is your pet. She cannot be removed from your party."

"Haaah. I see." Adam ran his fingers over his mask and closed his eyes for just a moment. "Okay then. Aris, Titania, Kureha, and I will form one party. Meanwhile, Fayte, Susan, and Lilith will form another party. Let's head to the Guild Association and look for some quests we can take."

"Sounds good to me," Aris declared.

"I am fine with whatever decision you make," the quiet Lilith added.

"I-I'm fine with it too," Susan said.

Fayte smiled as she removed her veil from her inventory and placed it over her face. "It seems we're all in agreement, so what are we waiting for?"

✳✳✳

They arrived at the Guild Association and were met by Clarise, who once more took them to the room where they chose missions.

The room, he learned, was actually Clarise's office. It seemed when associate employees were assigned to work with a specific guild, they were given an office space that could be used for guild business.

On a side note, Clarise had been very shocked when they introduced Kureha to her.

Clarise set two stacks of papers down on the coffee table for them to peruse through. Adam could only gawk when he saw how many more missions there were today.

"Is it just me, or are there even more missions than usual?" asked Aris.

"That's only natural," Clarise said as she sat back down, smiling at the group. "Word of your feat spread not long after you returned. It isn't often someone goes toe-to-toe with a demon commander and wins. Because of that, a lot of people have sent quests specifically to you."

"So these are all quests where we have been requested?" asked Fayte.

"Not all of them." Clarise corrected with a headshake. She then gestured to the stack on their right. "These are the normal quests that anyone can take." She moved her hand until it was pointed at the other stack. "And these are quests that you have been personally requested to take."

Clarise had already explained the difference between these two types of quests. Generic quests, as they were called, were quests that anyone could take regardless of what guild they were from. Personal quests were ones that could only be accepted by a specific guild.

Aside from that, the difference between a generic quest and a personal one was the difficulty level. Personal quests often had an increased difficulty but offered higher rewards. Adam picked up a personal quest from the top of the stack, read it, then blinked.

"Please teach my son how to wield a spear. That's a pretty unusual quest. Let's see… the reward is… thirty million gold?! That's a bit surprising. However, it doesn't offer many experience points. Just a paltry one million."

While one million experience points sounded like a lot to normal people, to Adam, it was minuscule. A pittance. A drop in the bucket. One million experience points wouldn't even fill up one-hundredth of his experience gauge.

"There are some quests like that," Clarise said. "These quests are from members of the nobility. The Sun Continent has a number of aristocratic families that are very powerful and very wealthy. They're more than willing to spend millions on their children. Of course, because these are quests to teach, the amount of experience you earn is far less than a normal mission of this level."

Adam glanced at the mission level requirements… only to find none. Instead, the level requirements had been replaced with his name, meaning he was the only one who could accept this quest.

Since that was not his goal right now, Adam set the quest down and picked up another one. There were quite a few teaching requests. Not all of them were for him. There was one that requested Fayte come and teach some nobleman's daughter magic, another that requested Susan teach an archery class for students of the Hunter's School, and one that even asked Lilith to become a young noble's personal bodyguard. All of them were quests that paid a large amount of money but offered very little experience points.

They ignored those for now.

"Th-there are so many quests to teach," Susan muttered. "They even want me to teach people archery."

"I think there might be more quests for you than there are for the rest of us combined," Fayte added as she placed another quest on the stack of ones they had rejected. It was another quest for Susan to teach a nobleman's son archery.

"It is likely because of your class," Titania informed her. "The Fairy Archer class is one that has not been seen for thousands of years, after all. Not only is your class rare, but the Fairy Archer class is considered the best among all the archer classes available."

"S-so that's how it is," Susan muttered.

"One of the aspects of the Fairy Archer Class that makes it so powerful is both its versatility and the power of its skills. I'm sure you've noticed, but a lot of skills were made available to you after reaching level 20, and all of them are quite varied. There are skills that allow you to shoot targets from afar, skills that can ignore all of an enemy's defenses, and even skills that can offer a wide range barrage and area of effect attacks. As a Fairy Archer, you can choose to specialize in just one aspect of archery, or you can diversify yourself and become a jack of all trades. No other archer class offers such a wide range of skills."

Titania was puffing out her chest as she spoke, showing the pride she had for her race, though she certainly had a reason to be prideful. It was true that the Fairy Archer Class offered a lot of skills.

Adam had helped Susan choose her skills the other day, so he knew how many she had available to her.

The skills Adam had Susan learn were meant to make her into a more jack of all trades type. He wanted her to be capable of fighting at both close and long range. Perhaps it was a result of how he was trained, but Adam believed that versatility and adaptability trumped complete specialization. That was why he could also use daggers, blowguns, various forms of weaponry, hand-to-hand combat, and even a sword on top of the spear.

Of course, he was still better at the spear than anything else.

"Adam. Adam. What about this one? It's a request from Watershore's Mayor," Aris said, leaning into him and showing off the quest she had grabbed. Adam looked at it with her.

Request: Several dozen women have gone missing in Watershore and the city is under attack by [zombie pirates]. Your mission is to defeat the pirates and, if possible, rescue the women who have been kidnapped. Level Requirement: 45-50. Reward: 10,000,000 gold coins; 160,000,000 experience points.

Adam noticed how high the experience points reward was and decided this quest was perfect. He didn't know if they would be able to rescue the women since it depended on whether they were still alive, but someone wouldn't post a quest that was impossible to complete. At least, that was his hope.

***

It took one full day for Adam, Aris, Kureha, and Titania to reach Watershore. They rented out a pair of horses and rode through the day, stopping only to log off, eat, and use the restroom. Night had fallen by the time they reached Watershore.

"Halt! Who goes there?!"

A large group of guards was standing at the front gate when they arrived. The gates were closed at the moment. Torches lit the area around it, revealing two guards standing by the gate and even more standing on the crenelations above. The ones above had their bows pointed at Adam and his party.

"This is quite the rude welcome. Are they so nervous they have become incapable of showing common courtesy?" asked Titania with a huff.

Adam ignored the woman as he pulled the reins of his horse to stop it from continuing. He climbed off. Behind him was the horse with Aris and Kureha. The younger of the two was seated in front. Though they looked nothing alike, Adam could not help but think they looked like sisters.

"We mean you no harm," Adam said, announcing himself. "My name is Adam. I've come here because the Mayor of Watershore has requested my help."

"Ah! You're Adam?! THE Adam?!" one of the guards shouted.

"Uh… yes?" Adam said, taken aback.

"I can't believe it's really you!" The guard, a young man with brown hair and eyes, came over to him, expression shining in the firelight. "I wasn't able to see the tournament, but I heard all about it from a friend who lives in Solum. I'm so honored to meet you, sir! Will you shake my hand?!"

"Er, um, okay…"

Adam felt uncertainty creep into his gut as he shook the man's hand.

"Aaaaaah. This is great. I'm never washing this hand again."

"Please do. Wash it. Not washing your hands is unhygienic."

Adam felt an odd sense of déjà vu. Hadn't Fayte had to deal with something similar not long ago with Clarise?

"Humans are so weird," Titania muttered to herself. Adam said nothing, but he agreed with her.

"Idiot!"

The other guard came up beside them and whacked his companion on the back of his head. As his fellow guard nearly doubled over, Adam studied this one, who was far older and much more composed. His dark brown hair was flecked with silver. He had a thick beard, and his features were far more masculine than the youngster beside him. Both guards wore gleaming steel armor and carried swords at their hips.

"I apologize for my companion's… enthusiasm," the older guard said. According to the status screen above him, this man's name was Alfred, and the other man was Aleck.

"It's fine," Adam mumbled as Aris dismounted from her horse.

"Big Sister. Big Sister. Can you help me get down?" Kureha requested, holding out her hands.

"Of course. And… hup!" Aris smiled as he lifted Kureha off the horse and set her on the ground. The young fox yokai smoothed out her kimono, then wandered over to Adam, her fox ears twitching and her tail swaying.

"Holy crap! Is this little girl a beastman?! I thought they only existed on the Moon Continent!"

"Can it," Alfred said before addressing Adam again. "I don't mean to question your identity, but do you have proof that you are who you say you are?"

"Of course. I take it this should suffice?"

Adam removed the quest scroll from his inventory and handed it to the man, who read it over and nodded to himself.

"This does indeed suffice." Alfred handed the scroll back to Adam, who stored it in his inventory once more. "Since you've come here at the request of the mayor, please allow me to take you to him."

"Ah? Are you sure we can't meet with him tomorrow?" asked Aris.

"If this were a normal quest, meeting him tomorrow would be fine, but I'm afraid we don't have time for that," said Alfred. "The situation we're in right now is bad. Real bad. The mayor can explain it to you in greater detail, so for now, let's—"

Before the man was even able to finish talking, several loud bells began ringing from inside the city. Alfred's face paled as he whirled around. Even the overly enthusiastic Aleck looked more serious.

"Is that the emergency bell?" asked Adam.

"It is." Alfred's face grew graver and more severe by the second. "There is only one reason that bell would ring now. We are currently under attack." He turned to Adam and Aris. "I apologize for the inconvenience, but could I request your assistance in repelling these invaders?"

It was already quite late. They should have been eating dinner. Adam wanted to reject helping these people, but doing so might jeopardize his standing and the quest. People in this world couldn't be revived, after all, and that meant those who survived would hold a grudge against him for not helping when he could.

"Of course we'll help! Right, Adam?"

There was also the fact that Aris looked raring and ready to go. She seemed more than ready to fight off a horde of invading pirates.

"You heard the lady. We'll help out," Adam said with a wry smile.

"We cannot thank you enough. The pirates are probably attacking the harbor, so please head over there," Alfred said before he placed two fingers in his mouth and whistled. With that, the guards stationed at the top began working a lever, and the massive gates slowly opened with the creaking of gears.

UNDEAD PIRATE ATTACK

“ “They be attacking the ships! Don't let them scallywags get away with this, arrrrrg!”

“Arrrg! Attack our ships, will ye?! I'll send yeh straight to the bottom of the sea!”

“What are these things?! There's no way they can be human!”

Davy Jones growled as the sounds of combat and shouts of fear rang out all around him. Ever since the young lass who trounced him in combat left, he and his crew had turned over a new leaf and become respectable members of society. They'd done their time, paid their fines, and now belonged to a small trading company that was willing to take a group of former pirates in. He thought they had been doing well for themselves.

But all that was in threat of sinking to the bottom of the sea.

The harbor was under attack.

Davy Jones backpedaled as he was assaulted by two pirates. They could not be called regular pirates. Indeed. Normal was not a word he would use to describe these two, or the others that were attacking the harbor. Their skin was sallow, pale, and smelled rancid—clearly dead flesh. It hung off their emaciated frames, which were covered in tattered trousers and shirts. Neither of his foes had eyes. Sitting within their sockets were burning red flames.

[Zombie Pirate]. That was the name of the creatures they were facing.

"Take this, ye scurvy cur!"

With surprisingly nimble feet, Davy Jones stepped forward, dodged a swinging sword, and swung his own blade. He activated his special skill. [Bisection] was an ability unique to him. It was a skill that cut all the way through someone, dividing them into two separate parts. With his skill activated, he sliced through the [zombie pirate] like it was made of paper mache. The two chunks fell to the ground with meaty thuds.

He expected that to be the end of his foe and turned to face the other one.

The second [zombie pirate] was already mid-swing, so Davy Jones raised his sword to block, sparks flying from their clanging weapons. He activated [riposte], parrying the attack before stabbing his sword into his opponent's throat. This would have been enough to kill a normal enemy. His current enemy was not alive, however, and so the attack did nothing but gain him some time.

Following through with his first attack, Davy Jones took two steps forward and used [slash] followed by [thrust]. The [zombie pirate] fell back as wounds became visible on its body. Yet no matter how much damage Davy Jones did, his foe refused to fall.

He sensed movement behind him. After parrying an attack, Davy Jones whirled around to find the [zombie pirate] he thought he had killed already standing. The two halves were whole again. It swung the sword in its grasp. Davy Jones had no choice but to evade since [parry] was cooling down. Yet the moment he moved out of the way, something powerful slashed into his back, causing him to stagger forward. It was the other [zombie pirate].

"Ye foul beasts! Gangin' up on a pirate like this'll be the last thing ye do!"

Despite his bravado, Davy Jones was very quickly pushed back. There was nothing he could do against an undead monster that could regenerate—never mind two. Attack after attack rained down upon him. His health dropped like a treasure chest sinking to the bottom of the sea, his sword was soon knocked from his hands, and he was forced to his knees. The two [zombie pirates], now looming over him, raised their swords high to deliver the finishing blow.

Was this it?

Was this the end?

Davy Jones might have been a fearless pirate, but he didn't want to die here, and yet he couldn't think of anything to do that would get him out of this situation. All he could do was accept his demise.

It really is a pity. Just when I thought I could turn over a new leaf...

Davy Jones did not close his eyes in the face of approaching death, for the pirate understood that death was just an old companion he walked beside for all his life. It was unfortunate. However, it seemed his old friend was coming to collect his dues.

Yet just when Davy Jones thought death would come for him, both [zombie pirates] lost their arms, heads, and even their legs. It happened so fast that Davy Jones thought he missed something. One second he was about to die. The next his two foes were lying in pieces. He was so shocked he nearly missed the young woman standing before him.

"You okay?" she asked.

He gawked.

The young woman before him was a beautiful lass dressed in something that resembled the belly dancers of the Earth Continent. She wore a skirt that trailed down to her ankles, but there were slits going up either side to reveal a glimpse of her fine legs. Her top was nothing more than a fitted bra. It didn't cover her white stomach or creamy cleavage at all. She wore a veil that covered the lower half of her face, and there were a pair of swords being gripped in her hands.

Davy Jones felt tears sting his eyes.

He knew this young lass.

"L-Lady Aris! Ye've returned!"

"Huh?" Aris blinked like she couldn't understand what he was saying, but then she squinted her eyes at him for several seconds before making a surprised exclamation. "Oh! You're Davy Jones, aren't you?"

"Aye! I'm glad ye remembered me."

"What are you doing here?"

"Protectin' the harbor, arrg. These damn [zombie pirates] be attacking us night and day."

"That's not what I—you know what? Never mind. Anyway, if you're protecting the harbor, you should do a better job. Letting these wimps get the better of you is pathetic."

"Yer words are harsh as always."

Davy Jones laughed as he climbed to his feet, picked up his sword, and prepared to fight again. Seeing the young lass had renewed his resolve. He wasn't the only one. Several of the pirates who had been with him saw Aris appear and let loose a loud cheer. They began attacking the [zombie pirates] with fiercer zeal, as if they had a goddess of war at their backs.

Among the crew and soldiers defending the harbor, one person was mowing down [zombie pirates] like nobody's business. He cut them down within seconds, leaving behind a line of corpses in his wake.

That person was none other than Adam.

***

-179,550; -179,550!

The moment he arrived to find the chaos taking place in the harbor, Adam initiated his attack with [Blood Sacrifice] and [Energy Sweep]. A powerful blue wave of energy erupted from his spear and swept over the [zombie pirates]. The attack, enhanced by both him and Titania's [Song of Vigor], dealt enough damage to drop the [zombie pirates'] health to zero. Nearly two dozen enemies were felled in a split second.

Adam was like a whirlwind as he attacked with several of his most powerful skills, which were far stronger now than they ever had been. Upgrading them all so much had been the right decision. Like this, he could easily mow down multiple foes in quick succession, even if they were several levels higher than his own.

Name: Zombie Pirate

Description: A pirate who died at sea and was brought to life through necromancy. This undead pirate will attack relentlessly until its enemy is dead. Be warned, this type of zombie will reanimate over and over until you kill the one who turned them.

Class: 1-Star

Lvl: 45

Health: 100,000/100,000

MP: 45,000/60,000

Strength: +1,000

Constitution: +1,500

Dexterity: +450

Intelligence: +10

Speed: +50

Resistances:
Fire: -50%
Light: -100%
Water: 50%
Healing: -12,000%

Skills:
Skill Name: Slash
Description: A basic skill where the [zombie pirate] swings its sword.
100% damage
MP Cost: 1,000
Cooldown Time: 0-seconds

Skill Name: Thrust
Description: A basic thrusting attack.
160% damage
MP Cost: 2,000
Cooldown Time: 5-seconds

The [zombie pirate] didn't have many attacks, but it had a lot of health, some very impressive stats, and it also couldn't be killed, which presented a huge problem. Adam looked behind him and grimaced when he saw the other [zombie pirates] he had killed getting back to their feet. Another glance around revealed Aris some distance away, dancing around a series of attacks and returning them with her own.

"Kureha! Open a path to Aris! Use fire attacks!"

"You got it, Big Brother!"

Adam would never get over Kureha calling him "Big Brother," but he said nothing as the fox yokai unleashed [Firestorm] from her first tail. The attack was... incredible. Instead of a simple wave bursting from her tail, it looked like an inferno had swept out and overtaken all the enemies in their path. The intense blaze was so hot that it scorched the ground, leaving charred stone in its wake.

-64,296; -64,296!

That was to say nothing for the damage she did. Adam had never seen anyone deal damage to so many in a single attack before. This was a result of her abilities being upgraded. These [zombie pirates] were also weak to fire, which meant they did two times more damage than normal.

As the flames dissipated, Adam saw that all the [zombie pirates] who had been trapped within the blaze were now on fire. Flames flickered all around them, dealing a constant stream of damage that further dropped their health.

Not one to miss an opportunity, Adam led Kureha and Titania to Aris, who was like the wind as she used her ridiculously high Movement stat to dart around the battlefield, helping people who were in trouble. Thanks to her, many of the soldiers and former pirates who had been on the verge of losing were able to reclaim their lost morale.

One thing Adam was surprised to see as he made his way to Aris was that it wasn't just NPCs who were taking part in this battle. There were a number of players also defending the harbor from attack. A young woman dressed in full body armor and carrying a massive kite shield was absorbing damage and pulling aggro as her two comrades attacked the [zombie pirates] she drew to herself. The one on her left was an assassin clad in black. He twirled the dagger in his hand and attacked with all his might. The other was a mage who launched fireballs from her staff.

Unfortunately, none of them were at a level high enough to do more than become fodder. They died rather quickly. Adam shook his head. Those people probably hadn't been higher than level 18 or so, but how could they have known about the power of these monsters? It didn't look like any of them could use [Scan] like Titania.

"Aris!" Adam called out.

"Ah! Adam! There you are. I was wondering when you would join me."

Adam almost rolled his eyes, but he refrained and instead told her about his discovery. "Listen, these aren't normal zombies. They were revived through necromancy. According to their description, they will keep coming back to life until we kill the one who reanimated them."

Aris was unable to say anything at first. Several dozen [zombie pirates] were closing in from all sides. The three of them—Adam,

Aris, and Kureha—formed a triangle with their backs to each other. In the middle of their group was Titania, who continued to sing.

Kureha let loose with another [Firestorm], which erupted like a furnace on high and burnt several [zombie pirates] to ash, though like magic, they just reformed from the ashes and attacked again.

"Whaaat? So that didn't beat you guys! Fine. Take this!"

Kureha held out her hand as flames swirled around it, forming a whip, which she grabbed a hold of and swung. The whip tore through a [zombie pirate] like its body was made of toilet paper. The two halves caught fire as they fell to the ground and burst into ash. Kureha didn't stop attacking after defeating one of them and attacked all the others on her side.

On the other side, Adam unleashed another [Energy Sweep], which overtook the enemy like a hurricane, the blue energy slicing into them and continuing on to deal damage to more enemies. While his attack did not contain the [zombie pirates'] elemental weakness, he did so much damage that a single technique was enough to drop every monsters' health to zero.

-2,100; -2,100; -2,100; -2,100; -8,400; -2,100; -2,100; -2,100; -2,100; -2,100; -2,100; -2,100; -2,100; -2,100; -2,100; -2,100; -8,400; -8,400; -2,100; -2,100; -2,100; -2,100; -2,100; -2,100; -8,400; -2,100; -2,100; -2,100; -2,100; -2,100; -8,400; -2,100; -2,100; -2,100; -2,100; -2,100; -2,100; -2,100; -2,100; -2,100; -2,100; -8,400; -8,400; -8,400; -2,100; -2,100; -2,100; -2,100; -2,100; -2,100; -2,100; -2,100; -2,100; -2,100!

Aris could not deal nearly as much damage as Adam or Kureha, but what she lacked in strength, she made up for in the sheer number of attacks she could unleash. After activating the [Blade Dance] skill, Aris danced around her enemies and swung the swords in her hands like extensions of her body. Damage signs began floating over the [zombie pirates] as Aris cut into them so quickly that their health dropped to zero in less than a second.

Yet for as much damage as they dealt, Adam knew it was only a matter of time before they were overwhelmed. The enemies they had already slain were rising again. Just fighting like this wasn't going to be enough to defeat them.

"Titania, can you find the person who reanimated these [zombie pirates]?" he asked.

Titania had no choice but to stop singing as she was addressed to answer Adam. He felt her power leave him as [Song of Vigor] ceased. The amount of damage he could do now was less than before, but that was fine for now.

"I can do my best, but do we even know what we're looking for?"

"We're looking for anyone who is acting suspiciously. Look nearby for people hiding in the shadows. If you can't find anyone, then expand your search radius until you do. Me, Aris, and Kureha will do our best to hold these monsters off until you return."

"Okay. Don't die on me," Titania said before flying high into the air and disappearing.

"Are you sure that was a good idea?" asked Aris.

He shrugged. "Not much we can do right now. We need to find the culprit, and she's the only one who can move freely right now. Anyway, get ready. The [zombie pirates] have regenerated."

Just like Adam had said, the [zombie pirates] they had already slain were back and ready for more. They surged forward like a school of fish. Adam soon found himself trapped within the throes of combat. He unleashed another [Energy Sweep] upon the horde, but his attack didn't do nearly as much damage now that Titania was gone and [Blood Sacrifice] had entered its cooldown time.

-19,950; -19,950!

Despite the fact that his attacks barely took a fifth of his opponents' health, Adam continued to attack, adopting the Form One stance and unleashing his newest attack. [Form One] was a skill based on the Form One stance of the Pleonexia Family's Seven Forms Style. Immediately after spreading his legs apart, Adam thrust out his spear hundreds of times in quick succession. So fast were his attacks that multiple spear shadows appeared all around him. It was as if several dozen spears were all attacking at the same time.

-13,300; -13,300!

Though [Form One] was only at level 1 and didn't do much damage per attack, it was a skill that attacked over and over again, allowing him to attack one enemy dozens of times without pause.

The only way to stop it was to disrupt it with an attack or for Adam to cancel the skill or run out of MP. He could also remain in the [Form One] stance for as long as he wished. It was more like changing attack styles than an attack itself.

Of course, as was the case with all attacks, this one came with its own set of weaknesses.

While the amount of damage he did was enough to reduce his enemy's health to zero, the other [zombie pirates] swarmed over him from all sides. Adam was forced to move out of [Form One] and unleash an [Energy Sweep].

-19,950; -19,950!

Once more, the amount of damage he did was negligible, barely a fifth of what his enemies possessed. Several of the [zombie pirates] came in and attacked. He blocked several sword swings by spinning his spear around in the Form Three style, though this wasn't a skill. It was just a regular block, which meant it was limited.

-1,000!

-1,000!

-1,000!

-1,000!

Adam was forced back as his health was reduced to 2,500/8,600. He kicked a [zombie pirate] in the chest, making it stumble into its comrades, removed a [high-grade health potion] from his inventory, and downed it in one go. It wasn't enough to bring his health back to full, so he downed another one. The [zombie pirates] were closing in once more, so after his health reached full, he adopted Form Five and decided to focus on defense instead of attack.

Behind him, Kureha and Aris were doing the same, and just like him, they were struggling. Aris lightly danced around several attacks, but there were so many zombies that one of them managed to slip through and wound her. A large -1,000 appeared above her head as she stumbled back. Even though she was injured, she didn't stop and continued to attack. More damage signs appeared above her. She retreated, downed two [high-grade health potions], then attacked again.

The one who had it hardest of all was Kureha. She had only recently gained her human form and therefore didn't know how to move very well. A scream of pain escaped her as two attacks slashed into her clothes. Gritting her teeth as tears formed in her eyes, she created another [Fire Whip] and attacked every enemy before her. The flames slashed into zombie flesh. Each attack removed a body part. Yet the [zombie pirates] continued to come.

"ADAM!"

Just as Adam was getting ready to cut his losses and order them to retreat, Titania flew down from overhead.

"Did you find him? The person responsible for this?"

"I believe so." Titania was hovering a little above Adam as she pointed away from the harbor, toward the ocean. "There is a small raft several klicks off the harbor. A woman dressed in a gaudy outfit was on the raft, chanting something under her breath. There are a few [zombie pirates] with her."

Adam clicked his tongue as he realized what that meant. There was no way they could attack her if she was that far out. This was just great.

"What if we use one of those canons?" asked Aris, pointing toward a ship. It was a bit larger than the average vessel, with three masts, a large deck, and several dozen cannons. This must have been a war vessel. It was painted in the colors of Watershore, that was to say it bore the symbol of Watershore on its flags and hull.

"It's worth a shot! Come on!" Adam shouted.

Now that they had a plan, the group of three moved cohesively toward the ship, fighting their way through [zombie pirates] with fire, swords, and spear. It took longer than Adam would have liked, and he nearly died on several occasions, but they eventually made it to the ship.

Aris ran aboard as Adam and Kureha defended the boarding ramp. She loaded the cannon with some gunpowder from below deck, placed a cannonball inside, and pushed the cannon until it was aimed at the small raft, which she could just barely see.

"How's it look, Titania?" she asked.

"I think your aim is accurate. Go ahead and fire," Titania commanded.

"Okay! Fire in the hole!"

Aris struck the cannon with her sword, creating sparks that lit the wick. The cannon went off seconds later with a loud *boom* that nearly deafened her. She covered her ears and watched the cannonball fly through the air and strike the water a few feet from the raft. She clicked her tongue, loaded the cannon again, adjusted her aim, and fired once more.

She missed again.

While her attacks didn't hit, her actions had not gone unnoticed. The raft had been rocked by the explosions of water. Whoever was on it realized that she was being attacked and began retreating. Likewise, the [zombie pirates] that had been attacking the harbor were also retreating.

"A-are they leaving?!"

"W-we managed to beat them back… somehow."

As the people defending the harbor realized their enemies were retreating, several loud cheers went up. Adam paid no attention to the cheers as an announcement screen appeared before him.

Ding!

[Congratulations! You have defeated 200 [zombie pirates]. Items dropped: x120 [steel cutlass], x50 [soggy boots], and 600,000 gold coins. +30,550,000 experience points.]

Ding!

[Congratulations! Aris has leveled up! She is now at level 19! +400 HP! +40 MP! +5 SP!]

As the announcement that Aris had leveled up was made, Adam felt a brief moment of happiness. The goal of this quest was to help Aris reach level 20. Now she was just one level away from their goal. He imagined she would reach level 20 or maybe even 21 if they completed this quest.

He was a little curious about how they defeated those [zombie pirates]. Technically, they had kept reviving over and over, so he didn't think they would have earned any experience from them, but perhaps the act of killing them over and over had given them more experience than they would have gotten otherwise? He mulled that over as Aris raced down the boarding ramp and threw her arms around him.

"We did it!" she cheered.

"We did it, Big Brother!" Kureha also cheered as she latched onto his leg.

"Hmph. You never would have been able to win had I not acted as your scout. I hope you appreciate the danger I put myself in," added Titania, who crossed her arms as she floated before him.

"You are right. Thank you, Titania," Adam said sincerely.

Titania's cheeks turned bright red at his gratitude. She turned her head and huffed. "S-so long as you are aware of my contribution. A-anyway, you are, um, welcome."

For as arrogant as Titania was, she did not take compliments well. He was tempted to tease her about it. He refrained. Even as they stood there, celebrating, several people were coming over to them. He spotted the pirate captain who had escorted Aris to Watershore when she first left the Village of Beginnings. He wasn't alone. Walking alongside him was a man dressed in silver armor that was dented and scratched, though Adam imagined it would have looked quite magnificent without all that battle damage.

"Looks like the welcoming committee is here," Aris said.

"Seems that way." Adam took a deep breath, then adjusted his mask. "Well, let's see what these people want."

THE PLAN TO SAVE WATERSHORE

The man in the dented armor introduced himself as Captain Raiker. He was the leader of all the soldiers stationed at Watershore. He struck Adam as a classic hard ass, the kind of by-the-books leader who was really good at what he did but had a "my way or the highway" approach to dealing with subordinates. Fortunately, because he was such a stickler for protocols and rules, Adam, Aris, Kureha, and Titania did not have to deal with him for long. They were led to the mayor's office shortly after his introduction.

Derek Waterton greeted Adam and Aris with a beaming smile as they entered his office. He wasn't the only one present. A younger man who looked like Derek but twenty years in the past was also present. This must have been his son, who Adam was directly responsible for helping cure.

"When I heard that you had returned to help, my heart became at ease. Thank you for helping defend the city."

"You're welcome," Aris said. Her cheerful voice caused the younger man to look her way, and Adam did not appreciate the look he sent his lover. He glared at the boy for several seconds—the time it took the mayor's son to realize he was close to death and look away.

"It wasn't a problem," Adam added after making sure the mayor's son wasn't stripping his lover with those lecherous eyes. "We were asked by the Guild Association to come, so this is all just in a day's work. That said, we are hoping you can tell us a bit more about the situation."

"Yes. Yes. I will definitely tell you about the predicament we have found ourselves in." Mayor Waterton dabbed at his forehead with a handkerchief as he began his tale. "It all started a few days ago when several people went missing. We didn't think much of it at first. People go missing all the time. Some fall into the water and drown, and others vanish out at sea. However, it soon became clear that something was odd about the people who went missing."

"What was odd about it?" asked Adam.

"The people who went missing were women, right?" asked Titania.

"Yes," Mayor Waterton confessed.

"I knew it."

"What's so odd about that?" asked Aris.

"Allow me to explain," Titania said before the mayor could speak further. The tiny woman flitted around until she was floating before Adam and Aris, coughed into her mouth, and explained what she knew. "There are certain dark rituals that can only be used by performing incredible acts of cruelty and evil. For example, there was once a dark magician who created a gateway to the Underworld by sacrificing pregnant women and their unborn children. This vile act tore apart the boundaries between our world and the Underworld, allowing minions of evil to invade the world until a group of brave heroes vanquished the dark mage and closed the gate. There are other, similar rituals that can only be activated with female sacrifices, the blood of male virgins, or torturing children."

"This is getting a lot darker than I expected," Aris muttered.

Adam nodded. This was a game that mostly avoided violence and didn't even have a bloodshed feature. Of course, he remembered the goblins from the Village of Beginnings. Titania had said they were creatures that made themselves seem harmless at first, then began kidnapping women and raping them to produce offspring. It was enough to make Adam wonder what sort of rating this series would have under the old ESRB.

"I'm guessing the women who went missing were used in a ritual of some kind?" asked Adam.

"So we assume." Mayor Waterton ran a hand through his hair. "It was several days after nearly a dozen women went missing that we suddenly began getting attacked by [zombie pirates]."

"It sounds to me like that woman I saw on the raft used a mass reanimation ritual to resurrect several hundred pirates as undead," Titania concluded, crossing her arms. "That is a highly complex spell that requires multiple human sacrifices to empower it."

"So it doesn't have to be women specifically?" asked Aris.

Titania shook her head. "It does not. The fact that only women were kidnapped simply means this killer prefers killing women."

So they had a deranged psychopath who kidnapped a bunch of women and sacrificed them in a ritual to reanimate the dead because she disliked women? That made sense. Adam almost sighed as he realized they were probably dealing with a psychopathic serial killer.

"Titania, I couldn't see the woman very well during the fight. What can you tell me about her?" he asked.

"I can tell you that she was not human," Titania said. "Her skin was blue, and she had four arms. I believe she is what you would call an Asura. Asuras are a type of demon who served under the [War Demon]. They are traditionally very good fighters and have strong magical abilities. Killing her isn't going to be easy."

Adam wanted to groan. First [Andras] and now this Asura lady? He was beginning to suspect all this movement from the demons meant the War Demon was on the move once more. Was this for an upcoming event? Limited time events were a fairly classic way of keeping people interested in playing a specific game, but he didn't think it was needed for this one.

"We can figure out more about our adversary when we do some reconnaissance," Adam decided. "For now, I would like to see if we can discover our enemy's location. Mayor Waterton, can you bring out a map of the surrounding waters? I'd like to see if there are any islands located a few klicks offshore."

"Certainly, we have several such maps. I'll have my son grab one for us," Mayor Waterton said.

Mayor Waterton's son nearly jumped at being addressed, but he was quick to rush out of the room and come back several minutes later with a large scroll in hand. It was a highly detailed map of the ocean surrounding the Sun Continent. There were a lot of markings on it showing the various trade routes.

"There are quite a few islands located off the coast of Watershore. I'll mark them for you now." As Mayor Waterton began marking the different islands on the map, Adam, Aris, and Titania tried to figure out which among those islands their wayward Asura was hiding.

After looking at the map for several hours, Adam, Aris, Titania, and Mayor Waterton were able to determine that the Asura woman was probably hiding out in one of three islands. They were located exactly fifteen, twenty, and twenty-two klicks away from Watershore and were known as Angel's Isle, Devil's Horns, and Phoenix Island. Their names came from their respective shapes, apparently.

These were the only islands close enough for someone to attack Watershore every night and retreat every morning. There were other islands, of course, but they were too far away for someone to travel with a horde of [zombie pirates].

"So we know their possible location. The only question I have now is how they're traveling here?" Titania muttered. "I didn't see any ships they could have been on. All that woman had was a raft, but there's no way something so small can safely carry her across the sea."

"She might have a ship hidden nearby." Adam shrugged. "We're not going to find out by just standing here. Let's get some sleep and head to those islands tomorrow."

"You realize we're going to need to board a ship to reach those islands, right?"

"Urk!"

Adam felt a sudden lurch in his stomach as he realized that, indeed, they would be on a boat. He still remembered the last time he was on a boat. The sensation of vertigo and the feeling of his contents spilling from his stomach hadn't gone away even after all this time. He didn't want to go through that again. He *really* didn't. But it wasn't like he had a choice. They needed to reach these islands, find the Asura woman, and defeat her.

"I feel like I'm missing something here," Aris muttered.

"You're not the only one," Kureha said. "Big Brother? What's Big Sister Titania talking about?"

"She's not talking about anything," Adam said, gently stroking the little fox yokai's ears. He soon realized that her ears were definitely her weakness. Kureha practically melted at his touch. Her face became slack, her shoulders slumped as she leaned into his hand, and her three tails wagged back and forth with exaggerated motions.

Mayor Waterton stared at the child as if just now noticing her. "Pardon me, young hero, but is that a beastman child?"

"Not quite." Titania was the one who answered him. "Kureha is a fox yokai—a divine messenger of the Moon Goddess, though you could technically classify her as a beastman."

"I see."

The look on Mayor Waterton's face spoke volumes about his feelings on the subject of beastmen, and it was a look Adam didn't appreciate, but it didn't seem like he was going to cause them any trouble either. If he did, then Adam wouldn't hesitate to cut this man down. He wouldn't let anyone harm a member of his party.

Once everything had been decided, Adam, Aris, Titania, and Kureha got themselves a room at one of the inns. It was a quaint place called the Sailor's Retreat. The rooms were one hundred fifty gold per night. Adam listened to the stairs creak as they traveled up them, wandered down the hall, and entered their room, which was little more than a seventy-five square meter space with a bed, dresser, and nightstand.

"Let's go back to our world. I'm hungry." Aris rubbed her stomach as she spoke as if to emphasize her hunger.

"Agreed. We didn't get to eat dinner," Adam said.

"Hmph. I suppose Kureha and I will just sleep here," Titania said.

"Awww. Are you guys going back home?" asked Kureha.

"We don't have much of a choice." Aris smiled as she leaned down and stroked Kureha's head. "Our real bodies are in another world, and they need maintenance to stay alive. We've got to eat and sleep properly."

"I understand," Kureha said, though her ears drooped, and her tails hung limply as she spoke.

While Adam did feel a bit bad for the girl, they couldn't remain here, and so he and Aris logged off. The last they saw of Kureha and Titania was of the two climbing into the bed. Then they were back in Fayte's apartment. The lights were off and Fayte wasn't anywhere to be seen.

Adam stood up as Aris stretched her arms above her head and yawned. He found a note on the coffee table, which read *"I figured you and Aris were doing something, so I didn't want to disturb you. There is dinner in the fridge. Please eat it when you log off."* Adam felt the smile pull at his lips as warmth spread through his chest at Fayte's thoughtfulness.

"Looks like Fayte made us dinner."

"Really?" Aris perked up.

"Yeah. Hang on a moment. I'll get it."

Adam went into the kitchen, grabbed two plates, two forks, and two glasses for water, then looked in the fridge. There were quite a few ingredients. What grabbed Adam's attention was the quiche wrapped in saran wrap. It looked like someone had already taken a slice out of it. He pulled the quiche out, undid the wrap, and cut two slices for him and Aris before serving it on the plate.

Aris's eyes lit up in delight when he returned and placed the food on the coffee table. Her stomach gurgled as she grabbed the plate and dug in. The moan of delight that escaped her sweet lips made Adam twitch, but he held back his desires... for now.

Once they had finished eating, Adam and Aris headed back into their bedroom. They were already in their pajamas, so they just climbed into bed. Aris lay on her side. Adam scooted closer until he was properly spooning the young woman, who wiggled her butt against his crotch.

"Minx. You're doing that on purpose."

"So you can tell. Hee-hee. What can I say? I'm horny."

"I can't believe you can say something like that so casually."

Despite his words, Adam was also feeling it, which explained why he slid his hand around to Aris's front, let it glide down her stomach, and cupped her crotch over her clothes. He began rubbing her from outside her clothes. Aris's breathing picked up a hitch as he stroked her. She arched her back against him and turned her head to stare into his eyes.

"Adam… haaah… make me feel good."

"That's one command I can't ignore."

Adam slipped his hand into Aris's pants and panties until he felt her smooth, bare skin, then her nether lips. He slowly rubbed his index finger along the length of her outer labia, applying gentle pressure. Then he spread her lips apart. He couldn't see what he was doing, but he judged his actions by the moans of his companion. Aris had closed her eyes and was breathing like she was jogging a marathon. After simply petting for, he found her clit and stroked it with rough circles.

"Ooooh! Adam! Li-like that! Haaah… mmmmm! That's… exactly what I want! F-feels sho good!"

"You're slurring."

"S'your fault… that I'm… ahhn… like this!"

Adam chuckled before he leaned down and began planting kisses on her neck. Aris tilted her head to give him more access to her skin, and he took complete advantage of that to nip and lick all of her pleasure points. At the same time, he rubbed and even pinched her clit until her entire body was shaking from an orgasm.

Her skin had warmed up by now. Adam could feel the heat from her body against his chest, feel the slickness of her skin as sweat droplets formed. It sent a thrill through his body.

Aris turned around, eyes hooded with desire, mouth parted in an expression so erotic it left him breathless. She smiled at him, but it wasn't her typical vibrant smile. Seductive. Sensual. This was a succubus's smile, and it enraptured him.

"You realize there's no way I'm going to sleep now, right?" she asked.

"I might have had an idea this would happen," Adam confessed.

"Good."

Like that, Aris rolled them over until he was lying on his back and she was straddling his waist, slowly lowering herself onto his cock. They spent the rest of their night locked in passion.

✳✳✳

Adam and Aris logged into *Age of Gods* after having breakfast with Fayte. They appeared within their room and were met with a sleeping Kureha and Titania. While Titania was simply resting on the pillow as if it were a bed, Kureha had buried herself inside the covers and curled into a ball.

"Awwwww. That is just too cute," Aris said in a whisper.

"It is," Adam agreed. Despite his words, he showed no hesitation in walking over to the bed and waking the pair up. "Come on, you two. It's time to get a start on our day."

"Mmmmm… is it morning already?" Titania woke up first, sitting up and rubbing her eyes. She glanced out the window to find the sun was just rising into the sky, grunted, and fluttered her wings until she could fly over to Adam's shoulder, which was basically her perch now. "If you ask me, it's still way too early for us to start doing anything."

"You should be used to this by now," Adam said.

"Being used to something does not mean I have to like it," was the quick retort.

"Big Brother? Big Sister? Morning," Kureha greeted next. She sat up in bed and cutely rubbed her eyes before looking at them both.

"Good morning, Kureha," Aris greeted.

"Are you ready?" asked Adam.

"Um. Kureha is ready," Kureha said.

With everyone ready, the group left the inn and journeyed over to the docks, where they were to meet someone who would be joining them on this mission. The early morning air was crisp and clean. Adam took a deep breath as he watched the sleepy harbor wake up. Bakers were beginning to bake their bread, and apprentices were helping them set everything up. Most of the stores were still closed. They wouldn't open until later when the streets became busy with people.

The docks were full of activity when they arrived. Sailors were loading crates and barrels onto a ship. Standing before the ship was a man dressed in armor. The armor was no longer dented and scratched, but shone with the vibrancy of silver. Now that it had been repaired, Adam could see the designs etched into the surface. There was a woman standing underneath a sun on the front. That must have been the Sun Goddess Stella.

"You're finally here," Captain Raiker said with a grunt.

"Someone's impatient," Aris muttered under her breath, though it was loud enough for the good captain to hear her. His glare was quite something to behold, but Aris just stuck out her tongue and pulled her eyelid down at him.

"Keep glaring at Aris and I'll skewer you upon my spear like a rotisserie. Are preparations ready?" asked Adam.

The man grimaced at Adam's very graphic threat, but he nodded nonetheless. "Everything is ready. We can leave at a moment's notice."

"Then let's not waste any time," Adam said. "I want to get this over with."

"You just don't want to be on a ship for any longer than necessary," Titania said with a snort.

Adam clicked his tongue. On the other hand, Kureha looked between the two, then tugged on Adam's pants.

"Big Brother. Big Brother. Are we going on a boat?"

He tried hard not to grimace. "We are."

"Aaaah! Yay! Kureha has never been on a boat before!"

Seeing the girl get so excited over the prospect of riding on a boat gave Adam mixed feelings. He did not want to get on another boat if he could help it. Just thinking about riding on a ship that he knew would make him seasick made him feel sick, but he didn't want to dampen the little girl's excitement, so he put on a brave face.

The group bordered the vessel alongside Captain Raiker and a crew of sailors. Most of them were dressed in plain steel armor, chestplates, gauntlets, and greaves that marked them as soldiers, but much to Adam's surprise, there were also several pirates onboard. Among them was Davy Jones, the pirate captain who Aris had beat the snot out of and forced to ferry her across the ocean.

"Lady Aris, looks like we'll be ferryin' ya across the sea again, aye," Davy Jones said with a toothy grin.

"Seems that way," Aris said with a grin of her own. "Looks like I'll be in your care again."

"Our goddess has returned!"

"Praise be for the return of our goddess!"

"All hail Aris!"

Davy Jones wasn't the only one excited. All of his men were cheering upon seeing Aris once more. The soldiers who were also going with them looked confused, like they couldn't understand what about Aris made these men so excited, though some of them seemed to at least have an inkling as they studied Aris decked out in her belly dancer outfit.

Adam wouldn't say it out loud, but he really wished she would cover up more. He didn't want anyone else seeing so much of her skin.

The ship soon began moving under Davy Jones' command. Adam tried to ignore the sudden lurch as the ship left the harbor, but his feet were unsteady, and so he soon found himself leaning over the side of the vessel and regurgitating the contents of his stomach. Aris was rubbing his back.

"I had no idea you got seasickness, Adam."

"Ugh… please don't say anything."

"Pffft! Heheheheheheh…"

"Stuff it, Titania!"

"Don't worry about it. I think it's cute."

"Urk… that just makes me feel worse, Aris."

"Big Brother, are you not feeling well?"

"Your big brother apparently has a problem with seafaring vessels," said Titania.

"Really?"

Adam was unable to ignore his seasickness, and the conversation among the three girls around him was just making it worse. Aris seemed to intuit this, fortunately, and she led him to the captain's cabin—gracefully provided by Davy Jones. There she had him lay down with his head on her lap and stroked his hair and face.

Adam closed his eyes. He didn't know why, but being in this position just made him feel so much better. The sweet sensation of Aris's soft thighs and the feeling of her delicate fingers running through his hair and over his face was something he couldn't get enough of. He wished this moment would last forever.

"How long do you think it will take to reach the first island?" asked Aris.

Adam didn't have an answer, but Titania did. "The closest island is Angel Isle. It is fifteen klicks from Watershore. Vessels like this can travel anywhere between five and eight knots depending on the size of the vessel, the route, and the weather."

One knot was roughly two kilometers per hour, which meant five knots was about ten kilometers per hour. Angel Isle was fifteen klicks away, so assuming they traveled at five knots, they would reach it within an hour and a half.

Just as Adam predicted, it took maybe a little over one and a half hours. Adam forced his body back into motion and walked onto the deck. The rocking of the boat made him want to hurl, but he forced the sickness back with sheer willpower and stared at the island visible in the distance.

He could understand why it was called Angel Isle. The island wasn't too big, maybe a couple of kilometers from one side to the other, but a large mountain sat in the very center of the island. Two large cliffs jutting from either side were roughly shaped like angel wings, deformed though they were. It made him think that perhaps that mountain had at one point been a statue that crumbled after thousands of years. Whatever the case was, the mountain was now overgrown with greenery like grass, flora, and a variety of trees.

"So that's the first island we're checking," Aris said.

"Yes. Angel Isle." Titania crossed her arms and placed her left leg over her right as she sat on Adam's shoulder. "It's said that long ago, an angelic messenger descended to this island at the behest of Stella, the Sun Goddess, and hid a treasure somewhere on the island. I heard that rumor before I was sealed."

"Ye are well-informed," Davy Jones said as he walked up to them. "That was an old rumor from long ago. No one has ever found treasure on that island, and so it has long since remained abandoned and forgotten. Only pirates use this island now."

"So you think we might run into pirates here?" asked Aris.

Davy Jones shook his head. "No. Considerin' all the [zombie pirates] we fought the other night, it is likely all the pirates who made this place their hideout have been turned into reanimated corpses."

"Got it."

As Adam stared at the island, he wondered if maybe there was actually some truth to the rumor about an angel descending to this island and burying a treasure. No one had discovered anything. However, Adam had found many hidden secrets that nobody knew about in this game.

The ship soon set anchor close to shore, and all the soldiers and sailors prepared smaller boats that he, Aris, Titania, and Kureha climbed aboard. They rowed to shore and Captain Raiker commanded his men to set up a basic camp.

The camp they were setting up was located several dozen meters off the shore. The island's terrain was quite simple. The beach was made of white sands. After cresting the hills further along the shoreline, sand shifted to gravel and grass. There were only a few coconut trees located this close to the shore, but a thick jungle that seemed near impenetrable covered much of the island surrounding the mountain.

Aris asked if Captain Raiker needed any help, but the captain just told her to stay out of his way.

"We can handle this matter. You just stand off to the side and try not to bother us," he said.

Aris pouted at the man before stomping over to Adam. "Can you believe how rude that captain is? All I did was offer to help, and he was like, 'you'll only get in the way, so just stand aside.' I've never met someone so rude."

"Some people are just gruff like that," Adam said as he rubbed Aris's hair. "Try not to let it bother you."

"Let us leave these men to their work. I believe we should begin searching the island while Captain Raiker and his men set up camp," Titania said.

"I agree," said Adam.

"Yay! Let's go exploring!" cheered Kureha.

"Time to set forth on a new adventure!" Aris also cheered. She thrust her fist into the air. Seeing this, Kureha mimicked the older woman, standing beside her and thrusting a fist into the air.

"I'll let Captain Raiker know we're going to do a preliminary search of the area. Then we can head off," said Adam. He went over to the captain, who was in the procession of issuing orders to some men trying to set up a tent. Captain Raiker listened as Adam explained what they were doing, then said he and his party could do whatever they wanted.

"We won't rely on you otherworlders to solve all our problems. You do what you want. Leave all the real work to us," he said.

Adam didn't understand where all this vitriol was coming from, but it was clear to him that Captain Raiker did not like otherworlders all that much. That was fine. If this man hated him and his party so much, then they would simply each do their own thing and only rely on each other when necessary. There was no need for him to play nice with this man.

As they left the camp, Adam wondered what sort of discoveries they would make on this island, or indeed if they would discover anything.

SURPRISE ATTACK

Adam, Aris, Kureha, and Titania scoured the highest peaks and the lowest plains, figuratively speaking, and yet they didn't find a single trace that the Asura they were after was there. Of course, they didn't find any trace that an angel had descended from heaven and left a treasure either. In all regards, this was just an empty island with an unusual shape.

They reported their findings back to Captain Raiker.

"Hmph! I could have told you that just from the fact that we haven't been attacked yet. It seems you otherworlders are lacking in both brains and brawns."

Captain Raiker remained vitriolic as he spoke to them in a manner so condescending even Adam was tempted to hit him. Aris's cheeks swelled with her pout.

"Why are you so insulting? What the heck did we ever do to you, huh?!"

"It's not what you 'did' that bothers me. It's what you don't do." Captain Raiker huffed and turned away. "I've got nothing more to say to you. Just stay out of our way and everything will be fine. We natives can handle this situation without your help."

Aris ground her teeth as the man walked away. "Can you believe that jerk? Just who does he think he is?"

"Unfortunately, there are many people like that." Titania crossed her arms, tilted her head, and furrowed her brow. "It is mostly jealousy. You otherworlders come here with incredible powers and the ability to return from death. People like Captain Raiker, who deal with death every day, are inherently jealous of you."

"That's… well, that's just stupid. None of that is our fault," Aris huffed, crossing her arms.

"You are correct, but no one said humans were very smart," Titania said.

The group made their way into the camp. It was close to becoming evening and everyone was standing around the fires, cooking food or drinking wine. Adam was almost shocked to see wine being passed around, until he remembered people in the Middle Ages only drank alcohol. Water back then was dangerous because of all the impurities and the lack of purifying techniques. The alcohol killed bacteria so humans could drink.

Adam went to set up one of his tents so Titania and Kureha could use it while he and Aris logged off—only to blink in surprise when his tent failed to load. He tried again. Again he failed. Just as he was about to try a second time, a window appeared before him.

Ding!

[Tents cannot be used while there are enemies nearby.]

Eyes going wide with surprise, Adam looked around but found nothing to suggest they were in battle. No one was fighting and there wasn't any sign of an enemy. It took Adam a moment, but he soon realized the enemy was likely hiding close by, waiting for the right time to attack.

"We need to speak with the captain again," Adam decided. "There are enemies hiding somewhere close by."

"What?! Really?" Aris asked.

"Is that what that strange screen was telling you?" asked Titania.

"Yes."

"Big Brother, what is that screen? Is it like Kureha's status screen?" asked Kureha.

"Something like that."

Adam ruffled Kureha's hair before making his way toward Captain Raiker, who was busy issuing orders to his men. He noticed when Adam and his group approached, but he ignored them in favor of continuing to issue orders. Adam waited for several minutes before growing tired of this man's treatment of them.

"Captain, I believe we should head back to the ship."

"What's that?" Captain Raiker whirled on them.

"There are enemies nearby. We should head back to the ship and travel to the next island quickly."

"Ha! Listen, you, I'm the one in charge here. You clearly don't understand logistics so let me lay it down for you in simple terms. We've already set up camp and my men aren't sailors. They don't do well at sea and the ship doesn't have enough room to let them all sleep comfortably. We need to rest to be at full strength for the enemy. Ergo, we're not leaving until tomorrow morning."

Adam had known plenty of people, so he'd met others who were this belligerent, but it was quite rare. Captain Raiker had a huge chip on his shoulder, or so it seemed. He would have gladly left this man and his troops to their own devices in most cases. Yes, *in most cases*. This sadly wasn't a case where he could just up and leave since Kureha and Titania were with them. That made this situation all the more frustrating.

"You are such an ass!" Aris snapped. "Are you stupid?! You must be! Only an idiot would not listen to others because he's jealous!"

"What did you just say to me?!"

"You heard me! Jerk! Prick! Cock sucking butt muncher! Blegh!"

Adam almost smacked himself in the face as Aris pulled down her eyelid and blew a raspberry at the captain. It was a childish thing to do. It was also effective at riling up Captain Raiker. The man's face turned red like a bonfire as several veins popped on his forehead, throbbing.

"You stupid little bitch. Don't think I won't hit you just because you're a woman."

"You're welcome to try, but you're so slow you won't even be able to hit my afterimage."

Aris and Captain Raiker were staring each other down now, ready to come to blows. It was something he had forgotten, but now he remembered how hot-headed Aris could be when riled up. She really would pick a fight with this man if he did nothing. With a sigh, Adam stepped between them, breaking the pair up.

"Let's go, Aris."

"Adam?"

"Don't waste your time on this man. We have better things we could be doing."

While Adam's words riled Captain Raiker up even further, he did nothing as Adam grabbed Aris by the hand and pulled her away. Kureha and Titania followed them as they wove their way between the soldiers, which had formed to watch a potential fight. Everyone seemed disappointed when the confrontation didn't come to blows.

"Kureha doesn't like that man," Kureha said at last.

"Neither do I," added Titania. "That man is quite insufferable. Aris was right about one thing. Only a fool does not heed the advice of others."

"Whether he's a fool or not, we have no choice but to accept things as they are." Adam paused to think about their situation. "We can't leave you two alone right now, but we need to eat to maintain our bodies in the real world. Aris and I are going to take leave in shifts. Aris, I want you to log off now to get some food and go to the restroom. Rest if you need to as well. I'll log off after you."

Aris frowned at Adam, who suddenly felt like he'd said something stupid.

"What's wrong?"

"Adam, did you forget? We can't log off when there are enemies nearby."

To emphasize her point, Aris tried to log off, only for a message to appear saying she couldn't log off when there were enemies nearby. Adam ran a hand through his hair. He wouldn't say he forgot, but the thought had simply not crossed his mind.

"Guess we're stuck here until we can deal with the enemy then," Adam muttered with a sigh.

Because there was nothing they could do, the group created a campfire, found some logs, and sat around it. The heat warmed them up as the sun began going down. Adam had some food in his inventory, so he brought it out for them to eat. It was just a simple meal of meat skewers and bread. He kept them on his person because Kureha and Titania liked them.

He wondered how Fayte and the others were doing right now. Were they also on a quest like this? Was it dangerous? He hoped their quest was at least going more smoothly than theirs. While they hadn't run into any danger yet, Captain Raiker had already made their quest unbearable.

"Hey, Adam. Can I ask you something?"

Adam glanced at Aris. She sat beside him, her knees drawn up to her chest, arms wrapped around her legs as she stared at him. Her skirt had fallen away, revealing a long expanse of glorious thigh and butt. Adam glanced around to make sure the other men weren't looking their way.

"What is it?"

"I want to ask… why have you been ignoring Fayte's feelings? I'm sure you know that she likes you."

Adam couldn't say anything at first, but he soon swallowed the lump in his throat, sighed, and ran a hand through his hair. "I should have expected you would ask this question eventually. Of course I'm aware of Fayte's feelings for me. I've been aware of them for a while now. But it's not like I can do anything about them. I'm with you."

Polygamy was still illegal in the American Federation. Of course, this didn't stop the rich and powerful from having mistresses, but it was an unofficial relationship. A mistress would never be anything more than a woman whom a man slept with on the side. They would never be acknowledged.

"Is the reason you're not accepting Fayte's feelings… because of me?" asked Aris. "Do you think I would be upset and tell you not to?"

"No." Adam blew out a deep breath, then smiled. "It's the opposite actually. I know you'd be perfectly okay with it, but that's also why I can't do it. I don't want to take advantage of your open-mindedness and feelings toward me. Of course, that's not the only reason. Just one of them."

"What's the other one?"

"Aris… have you considered Fayte's feelings?"

"What do you mean?"

"I mean have you considered whether or not Fayte would be okay being in a polyamorous relationship?" Aris furrowed her brow like she didn't understand. Adam looked at Kureha and Titania, who were pretending to eat while listening into their conversation. "I haven't known Fayte for very long. Certainly, I haven't known her for nearly as we've known each other, but if there's one thing I have learned about Fayte from our interactions every day, it's that she dreams of one day falling in love and marrying a man who will dedicate himself only to her. If she joined us, Fayte would become nothing more than a mistress, and that's not what she wants."

Had Fayte been a normal woman, she might have accepted being in a polyamorous relationship. Every woman who belonged to the nobility had to steel themselves for the possibility that their husband would sleep with one or more women on the side.

While polygamy *was* illegal, it was also an accepted practice—all off the record of course. World War III and Mortems Disease had ravaged the world to such a degree that less than half the population had survived. For this reason, the government turned a blind eye to it in the hopes that the nobles who engaged in this practice would help rebuild the population.

This was, of course, heedless of the fact that many babies birthed in recent years had been stillborn and quite a few women had gotten Mortems Disease and died during the birthing process. The power of bribery was strong. Combine that with the American Federation's desire to rebuild what had been lost, and you had a group of spineless government officials willing to turn a blind eye to the illegal actions of powerful nobles.

"I guess I didn't consider that," Aris admitted after a while.

"I figured. Anyway, I don't think Fayte is thinking about romance right now," Adam said. "She's currently trying to get out of an arranged marriage with Levon Pleonexia, so courting is probably the last thing on her mind."

Courting. Not dating. Nobody dated for fun anymore. If you went to someone with the intention of engaging in intimacy, it was always with the intention of marriage and children now. That was just the kind of world they lived in—at least officially.

Aris didn't say anything. Adam hoped she was considering what he said.

"It seems you otherworlders have quite a few problems of your own to deal with," Titania said.

"We do," Adam agreed.

Kureha tilted her head and frowned. "Kureha doesn't get it."

"Don't worry. You'll understand when you're older," Adam said, causing Kureha to pout at him.

A scream echoed from the opposite side of the camp. Adam and Aris leapt to their feet as Titania and Kureha whirled around. He couldn't see anything at first. Whatever was happening was too far away and there were too many people between him and it, but as the seconds ticked by, the people closer to them panicking as well.

And that's when Adam saw them.

[Zombie pirates].

He and Aris were furthest from the shore, which meant the [zombie pirates] must have been hiding beneath the waters, waiting until night fell to launch their attack. Firelight cast gloomy shadows against their disgusting faces. Most of them were covered in seaweed, but the ones that weren't revealed hideously scarred flesh and skin that sloughed off their bones.

"Titania! Song of Valor!" Adam shouted.

They normally had Titania sing [Song of Vigor] because it increased their attack power by 300%, but that was for when they were in a situation with only their party to worry about. Right now there were over a hundred soldiers who would drop like flies if they weren't well defended. [Song of Valor] increased their defense by 300%. It should help keep these soldiers alive for at least a little while.

"Let's find Captain Raiker!" Adam recommended. "Kureha, I need you to provide me and Aris with support! Aris, we're going to cut our way through!"

"Got it! I'll be your wingman!" Aris said as she readied her swords.

"I'm not sure you're using that term correctly, but sure."

Adam and Aris rushed into the crowd of panicking soldiers and [zombie pirates], immediately going to work.

Adam used [Energy Thrust] to impale one enemy, then lifted them by the spear and tossed them into their fellows. That attack didn't do more than -1 damage, but it did knock down the [zombie pirates], which gave the soldiers time to attack them. Next to him, Aris danced across the ground as she swung her blades in complex patterns that left streaks of light in their wake. He didn't know if she was doing it on purpose, or just getting lucky, but each of her attacks would sever a body part. Maybe this was the result of her high luck stat.

[Firestorm]

-14,288; -14,288!

There were so many enemies surrounding them that Kureha's attack swept over dozens of [zombie pirates] and lit them on fire. Now they looked like flaming humans. The [burn] status effect generated constant burn damage, so even after the wave of flames passed over them, their health continued to drop.

"Ugh… that smells awful," Aris complained as she ducked under an attack and launched her blade up, impaling a [zombie pirate] through its jaw. Her weapon punched through the mouth and emerged from the top of its skull. She kicked it away, nose wrinkling.

The scent she referred to was the smell of burning zombie flesh. It was acrid and awful, an invasive scent that made even Adam want to vomit. Times like this made him wish *Age of Gods* wasn't so realistic.

Adam swung the spear around and unleashed [Energy Thrust], following Aris's example and attacking what he believed was a weak spot. The larynx. It was an area of the throat just below the head. Anyone cut there would generally die within a couple of seconds as their life bled out and they were unable to pull in oxygen. When Adam launched his attack, however, every [zombie pirate] nearby lost their heads.

-53,200; -53,200; -53,200; -53,200; -53,200; -53,200; -53,200; -53,200; -53,200; -53,200; -53,200; -53,200!

His attack didn't reach as many enemies that Kureha's had, but it did a lot more damage. Slashing attacks must have been more effective than magic attacks on the undead. He wasn't sure if that was true, and he didn't have time to ponder it further. Adam continued to move until he, Aris, Kureha, and Titania reached Captain Raiker.

The man was having trouble.

He was in combat with several [zombie pirates] and being pushed back. Sweat beaded on his forehead as he swung the sword in his grasp like it was a cudgel. There was no grace to his movements, no methodical maneuvering. He was surrounded on all sides. This was all he could do to keep the enemy at bay.

"Here I go!" Aris shouted as she put on a burst of speed so intense even Adam couldn't see her.

[Blade Dance].

-700; -700; -700; -700; -1,400; 1,400; -700; -700; -700; -700; -700; -700; -700; -700; -700; -700; -700; -700; -1,400; -1,400; -700; -700; -700; -1,400; -700; -1,400; -700; -700; -700; -700; -700; -700; -700; -700; -1,400; -1,400; -1,400; -700; -700; -700; -700; -700; -700; -700; -700; -700; -700; -700; -700; -1,400; -700; -700; -700; -700; -1,400; -700; -1,400; -700; -700; -700; -700; -700; -700; -700; -700; -700; -700; -700; -700; -700; -700; -700; -1,400; -700; -700; -

700; -700; -700; -1,400; -700; -1,400; -1,400; -1,400; -1,400; -1,400; -700; -700; -700; -700; -700; -700; -700; -700; -700; -1,400; -700; -1,400; -700; -1,400; -700; -700; -700; -700; -700; -700; -700; -700; -700; -700; -700; -700; -700; -700!

Aris was like the wind as she raced through the crowd of [zombie pirates]. Wielding her blades with grace and skill, she sliced through the enemy like they were wheat before a scythe. Heads flew. Arms fell. Several of the undead had their legs removed. One was even cleaved in half. While the amount of damage she did per attack wasn't very much, the cumulative amount of damage she dealt was astounding even to Adam.

She stopped attacking after her MP reached zero, removed a [high-grade magic potion] from her inventory, and downed it. Adam used the opening she created to launch another [Energy Sweep]. A blue wave flew from his spear as he swung it. As the wave sliced through numerous [zombie pirates], Kureha came in and fired another wave of [Firestorm], then created a whip in her left hand and attacked any enemy that was nearby.

"Captain Raiker!" Adam shouted to get the man's attention. "We need to get out of here! These zombies won't die unless we kill the one controlling them!"

Thanks to Titania's song, their forces were still holding on, but an increased defense wouldn't be enough to turn the tides of battle when the enemy was undead. The only thing they could do was find the woman controlling these monsters and defeat her.

Captain Raiker grimaced. "I believe you are right… but we can't retreat anymore. The first thing those bastards did was destroy our boats."

A glance at the shore revealed what he meant. All the boats they had come on with had been reduced to scrap. The Asura who was controlling these zombies obviously wanted them to remain here, where she could take care of them at her leisure.

Damn it.

Adam didn't want to admit they were in a bad situation, but they were basically sitting ducks now. Even he wouldn't survive indefinitely against such an overwhelming onslaught. Once more, he realized how stupid the captain had been when he decided to set up camp on this island instead of going back to the ship. At least then they would have had a chance of kicking the zombies overboard and sailing away.

A [zombie pirate] stumbled up to him. Adam impaled him through the face with [Thrust], kicked him off the spear, then adopted the [Form One] stance and attacked so quickly that numerous spear shadows appeared, making it look like he was wielding over a dozen spears at once. His attack put several holes in the zombie's body. Sadly, that zombie was just one among many.

"Aaaah! Dang it! That hurt!"

Aris grunted as she received a gash on her side. Adam turned around to see her holding her torso, and while there was no blood, he knew the pain she felt was quite real. Despite this, or maybe even because of it, Aris was grinning as she picked up her dropped sword and attacked with renewed ferocity. Her multitude of sword swings pushed back several [zombie pirates] at once.

Adam's thoughts raced like lightning as he considered their situation. They couldn't keep this up. It was surely only a matter of time before they died if they remained like this.

Think, Adam. What are zombies weak against? Healing magic? Holy magic? In most video games, you can cast spells like heal and cure to damage them, but we don't have any...

"Titania! Can your [Song of Refreshing Rain] damage these [zombie pirates]?" asked Adam. Titania did not stop singing at first, but he could tell from her narrowed eyes that she was thinking about it. She nodded after a moment. "Then do it. Sing [Song of Refreshing Rain]."

Titania hesitated, but then switched songs. The [Song of Refreshing Rain] was a melody that reminded Adam of spring rain washing away the dreariness of winter. It was a beautiful song and even though he didn't know the lyrics, he could appreciate the harmonious sound of Titania's beautiful voice.

-7,200; -7,200;

-7,200; -7,200; -7,200; -7,200; -7,200; -7,200; -7,200; -7,200; -7,200; -7,200; -7,200; -7,200; -7,200; -7,200; -7,200; -7,200; -7,200; -7,200; -7,200!

The first thing Adam noticed about Titania's song was that while it didn't do much damage, it did far more damage to these [zombie pirates] than it healed. He assumed that was because healing attacks were something they were weak against. Now that he saw the damage the attack did, he remembered their stats said they had a -12,000% resistance, meaning it did 120 times more damage than it recovered on a normal person.

We should have done this at the beginning.

Adam could only put his mistake up to inexperience. He always used to play games solo, and he'd never been a healer. There also weren't any members among his assassins who had healing ESP powers. Of course, those were all just excuses. The truth was he simply didn't think about how this could turn the tide of battle.

With the constant damage Titania dealt to the [zombie pirates], they were able to make quick work of them. Adam noticed immediately that zombies who died did not get back up. Since they were undead, they should have risen again. He could only assume Titania's healing spell had somehow severed the connection between the [zombie pirates] and the woman controlling them.

Ding!

[Congratulations. You have defeated 150 [zombie pirates] and one 2-star [zombie pirate lieutenant]. Items dropped: x260 [dull cutlass], [jagged cutlass], [pirate boots], [pirate pants], [pirate

coat], and 1,500,000 gold coins. +22,000,000 experience points. +2,000,000 ability points. +1,500,000 reputation.]

"Looks like that's the end of them," Aris said, wiping the sweat from her brow.

"Seems so." Adam finished reading the announcement, which said they had earned quite a lot of experience points but sadly not enough for Aris to level up, then turned to Captain Raiker. "How many people have we lost?"

Captain Raiker grimaced but answered him. "Half our forces were decimated during the surprise attack."

Adam nodded. He had expected as much.

"Aris, Kureha, Titania, and myself are going to continue on alone. I think you should get your men back to Watershore."

"Now hold on just a—"

"You do not have any right to argue." Adam cut off coldly. "You've lost half your forces, our boats are all destroyed, and the survivors are too exhausted to continue. Just look around if you don't believe me."

Captain Raiker looked around at his men, most of whom were lying on the ground, groaning in pain or completely still. The few who were strong enough to move were limping in exhaustion as they tried to help their comrades. More than their exhausted bodies, however, it was their spirits that had taken the greatest beating. Adam could see it in their worn, haggard faces. These people had fallen into despair.

"I... concede that you are right," Captain Raiker said at last.

"In that case, you should do what's best for your men. We'll complete this quest on our own," Adam said. Captain Raiker glared at him, but it was the glare of a man who knew he could offer no rebuttal. Adam paid it no mind as he turned toward the shore and began walking. They would need to cobble together a vessel if they were going to keep going.

THE ASURA

After creating a raft from broken parts of the various boats they had used to reach Angel Isle, Adam, Aris, Kureha, and Titania traveled back to the ship where Davy Jones was waiting. He had been surprised to see them appear in such a roughshod vessel. It seemed the [zombie pirates] had not attacked the vessel, and so they hadn't known about what happened.

The first thing Adam and Aris did was have him travel back to Watershore with them. Once there, they informed Mayor Waterton about what happened and requested he send a rescue force to pick up the soldiers that had gone with them. The mayor had, of course, said they would gather a rescue force immediately.

It was late by the time they had finished, so Adam and Aris logged off after reaching an inn, slept until morning, then logged back on after breakfast. They met up with Davy Jones again. The former pirate turned trader had already prepared the essentials they would need, and so they boarded his ship and set sail for Devil's Horn.

Unlike Angel Isle, which looked like an island with a pair of angel wings in the very center, Devil's Horn was a small island surrounded by a crown of horns that rose from the water's surface like an abominable horror from the deep. The waters were treacherous with coral reefs and dangerous monsters. Adam was unable to see them because he got motion sickness whenever he was on a ship, but Aris said she had spotted several large shadows swimming underneath the boat.

"We be here. The question is where should we go now? Have ye any idea where that Asura woman is hidin'?" Davy Jones asked them.

They were inside of the captain's cabin, graciously provided by Davy Jones himself. Adam was lying on the bed. Aris was sitting and letting him rest his head on her thighs. Meanwhile, Kureha was curled up on his chest, which felt quite different now that she had a human form. Adam wouldn't lie. He felt slightly uncomfortable with this little girl lying on him like this, but he didn't push her away either.

"Urb… are there any… caves?" asked Adam, trying his hardest not to vomit. Even talking made him feel woozy.

Davy Jones nodded. "Aye. There be several caves in Devil's Horn. The biggest of 'em used to be a well-known pirate hideout, but it's since been deserted."

"Go, ugh… go there."

Davy Jones looked at Aris, who merely nodded, then said "aye" and left. Once he was gone, Aris went back to stroking Adam's face. He sighed and closed his eyes. Her actions didn't help his motion sickness recede, but he felt slightly better for it anyway.

"For such a strong human, you certainly are weak against the strangest things," Titania said.

The tiny fairy was sitting on a pillow, her legs stretched out in front of her, arms behind her back to hold up her torso. She stared at Adam with an amused smile.

"Everyone—urb!—everyone's got a weakness or two. Don't judge me for mine."

"I am not. Do not misunderstand me. I'm just saying this makes you more human."

"I'm not sure I… like what you are implying."

"She's just saying you're so amazing you sometimes don't seem human." Aris looked at Titania and raised an eyebrow. "Right?"

"Just so," Titania said with a nod.

Adam wasn't sure he believed them. In either event, they reached the hideout that Davy Jones spoke of after a few more hours inside the ship.

The hideout was located between the two largest horns, which reminded Adam of the horns found on the classical appearance of the Devil of Biblical literature, on a small island with a high cliff. There was a cave located in a corner of the cliff face. A cavernous space lay inside the cave. Located there was a tiny dock made of wood planks, which connected to a rock surface that had several tunnels leading deeper into the island.

Even though it had been a long time since the pirates had been using it, there was evidence that someone had been there recently. Boxes sat stacked together. When Adam peered inside, he found food and wine. Someone was using this place. The Asura woman? He didn't know, but he was determined to find out.

"I guess we'll begin searching the cave," Adam said.

"What should we do?" asked Davy Jones.

"You guys stay here," said Aris. "We'll need you to return to Watershore."

"Aye. We can do that."

Sniff. Sniff. Kureha raised her head and sniffed the air. She then grabbed Adam's sleeve and tugged on it.

"Big Brother, Kureha smells something coming from over that way," she said, pointing toward one of several tunnels.

"What does it smell like?" asked Adam.

"Miasma."

"Miasma?" asked Aris, tilting her head.

"Miasma is a type of vapor released by undead and magicians connected to it," Titania explained. "If she's saying there is miasma coming from that tunnel, it means the Asura woman and her undead army are likely there."

Adam cupped his chin. "We don't know how large her army is or how powerful this woman is. Let's do some reconnaissance first."

Leading the way, Adam traveled into the cave Kureha had indicated. They moved in a basic formation with him in front, Kureha and Titania in the center, and Aris acting as their rearguard.

Adam would have preferred to have Aris up front with him and Lilith behind them, but she was on a quest with Fayte and Susan.

The tunnel had an uneven floor that made travel difficult for the average person. It also sloped, curved, and branched into more tunnels. Were it not for Kureha and her incredible nose, they would have never been able to find their way, but they soon reached the end. The tunnel widened into a large room that looked like a gigantic conch shell. A spiral along the wall traveled upward to create a walkway. They ended up close to the middle.

Noise from below caught their attention. Adam and Aris crouched low and crawled toward the ledge. They looked down. What they saw stunned them.

"It really is an army," Aris whispered in shock.

"I count at least one thousand [zombie pirates]," Adam muttered incredulously.

"That woman sitting on the throne must be the Asura."

"Titania." Adam turned to the fairy.

He didn't need to tell her what he wanted. Titania cast [Scan] on the woman.

Name: Astarte

Description: A duke under the War Demon's command. Astarte is one of demonkind's most powerful sorceresses. She seduces men with false promises and drives women into despair by stealing their lovers and turning them into slaves.

Class: 4-Star

Lvl: 60

Health: 5,000,000/5,000,000

MP: 50,000,000/50,000,000

Strength: +400

Constitution: +2,000

Dexterity: +200

Intelligence: +15,000

Speed: +500

Skills:

Skill Name: Turn Undead

Description: Turns a corpse into an undead monster

Corpse remains undead indefinitely or until Astarte runs

out of mana or is killed

MP Cost: 50,000 MP

Costs 1,000 MP to revive corpse whenever it is killed

Cooldown Time: 0-seconds

Skill Name: Command Undead

Description: Astarte can issue orders to her undead legions.

MP Cost: 0

Cooldown Time: 0-seconds

Skill Name: Cloud of Calamity

Description: Creates a cloud of poisonous miasma

Miasma covers a 40-meter radius around Astarte

100% chance of causing poison status effect

Damage = player's Constitution * 2 per every 10 seconds

Skill lasts for 30 seconds

MP Cost: 10,500

Cooldown Time: 60-seconds

Skill Name: Underworld Gate

Description: Gathers mana to form a gate that leads to the underworld

Skeletons burst from the gate and drag whoever is caught in their grip into the Underworld

This attack does no damage, but players caught within it are forever trapped with no way to return

MP Cost: 15,000

Cooldown Time: 24-hours

Skill Name: Hypnosis

Description: Astarte can cast this spell by looking at someone

Spell can be resisted if player's Intelligence is over +500

Hypnosis lasts for 60 seconds or until spell is disrupted

MP Cost: 5,600

Cooldown Time: 30 seconds

Four Arm Sword Stance: Astarte uses four swords to attack when players get close

Damage = Strength * 2

MP Cost: 0

Cooldown Time: 0-seconds

It looked like she was something of a glass cannon… at least compared to demons like [Andras], who was physically powerful and possessed a large amount of HP. But it wasn't like she needed a lot of health since she had an army of undead at her command. Adam assumed her army was her main weapon. If her army was ever wiped out, she would rely on [Cloud of Calamity] and [Hypnosis] to defeat her enemies. In the event they somehow managed to get close, she had [Four Arm Sword Stance] to defend herself with, though it didn't do much damage. And finally, there was her trump card.

Adam didn't know if [Underworld Gate] really kept players from ever returning or if that was just how the description depicted it. He didn't want to find out either. Even if it didn't drag them into the Underworld and keep them there for the rest of time, it would still remove them from battle.

"There's no way we can beat her in an even fight. Let's return to Davy Jones and come up with a plan," Adam said quietly.

No one disagreed, and yet, just before they could move back, [Astarte] looked up at them and smiled.

"The rodents who are hiding up there. Come down here before I get my beloved army to drag you down."

Everyone froze. A chill ran down Adam's spine. Had they not been quiet enough? No, they had been so silent there was no way their voices could have reached the bottom of this cavern, which meant this woman just had really good perceptions. He thought fast.

"Titania, hurry to Davy Jones. Tell him to grab all the explosives he can, set them up inside this cave, and detonate them," Adam said as he stood up.

"What about you?" asked Titania.

Adam forced a smile. "I'm sure we'll think of something."

"Hurry up before I lose my patience," called [Astarte].

There was no more time. Titania flew off as Adam, Aris, and Kureha walked down the spiral walkway until they reached the bottom. The [zombie pirates] moved out of the way as they walked, parting like the Red Sea. Now they were surrounded. Adam held off his grimace at the stench of rotting flesh, but Aris and Kureha didn't bother hiding it. They covered their noses in disgust.

"How curious." [Astarte] rested her elbow on her throne made of human bones and placed her chin against her knuckles, observing them with a collected smile. "A pair of otherworlders and a young fox yokai. You must be the ones who caused me so much trouble recently."

"We might have been," Adam allowed.

[Astarte's] bewitching smile widened. "In that case, I hope you don't mind if I take my revenge on you. Don't worry. I just plan to make you my slaves. Mmhmhmhm. Though I might just make you my pet. You're quite handsome and it has been so long since I laid with a man."

"Sorry, but you're not my type," Adam said.

"You say that like it matters," [Astarte] fired back.

Adam, Aris, and Kureha closed ranks as the [zombie pirates] became restless. Knowing battle would be upon them soon, he decided to see if he could at least get some information out of this woman.

"Tell me what the War Demon is planning," he demanded. "We already discovered that [Andras] was mining [magicore] in a dungeon and now you're creating an army of undead. Your leader must be planning something big. Am I wrong?"

"I don't have to tell you anything. If you want that information, why don't you try prying it from me?" [Astarte] pointed her free hand at the group. "Kill them."

Just as Adam expected, the army of [zombie pirates] descended upon them like a tidal wave. Fortunately, they were limited in this small space. As the first group moved upon them, Kureha unleashed [Firestorm] to devastating effect.

-14,288; -14,288!

The flames swept over all the [zombie pirates] and lit them ablaze. Despite having become human bonfires, they continued to move forward even as the burn damage ate into their health. However, Kureha unleashed her next two attacks in quick succession: [Overflowing Cascade] and [Thunder Storm].

-11,280; -

11,280; -11,280; -11,280; -11,280; -11,280; -11,280; -11,280; -11,280; -11,280; -11,280; -11,280; -11,280; -11,280; -11,280; -11,280!

The first attack, [Overflowing Cascade], creating an incredible downpour of water that descended on the group of undead from above, slamming into them and sweeping many of them away. Adam, Aris, and Kureha were safe in the center. To them, it was like standing in the middle of a vortex and watching as all their enemies were crushed between the water and the wall.

[Astarte] was quick to realize what was happening and leapt off her throne. She had enough power in her legs to jump all the way to what could have been considered the second floor. She watched dispassionately as the wave spread out from the center and engulfed her army of one thousand.

-43,616; -43,616!

Immediately after her second attack, Kureha unleashed her last attack. Storm clouds gathered overhead. Flashes of lightning appeared within them. The storm clouds built up within less than a second, then all that power rained down as several dozen lightning bolts struck the [zombie pirate] horde.

Thunder crackled. Adam felt his ears burst. He would have covered them, but he couldn't afford to in case one of their enemies attacked.

The amount of damage done by Kureha was astronomical. Even Adam was stunned by the raw damage she dealt, but he realized why her last attack had been so effective, though he had no time to think on it as the [zombie pirates] recovered and charged toward them.

With little time to think, Adam activated [Blood Sacrifice] and [Form One]. His health and MP dropped. He narrowed his eyes as, behind him, Aris readied her twin blades. Then the undead army was upon them.

***

Titania was glad she had such a good memory. She raced through the maze-like passages and burst onto the dock, where Davy Jones and his men were waiting. The former pirate stood on the deck of his ship. He seemed to be contemplating something as he looked out the cavernous mouth.

She quickly flew up to him. "There's a large army of undead and a duke under the War Demon's command. I need you to gather all the explosives you have and set them up around this cave. We're going to bury [Astarte] and her undead army."

Davy Jones glanced at her, then came to himself. He nodded once. "I understand." He turned toward his crew, who were all busy doing their own thing, then shouted. "Alright, yee scurvy sea dogs! Gather the explosives! We're gonna bury this place seven leagues under the sea!"

"ARRRG!" the former pirates under his command released something akin to a war cry.

Titania watched as Davy Jones and his crew got the work. She wondered at first if she should stay where she was, but then shook her head and took off back down the passage she came from. These men could handle their tasks without her. She needed to hurry up and return to her party's side so she could support them.

She just hoped she wasn't too late.

***

-600!

-600!

-1,200!

Adam grunted as he backpedaled to avoid several attacks from a pair of [zombie pirates], but he wasn't fast enough to avoid the third one that attacked him from the left. Phantom pain lanced through him. He ignored it and quickly struck the [zombie pirate] with several spear shadows, then ducked when Aris flew over his head, spinning like a top as she sliced into a zombie, removing its left arm, right leg, and head. As the zombie fell to the ground, Kureha lit it on fire with [Fireball].

Adam quickly downed two [high-grade health potions] to fully restore his HP. He blinked the sweat from his eyes and looked at the undead surrounding them. There was no telling how many they had cut down since they just rose back up. He, Aris, and Kureha had managed to avoid being buried underneath the horde of bodies by using teamwork. Adam used his Strength to demolish enemies that got close, Aris used her Speed to keep the enemies at bay, and Kureha used her magic to launch AoE spells. It had worked well so far, but there was a problem.

They were running out of health and mana potions.

On top of having activated [Blood Sacrifice] multiple times, there were so many enemies that Adam could not dodge every attack, and though he managed to deflect a lot of them, several had gotten through, forcing him to use his [high-grade health potions] like they were candy. He was already down to just ten more.

Aris had similarly been unsuccessful at dodging attacks. Her incredible speed had been an asset, but it was also hindered by the sheer number of undead surrounding them and the enclosed space. No matter how fast someone was, it didn't matter if there was little room to maneuver. Aris's only saving grace was her nimbleness. She had become much more adept at abrupt turns and twists, which allowed her to remain alive so far.

Kureha had not received any damage thanks to him and Aris. They were good enough at watching each other's backs that they hadn't let a single [zombie pirate] through their stalwart defenses. Yet even she was limited in what she could do. Her cooldown times for all her spells were between ten and thirty seconds, which meant they needed to wait until she could launch an attack. She worked around this by launching one spell every five seconds, but even that meant there was a five-second pause between AoE spells.

In battle, five seconds was more than enough time for the enemy to close in.

Especially in such an enclosed space.

"Kureha! Mist!" Adam shouted.

"Mist? Ah! Got it, Big Brother!"

While Kureha was confused at first, she soon cast another of her spells. [Blinding Mist] was a spell they had not used yet. The young fox yokai waved her third tail around in the air, gathering moisture that soon turned into a thick vapor. Mist swirled around them like a spiral before covering everything within a ten-meter radius. Adam had judged this bottom floor to have a twenty or thirty-meter radius, or thereabouts, and so he knew this wasn't enough to completely conceal them.

But it would be enough for what he had planned.

Adam wrapped one arm around Aris's waist and grabbed Kureha with the other. Then he bent his knees, leapt into the air, and activated [Double Jump]. The skill took him far above the mist. He looked around and spotted [Astarte] standing several meters away on the spiral walkway. She had already spotted him, but it didn't matter.

He activated [Flight] next, soaring through the air quickly, his destination the woman with four arms.

"Kureha! Attack her!"

Kureha didn't speak as she used her first two tails to attack. A massive ball of flames burst from her first tail, then a bolt of lightning shot from her second tail. Despite [Fireball] being launched first, [Thunder Bolt] reached [Astarte] first. It was so fast the woman had no time to leap backward.

-24,816; -18,800!

The two attacks struck. The first one staggered [Astarte], while the second one lit her on fire. Their enemy screamed in shock as the two attacks struck.

Adam wasted no time. He dropped Aris onto the floor. She landed with a crouch, then pushed off the ground and flew at [Astarte], swinging both blades so quickly they were nothing but flashes of silver.

Thanks to [Blade Dance], Aris was able to constantly attack [Astarte] with a relentless barrage of sword strikes. Her attacks were too fast for the eye to follow. Or so it seemed to Adam. He was more than a little shocked to see that [Astarte] was able to keep up well enough to block them. Sparks flew from their clashing swords. Their enemy's four blades allowed her to keep up with Aris's faster than normal speed.

Adam didn't hesitate to rush behind [Astarte]. He had already activated [Blood Sacrifice] again. He was ready to unleash [Dance of the Sakura Blossoms]. That was his plan, at least, but those plans were dashed when [Astarte] kicked Aris away and turned around to face him.

[Hypnosis]

Before Adam realized what was happening, his world went black.

✳✳✳

"Uh oh."

Aris realized they were in trouble the moment Adam turned to face them. His expression was blank, like a zombie's.

[Astarte] laughed. "You fool! Did you forget about my ability? Now, be a dear and go kill that friend of yours. Don't worry. I'll resurrect her as one of my undead. That way you can be forever tormented with the knowledge that you failed to protect her."

Adam rushed forward and thrust out his spear at Aris, who used her Speed to withdraw fast enough to avoid his initial strike. Her lover was relentless, however, and he moved swift as lightning to chase after her. She gritted her teeth as he attacked with the [Slash] and [Thrust] skills.

Aris knew better than to let herself get hit. If she was hit even once, that would be the end of her.

"Adam! Snap out of it! It's me! It's Aris! Stop attacking!"

"He can't hear you, dear. [Hypnosis] blankets a person's mind in a thick mist that makes them unable to resist my orders. Not even someone with the strongest will can dispel my mind control," [Astarte] laughed.

"Ugh!"

Aris tried several more times to make Adam snap out of his hypnotized state, but nothing she said got through to him. It was like he didn't hear her at all.

She knew Adam had a strong will. Had this been real life, he could have certainly broken free, but while the game mechanics for *Age of Gods* mimicked real life to an extent, there were some things it didn't mimic. Spells like this were one of them. Even if Adam's will was powerful, he could not break free of an attack like this unless his Intelligence stat was high enough. Unfortunately, Adam had neglected Intelligence since its only use was to build his reserves of MP.

I really hope Adam decides to invest more skill points into his Intelligence when this is all over.

Because she couldn't get through to him, Aris made a snap decision. She sheathed her weapons, grabbed Kureha, and ran away.

"Are you running?! There's nowhere for you to run! Go forth, my new minion, and kill your friend!"

Under [Astarte's] compulsion, Adam raced forward to chase after Aris, but it was useless. Her Speed was not something even he could keep up with. Before he could even catch up to her, she began running right up the wall, reached the next ledge up, and disappeared into one of several tunnels.

If she couldn't fight Adam head-on, she would just play a game of cat and mouse until the [Hypnosis] wore off.

ARIS BLURTS!

Aris had no idea how long she had been running, but her body was giving out. Exhaustion seeped into her bones. Her legs felt like brittle twigs. Yet she continued to run because that was all she could do.

Adam was hot on her heels.

This is not the kind of chasing I had in mind for us after my rehabilitation.

Rather than chasing her down so he could ravish her body, her lover had been hypnotized and was now trying to take her out. It was all thanks to that cunt sucking whore. If she were strong enough, she would have stabbed that woman's eyes out. Aris hated this. More than her situation, however, she hated seeing her lover in this state.

"Haaaah… haaaah… is he… still following us… Kureha?" asked Aris.

"He's right behind us, Big Sis!" Kureha shouted.

She was carrying Kureha piggyback because it was just easier. The girl could look behind them and what she saw was apparently Adam hot on their heels. Even though her Speed and Movement far outclassed his, he was able to make up for that by using the enclosed space and sharp turns to his advantage. He also had far more energy than her. Was this the result of his higher Constitution?

"A-Aris!" a shout came from behind her. "Hold up! The [Hypnosis] wore off!"

"Oh, thank God!" Aris pressed her heels into the dirt and ground to a halt, whirled around, and glared at Adam. "Do you know how long I've been waiting for you to recover?!"

Adam gave her a sheepish grin. "About sixty seconds, I'd say. But anyway, we don't really have time for this right now. I'll listen to you complain after we deal with [Astarte]."

"Ugh. Right. Fine. But I reserve the right to complain as soon as we're finished."

"Noted."

"Are you back to normal, Big Brother?" asked Kureha.

"I am," Adam said.

"Yay! That makes Kureha happy!"

Aris felt a lot better as she and Adam walked back into the spiral room together. [Astarte] was still there with her [zombie pirate] army, and she looked none too pleased as the pair emerged from one of several exits. Her glared locked onto them the moment they emerged.

"I can't believe you managed to last long enough for my [Hypnosis] to wear off. Perhaps I should have cast it on you instead."

"Had you done that, I would have gutted you," Adam said, readying his spear. "Now, where were we."

Aris grinned as she set Kureha down and twirled her curved swords around. "I believe we were about to kick her ass."

"Butt. Kick her butt. Don't swear," Adam said.

"You're not my mother, Adam. Though I'll let you spank me later if you want."

"Tempting."

"Tch!" [Astarte] clicked her tongue. "You two make me sick. But it doesn't matter if the [Hypnosis] wore off. Did you forget? I have an entire army on my side."

That much was true, and Aris eyed the undead army that stood between them and her with apprehension. Even she knew that attacking this army head-on was a bad idea. And yet, just as she was about to consider retreating again, a song came to them as if on the wind. It refreshed Aris. She felt like she was being engulfed in a light spring rain as her HP was restored.

+60; +60; +60; +60; +60; +60; +60; +60; +60; +60; +60; +60; +60; +60; +60; +60; +60; +60; +60; +60; +60; +60; +60; +60; +60; +60; +60; +60; +60; +60; +60; +60; +60; +60; +60; +60; +60; +60; +60; +60; +60; +60; +60; +60; +60; +60!

It wasn't long before her health was replenished to full. The [zombie pirates], on the other hand, were not so lucky.

-7,200; -7,200;

-7,200; -7,200!

"W-what is going on?! My army!!!"

[Astarte] could only watch in horror as her undead forces received damage from the song that refreshed and healed her enemies. Maybe she would have made a move, but neither Adam, Aris, nor Kureha had any intention of letting that happen. They attacked before she could get her shit together. Kureha released a [Firestorm] that swept over the enemy and set them all ablaze. Aris ran headlong into the blazing throng, side by side with Adam, and cut through them like Ryu Hayabusa cutting down demons.

Ding!

[Congratulations! You have defeated 1,000 [zombie pirates], two 2-star [zombie captains], and one 2-star [zombie generals]! Items dropped: x900 [cutlass], [Sword of the Betrayer], [ancient buckler], and 30,000,000 gold coins. Inventory is full. Items have been sent to guild storage. +146,666,000 experience points! +4,200,000 ability points! +660,000 Reputation!]

Ding!

[Congratulations! You have leveled up! You are now at level 20! +400 HP! +200 MP! +5 SP!]

Ding!

[By reaching level 20, you have increased the level cap on your old skills. You can now increase the level for all of your skills by 5.]

With a click of her tongue, [Astarte] leapt backward and swept out her hands as if to summon something. Aris felt a tingle run down her spine seconds before a magic circle appeared on the ground beneath her feet.

"That doesn't look—whoa!"

Adam wrapped an arm around her and leapt backward just before a massive gateway appeared between them and [Astarte]. This must have been the woman's trump card. [Otherworld Gate]... or something. Aris was sure that was its name, but she didn't particularly care enough to remember.

"That was a close one," Adam said.

Though he said this like they had escaped, the gate burst open, and skeletons rushed out to grab them, but Aris had recovered now, and she was even faster than Adam. She yanked him along as she leapt back, moving out of the skeletons' reach.

The undead horde was already gone thanks to Titania. She and Kureha stood a ways back. The small fairy had already switched from the [Song of Refreshing Rain] to the [Song of Vigor].

As Adam and Aris cleared the way, Kureha spun around and lashed out with her tail, creating a wave of fire that swept over the skeletons and pushed them back. It was only temporary. Whatever these things were, they were far more powerful than anything she had seen so far. Kureha's attack also didn't seem to damage them. It just slowed them down.

"What do we do now?" asked Aris.

"We retreat," Titania said. "Davy Jones and his men have already planted the explosives. They should be going off in—" A loud explosion rang out, rocking the entire spiral room and causing the ceiling to fall off in chunks. "—now, apparently! Let us not dally here! We should move!"

"Where do you think you're going?! Don't run away from me!!"

[Astarte] shrieked behind them, but Aris and her friends were already heading into one of the tunnels. Aris didn't know if this was the right way. She was just following Titania. They took several turns, then screeched to a halt because the roof had caved in. Just as they turned around, they found [Astarte] standing behind them, looking pissed.

"I won't let you escape! You've ruined all our plans! All my plans! And I will see you dead!"

"Titania!" Adam shouted.

Titania began singing once more. Adam's body glowed red as he raced forward. It was like his blood was boiling and coming out of his pores as steam. He didn't seem injured, however, and as he raced forward, he attacked the woman with the strange flower-patterned skill that Aris had seen him use many times now.

-59,850; -179,550; -538,650; -1,615,950; 4,874,850!

Adam's attack tore through the woman like a hot knife. [Astarte] didn't even get to shriek as he killed her in one shot. It was almost anti-climactic. They had put in so much work getting close to her back there, just for Adam to come in and one-shot the skank… but, oh well. Aris was just glad she was gone.

Ding!

[Congratulations! You have defeated the 4-star demon general [Astarte]! Items dropped: x4 [Blade of the Damned], [Charmed Necklace], [Damned Queen's Dress], and 45,000,000 gold coins. +150,000,000 experience points. +850,000 ability points. +1,000,000 Reputation!]

Ding!

[Congratulations! You have leveled up! You are now at level 21! +400 HP! +200 MP! +5 SP!]

Ding!

[Congratulations! Adam has leveled up! He is now at level 22! +1,500 HP! +620 MP! +5 SP!]

"Oh! We leveled up!" Aris exclaimed in surprise.

"Never mind that! Let's keep moving!" Adam shouted.

Aris shook her head, slapped her cheeks, and chased threw herself into a sprint as she, Adam, Kureha, and Titania raced down the collapsing tunnels.

***

Adam stepped into the chilly winter air, walked around to the other side of his car, and opened the door for Aris and Fayte. The two women thanked him with a smile. While he wore his normal jeans and a t-shirt, Aris and Fayte were bundled up. Fayte was, of course, wearing her hideous clothing and veil, but Aris had gone with a pink duster, leg warmers, and UGGs.

"So this is where you went to get medical care?" asked Fayte.

"That's right," said Aris.

"The New York City Hospital is the best one on the east coast," Adam added.

"It is. I've heard many good things about it," Fayte agreed.

They left the parking garage and made their way across the street, entering the hospital through its automatic sliding door. There were already a number of sick patience sitting in the waiting room. A young man kept coughing into his hand. A little girl had the sniffles and her mother kept wiping her nose. One person sitting in the far corner had broken out in hives.

Walking up to the front desk with Fayte and Aris behind him, Adam announced his presence to the young woman. "Hello. I'm here for my appointment with Dr. Sofocor."

The young woman who appeared thinner than was probably healthy looked up. She glanced at him, then at Aris, then at Fayte. She did a double-take upon seeing his companion's ugly clothes, but she at least retained enough professionalism not to say anything.

"Um… just fill out these forms please."

"Thanks."

She handed Adam the forms, and he filled them out before handing them back. The woman told him that Dr. Sofocor would be out shortly, and they should sit down and wait.

Unlike the last time they were here, no one was actively avoiding them, though Fayte did receive many an odd look from the people present. No one seemed to know what to make of her outfit.

The wait wasn't long. A few minutes after they sat down, Dr. Sofocor appeared in the room. She looked the same as always. Her brown hair was tied into a tight ponytail. She wore a knee-length black skirt, a long-sleeved black shirt, and a white lab coat. Wrinkles lined her mouth and eyes, denoting her age. Adam thought he saw a few new gray hairs, but he had enough sense not to tell her that.

"Adam… I was beginning to think you'd forgotten our promise," Dr. Sofocor said immediately upon seeing them. She smiled at Aris. "Hello, Aris. You are looking well."

Aris beamed at her. "I'm feeling well! Adam has been taking very good care of me!"

"I'll bet he has," Dr. Sofocor said, tone dry.

"Jealous?" asked Adam.

"Don't even get me started." Releasing an annoyed grunt, Dr. Sofocor finally looked at Fayte. It was a testament to her mental fortitude that she didn't freak out upon seeing the woman's ugly outfit. "Is this the person you spoke of?"

"Hello," Fayte said, clasping her hands together in front of her. She performed a short bow from the waist. "I'm Fayte. Adam has told me a lot about you."

Dr. Sofocor raised an eyebrow but responded all the same. "Dr. Sofocor, but you can just call me Julia. I'm not your doctor, so calling me by name will make this conversation go a lot more smoothly."

"Pleased to meet you, Julia."

"Likewise, Fayte."

"Perhaps we should change venues so we can talk," Adam suggested.

Dr. Sofocor nodded and headed back into the hallway. Adam, Aris, and Fayte followed the woman as she took them to her office, which was little more than a large space filled with equipment and some seats. Adam's nose twitched as the scent of antiseptics hit him. The moment they were inside and the door was sealed shut, the good doctor whirled on Fayte.

"Are you really Adam's benefactor? The one who cured Aris of Mortems Disease? How did you do it?! Can you tell me? What would it cost to make you part with that knowledge?"

Adam almost facepalmed when Dr. Sofocor moved into Fayte's personal space and peppered her with questions. Almost. Aris held a hand to her mouth and giggled. For her part, the one on the recipient end of the doctor's onslaught merely glanced at Adam as if asking for help.

He sighed and pushed his way between them. "She can't answer you if you don't even give her a chance to talk."

"Ah. You're right. I'm sorry. Lost my composure a bit there." Dr. Sofocor smoothed out the ruffles in her skirt.

Adam raised an eyebrow. "A bit?"

"Fine. A lot," Dr. Sofocor growled, her cheeks red. "You can't blame me."

"I suppose not."

Now that Dr. Sofocor was calm, Fayte removed her veil, ignored the doctor's sharp intake of breath, and smiled. "I would be more than happy to tell you about the cure I have for Mortems Disease. In fact, I would be willing to let you take the capsule that cured her. However, I do have a few stipulations that I hope you'll agree to."

"What are they?" asked Dr. Sofocor immediately.

Fayte held up a hand and extended a single finger. "One, nobody except yourself and people who have been personally vetted by me can study the capsule with you. You can recommend people. But I get final say in who can and cannot examine the capsule. Two, I'm willing to offer you the chance to study and reproduce the method of curing Mortems Disease for free, but when you release the cure to the world, I want you to let everyone know it came from me. My full name is Fayte Dairing, by the way. If you can agree to these two terms, I'll let you study the capsule to your heart's content."

"Deal!"

It amazed Adam how the woman didn't even think about Fayte's offer before accepting, but this was something she had been researching for over a decade without success. He imagined the woman was prepared to accept a deal with the Devil if it meant acquiring a cure. As the two shook hands, sealing the deal between them, Adam wondered how long it would take before the name Fayte became synonymous with saint.

✳✳✳

Adam was sitting in the Guild Association office that belonged to Clarise. It wasn't just him either. Titania was sitting on his shoulder like she always did, and Kureha had taken his lap for her seat. It used to be his head that she sat on, but ever since she gained a human form, his lap seemed to have become her personal chair.

He felt a little awkward about it. Adam wasn't what you'd call a family man. The only person he had ever loved was Aris, and even her parents had just been background decorations to him. Now he had this child who called him "Big Brother" using him as her chair, demanding affection, and he just didn't know what to do.

Perhaps that's why he let her do what she wanted.

He was out of his element.

Aris, Fayte, Lilith, and Susan were not with him today. His lover had told him that today was going to be a "girls talk" day and that boys weren't allowed, and thus he'd been expelled from the Guild House until their talk was over. Adam had no idea what they were going to talk about. However, he remembered an old saying that Lexi had once said to him.

"A girl needs to have her secrets."

Adam had no idea what that meant, but he had always taken those words to heart. That explained why he didn't know Aris had been masturbating as she fantasized about him when she was younger. He needed to let a woman have her secrets.

At least, that was what Adam told himself.

"Thank you for coming today. I delivered your report to Mayor Paxton, and he has expressed concern regarding the movements of both [Andras] and [Astarte]," Clarise, sitting across from him with her hands in her lap, said. The expression she wore was grave indeed. It belied how serious this situation was. "Now that we are aware that commanders under the War Demon are on the move, we've begun to realize that several similar situations are likely being caused by his forces. Adam, we have several quests with similar circumstances that we believe his forces are causing. I would like you and your guild to handle all matters pertaining to this. This is an official request from Mayor Paxton as well."

"Will my guild be compensated appropriately for handling these quests?" asked Adam.

He removed his hand from Kureha's tails, which he had been fluffing because they were there and not because her tails were so irresistibly fluffy, and reached for the teacup, bringing the porcelain object to his lips. Warmth blossomed on his tongue. It was spicy. Chai? Not quite. Though it tasted similar to chai tea, there was an unquantifiable flavor that he couldn't identify. Either way, it was good.

Kureha turned to him with a pout. "Big Brother? Pet Kureha's tails more."

Adam sighed but placed the cup down and willingly pet the girl's tails. They were very soft. Kureha giggled and leaned against his chest.

"You're quite the accommodating big brother, aren't you?" Clarise smiled. Adam grunted. Coughing into her hand, the woman got back on track. "The Guild Association is willing to give you proper compensation. We have been vested with the authority to handle this matter as we see fit. Each commander you slay will earn you a total of two hundred million experience points and fifty million gold coins. We actually wanted to offer you more, but our coffers are limited. This was the best we could come up with."

The gold was not as important as the experience, so he honestly didn't mind. What he and his guildmates needed was to increase their levels until they were so powerful that even if the Pleonexia Alliance came at them with all their forces combined, they would still come out on top. He wanted to be able to crush a guild with millions of members with a small guild of just seven.

That would send the entire world a message.

That was what he wanted.

"If the War Demon and his forces are on the move, then it is true something needs to be done, but are you sure we're right for the job?" asked Titania. "I do not mean to cast doubt on myself or my companions, but we are still just a small force of seven people. Our individual combat prowess aside, I'm not sure we can deal with every single one of his commanders."

"This is completely optional," Clarise confessed. "You don't have to accept this if you don't want to. However, if you don't accept this, we will have no choice but to rely on our own forces. I don't have to tell you this, but very few of our soldiers are over level 50. Only our captains and commanders have ascended the limits of human strength, and even they pale in comparison to the War Demon's commanders. There's no telling how many lives will be lost."

"So you hope to use otherworlders who have no reason to fear death in your battle against the War Demon and his forces?"

"Yes."

Titania huffed and crossed her arms. She didn't like their plan one bit and made that clear through her actions. Adam wondered if the reason she was against this had to do with her own mortality. Unlike him, Aris, Fayte, Susan, and Lilith, she and Kureha would die if they were killed. There was no reviving them.

People die when they are killed.

"What's so funny?" asked the irritated Titania.

"Nothing," Adam coughed into his hand to cover his chortling.

Ding!

[You have been offered a new quest: [Slay the War Demon's Commanders]. Will you accept? Yes or no?]

"All right." Adam pressed the "yes" button on the screen that appeared before him. "I accept your request. However, my companions and I will decide how and when we will fight these commanders. Let Mayor Paxton know we'll be completing these on our terms."

"Thank you very much." Clarise stood up and bowed to him. It was a low, formal bow, showing just how important this quest was to her and the entirety of the Sun Continent.

Ding!

[You have accepted the quest: [Slay the War Demon's Commanders]!]

✳✳✳

"I know it's an old game, but there's just something about *War of Worldcraft* that I really love. I think it has a certain charm to it that newer MMOs lack."

"Do you think maybe it's the lack of VR experience? I know that virtual reality has become all the rage since the end of World War III, but I remember playing a bunch of old console and PC games with Adam and enjoyed them greatly. Of course, I like *Age of Gods* too, but I think the older games that don't rely on VR technology are very charming and fun."

"Yes! That's exactly it! Virtual reality allows you to fully immerse yourself in any game you play. Don't get me wrong, I love that. But! I just think there's something innately authentic and entertaining about retro games you can play on PC and consoles."

Aris sat around a table with Fayte, Susan, and Lilith. The four girls had been chatting away ever since Adam left. Aris had wormed her way past Susan's shy exterior by bringing up old video games. The girl was apparently a fanatical enthusiast and loved old console and PC games, to the point where her shyness evaporated like moisture on a hot summer's day. She was glad that she had been able to find something she and this girl could talk about.

She's so cute.

Adam had once confessed that Susan brought out his protective instincts, and she could totally understand where he was coming from. There was just something about the young woman that made Aris want to protect her. Of course, she was so cute that Aris also wanted to bully—er, she wanted to tease her. Yes, the idea of teasing the younger woman was so appealing that it took every ounce of willpower Aris had not to launch into an innuendo-laden assault.

Gosh, I want to embarrass this girl so badly.

"It could also be because of the change in storytelling," Fayte theorized. "I know older games always had a story you can follow, but virtual reality games no longer have a main story quest. It's all about PvP battles now. Come to think of it, I think *Age of Gods* is the first VRMMO I've played where there appears to be a complex story hidden in the game's background."

"That might be part of it too," Susan agreed, nodding several times.

Aris hadn't stopped smiling since they all began speaking. She hadn't been this happy since before she got Mortems Disease, back when her parents were still alive, and she and Adam lived without a care in the world.

She frowned.

My next few words might change that...

Aris had been thinking long and hard about what she wanted now that she was cured, about how she wanted to live and what her goals should be now that she was not going to die. The conclusion she had arrived at was unconventional. However, she hoped these three women would be able to accept what she planned to ask of them.

"Ahem." Coughing into her hand, Aris gathered everyone's attention. Even the quiet Lilith who had not said anything up to this point was now looking at her. "Everyone, I wanted to talk to you about something important."

"I thought so." Fayte smiled. She was not wearing her veil, so Aris could see just how truly resplendent a smile it was. "You seemed to have something in mind when you told Adam you wanted to have a girls talk. What did you want to discuss?"

She raised a hand to her chest. Her heart was hammering. It was with shock that Aris realized she was nervous. Ever since she had been cured, Aris had made her decisions in a way that others would have considered recklessly carefree, and that was because she had based her choices on what she wanted to do and not what was necessarily good for her. If Adam didn't act as her logical dictator, she would have probably done many more stupid things in the name of enjoying her newfound freedom.

However, ever since her conversation with Adam, Aris had been thinking seriously about the matter she wanted to bring up, and now that she had finally resolved herself to do it, she was incomparably worried about how these three would respond. Would they accept it? Would they agree with her? Or would they not accept it? What if her words irreparably damaged the friendships she was only now beginning to form? Those thoughts swirled through her mind as she screwed up her courage.

Aris took a deep breath, held it for several seconds, then expelled it in a single woosh. She looked at the three before her. They were waiting patiently for her to say what she wanted. Aris opened her mouth…

"I want you three to form a harem with me!" she blurted out.

To Be Continued…

AFTERWORD

Can you believe that Aris? How could she blurt out something like that after Adam specifically warned her to think about this very subject just a few seconds before?

I'm just kidding. That sort of thing is very Aris-like.

Hello one and all. It is I, Brandon Varnell, that guy who writes so many light novels he often forgets what he's writing and mixes up his characters' names.

Before I forget, I'd like to ask if everyone who read this could please leave a review? Books live and die by their reviews. You would be helping me put food on my table by writing one, and I would be very grateful.

Now with that out of the way, let me talk a bit about Aris. She's a mischievous minx, isn't she? As someone who has walked hand-in-hand with death for so long, Aris is pretty determined to live her life to the fullest—a very natural reaction if you ask me. However, this often means she causes a lot of trouble. That last statement about forming a harem is sure to cause no end of trouble in the next volume.

A lot happened in this volume, but a good portion of it was setup. The next volume is going to be dealing with a few major plot threads I set up in this one. I'm sure anyone who has been sticking with me for so long knows how I operate. I like to create plot threads that don't become relevant until much later in my series—foreshadowing events are one of my favorite things to do when writing. I just like that moment when people reading my books go: *"Oh, shit! So that's why this happened two volumes ago!"*

As always, my harems are very, very, *very* slow burn. I never have my protagonist get with a bunch of women right off the bat, so Adam is gonna have to work for it. I think it's much more rewarding when the protagonist earns the right to have a harem rather than having a harem just given to him.

Now then, I have some last minute thanks to give to a few people.

First and foremost was my editor and proofreader for this series. I've been having some major problems with this particular series, though a lot of it has to do with me mixing up my manuscripts. My editor and proofreader has been doing a nice job of keeping things stupid simple for me—cuz I'm a stupid simple guy. Thanks for helping fix my bad grammar.

I also want to thank Lonwa_A. He's my artist for this series. He had some issues with the art this time, but I hope he and I can continue to work together on this series. I really do love his art. It's amazing, and the more realistic style fits the aesthetic I'm doing for.

My last thank you is to all of you who read this story, who wrote a review for it, and who continue to support me. You're awesomesauce. I can't show my gratitude enough times. I hope you all enjoyed this volume and will join me in the next one, where Adam and his harem face off against their most powerful foes yet!

~Brandon Varnell

BRANDON VARNELL IS
WRITING STORIES AND CRE-
ATING COMICS ON PATREON!

HAVE YOU EVER EXPERIENCED ONE OF THOSE LIFE-CHANGING INSTANCES? AN EVENT SO MOMENTOUS THAT, YEARS LATER, YOU'RE STILL MARVELING AT HOW IT CHANGED YOUR LIFE?

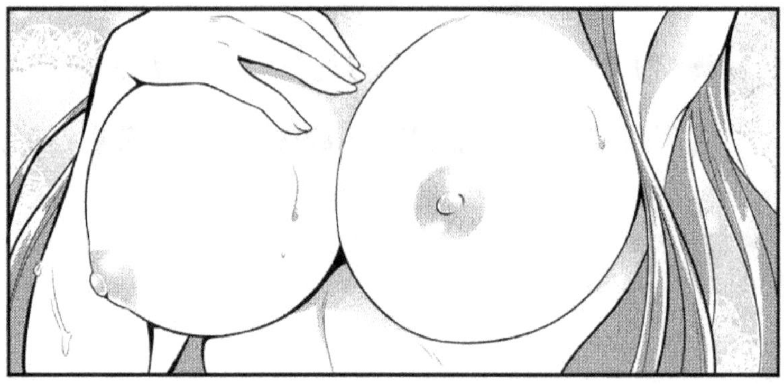

I HAD ONE OF THOSE. IT HAPPENED A WHILE AGO

EVEN TO THIS DAY, THROUGH ALL THE CHANGES THAT HAVE HAPPENED, THROUGH ALL THE EXPERIENCES THAT I'VE BEEN THROUGH, I STILL CAN'T BELIEVE HOW THIS ONE MOMENT CHANGED MY LIFE FOREVER.

NO MATTER WHAT CAME AFTER, OUR FIRST MEETING IS SOMETHING THAT I'LL ALWAYS REMEMBER.

ESPECIALLY SINCE, AT THE BEGINNING OF THIS TALE, I THOUGHT SHE WAS NOTHING BUT AN ORDINARY FOX WITH, UNORDINARILY ENOUGH, TWO BUSHY RED TAILS.

LIFE

．
．
．
．
．
．
．
．
．
．
．

IT HITS YOU WHEN YOU LEAST EXPECT IT TO.

American Kitsune

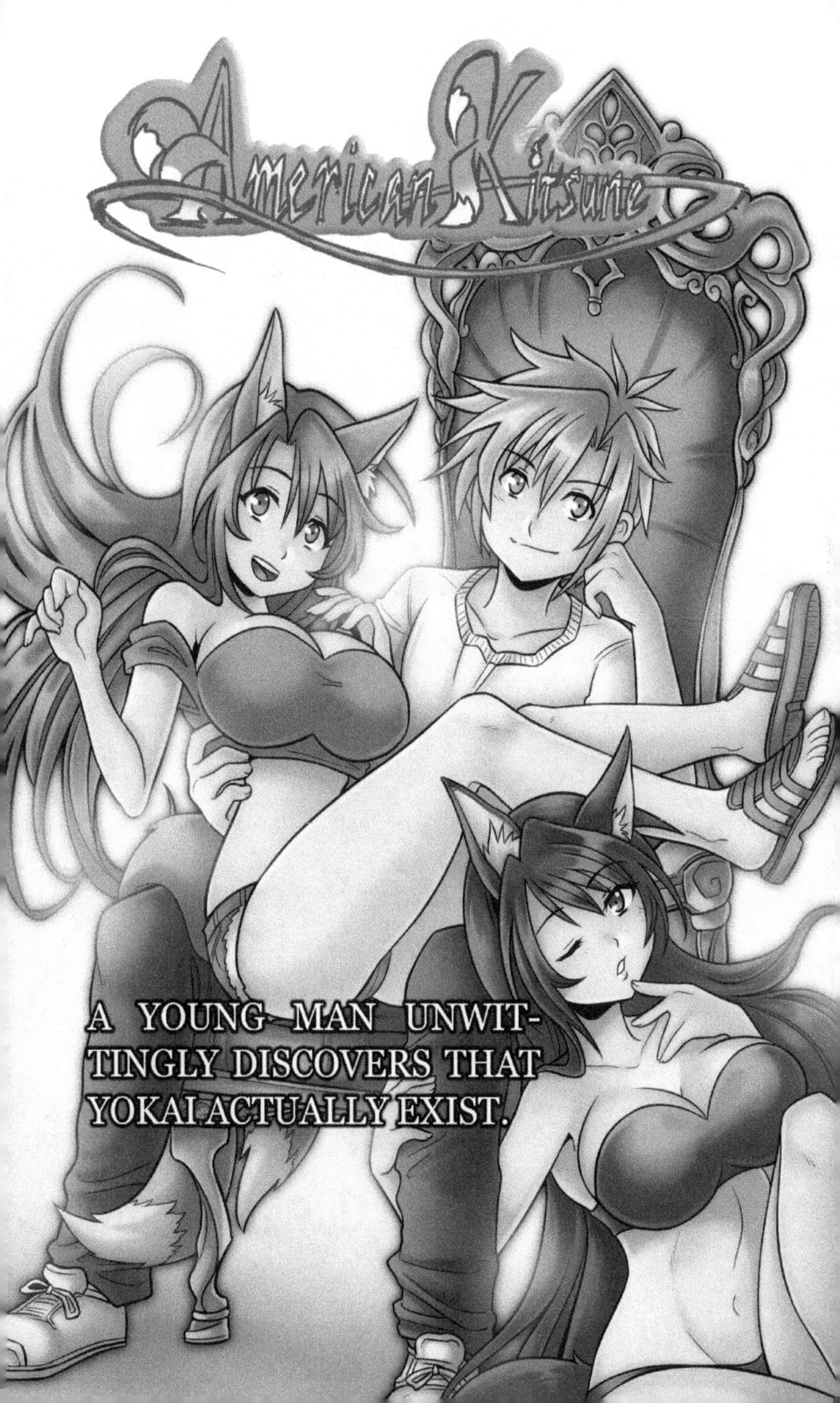

American Kitsune
A YOUNG MAN UNWITTINGLY DISCOVERS THAT YOKAI ACTUALLY EXIST.

catgirl doctor
THE STORY OF A YOUNG DOCTOR-IN-TRAINING AND CATGIRLS.

INCUBUS
VERTICAL
THE WORLD'S ONLY INCUBUS
MUST BOND WITH SEVEN
WOMEN!

MMG:001
A MAN DESPERATE TO SAVE HIS LOVER JOINS FORCES WITH A WOMAN LOOKING FOR A WAY OUT OF AN UNWANTED MARRIAGE.
MAN
MADE
GOD

He just wanted to be a hero.
She didn't want to be stuck in a loveless marriage.
A Most Unlikely Hero

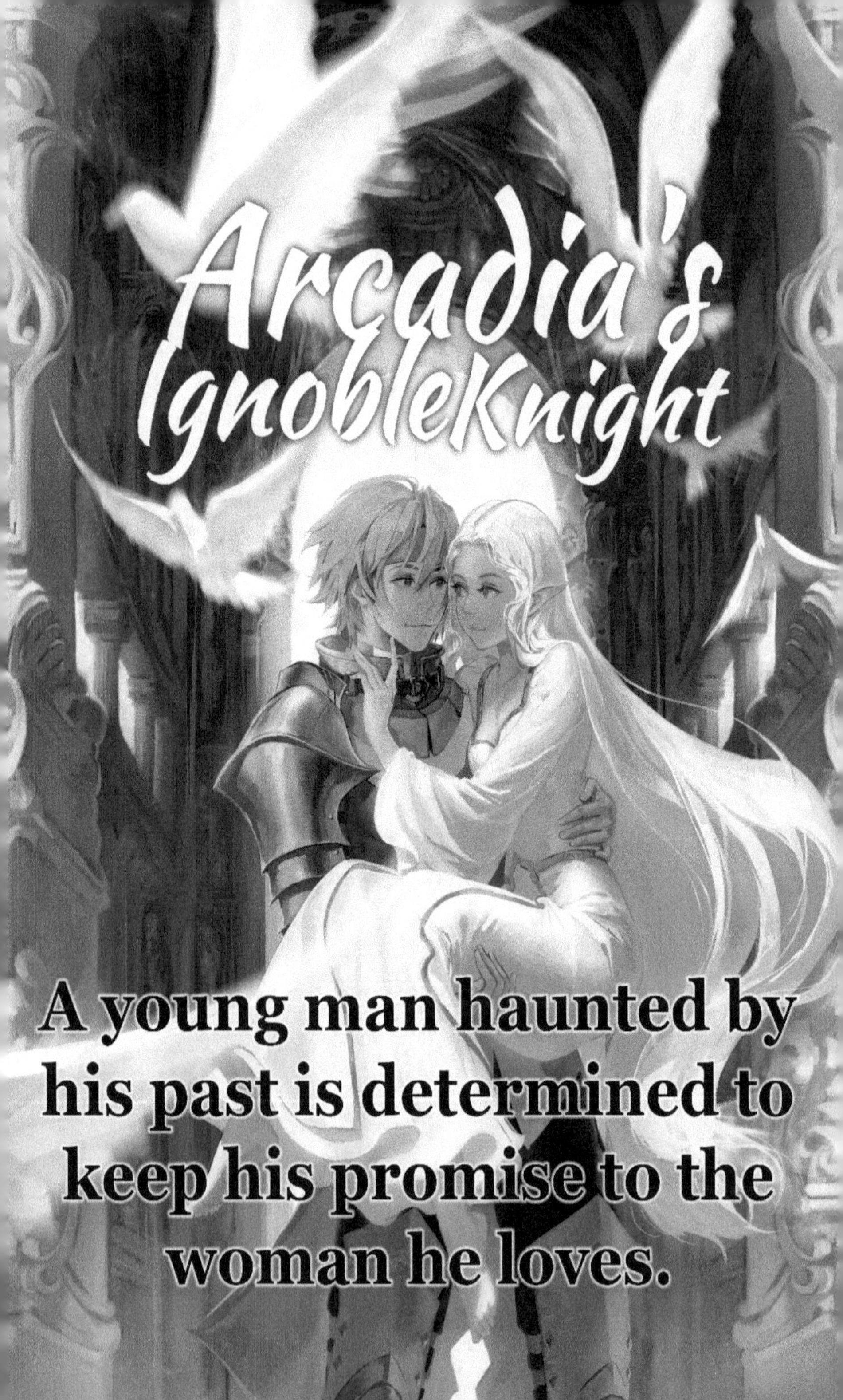

Arcadia's
IgnobleKnight
A young man haunted by his past is determined to keep his promise to the woman he loves.

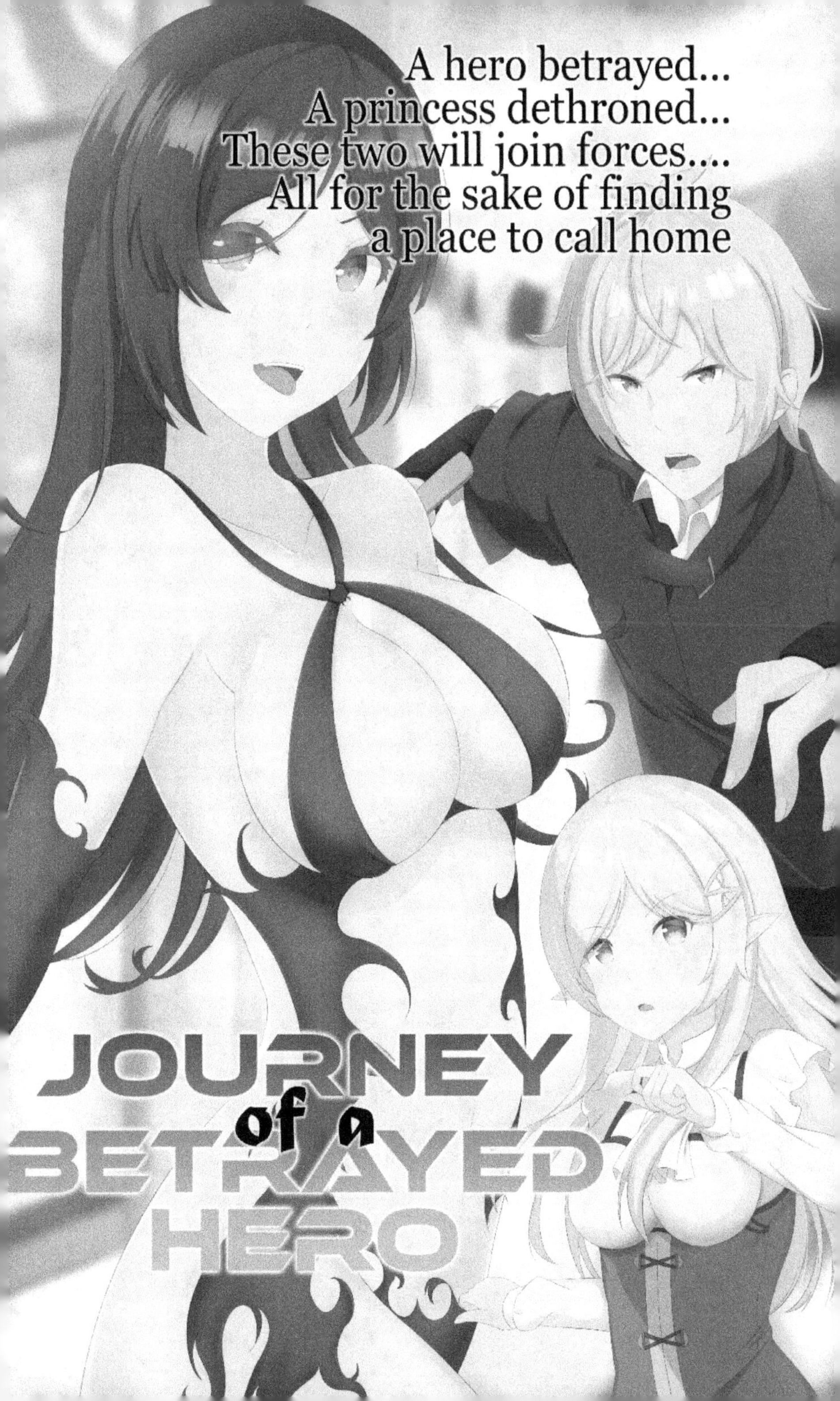
A hero betrayed...
A princess dethroned...
These two will join forces....
All for the sake of finding
a place to call home
JOURNEY of a BETRAYED HERO

A former Marine running from his past.
An angel with nothing left to lose.
A succubus at the bottom of the food chain.
What do these three have in common?
A goal: To escape the hellish nightmare
they've found themselves in. Together.

Swordsman
Of the
Rift 2

WIEDERGEBURT
LEGEND OF THE REINCARNATED WARRIOR

HE RETURNED TO THE PAST
IN ORDER TO CHANGE THE
FUTURE.

The Executioner Series
The complete series
is available now!